CREATURE FROM HELL

As he pedaled furiously through the darkness, Johnny watched with horror as a grisly, pale man, covered with scars and dried blood, stumbled into the bike's path.

He ran straight into the thing, managing somehow to keep the bike upright.

The man hurled his rotting body over the handlebars, growly not with pain or exertion, but with unmistakable *hunger*.

The thing was aiming for his neck, but Johnny twisted his head at the last second. Its teeth tore Johnny's ear; warm blood streamed down the boy's chest.

Then the mystery happened. The creature flinched, shook in spasms, and *smoke* erupted from its mouth, pushed out by its horrible cries of pain.

As most of the creature's lower jaw began to dissolve in a haze of green fire, Johnny screamed as loud and as long as he could . . .

Paperback
Book Exchange

1811 S. Mission
Mt. Pleasant, MI
(517) 772-5473

TERROR LIVES!

THE SHADOW MAN   (1946, $3.95)
by Stephen Gresham
The Shadow Man could hide anywhere—under the bed, in
the closet, behind the mirror . . . even in the sophisticated
circuitry of little Joey's computer. And the Shadow Man
could make Joey do things that no little boy should ever do!

SIGHT UNSEEN   (2038, $3.95)
by Andrew Neiderman
David was always right. Always. But now that he was growing up, his gift was turning into a power. The power to know
things—terrible things—that he didn't want to know. Like
who would live . . . and who would die!

MIDNIGHT BOY   (2065, $3.95)
by Stephen Gresham
Something horrible is stalking the town's children. For one
of its most trusted citizens possesses the twisted need and
cunning of a psychopathic killer. Now Town Creek's only
hope lies in the horrific, blood-soaked visions of the MID-
NIGHT BOY!

TEACHER'S PET   (1927, $3.95)
by Andrew Neiderman
All the children loved their teacher Mr. Lucy. It was aston-
ishing to see how they all seemed to begin to resemble Mr.
Lucy. And act like Mr. Lucy. And kill like Mr. Lucy!

*Available wherever paperbacks are sold, or order direct from the
Publisher. Send cover price plus 50¢ per copy for mailing and handling to Zebra Books, Dept. 2651, 475 Park Avenue South, New
York, N.Y. 10016. Residents of New York, New Jersey and Pennsylvania must include sales tax. DO NOT SEND CASH.*

DARK SOULS

Barry Porter

ZEBRA BOOKS
KENSINGTON PUBLISHING CORP.

ZEBRA BOOKS

are published by

Kensington Publishing Corp.
475 Park Avenue South
New York, NY 10016

Copyright ©1989 by Barry Porter

All rights reserved. No part of this book may be reproduced in any form or by any means without the prior written consent of the Publisher, excepting brief quotes used in reviews.

First printing: May, 1989

Printed in the United States of America

Chapter 1

She wished she could scream herself awake.

Like before, they were alone, on their honeymoon. In a cabin in the mountains of Colorado. Janet stood on the stairs, dressed in a negligee, watching her husband prepare a fire in the hearth. It was warm, inviting. The furry rug in front of it would be perfect for making love. Her thoughts grew more erotic, but she didn't move down the stairs to Tom.

The phone rang; it was a message from the outside, where they would not return for ages — an intruder. Tom sighed and moved to answer it. She wanted to follow, but she was frozen solid.

Scream, dammit, scream!

He grabbed the receiver, turning toward her. He froze, the phone halfway up, staring at her. His expression seemed to show that he could see her discomfort. If he only knew it was absolute terror, maybe he wouldn't —

The receiver touched his ear.

Suddenly, Janet was moving. She had anticipated the release, was ready for it. She raced toward the man she loved, arms outstretched, ready to hold him close, to tackle him if necessary, and never let him go.

Go! Go! Almost there —

The familiar, yet still terrifying rumble caused her to

stumble. Her fingers were just grazing him when the floor beneath them exploded.

Janet was pushed away from Tom—though she tried desperately to hold on to him, grabbing his neck, his arms, his hands, *anything*. Her body flew across the room and landed against the opposite wall, without pain, though she felt the shock of the impact.

When she looked up again, Tom was lying in a corner, bloodied but conscious. He reached for her, but he could not move closer. It was impossible.

Between them stood the creature that had erupted through the floorboards. Janet thought it had the shape of a dog, though the rest of it was far from a normal beast. Muscles bunched across its back, where glands secreted some sort of green syrup that bubbled along the spine. Patches of hair sprouted here and there on its powerful body, giving the creature a haggard look. Its paws were oversized, the toes spread out like human hands, long, twisted claws digging into the carpet. The shoulders hunched down to a bulb head and a long, thin snout. The red forehead glistened, as if it had been rubbed with a stone for eons. Janet would have sworn it was a jewel embedded above the thing's eyes.

Don't look at the eyes!

Teeth sprang crookedly from the dripping gums, deforming the lip, as if there weren't enough room for all of them in the beast's mouth. And the eyes . . .

Wake up, wake up, wake UP!

But a grip as powerful as the beast's jaws forced her down into her own subconscious. It made her watch. She became so rigid that she couldn't even avert her eyes from the creature.

It turned to stare at her.

Janet tried to scream but her throat produced nothing. The dog-thing eyed her carefully.

Those eyes—so dark, so black—look somewhere else!

It growled, starting like the rumble before the floor ex-

6

ploded, but then it went deeper, shaking the bones inside of her body. Janet's eyes darted about, looking for something normal, something comforting, to lock on to.

Tom.

He was there, behind the beast, reaching out for her. She saw his mouth moving, but couldn't hear the words. She tried to read his lips.

Honey! Hurry! Come to me! Come here!

The beast growled again, breaking her concentration. But the growl didn't die this time. It grew into words, understandable words, that sank deep into Janet's mind.

"Who am I?" the beast asked.

"I don't . . . I don't know."

"Who am I?" the beast repeated. Its eyes bored into her. The jewel in its forehead seemed to glow redder, hotter.

"I don't know!" she screamed. But she did. The answer was right on the tip of her mind, if she'd just let it roll toward her, take that quick peek —

"Tom!" she cried. She ran toward her husband. He opened his arms wide. If she jumped over the creature, he would catch her. She *moved,* splinters digging into the dirty soles of her feet. The creature's stare weighed her down, trying to keep her from her husband, but the farther she ran, the freer she felt. The beast stood before her, not quite waist high. The hold was lessening. She could do it. She felt sure.

But as she jumped, the creature stood on its hind legs. It revealed a stomach of rotted flesh and worms and black things she knew had to be maggots. It opened its arms, like Tom, to catch her.

"Who —" it began.

"God!" she screamed.

And then she awoke.

She lay there sweating for a while, trying to regain her breath. As the dream receded into silliness, she looked

7

around. She had awakened, as most mornings, curled in a ball, with her arms wrapped around her pillow. She sighed. The dream was startling, but the position was familiar.

She blinked rapidly, dispelling the nightmare by concentrating on the present. She was in their bedroom, thin rays of light filtering through the window blinds, spotlighting a million dancing particles of dust. Outside, the parading cymbals of the trash men echoed down the deserted streets, no doubt waking others who had slept late. Peering through half-closed eyes, she checked the clock on her dresser. 8:43 a.m. Tom was already on the road, halfway to work.

She sat up, a stifled curse on her lips. She stretched, grunted at the morning stiffness in her back and shoulders, and finally stood upright in the morning light.

Her first stop was the bathroom, where she washed her sweaty hands, face, and neck, and hastily evaluated herself in the mirror. Tall, smooth body. Perhaps shapely if the breasts were fuller. Thin waist — good for now, but beginning a long battle with middle age. Long brown hair, curling naturally at the ends. Clear skin, slightly pale, maybe needed a bit more sun.

Soft hands roamed her thighs and stomach. *Something missing in there, Janet. Something important.* The thought made her feel incomplete, and she caught herself checking the rest of her body, taking inventory of her limbs. She sighed and blinked slowly. "Maybe a part of my mind is missing," she whispered with a wan smile. Then she frowned. She remembered the beast. *That* wasn't funny.

The body check hadn't ended so badly, though. *Tired,* she thought. Not really old, not really showing her nearly forty years, but tired. She decided, then, that she was too tired to take a shower right now, so she dressed quickly in a T-shirt and jeans from the day before, changing only her underwear, and sauntered out into the kitchen. Tom's breakfast dishes were piled neatly in the sink. She washed them out, put them in the cupboard, and gave a drink to each of her plants on the kitchen window sill. Her hands shook a little as she poured the water. She was still affected by the nightmare. She felt confident, however, that time would wipe its memory away. It had in the past. Of course, it did take a little longer each time . . .

The damned beast!

It ravaged her dreams after their honeymoon had been cut short—"Pressing business," Tom had explained, unable to look at her—and continued to this day. Seven months. All because of a single phone call from Tom's office—a doctor's office—concerning his new wife.

No use talking to him about her dream after that. No mention of the beast. The prophecy was obvious, perhaps even dangerous. But she wasn't about to give up without a fight. It had taken her days to dismiss the need to tell him, but she'd done it. Now there were greater problems to deal with—problems much more real.

She had a vacation to get through.

Back in their bedroom, she dragged out two large suitcases from the closet—last used during their abbreviated honeymoon. She packed only her own, ignoring the good memories that rushed at her—*only the two of us, four dark walls protecting us from the cold, warmth in each other's arms in front of the fire, light dancing on the sweat of our bodies*—filing them away until later when things were right again and they could be shared.

She left Tom's empty luggage next to her full suitcase. He preferred to do his own packing, she remembered.

Downstairs, she made a few phone calls. Jim Buxley, next door, would be happy to feed their cat and keep an eye on their house. The newspaper and mail were held until further notice. Next, she made sure all of the gas in the house was turned off and activated the automatic light switches to confuse would-be burglars.

She stood in front of the kitchen window in the warmth of the sun trying to think of anything she'd forgotten. Nothing

9

came to mind, so she made herself a cup of tea and sat down at the dining room table. She sipped at the hot liquid, staring into space.

Outside, a spring breeze blew against the Howards's home. The sun was moving higher, scaring away the shadows.

She could feel a change in the air. Something new was waiting for her in the mountains. The beast was forgotten for the rest of the day.

Doctor Tom Howards, six-foot-one, slim though not too taut, with a carefully pruned mustache, black hair cut short for his patients' sake, and a constant five-o'clock-shadow, stepped outside into the evening air with a frown on his face. He locked the office door behind him and walked to his car, his mind filled with half-thoughts and half-emotions. He didn't want to give in to any of them, but he knew the familiar drive home would provide too fertile a ground for him to avoid them. He crawled into the front seat, tossed some files in back, closed the car door, but did not start the ignition. He just sat there, staring out at the falling sun, afraid of his idle mind.

Soon, of course, so that he never knew they had arrived, his thoughts took over. They picked at a painful scab, one he normally avoided even when he was alone. Unknowingly, his fingers pushed against the ignition key and started the car. He was never truly conscious of the act.

The long drive home began. Another nightmare.

He wondered about the "vacation" he and Janet were about to embark on. It scared him, seeing Janet so enthusiastic over it. The abrupt change in her manner was disturbing — no, more than that. It was *demanding*. She was placing a lot of hope in this trip and he felt she wanted him to do the same.

Not his fault. Not her fault. A family was all he had

wanted. It had become a burning desire after falling in love with Janet, a burning desire he now knew could not be satisfied naturally.

No one's fault, yet the guilt remained. Even worse, it isolated him. He *knew* he was selfish to believe he was suffering alone, but he'd never shared pain before. How could he share pain this large with the woman he loved?

If she can't, Tommy, maybe another woman, a different woman —

He caught the dark, stray thought this time. Squelched it. That was something else that disturbed him. Those thoughts, thoughts he would swear were foreign to him, were becoming more frequent . . . and harder to kill.

He concentrated on his wife and his love for her. No, he assured himself, there was nothing that could break that. Children had been important to him, but not more than Janet. Never more than her.

But what if her love for you has been broken?

He let it go. He wasn't sure if it was a stray thought, or a truth from deep in his heart.

I can't go on like this . . .

Turning onto his street, he prayed this vacation she'd talked him into would prove beneficial. Maybe it would snap him out of his depression so they could begin searching for a compromise — if one existed.

But as he steered into the driveway *(endless, sleepless years of internship to buy this driveway — was I happy back then?)*, his thoughts took advantage of the silence and his exhaustion, and whispered: *Compromise? No fucking way.*

The garage door slammed behind him, and he sat in the darkness for a long while, alone, listening to the car's cooling engine tick out the minutes.

Cathy Simon watched the butterfly dip and rise, again and again, occasionally fluttering close enough for her to touch. But she didn't try. She was content merely watching the aeronautic display, performed only for her.

She loved to sit in the grass like this, the small flowers bending against her, a cool breeze from the bay exhaling from its long journey across the ocean to play with her hair. She never felt this way in the city, with all of its harsh, exploding sounds and disturbing scents. This was pure nature, clean and sharp. She felt as if she were a million miles away from anything real. This was *true* freedom. It kept her to herself, away from people. It let her dream of impossible events. It let her think about her mother.

She lowered her head and noticed a column of ants bringing home the bread. She didn't stir. The few bugs didn't bother her, even when they took shortcuts over her feet and legs. She watched them quietly, their work of survival merely a dance to her eyes. Silently she wished she too could become part of the show.

A smile tickled her lips. She laid her head back and stared up at the clouds. The balls of cotton, huge and soft, moved gracefully, observing.

"Cathy."

The call was long, the syllables drawn out. The wind tried to steal the sound away, but it wasn't strong enough. She turned and sat up. Over the dancing hills, a stout man dressed in a grey shirt and jeans waved to her and called her name again.

Cathy whispered goodbye to the butterfly and fond farewell to the ants, saluted the mighty clouds, and sprang to her feet. As she ran, brushing dirt from her behind, blades of grass reached for her legs, trying to hold her back with them.

But she ran on to her father. She thought he looked younger somehow. Perhaps it was the distance, but his hair seemed darker, his face smoother, his complexion pinker. As she grew closer, though, there was a hurried transformation. His head sprouted grey straw, his eyes had folds beneath them, and deep lines outlined his face. He became old. He wasn't *really* old, she knew, but with her mother gone . . .

12

She was giggling now, and jumped into her father's powerful arms.

"Good girl," he said, brushing the blond curls out of her eyes as he always did. "Let's get in the car and get going, hon. We've got a long drive ahead of us."

"Okay!" she shouted excitedly. She loved riding in the car and watching the varied landscapes glide by. She was going to be a painter or a photographer when she grew up, and she thought seeing the world was the best experience she could hope for.

Patrick smiled, opened the door for her, and she climbed in.

"How long a drive, Daddy?"

"Quite a few miles."

"As far as the moon is?" She watched her father with complete innocence as he walked to the front of the car and stepped in.

"No, hon, not that far. But still a long way over hill and dale."

"Dale? What's a dale?"

"Oh . . . I'm not sure. I think it's a tiny valley."

But she didn't hear, wasn't really that interested. Just hearing his voice was comforting enough. She still remembered a time when he barely spoke at all.

Patrick started the car and pulled out of the rest area onto the main road. Cathy held her head out the window, her mouth open to catch the warm breeze. Outside, the grass waved farewell forever.

After a while, he put the car on cruise and stretched his legs. His body cracked, then sagged, but he smiled in satisfaction. It was still taut — and squat. The Bull, Margie had always tagged him. ("It's not because I'm horny, is it?" he had always replied.) Oddly, he couldn't remember if his daughter had ever picked up the nickname. Had it really been so intimate a thing?

He twisted around and saw that Cathy was stretched out

on the back seat, fast asleep. He marvelled at how much she looked like Margie. He remembered when the comparison to his dead wife would have stabbed at him, painfully, but now the love of that woman was so precious to him that he sometimes *wanted* those memories to haunt him.

He returned his eyes to the road stretched before him — a long way to go. He'd let Cathy sleep for now, but she'd want to be awake when they reached the mountains.

He smiled at that. The first thing he'd really known for sure about his daughter was her love of nature. After Margie's death, and his long illness that followed, he found himself involved in Cathy's school activities, particularly her drawings and paintings. She went mad over the beauty of the outdoors — his regular little nature nut. So, his announcement of an impromptu vacation in the Colorado mountains was an exciting offer.

He was looking forward to it as well, though Avilon had warned him of the real reason behind the reunion. Still, he thought a few weeks in the country might help to bring he and Cathy closer — not that they were distant now. In fact, since he'd stopped patronizing her talents and started treating her like a daughter rather than a student, they had become each other's natural support.

It dawned on him, then, that this was the first vacation of any length they'd taken since Margie's death. The thought disturbed him.

The pain of Margie's passing still existed, but not as severe. He had thought that riding away from their home like this, just the two of them, would be more painful. He guessed he could live with what there was, but it still concerned him. The entire vacation now concerned him.

Cathy entered his thoughts again. Naturally, with three years of single parenting behind him, he recognized the small chill of insecurity that circled the bottom of his spine. But now, as they left the city, it increased. He couldn't shake it, couldn't understand why it was even there. It gave him

14

pause, though, and that was enough for him to start feeling scared again.

Forcing another casual look behind at her, he wondered what could possibly harm such an angel. Nothing that he'd allow.

He cleared his head. It was a long road to Colorado. And a change, he hoped, was waiting for them at the end of it.

He tried not to pause before pushing the gas pedal.

Avilon Jersey blew at the steam rising from her tea cup. She closed her eyes and sipped the contents, grimacing at the sting the hot liquid brought. Her body tensed, and she pulled the covers up around her ears. It was unusually cold for spring, even for evening. Hell, it was outlandishly cold for a house that was supposed to have insulation. But what could be done? She was an old woman at the mercy of the world.

She shook her head and tried to smile. Her husband would have been cackling if he'd heard her say that. Her reliance on a sharp tongue and not-so-empty threats were well known throughout the little village of Harkborough.

She wondered how she could use that strength to help her daughter now. She recalled the frantic phone call, the fear in Janet's voice, and her own loss at how to console her with mere words. She had to hold her daughter, wipe the tears, bring her closer.

And then the idea of a reunion came into being. Not that she thought it a great idea, but it was one she had chosen on instinct, and she usually trusted her instincts. Janet had sounded enthusiastic about it, so maybe there *was* some wisdom left in her old, doddering head after all.

"Doddering because of the cold," she mumbled to the empty room. Quick as she could, Avilon hurried over the freezing wood floor to her bedroom window, making sure it was closed tight. As she did so, the wind outside blew hard, rattling the window until it nearly sprang open. Avilon

15

grunted and was sweaty by the time she got it securely latched.

So cold . . . so cold . . .

She hurried back to bed. The temperature was diverting, but not enough to push thoughts of her daughter from her mind. God, what a mess it was going to be. She knew the toll infertility could bring to a marriage, especially when it was such a surprise. She had become barren herself after having Janet. If not for society's opinion of divorce back then, she and Peter might not have stayed together until death took him away. That was too horrible to think about. They would have missed so many good years.

Fortunately, they had also had Patrick, Avilon's nephew, to keep little Janet from loneliness. He was so young when his parents died that bringing him up was like bringing up one of her own. She wondered if Tom and Janet had discussed adoption. Probably. And then Tom had probably dismissed it out of hand. He was like that.

She pressed her lips together until they were white, and closed her eyes. In the cold silence, she wished that the strain between her daughter and son-in-law was due only to the unexpectedness of the news. That all they needed was time. And that she could give them that time up here, where their love was committed.

Strength. Give us all strength.

Outside, the wind answered in howls.

And please warm this place up, huh? Avilon shivered. Maybe sleep would help. She reached up and turned the lights out, then burrowed under the covers. The tiny chimes of her wall clock told her that it was only nine, but she wanted to retire early so she could prepare for her family's arrival.

She drew the covers tighter as she shivered again and again. *Damned cold for spring,* she thought.

A block down the street from Avilon Jersey, a figure sat in

16

a pew in a church, and he too shivered. However, it wasn't a chill that disturbed Father Tilkan. It was fear.

The electrical lights had been turned off at eight o'clock, as they were every weekday night, but he had gone to the trouble of lighting twenty candles — including the one housed in the lantern over the altar that signified Christ's presence in the church — and had placed them conveniently about the vestry. They flickered and bowed, seemingly in unison, but the father paid them no mind. They were not there for light, for he could perform his duties in the dark if it was required. They were not there to keep the room warm, for their collective heat would hardly be enough to keep a large closet comfortable. They were, however, necessary to illuminate a clear path in his mission, and to warm his soul so that he would not feel completely alone.

They did not meet his expectations.

Father Tilkan lowered his eyes from the candles' hypnotic glow and swallowed hard. He felt the nausea rise again in his throat. He breathed deeply, forcing it down once more, one hand clutching his stomach while the other caressed his rosary. Something was wrong. Not something a doctor could remedy, but a sickness from without, pressing against him. He couldn't breathe, and his skin was clammy and slick with sweat. Something was pushing up against him, locking out the air, smothering him.

I should be at the altar, he thought, his anger with his limitations rising. *God forgive me, I should be kneeling on the prie-dieu, praying, hoping,* demanding *guidance!*

With difficulty, he looked up to where he should be. The figure of Christ looked down at the same spot, and Father Tilkan swore he saw a puzzled expression on the statue's face, shifting in the red light of the altar's lantern, asking, *"Where? Where is he? Where is the one I must help?"* But the act of moving . . . it was too difficult . . . too obvious for the one at the window.

At the thought, his gaze wandered to the nearest stained-glass window, an expansive and colorful depiction of angels rising to their heaven. But he looked beyond the ornamentation, to the silhouette that was there, but wasn't. That is to say, it was almost fully formed, but it still flickered in intensity, as if it were pulling particles from the wind and the earth to form a whole. Swirling, expanding into darkness, contracting into evil, feeding upon itself until it could feed upon others. And always, always growing. Nurturing into a plague.

Am I going crazy? Is this insanity? he thought to himself, not for the first time. *Cold winds turning into plagues . . . evil growing, ready to feed on human beings . . . shapeless creatures looking in on me from the window . . . Are these the thoughts of a sane man?*

But he knew it to be true. The answers had come to him so clearly. It was a warning of things to come. And only he could stop it. Or so the voice inside him told him.

A spasm attacked him again, forcing him into a cold sweat, white knuckles pushing his fingers into the wood of the bench. When he could, he jerked his head up to the figure of Christ at the front of the church. His broad majesty was illuminated by the red glow. *A single light,* he thought morosely, *like me?* He clutched his cross to his chest, his body warmed its iron core, the symbol exchanging its strength for his faith. The chill passed, and he brushed sticky hair back from his face. He grimaced at the taste of bile around his dry tongue.

He looked at the window again, but only to confirm what he already felt from within. The figure was gone.

Tonight it would start. The disease was around him now, laughing, but unable to penetrate his faith. He wasn't sure that would last, though. The evil would soon be embodied, ready to lure and strike. He would have to act fast. His death would mean little unless he was allowed to complete his mission.

"Today," he gasped to his Lord, "it shall be an infant. Tomorrow . . ." Father Tilkan leaned forward, trying to control the first icy fingers of the chill.

The Christ visage looked on, a face of sculpted indifference. Father Tilkan studied the face, releasing the pew to grip his cross with both hands. "I am ready. I swear, I am ready . . ."

Outside, the wind blew harder against the church walls.

Chapter 2

The morning was crisp, and when the sun touched the mountain frost there was a light fog, as if the world were exhaling air long held. Then, like a gasp, it was gone.

Small wisps of fog did survive, however, and attached themselves beneath a large cottage atop a hill. The cottage had been standing there for many decades, and it welcomed the curling fingers of mist into the depths of its foundation.

It was 8:00 a.m., and Avilon was awakened by a sharp knock at the front door. Dragging herself out of bed, she cursed the visitor and the cold, her lips moving silently, and slipped on her robe.

The low morning light drew checkered silhouettes on the floor, and where the sun was warmest, a tiny trail of smoke rose from between varnished boards. Soon, other ghostly snakes found their way to the surface and married with the warm air above.

But Avilon was unaware of the invaders. She was conscious only of the incessant knocking at her front door and the cold prickling of her feet. Warmth and silence were foremost in mind, and both could be found only under her bed's covers. She hesitated for just a moment, then felt her feet move forward automatically as the knocking grew louder.

At the entranceway, she finished tying her robe and

reached for the door. Opening it a crack, she grimaced at the wind pushing its way past her, but pulled the door wider. Warmth and silence were forgotten when she saw who was standing on her doormat.

"Patrick! Cathy! Please, please come in!"

Patrick smiled and they walked in together. "Aunt Avilon, it's been a long time." He kissed her cheek and Cathy did the same.

"Hello, Auntie," said the girl.

"Welcome, dearest, welcome."

Avilon closed the door behind them, surprised that she had to exert herself to latch it against the wind, then ushered the pair into the den. Without waiting for answers to her offer, she whipped up some instant hot chocolate, dropped a few marshmallows into Cathy's cup, and reclined in her rocker as her two guests sat on a nearby couch. She felt warmed already.

"I'm sorry we're early, Avilon," said Patrick. "We wanted to get started as soon as possible since we didn't know how long the drive would take us." Beside him, Cathy yawned and smiled at the attention it received. "Cathy was supposed to sleep on the way up last night, but you know how she loves the country."

Cathy had, in fact, nodded on and off, and didn't exactly feel exhausted, but she thought it more prudent to say nothing at all.

Avilon sipped her chocolate, nodding her head in agreement all the while. "Oh, that's all right. I should be getting up anyway to get ready for the rest of the family. They should be here early this afternoon."

The greetings out of the way, the conversation turned more personal. Cathy listened with polite interest, but soon found herself drifting off. She began to believe a nap wasn't too bad an idea after all. *Strange,* she thought, as she began to lose consciousness, *strange how it looks like the floor is melting . . . can even see steam rising . . .*

Her eyes were about to close when her father's hand slapped her knees and he stood to his full five-and-a-half-foot frame. "Well, then, let's get cracking! Cathy can help dust and I can do whatever yard work needs to be done. And you, sweet Aunt, can put all of your concentration on the huge feast I'm sure you have in store for us."

"Patrick!" Avilon objected halfheartedly. "I'll hear nothing of it! You've driven all night long—"

"Yeah, but I primed myself. I slept all the day before."

Cathy backed him up. "He didn't do *anything* but sleep."

Avilon had started to argue again—Cathy could obviously use a nap now—but she'd raised Patrick since he was six, and was certain her exertions against him would end in failure. At times Patrick's dedication to emulating the world's best single parent was more than transparent—and often times not a little damaging.

Instead, she nodded wearily and rose from her rocker. "All right, you two. Let me get dressed and we'll start."

By midafternoon, the entire house, inside and out, was clean and proper for guests. After finishing what little work the yard required—Avilon spent most of her time outside, so the surrounding gardens, shrubs, and trees were in pristine order—Patrick had done more menial chores, such as sweeping. Cathy dusted and was properly praised, although she was well aware that the furniture was kept in perfect condition by her great-aunt. Still, she accepted the acclaim from her father with very little modesty. Both then joined Avilon in the kitchen—and were promptly chased out and told to rest up for the evening. Dutifully, they followed orders, and Avilon returned to the turkey.

A turkey, Avilon reflected, *means a celebration.* Then she smiled. She could think of nothing more festive than having her family back together again. It had been nearly a year— not since the wedding—and she was reminded now how lonely her house could be when nestled about a single soul. She, too, was looking forward to the weekend—and she was wise enough to recognize why. She felt needed, more than she had felt in years. *She* would be the anchor for the others this weekend. *She* would be the strong one, the comforter.

She would feel *useful* again.

While Avilon was submerged in private thoughts and Patrick was puttering around the living room, Cathy stood at the opposite end of the cottage, in the doorway of a room she had just discovered.

She was amazed at the cottage, how it could turn up a hidden room at every turn. Her life had been spent in a three-room apartment on the third floor. She had driven by mansions and large houses with her father during their occasional excursions, but she'd never actually entered one and investigated its every corner.

And this place was big. She remembered the main parlor room and the bathroom down the hallway and around the corner—the only two rooms she had seen when she and her father had attended the wedding of his cousin, Janet. Those two rooms seemed smaller now, but she attributed that to being a whole year older . . . she was almost nine now.

Still, when she had been dusting, she thought she had seen all of the rooms, yet she had missed one. It wasn't very large, probably just a den, but the dust on the table and chairs disturbed her. Her job was not complete.

She looked down the hallway to where her father had disappeared. She heard nothing and decided he might have fallen asleep on the couch. Quickly, she retrieved the dust rag she'd left on a chair in the parlor and raced back to finish her job. The rag swiped across the table's surface, then across the chair, and she stopped, recognizing the two. They matched the furniture in the dining room, where she had spent most of her time before trying to clean the elegant twelve-foot table and matching oak chairs surrounding it. It had been a large job compared with the minor dusting needed in the other rooms. She had had to kneel on the chairs to reach the center of the table. When she'd finished, she had placed a small vase of roses at the center of the table.

She wanted to do the same with this tiny table now, but could find neither a vase nor a flower. She stood back, hands on hips, and blew a lock of golden hair from her eyes as she surveyed the job.

"Sparkling like silver, hon."

She turned and found her father peering around the corner, smiling. "Thanks," she said. "Can I go outside now?"

"What?" He frowned. "I thought you wanted to take a nap. You were yawning every five seconds the last ten miles up here."

"But I feel like going out now."

He sighed, then smiled wearily. "All right, all right. Stay around the house, and don't go wandering off into the woods. And be back before dinner."

"Okay."

She turned and ran out on the den's veranda, leaving the doors open in her haste. Patrick shuffled the length of the room and started to close them. He paused a moment to watch his little girl run down a small grassy path, chasing another butterfly, her curls bobbing madly in the air. He shook his head admiringly.

So beautiful.

He shut the doors — then stopped again and frowned. He reopened one and looked outside.

Strange, he thought. The wind had been blowing like a banshee when they first arrived, but it was barely a whisper now. Not even cool anymore . . . almost stale . . .

He shrugged and smiled at the sound of his daughter's laughter. He watched until she disappeared around a bend, then pulled back inside, closed and latched the door, tingling with the beginning nibbles of guilt.

* * *

24

Janet marvelled at the Colorado mountains. She'd grown up here — and was suddenly aware of how painful the separation had been even for little more than a year. Smiling, she rolled down her window, leaned back in her seat, and took in a long breath of air — air that had never mingled with a smokestack.

The sun was high to the west, the mountains like huge jagged glaciers dimpled with violet diamonds. The magnificent pines in the foreground did not move, did not scamper from the path of these icy giants, nor did the fields of columbine, named the state flower because one could not look anywhere without seeing their bursts of color. There was no wind to disturb any of them, yet they were still alive and active. The scene could have been from a picture postcard, it was so calm and breathtaking. *There's gold in them thar hills,* she thought, amused. She allowed a small laugh to pass her lips. It felt good. She crossed her arms over her chest, wanting to hold the good feelings inside for as long as possible.

By late afternoon they were driving slowly through the Harkborough streets, afraid that even their engine was too loud for the sleepy hollow. Many of the buildings, although nestled deep in the mountains, looked strangely out of place. They were an odd mixture of fishing village and Old West ghost town. The main ones, most of them early landmarks, were built of dark timber, splinters sprouting at intervals like whiskers on an old settler. Fishing nets — used in the nearby river during the thaw — hung from posts and porch eaves like giant spider webs. All the buildings on the main street had raised porches, creating an uneven sidewalk. Even the store signs — those still in business — were made of wood, the letters burned-in and faded.

Janet suddenly bristled at the sight. She hadn't remembered the older buildings looking so . . . ominous. The end of the street appeared better, however. This part of town had been built when she was a girl. Concrete. Wood decorations. Modern, but designed to match the older buildings, these shops seemed to have more life to them. Maybe it was the people, she thought. The older part of town somehow looked deserted.

Fifteen minutes past the main street, their car climbed the rising road, and they arrived at the cottage just as evening was setting in. As they pulled up into the sandy driveway, Janet felt as if she were entering another world; a fairy tale land of her past that would never disintegrate with age. The cottage, even the land around it, had looked the same since she was a little girl — with no little effort from her mother, she knew. The walls were still off-white, decorated with red curves and borders, almost Spanish in style, and what had long ago seemed a small line between where a building ended and the land began was now invisible. The cottage was now a part of the landscape, as strong and unchanging as a redwood. The roof was still watertight, a sea of old shingles, chipped and lightly showered with leaves from the trees above. Below, the eyes of the house — the windows — remained checkered, supporting the sense of a fairy tale, as did the walkway to the front door bordered by sweet, red columbine.

Tom and Janet had rushed down that walkway in laughter as husband and wife once, rice raining on them. The flowers had still been in bloom then, too, and they had reminded Janet of tiny, red infantrymen raising their swords to salute the happy couple.

As Janet strained to see the whole house from the car window, Tom parked at the end of the walkway. The door to the cottage opened as soon as the engine was cut, and Janet burst into a wide smile.

"Mom!"

They moved together quickly, hugged, close and warm, mother and daughter against the cold. Clasping hands, they looked the other over, and found each healthy.

"I'm sorry we're late," Janet said. "It was a longer trip than we expected."

Janet felt like a little girl again under her mother's scrutiny. She was a tiny tot now with a blue ribbon hanging from her curly hair—long before it had straightened, leaving only small curls at the ends. Avilon, her mother, would cradle her, protect her, shelter her, and feed her for the next few days. There would be nothing but the sweet warmth of security.

And a lousy marriage to deal with.

The jar of reality must have shown in her face. Something unspoken, but important, passed between mother and daughter, and Avilon smiled back, squeezing her hand. "I've missed you so much. And you're not late. You're just in time for dinner." She winked and added, in a whisper, "This is going to be a wonderful weekend, I promise you."

The car trunk slammed behind them. Tom had the suitcases out and stood at the foot of the walkway, his attention occupied, distant. He smiled at Avilon's greeting and returned a short kiss. When Avilon began leading her daughter away, he took a deep breath of that mountain air he kept hearing so much about and busied himself with the luggage.

The two women walked casually up the walkway. Avilon's voice was chatty, revealing none of her apprehension.

"How was traffic?"

"Not too bad. Everyone seems to be moving away from the mountains this time of year."

"It's the cold. I can't remember it being this bad." Avilon peered intently from the corner of her eyes. "Was it a long trip?"

Janet sighed but managed a smile. "About what we expected."

She and Tom had spoken very little during the trip. Tom was, as usual, moody, accentuated by the strain of a three-hour drive. Only when the wilderness began to descend on them did he relax and actually smile. It bolstered Janet's hopes.

On the threshold, a bulky figure blocked their way. Janet stopped suddenly, for some reason instantly afraid. *The beast!*

"How you doing, Janet?"

Patrick leaned out of the shadows and hugged her. Janet's anxiety melted and she managed a relieved smile as she returned the hug.

"Good. Feeling very good, Pat."

Patrick nodded knowingly. "It's the house. It hasn't changed an inch. I figured it would seem smaller because I haven't spent too much time here since I was a kid, but it's still a monster." He rested a hand on Avilon's shoulders. "I don't know how you do it, Auntie. Just the quick cleanup today nearly killed Cathy and me."

"How are you two?" asked Janet.

"Much better." His gaze dropped for a moment, then came right back with renewed strength. "We've . . . appreciated all the support over the years. I know I haven't seen you two since your wedding, and before that not since the accident. Still, it felt like you were there."

Janet touched his hand and kissed his cheek. "So where is the little one?" she asked, looking around.

"Out back chasing rabbits and butterflies. She's still my little nature girl." He smiled shyly. Janet understood then just how much he must depend on Cathy. The fact abruptly left her without anything to say.

At a loss for words himself, Patrick moved past her. "Better help Tom with those bags," he said. He walked to the car where he and Tom greeted each other as if they were old friends rather than distant acquaintances.

Avilon watched them, then squeezed Janet's hand again. "Come on, everyone," she said, taking command. "Let's get in the house before we all turn to ice in this weather. Patrick, call Cathy in. Dinner's ready."

They all scurried inside, away from the enveloping night.

The sun was sliding out of the sky quickly, disappearing behind the distant mountain ranges. The halo of clouds around it were gold and silver. Earlier, the sky had paled, but it was now exploding with the colors of a butterfly's wings.

Watching this metamorphosis, Cathy finally wiped the last rays of the sun from her eyes and stopped walking. Her own butterfly continued on, seeking shelter in the shadow of a rock or under a tree. The sky darkened. It must be near dinner time, she thought. With some regret, she turned and started back. It wasn't too far, for she could still see the cottage through the aspen trees.

Then she stopped, looking around. Something was wrong. No, not wrong. Just different.

She was standing in the center of a circular clearing. There was no grass, no trees, no shrubbery; just dark, dry earth. The forest path led unwaveringly up to the clearing, disappeared, then emerged at the other end, unaffected.

Cathy bent down and looked closer. No ants. No flies or other bugs. Nothing moved in the circle. She looked up and discovered there were no overhanging tree branches or birds gliding above. Even the long, deep shadows of dusk avoided the area.

The strangest part was that Cathy was positive it had not been there before. She must have walked over the spot earlier, but she had not been so preoccupied with the butterfly that it would have gone unnoticed.

She kicked a small clump of dirt, frustrated and somehow anxious. The dirt fell heavily, instantly mingling with the earth again. Dust did not rise. Looking around, she felt a chill run through her body, yet there was no wind. No, the wind wouldn't dare venture this far into the pit's center. It was too dark, too foreign, as if it belonged in a land far away, not in the sleepy mountains of Colorado.

Shivering, she heard her father call. She took one last look around, then started up the incline, to the cottage. It had been nearly a year since she had been here last, so it was easy to get turned around. Perhaps she had come another way. Perhaps there had been a fire here, luckily contained within this small perimeter. She would check with her great-aunt during dinner.

The thought comforted her, brought a reality and logic to the foreign land. As she walked, her breath grew easier, her body warmer. Still, her walk turned into a run, and she found herself anxious to jump into the solid arms of her father.

To the west, the last wink of the sun tipped under the mountains and plunged Harkborough into darkness.

After Avilon and her guests were seated, there remained a single empty chair at the large table Cathy had dusted earlier. Avilon received amused glances when she revealed that there would be a surprise guest for tomorrow night's dinner. "Someone," she said, grinning, "that Tom will find particularly interesting."

A divorce lawyer, Tom thought, and cursed himself. He'd never thought of such things before.

It was well into the meal before Cathy mentioned her discovery. "Auntie, was there a fire up here?"

The others grew silent. Most thought she had spoken merely to attract attention in the midst of grown-up talk. Avilon dabbed at her mouth and looked into the child's eyes — and was disturbed to find no humor in them.

"What were you saying now, dear?" she asked.

"Was there a fire up here?"

Patrick snapped, "What are you talking about, hon?"

Cathy carefully explained the clearing. Although she had been uncertain before, she was now adamant — with so many speculative expressions fixed on her — that she had not seen the clearing when first passing through it. It had materialized out of nowhere.

Patrick looked around the table, a bit embarrassed. *Well,* he thought, *can't expect her to be an adult all the time.* "Obviously you've made a mistake, hon," he said. "You must have gone another way or been thinking about something—"

"Where's this clearing, Cathy?"

Everyone turned to Avilon. She did not appear to share their dismissal of the subject.

"Straight from that window." Cathy pointed out the tall glass veranda door at the end of the table. Outside, the dark cold cried to be let in. "Down the path," she continued. "That path goes right through the clearing."

Avilon's brows furrowed. "Why . . . I was just down there yesterday. I didn't go too far, though, because of the cold." She leaned forward, and everyone at the table sat up in their chairs, intrigued. "Was this clearing very far from the house?"

"No, Auntie. It's down the trail a ways, but you can still see the cottage through the trees."

Avilon looked disturbed.

Janet asked, "Mom, was there a fire here recently?"

"No, no, not to my knowledge. Not unless it just recently happened. But if it was that close, I think I would have seen or smelled the smoke or heard a fire engine or something." She laid her napkin on the table, almost a clear signal that dinner was at an end. She stared at the little golden-haired girl who had disrupted the first night of her family gathering. "Cathy," she said slowly, "are you *sure* a fire caused the clearing?"

"To have burned a complete circle, it *must* have been manmade," Tom interjected. "The ground would have thick deposits of ash and a horrible smell. It would probably be difficult to breathe." He looked to Cathy for confirmation.

"The ground was dark, but it didn't look like ashes," she answered carefully. "It was level and crumbly."

Patrick spoke up, annoyed with his daughter as well as his own unnatural curiosity. "I can't believe you're getting all worked up over a clearing in the forest."

"But there's never been a clearing there, Patrick," Avilon said. Her face revealed her concern.

31

"There is now," Cathy whispered, playing nervously with her potatoes.

"And if there was a fire," said Avilon, "I'd certainly like to know about it. It could still be dangerous if it hasn't been properly treated."

"Maybe some animals made it," offered Janet.

Avilon shook her head, still staring at the girl. "Animals, no. Animals wouldn't make a complete circle of the size Cathy's talking about."

"*If* Cathy's not exaggerating," Patrick remarked. He glowered at his daughter.

Cathy did not look up from her plate, but said, weakly, "I am not egg-sat-u-rating." However, she *was* sorry that she had ever brought the subject up.

Janet smiled and rested a hand on the girl's shoulder. "Well," she said, "your dad and Tom can check it out in the morning. I'm sure there's some explanation for what you saw."

Cathy looked up sharply. "I'm going too!"

Feeling rather foolish for getting so worked up over nothing, Patrick stabbed at his turkey. "Yes, you can come," he said in a low voice. "Now, stop sculpting your potatoes and start eating them."

Easy laughter broke the discomfort. Avilon took up her napkin again. Cathy was about to take a bite of her potatoes, but stopped and looked up at her father.

"What's skull-ting?"

More laughter led to a change of subject. Into the night, the chatter went on. When Avilon was given a turn to relate a story about her dead husband, Patrick's face lit up and he turned to her with an excited expression.

"Avilon, you must, absolutely *must,* give us a demonstration of your mysterious 'powers' tomorrow night!"

Avilon blushed and turned her attention to her plate. A smile wrinkled her lips.

Janet smacked her forehead and moaned, "Oh, no!" but

then, as Tom leaned over to ask what it was all about, she took up the appeal. "Yes, Mother, you must give us a performance."

"What would a family reunion be without that!" laughed Patrick.

Tom's face brightened with understanding. "Oh-ho! Is this the famous Harkborough Medium I've heard so much about?"

Patrick leaned back in his chair, and sipped at his wine. "The one and only, sir. The Madam can contact any spirit, be it real or imagined — more likely the latter — anytime, any place. Right, Auntie?"

Avilon looked up, her face still red. "It was just something to keep you kids occupied on rainy nights. You're not supposed to remember that stuff now!" Actually, it had once been a wage-earning act with her late husband, but that was something she would always keep secret.

The three enchanted adults continued to push and plead for a show.

Finally, Avilon laughed and said, "Well, I suppose I could give a small demonstration. For old time's sake."

Her guests applauded with delight and triumph.

"But," she warned, "I must insist on no laughing."

"We promise, Mom," said Janet. "Not a snicker."

"Not *during*, but *after* . . ." Patrick hooted a few times, taking another sip of his wine.

"Dad's drunk," Cathy said, louder than she had intended. The others stared at her in silence for barely a second as the statement was suspended in the air like a hatchet before the final blow — then broke up into laughter, except for Patrick, who could only manage a nervous grin. Cathy did not look at him.

The adults stood and started to clear the dinner table. Cathy sat for a while, not sure why, but feeling almost frozen to her seat. The others paid her no mind for now. They were discussing cryptic balls or something, and she wasn't really interested. Not now, anyway.

Her gaze wandered to the tall window at the head of the table. Outside, the wind was screaming, surrounding the house with its chill. Almost on cue, it rattled the pane of glass, trying to get in. She'd have a hard time sleeping tonight, she knew, wondering about the clearing and the strange feeling it had given her.

In abject concentration, she sat for a very long time staring out the window into the darkness beyond, her hand mashing a circle of fork trails in her potatoes.

Everyone in the cottage retired early that night, half eager to hike out to the clearing the next morning, the rest merely exhausted from their journeys. Patrick was the last one to bed, volunteering to secure the doors and windows of the cottage — and, privately, wanting to get some fresh air. During dinner, he and Janet had talked of a time when the cottage doors could be kept unlocked all night, the windows open in the summer, and they could sleep peacefully without fear of thieves or intruders or murderers. They were days long gone that could never be brought back, and Janet had somehow seemed more upset than reasonably expected at the change.

He made his way upstairs, hesitating outside Tom and Janet's door, listening and hearing nothing, before moving on to his own room — his old room, the one he'd grown up in. He clicked the door shut behind him, careful not to wake his daughter. The room was meant for one little boy long ago, and he now found himself unconsciously hunched over to not hit his head on the imagined low ceiling.

Moving to the bed, he looked down at his girl, fast asleep. Her freckled face was expressionless, revealing neither dream nor nightmare, save a tiny crease at her brow. *Probably dreaming of that damn clearing,* he thought.

Or maybe . . . maybe . . .

He shook the idea away, but it left a cold slime in the back of his mind. He reached out to pull the covers higher on her, then checked himself. Distant memories, blurred by the intoxication of those times, seeped behind his eyes . . .

A strong, beefy arm, white in the moonlight, touching her as she slept, wanting to wake her, to hold and caress her . . . like her dead mother . . .

. . . Ugly thoughts that made him shake again. He reminded himself that those days were past. He'd been stone sober for two years, though he still took a drink now and then, but never to excess. He was sure Cathy recognized the effort, too.

If not for that crack at dinner —

No, it was over. That had merely been a slip, maybe even just a joke. Or a warning. She must know things are all right now.

He watched the steady rise and fall of her chest under the blankets for a while. He thought of their life together since Margie's death. He was proud of her, how she'd come through it. Better than he had.

With the thought of Margie, a familiar chill drove through him, but passed quickly: signs of a scar nearly healed. He found it difficult to smile at the victory, however.

He undressed swiftly and went to bed. The nap had not been nearly long enough, and he could still feel a sharp pain in his back from the long hours of driving. In minutes, he fell into the untroubled darkness of sleep.

The figure moved smoothly, dipping each vial into the water and blessing the liquid two, three, even four times. He raised his cross and held it to his heart, praying silently, relentlessly, that his mission be seen through. He was not a young man, over the hill some would say, but he had dedicated his life to his Lord and His Word. That, certainly, was enough, wasn't it? Never had he realized, however, that his dedication would become so strained.

During the day, he had boarded the windows of the church. The wood barred the sunlight, but it also kept away the cold. As for the door, he would not lock it until he was ready. He was assured that the evil would not enter the church until everything else had been taken.

Father Tilkan submerged another vial and whispered the holy words. His cross was held tightly in his blistered hands. Calloused fingers held the vessel close. The dried blood on his fingertips washed off as he put them in the holy water.

Pausing, taking great gulps of air, he looked up into the compassionate face. A dry tongue licked chapped lips. He spoke louder now, a pained growl. "Soon. It will be soon. When it is ready, I shall meet it with confidence." He blinked the sting of sweat from his eyes, tried to ignore the quivering in his voice. "*We* shall meet it."

The statue's face flickered uncertainly in the light of a hanging lantern.

Outside, the air moved carefully, building ice crystals on the church's facade.

The evil had begun.

Adam Louis set his final beer down on his nightstand and belched. The gas warmed his insides as he snuggled into bed. With the lights turned out, Adam, in the silent night, reflected on the past few hours.

As usual, he had gone over to old Greg Wesson's house and played checkers. The game was a simple one, and he had whined, years ago, that it just wasn't a man's game. He was a New Orleans gambler, born and raised, and he was partial to poker. Nowadays, though, he wondered if he could remember anything about the card game. Checkers was the choice of Colorado mountain men — those who couldn't afford to lose at cards — and checkers he was forced to play. Being a novice — an excellent excuse he used at every opportunity, usually when they complained that they couldn't play poker—it was rare that he would win, but tonight was a special night. He had felt it that morning, hadn't he? Hadn't he woken up and said, "Damn if I'm not a-goin' to win big tonight?" He had, and he had won several games in a row. *Definitely,* his backwater faith told him, *an omen of good luck!*

Wesson, naturally, was not upset. Nothing upset the old goat. He was too damn easygoing, too damn unexcitable—probably due, Adam decided, to living so many years alone in the mountains. He wouldn't have lasted two days in rowdy New Orleans, nor would he have wanted to.

Still, Adam Louis and Greg Wesson had taken a liking to each other immediately, not because they were both alone and elderly, but because they shared common interests. They both enjoyed beer, liked burping, loved a good game of checkers (Adam would never admit this out loud), hated shit-sucking liberals, and felt comfortable when they could talk dirty without fear of admonishment. Compatibility bred a lasting friendship, which in turn bred the two best damn checker players in Colorado.

Already Adam was feeling anxious about tomorrow after-noon's rematch. The basic strategies were playing themselves out in his head when, out of the corner of his eyes, he caught something, he didn't know what, darting around his room. Whatever it was, though, it was definitely *in* his room, and he welcomed nothing there but his friend Wesson and himself.

He sat up abruptly, more angry at the intrusion into his scheming than the trespassing. He rubbed at his eyes until they adjusted to the darkness.

When his vision cleared, the first thing he saw was his bedroom window. It was open. He knew for a fact that he had shut that window because of the cold weather of late. A chill tickled the back of his neck, trying to tell him something, but he ignored it. Instead, he stared at the quarter moon for a moment, its light illuminating the forest below.

He watched the milky-white light for a long time. Then his mouth opened wide. His breath stopped short, making him gasp.

A shadow had risen in front of the window. It was neither a bird nor a spider web.

"What the hell . . . ?" he managed to whisper. As he went to pull the light switch, his hand froze. In seconds, it grew numb and heavy as he watched. He knew that it was not fear that had paralyzed it.

Something was holding his arm.

Blood rushed from his face as the shadow leaned in close. Adam was sickened by the powerful stench that hit him, reminding him of the time he had nearly tripped over a dead dog in the backwoods of Louisiana. Dead meat. Then the air was suddenly colder, and the smell lessened, though it never quite disappeared. He tried to speak. His tongue wouldn't move. His mouth was too dry.

A strange voice broke the silence. It spoke with control, almost exaggerating its pacing so that Adam would not miss a single word . . . or, thought Adam, like a child learning to speak.

"It would be best for us to stay in darkness," it said in a smooth, almost hypnotic voice. "It will be easier for you. More natural."

Bile struggled up Adam's throat. He had to force himself to breathe or he would suffocate — *but, God, that stench!*

As his lungs noisily sucked what little air they could, his eyes adapted fully to the darkness and made out a pair of fat, round orbs staring back. Like an animal's, they seemed to glow brighter the longer he looked into them, seemed to read right through him, to his very soul. But it was a black glow. It sucked at him, swallowing him in a pool of shiny ink. His neck muscles strained to turn his head, but he could not. He couldn't even blink. A painful tear floated down his cheek. A whimper slipped through his lips.

My goddamn eyes are being sucked out of their sockets! he thought, and panic rose like a ghostly hand, fingers squeezing his throat, strangling him.

"You know who I am," said the voice. "You've been waiting for me for a long time."

The orbs grew as big as half dollars, circling their victim. Adam thought he heard a distant *pop!* Tiny blood vessels in his eyes throbbed and expanded, blurring his vision even more — yet the round pools of darkness remained so clear, so sharp. Soon the tears were gone, wasted on his face. They were no longer needed. He had become part of the orbs: glowing, growing, forever. They'd eaten him up.

"Say it, Adam. Who am I? What am I?"

Adam tried to answer, but he choked, spitting out vomit. There was no struggle. Instead, a part of his mind, hidden, protected, was snapped open — and he smiled.

The answer was simple; he'd known it since the beginning. He was part of the answer. It had always been his destiny, a destiny he would soon share with everyone. It was the shape of the world yet to come. The New World.

A dark, cold hand, unseen in the darkness, unformed but powerful, circled his neck and tightened. Sharp daggers sprung from the fingertips and dug into Adam's flesh. There was no pain, but he could faintly feel the trickle of blood moving down his chest.

"Who am I, Adam?" demanded the voice. "*Say it!* What *am* I?"

The words came. They were easy now. He floated forward, the darkness lifting him, and he whispered the answer.

"God."

The shadow smiled. Its teeth became visible beyond the pale lips, tapering sharply and glistening. Hungry.

Adam Louis smiled back as he was pulled into the maw, and became part of the darkness forever.

Chapter 3

Patrick woke his daughter early the following morning and they dressed quickly, eager to have a look at the clearing. Their reasons for doing so, however, were completely different. Patrick was seeking a rational explanation for the doubts that had plagued him through the night, doubts he could not account for but made him edgy, even frightened. Cathy was also filled with doubts, but they were based on what she had seen and whether she had been mistaken. Her greatest fear was not that the clearing *did* exist, but that the servants of the night had moved it to a new location.

They closed the door behind them and tiptoed down the hallway, careful not to wake the others.

But they met Tom in the kitchen. He poured Patrick a fast cup of coffee, handed Cathy some toast. After the toast and coffee, they were off.

Cathy led the way down the dirt trail, ignoring the butterflies swarming nearby. Tom and Patrick smiled as they watched her. It was a beautiful day, slightly cool, yet not a trace of the wild wind that had been ravaging the mountains lately.

Patrick surprised himself. He was enjoying the morning so much, actually noticing the sweet sounds of birds and the sunlight on his cheeks that it took him a few moments to notice that Tom had fallen back. He slowed his pace.

"She's a beautiful child, Pat," Tom began.

"Thanks. I know. She's saved my life nearly every day."

"I'm sure you've done the same for her."

His eyes went to his feet, which were kicking up dust on the path. "I never did meet Marjorie."

Patrick was surprised how calm he remained at the mention of his wife. "Well, how could you?" he said. "She died before you even met Janet."

"Yeah . . . Janet's told me a lot about her, though. Sounded like a wonderful woman."

"She was."

"How'd you two meet?"

Patrick's hesitation was due, in part, to the tremor he detected in Tom's voice. *Be very careful here,* he thought. *There's something more he's looking for.*

"At a ball game," he finally answered, trying to retain his easy tone. "I'd decided that I probably wouldn't be much use on the youth center basketball team, so I signed up for baseball. She was one of the coaches. It was toward the end of the summer, the big game, and we ended up playing each other's team. Bam! Love at first sight. At least for me. I think it took her some getting used to me."

"Really? Why?"

"She was taller."

"Oh. Why'd you get involved with the youth center?"

Watch it! Patrick warned himself. "Well . . . I liked kids. I liked baseball. It was a natural. Anyway, we made a bet during the game: Whoever lost would pay for a pizza dinner for the two teams."

Tom's initial seriousness dissolved in a grin. "You mean your first date together was with a bunch of kids?"

"Thirty of them. Worse yet, my team lost."

This actually got a laugh from the other man.

Patrick shrugged, a pleased expression on his face. "Not so bad really. We went out that weekend—just the two of us—

41

and had a great time."

"Is that when she fell for you?"

"Naw. She said it took a few more dates to be sure. But I think she had me set up from the beginning. It turned out that she had signed up with the center because she figured it would be the ideal place to find guys who liked — and wanted — kids."

They laughed together at that, and the laughter somehow brought them a step closer to a deeper friendship. They let the comfortable quiet that followed drift on.

But soon both realized what the conversation had been leading to, and that the tragedy had to be brought up, no matter how briefly.

"Janet told me some of how it happened," said Tom carefully, "but never much detail. A traffic accident, right?"

Patrick found his head shaking in disgust. He pushed his hands deep into his pockets so Tom would not see the fists bunching. His own vehemence disturbed him, but then he'd never really talked a lot about the death out loud. He'd worked it a million times in his head, had even managed to accept it there, but to *speak* the words brought back some sharp feelings he'd long thought dulled.

"Yes," he said, trying not to grit his teeth, "a goddamn stupid traffic accident. Crossing the street with Cathy's birthday presents in her arms. She didn't see the car, and the half-blind, little old lady didn't see her or the stop sign." He took a breath. "It was over quick, though. Thank god."

Tom nodded. It was enough. He let it drop there.

They walked a little farther in silence. Patrick took the opportunity to study his friend. What he saw made him cold.

Tom appeared uncomfortable. Yes, he'd just asked about a very personal matter, but there was more than embarrassment and mourning in that face. For the first time since their arrival at the cottage, Patrick noted the dark folds under his eyes and around his mouth. Not even the dark mustache could hide the scars. And the *eyes*. Patrick had seen those eyes

42

before, in his bathroom mirror every day after Margie had died.

Patrick closed his eyes for a moment, pretending it was due to the sun. He debated with himself whether his interference would be beneficial or build a wall between Tom and himself. He thought back to his counseling days in school, to the help he himself had sought a long time ago . . . and came to a decision.

He put his hand on Tom's shoulder. Tom was a half foot taller than Patrick, but Patrick felt him wither under his touch. In silence, they slowed their pace even more, letting Cathy run ahead.

Softly, Patrick began. "Has this trip helped things at all between you and Janet?"

Tom let out a long breath that carried with it a hidden burden. *How much to tell?* he thought. Things were going better between him and Janet . . . sort of. The night before, they had tried to make love again for the first time in a long time.

Tried, he thought, and a flash of embarrassment and anger rose in his face.

She had tried, god how she'd tried. Her emergence from the walk-in closet dressed in nothing but a skimpy, purple negligee . . . that cloying scent . . . those large, round, deep eyes that he could once become lost in . . . He'd felt a response, felt himself drawn to her, all their differences forgotten. Their loving had been uncertain at first, like their first time together. But then the act grew fierce, burning with frustration, each trying to recapture the passion of the past.

He wasn't sure if it was the guilt he'd been feeling or something else. Whichever, his body hadn't responded. Janet had pulled away with tears in her eyes, whispering, "What is it? What can I do?" He'd had no answer. They had rested until morning in each others arms.

First a failure as a father, and now a failure as a husband.

Tom squelched the ugly thought, sensing somehow that it

43

was not his true feeling.

"Too soon to tell," he finally told Patrick. He couldn't look the other man in the eyes. He felt guilty for not being totally honest.

Patrick said, "You're torturing yourself just thinking about it. You know that, right? It won't change things."

"I know. But I'm pretty sure things will work out. This vacation helps." He found the courage to look Patrick squarely in the eyes. "I love her. She's your cousin, I know, and I could lie to you about some things, but I swear to you I love her. I won't let her go . . . unless she wants me to."

"She won't." Tom wished he could feel the same conviction as Patrick. "It's just the shock of finding out all of a sudden—"

"Right." Tom bit off the word. He'd been trying to tell himself the same thing for the past months. But how long does shock like that last? He'd delved deep into his feelings once to see if there were other emotions hidden there. But only once. And there he'd confronted a monster: betrayal. *We'd both wanted children so much, deserved children—and she cheated both of us!*

Before the monster had been set free, though, he'd shut the door tight, vowing never to venture to that corner of the dungeon again. He was afraid, very afraid, of that creature. Still, feelings change. Outlooks change. And more and more, he'd been feeling as if that monster had come from somewhere else, somewhere *outside* his body . . .

Strange happenings, man . . .

He wondered if he should take another peek below the surface.

They walked on, continuing their slow stroll through the burly pines and thin aspen, stepping in and out of the spotlights the sun managed to sneak through the branches. The morning dew still fell. It created a sparkling shower. Both men felt washed clean by it. They forestalled their conversation to appreciate the beauty. All could be wrong in the world, they thought, their very lives crumbling in despair, but this forest would always be here, breathing, waiting for someone to take a stroll in it. What the hell, it had all the time in the world. And there was something very comforting in that that neither man attempted to explain.

"You know," Patrick said, his voice as soft as the surroundings, "when Marjorie died, I had to make a decision. I had two choices. I could continue grieving her death"—*mostly through drinking,* he thought grimly—"and let my life and Cathy's go to hell. Or I could get on with my life. My life with just my little girl." He took a deep breath. He couldn't understand how women could reveal themselves to friends so easily. It was like wrenching a gut out. "I decided on the latter, and it was like Margie was dying all over again. It really was. I had to let go of the last piece of her, and that was the hardest part—even more than learning about her death."

He turned to look at Tom. "No matter what disaster hits your life, you gotta decide which new path will make you happiest. And when you do, all the other ways disappear." He shrugged, looked away. "Choose a path, man, or you're going to be standing at that fork for a long, long time."

They continued forward, together. He was about to add something more, something inane to calm the raging silence between them, when suddenly they were jerked back into the present.

Before them lay the dark clearing. Fat. Empty. Alone.

Patrick turned away from it and saw his daughter sitting patiently on a nearby rock, elbows on knees, head rocking in her palms.

"Daddy! Finally!"

Cathy was off the rock, her pudgy hands held angrily at her hips. In mock fear, Patrick hurried ahead and cried out in a tired, country, twang, "I'm here, Missy, I'm here!"

Tom stood back and surveyed the area. "This is the place, then."

"Yes, right here," Cathy said. "See the circle?" She pointed along the outside of the clearing. Trees and high grass bordered the area, but nothing of any color or shape passed within.

Patrick looked closely at the ground. Cathy was right. There was no life of any kind; no weeds, no plants, no insects. Nothing. Just lifeless earth, like some dark desert.

Standing at the edge, Tom kneeled and rubbed his hands in the dirt. It didn't feel like ash, certainly didn't look like it. The ground was not hard, but somehow it conveyed a feeling of sharpness, as if there were thousands of tiny pins waiting beneath.

Not even the merging of grass and columbine around the circle showed signs of singeing. However, they did reveal some activity. Tom circled the clearing with his eyes, determining whether the occurrence was identical all the way around. It was.

"Pat, look. The bordering grass. The blades and flowers all bend counter-clockwise, like there was a small tornado pushing them."

The other man moved to the border. A foot of grass and flowers around the area, broken in only a few places by tree trunks, leaned to the left. The grass beyond that twelve inches was tilted at varying degrees. Normal.

Tom stood, still looking around. "What do you think did it?"

"Tornado's the only thing I can think of, but then the rest of the grass . . ." His voice trailed off.

"What do you think the radius is?"

Patrick briefly measured the area in his head. "I'm not very good at estimates, but I'd say about ten feet. Can't be any more than that."

"I figure about eight, eight and a half."

Their investigation continued for nearly an hour. They inspected the dirt inside, compared it to the dirt outside. No real difference was discovered except for the color and hardness. The dirt outside was muddy and tough, like dough. The dirt inside, dry and course. They looked for scars on the neighboring tree trunks, but came up empty. They searched for branches that might have been torn from trees, but found nothing.

They did find, however, that the leaves of the bordering trees were bent in the same direction as the grass. This made them inquire further when they'd been ready to quit.

As the two men busied themselves, Cathy sat on a boulder and watched a large black ant crawl up the side. She picked up a twig lying nearby and put it in the ant's path. The insect climbed onto it and stopped, its antennae twitching. Cathy held on to the end of the stick and slowly brought it to the clearing's border. There she watched the ant with morbid anticipation. The bug remained unmoving on the twig, except for its antennae twitching.

Cathy stepped into the clearing.

The ant's antennae stopped and the bug released its grip of the twig. It hit the ground, its black shell nearly making it invisible against the dark earth. Cathy shuffled her feet and eventually found it rushing to the edge of the clearing, back to the green grass, towering columbine, stable ground, and predators of all kinds. She put her foot in its path, but it easily hurdled over the top and continued on its panicked course. Cathy followed it to the edge, where it paused and attempted to gain its bearings again.

Cathy nodded with understanding. "I know just how you feel," she whispered. "It's cold in there."

Nearby, Tom was studying something of interest above him. He called to Patrick and pointed. "This branch, see it? We must have missed it first time around. It's been cut or burnt or something." What he was pointing at was a thick pine branch, low on the tree, that had sprouted from its trunk many years ago. The end was severed, matching perfectly with the edge of the clearing below. From what they could make out, the amputation seemed to be clean, without discoloration or splinters.

"Jesus, whatever made this clearing must have been a tall

son-of-a-bitch."

"Or it was lifted upwards," Patrick suggested. "Come on. There might be others around."

They hastily inspected the trees within the affected range of the clearing's birth, and they counted seven definite cuts — plus a few possibilities.

Tom looked to the other man for help. "It's like a giant hole lying on *top* of the ground. An eight-foot circle going from ground to sky."

"Destroying everything in its path," said Patrick, looking straight up.

"Except us," added a tiny voice.

They turned and saw Cathy standing on the border, her hands wrapped behind her back.

Patrick took his daughter in his arms and turned back to Tom. "Well, we've had our little look around. It just gets more puzzling, so why don't we go back and get some breakfast. Give us time to think."

Tom nodded. "It was a pleasant morning for a walk, anyway."

Patrick agreed. Despite the mystery surrounding the clearing, it was a beautiful day. Almost unbelievably so.

As Tom hiked by them, Patrick looked at his daughter. Her chubby arms were wrapped round his neck, her face only inches from his. She smiled before he could avert his eyes.

"I'm sorry I doubted you last night," he said, the words strangely catching in his throat. "This is really weird out here."

"What made it?"

"I don't know. We'll talk about it back at the cottage. But in the meantime" — he redistributed her weight in his arms; God, she was getting bigger! — "do you want to ride or would you rather walk?"

She wrinkled her stubby nose. *That's a trait from me,* he thought, imitating the twitch.

"I want to race home," she said.

Patrick feigned exhaustion as he put her on her feet. "Race home? *Race home?*" Cathy knew what was coming and she readied herself, leaning forward on one leg.

"*—Race home!*"

They were off, running up the cant, the girl's squeals echoing through the forest until the shadows swallowed them.

Tom was taking a leisurely pace home, enjoying the fresh air, when the two hurried past him. He nearly called out something, but thought better of it. Let them have their fun. They looked great together. He hoped that he and Janet would one day become as inseparable.

But with the mystery of the clearing tugging at his thoughts and the cold mountain air working through his lungs, he never really noticed that it was all too late.

Father and daughter came running up the trail and burst into the house through the dining room veranda. Cathy had won fairly, but both had worked hard and were gasping for air. The trail had been uphill the whole way, and Patrick could feel his heart pounding against his ribs, demanding more room.

Mother and daughter were up by then, standing in their robes, frying eggs and bacon on the stove. They greeted the two competitors with a plate and told them to help themselves. Tom walked through the open door just as Janet was asking about him. He smiled on hearing the concern in her voice.

During breakfast, Janet and Avilon queried the others about the clearing, and grew more curious about the mystery as it was uncovered—and expanded. But by the end of breakfast, when the conversation had turned to lighter subjects, the clearing was stored in the back of their minds, too large to contemplate during what was supposed to be a vacation. The residue was slight and unduly affected only one person. Avilon wrote a short note to remind herself to

49

call the sheriff later in the week about the problem in the forest.

At that time, other inhabitants of the town were just awakening.

Mavis Thrumond opened her door quickly to get the morning paper from the front parkway. She put a wrinkled hand over her eyes, as a visor, and stepped out, kicking her feet along the concrete.

"Damn sun," she muttered. She had cussed the sun every day for the past forty years. She had been young once, and new to mountain life, and she had at one time even thought it romantic that her cottage was built with the bedroom window—and, consequently, the front door—facing east. Waking with her young husband in the sun's first glory had been dreamy—for a while. Age takes away those fantasies, though, and replaces them with the inconveniences of reality, and it was now, as it had been for several decades, that she was forced from slumber by the sun's blades, always finding their way through her thin curtains. What's more, she had to endure the rays the sun threw as she moved blindly to find her paper.

Life hurts, she thought. But it would be infinitely worse without her paper to read during breakfast.

Her blue-streaked legs kicked out here and there, and she cussed the paper boy. He never landed it on her front step, even when she would promise to give him a dime more each week. He usually got close, though, and it was the sun that caused most of the problems. Doctor Newton had said it was a sign of old age and environment. Her eyes were deteriorating and she stayed in the house too much, not enough sun. Mavis considered this to be hogwash, so she cussed the doctor out, too.

Finally, her leg made contact with something to her left. She bent over and picked up the elusive paper, then turned her back on the enemy, the victor once again.

She made her way back to the friendly shade, tucking the paper under her arm. Then, she stopped, squinting, and craned her neck forward.

There was another shadow under the porch's roof. It had a distinct shape, one she might have described as tall and elegant had she ever been able to speak to anyone again.

It reached for her, beckoning.

Mavis stepped forward, the paper slipping from under her arm, and put her hand in Its. It was cold, dark, like the shade she had holed up in all her life. It was comforting. Her eyes met Its. Immediately, the sun behind her was more than an inconvenience — it was a threat. Cool shade, always her preference, was now a necessity.

Licking her dry, wrinkled lips, she stepped into the shadow that was her home. She felt strange now, her body tingling with an excitement she had not felt since waking with her young husband in the sun's light. . . .

Her eyes watered with — *Love? Pain?* They seemed interchangeable in this lover's presence.

The black holes drew closer, almost floating in front of that distant, indistinct face. "Who am I, Mavis?" the voice asked, so smooth, like her late husband's, she thought. "What am I?"

Mavis smiled, enjoying the attention this shadow gave her. She loved the cold, couldn't understand why people enjoyed the warmth of bodies. She wanted to be seduced by the darkness, to love it as it loved her.

"Who am I?" the voice asked again.

"Lordy," she cooed.

She felt the sharp clamp around her throat only for a second. Then the ice rose in her veins, through her heart, up her neck and into her head, exploding nerves in a final orgasm. At the end, Mavis Thrumond closed her eyes and fell into the waiting arms of her old friend, darkness.

The checkerboard sat untouched, twelve pieces of plastic awaiting the onslaught of their equally numbered enemies.

Greg Wesson sat at the table in his shack, moving his eyes from black square to red square, his thin face supported by a cupped hand and an arm stem. His eyes finally veered from the pattern and glanced at the clock above the fireplace.

It was 1:00 p.m.

Adam Louis was an entire hour late. Yesterday they had played a few late evening games. "Just one," Adam had promised. He had won the game and had begged his friend to play another. Wesson had considered where the night was going. He had shopping to do the next morning, something he did only once a month, and he'd wanted to get an early start. Still, rarely did Adam have a look of triumph on his face, so they had played a few more games — Adam winning most of them because Wesson had been concentrating on his shopping list — then had retired early.

He stared at the checkerboard now, the same one his friend had been so enthused about, had been practically *drooling* over in anticipation of the afternoon game. Well, it was afternoon. Where the hell was he?

Scenarios filtered through his mind. Maybe he got hurt on the way over — or on the way back last night. Maybe he had a heart attack. Maybe he had some disease and was quarantined. Maybe . . .

Maybe he should give Adam a call. Once decided, it took him a good five minutes to remember the number, as he rarely used the phone and he'd forgotten where he'd written Adam's number. "Damn memory," he cussed, as he dialed. He let it ring ten times, then hung up. "Damn *his* memory," he muttered. "Old fool's probably gone vegetable on me."

Many tragedies assailed his mind. Adam drank a lot — too much. Perhaps he was lying drunk somewhere . . . or dead on some road after an accident . . . or the ticker gave out . . . or . . .

52

Fifteen minutes later he was shaking with worry, torturing himself with gruesome pictures of what might have happened to his friend. Eventually he did the only reasonable thing he could think of. He sat down in front of the checkerboard and tried to remember the telephone number of the Harkborough sheriff.

An hour after the sheriff's phone began ringing, there was a knock at Avilon Jersey's door. The family inside was enjoying a light lunch of crackers, cheese, and small salads. When the door was hammered, everyone was silent, and only Avilon looked excited. She turned to Tom, leaning in close as though she were passing on a bit of gossip. "Tom," she said, "this is the surprise guest I wanted you to meet."

Tom looked to Janet for a clue. She shrugged, as puzzled as the rest of them. But before anyone could begin asking questions, Avilon was out of her seat and hurrying to the door.

She returned with a large man—more in build than height—whose face resembled two milky pouches with a glowing, bulb of a nose in the middle, and a pair of spectacles magnifying a squint. He was dressed in a dark-green suit and carried a boxlike leather bag. As Avilon moved to the side, the guest momentarily snatched his crusty cigar from his mouth and rumbled out a greeting between lips resembling two red tires.

He was introduced as Doctor Timothy H. Newton, the one and only physician of Harkborough.

"What a wonderful surprise," Tom breathed dryly. Janet grinned at him and stood to greet the good doctor.

Newton, however, did not meet her hand with his, but stood back and studied her with mock astonishment. Slowly, his beach ball shaped head began to nod, satisfied with what he saw.

"Janet Jersey," he rumbled, offering his hand, "it's an abso-

53

lute pleasure to see you. I remember when you were nothing but a little seed sprout inside your mother."

Janet's face grew red. She quickly grabbed Newton's outstretched hand and tried to look pleased. "Hello, Doctor. It's Janet Howards now."

"Yes, of course. I remember, now. I was at your wedding, but you wouldn't have seen me unless you were at the buffet table."

The small slice of tension in the room was eaten away as everyone laughed.

Newton bent over and looked up into Janet's face. "Oh, now, girl, don't start storing blood up there. We have no secrets. Remember, I was the first man to see you naked."

Janet couldn't help turning away, so she disguised it with a smile and returned to her seat next to Tom. Her husband studied her with raised eyebrows and a slightly amused look on his face. She said nothing, but her mind was a whirl. One never really forgets a man like Doctor Newton.

He had delivered her into the world, had performed her first operation — removel of her tonsils — had given her her first shot and her first lollipop. And years later, had been her gynecologist, therefore honestly the first man to see her naked, adolescent body — when nudity really matters.

But there had been something harmless, even comforting, about the old man. He'd always seemed the same age to her, consistently the oldest man in the world, and even now he looked unchanged but for a few more folds in his skin, a bit more gravel in his voice, and a little more shock in his hair — all the accessories of age that he liked to complain about. Funny how she could still be embarrassed by this man who reminded her of Santa Claus, a man who knew her every secret. But the discomfiture always led to a sense of belonging. He was a part of her home, too.

And God, she thought, coughing, *he still smokes those crusty, smelly, nickel cigars. Some things just won't change.*

Newton turned from her and allowed Avilon to lead him

by the arm to the others.

"And this over here," she said, "if you remember, is my nephew, Patrick Simon, and his daughter, Cathy."

The two men shook hands cordially. They had never really gotten along since Patrick, as a boy, had kicked the doctor in the shin and called him an old slob after the older man had given him an injection—a distant, childish grudge, but one that had grown along with the individuals.

Newton passed Patrick off with a nod. However, he waxed over Cathy, bending in front of her, smiling ruefully, and gently shaking her hand. Her arm flailed helplessly up and down as he pumped.

Next was Tom, and he stood tall, holding out his hand in greeting.

"And this is the man I wanted you to meet," said Avilon, eyes twinkling. "Doctor Newton, meet Doctor Tom Howards."

Newton consumed Tom's hand in his own, turning the young doctor's knuckles white. Newton's cigar turned upward in his mouth. "Ah . . . a man of my own bank account. How you doing, Doc? How's business in the big city?"

"Oh, just a rampant flu bug, uh, sir. Nothing serious."

The big man grabbed the cigar from his mouth and burst out laughing. His good cheer was drowned in a fit of coughs, and Avilon took his arm again, helping him to a chair. Janet went for some water. He drank it greedily and breathed deeply for a few moments. When the coughing fit was over, he looked up at Tom. "Sorry, Doctor. When I was your age, an influenza bug could wipe out entire families. Now I find it's nothing but a little poop on the collar."

"Well, influenza wasn't what I—"

"You know," Newton cut him off and turned to Janet, "it's really good to see you folks again. I've been delivering babies for, oh, a hundred years or more, and I've never come upon a bigger bundle of trouble than what you were."

Janet was speechless again. *This is what you wanted,* she told

55

herself, *old memories*. All she could answer with, however, was a grin.

Recognizing her discomfort, Patrick filled in the space. He looked over to Cathy and winked, saying, "I bet my little girl is twice the bundle little Janet was."

Newton stared over at the girl, stretching his layered neck. His face grew grim. "Is that true, young lady?"

Cathy was also speechless, and looked to Janet for help. There was none there. She turned to her father and recognized the expression. Then, with her head held high, she answered the doctor, "Yes, sir, I am."

Newton stared at her soberly for a moment longer. Cathy's expression did not waver. Eventually, one of his thin eyes winked and his mouth wrinkled into a grin. He spoke very softly.

"Glad to hear it. Kind of a tradition."

As Timothy Newton's good cheer was devoured by Avilon's family, Sheriff Kinkade rolled one of Harkborough's two squad cars up Adam Louis's parkway. He stepped out into the afternoon's waning light and looked around.

Quiet.

Nothing out of the ordinary.

He slapped a cigarette from its packet and lit it. A ghostly trail of smoke followed as he stomped to the front door. *Always good to stomp,* he thought; *let them know you're not here on a social visit.*

He stood on the front stoop for a moment, sucking in smoke, listening. Still nothing. *As they say in the war movies, it's quiet . . . too quiet.* Kinkade smiled at the line, as he always did when he caught it on the late show. This trip, he felt, was almost as embarrassing. Some duty. He checked his gun at his hip, pulled his flapping pants up around his plump middle, and, having no other choice, knocked.

No answer.

His hairy, stubby hand drummed on the door again, louder.

Still nothing.

"Goddamn it, Adam," he bellowed at the door, "this is Sheriff Kinkade. I got interrupted in the middle of the *Battle of the Bulge,* so you sure as hell better answer if you're in there." He and Louis had been friends for all the years Louis had lived in town. He knew him well enough to know that the man was probably watching the same war movie and didn't want to be disturbed. This made Kinkade even angrier. If he wasn't going to be bothered by a sheriff, it probably meant there was a good scene on, which meant the sheriff was missing it.

"Damn you, Wesson, you senile old fart," he cursed under his breath.

The air pressing on him didn't help his disposition any. It was uncommonly humid for the late afternoon, and it made him sweat under the cumbersome and, in his opinion, quite unnecessary uniform.

He pounded the door once more, waited, threw his cigarette down in disgust, and tried the doorknob. He hadn't really expected it to turn. Greg Wesson was such a notorious drunk that he figured Louis had told him he was going out somewhere today and the old fart had clean forgotten. Still, the rusty knob *did* crunch clockwise, and the sheriff was further surprised to find he had to put some considerable weight behind the door before it would snap open.

"What the hell . . . ?"

The first thing that shook him was the smell. He had been concentrating so hard on the door that the abrupt stench nearly pushed him back outside. When his senses returned, he realized that the odor was not new to him. He had encountered it a few times before, during the long course of his career, when some of the older residents of Harkborough had died.

"Christ," he muttered, removing his hat. "Adam, I'm . . ."

57

He realized he was about to apologize, and stopped, embarrassed. He hadn't even checked the house yet to make sure.

It was not an easy task. Even after years of service, his face still paled when looking for death. It would be so much better he thought morbidly, if they would just die out on the porch or in the street, where everyone could see them plain as day. He hated searching from room to room, inevitably opening each door of the house slowly, his lips dry, waiting for that first glimpse of a stocking or hand so that he could exhale the fear he'd been carrying. It was worse than looking for a dangerous criminal in a dark alley — at least *they* had a chance of running away and never being found.

Like all those other times, he now had an image in his mind, one he tried to prepare himself for should his eyes actually meet it. Adam Louis, dead less than twenty-four hours. Couldn't look too different, definitely not rotting away. He'd be lying across a bed or table, one hand clutching a warm beer, the other pushing his fingers into his cold chest, trying to stop the pain. His eyes would either be bulging or, if Kinkade were lucky, closed, and his tongue would probably be peeking out from between blue lips.

That was death. Undignified to the dead, terrifying to the living.

Kinkade shuddered and waited till he got it under control. He didn't want to see those eyes — pupils so large they looked like bullet holes, eyelids so red they looked like tears of blood brimming over. He knew, just smelling the stench, just thinking of that image and being in that house, he would be sick for a week.

And if he actually found the body . . .

Ten minutes later, all the rooms had been searched twice. There were no signs of foul play, no evidence that the dying man had dragged himself across anything. And there was no body of Adam Louis. Only the smell he'd left behind.

Kinkade, breathing a little easier, scratched his bald head and patted his cigarette packet again. It was empty. He crumpled the packet, stuffed it deep in his pocket, and continued his preliminary investigation. He checked all the windows, found only the bedroom's unlatched. He checked the back door and kitchen door, but both were locked and chained. He couldn't think of anything else, so he left, closing the front door behind him and making a mental note to have it padlocked before nightfall.

Quickly, as the sun was being caged behind the forest of branches, he stepped around the cottage, searching for any prints, human or animal, near the windows and back doors. There were none. He returned to his car, wishing to hell the radio wasn't busted, but figured Louis's cottage to be far enough from nosey types that he could make a quick run to the station, use the radio there, and be back before anyone was the wiser.

During the ride back, he tried to fight the nausea pushing at his throat. The smell, he was certain, had been that of a corpse. But where was the body? The doors had been closed, as had the windows. Still, Adam must have been dead for quite a while to have left such a powerful reek in the cottage.

A frightening conclusion came to mind. Although, like the investigation, it was only a scratch at the surface.

Adam Louis must have been murdered.

Kinkade had searched that house twice, under and inside every corner and shadow, and had come up without a body. So the decedent had to have been moved by someone. *Now, he asked himself, who would do such a thing? And how the hell did murder find its way to Harkborough?*

"Whoa . . . back up, son," he grumbled to himself. He was a career man, and knew his job. No body, so he couldn't prove murder. All he had right now was a worried checker friend who liked to drink and a man who had disappeared.

And, of course, the stench on which Kinkade laid his whole theory.

When he got back to the station, Sheriff Kinkade grabbed a padlock and chain, rounded up his deputy, and both men met at Adam Louis's empty cottage to talk of murder and search for a body.

Dinner went smoothly. Though his initial introduction had been awkward, Doctor Newton's history with the family helped put everyone at ease. With very little effort, he'd soon found his place at the table.

Janet watched the man who she had once admired, and thought comically that he certainly ate like one of the family. Avilon had prepared a roast, garnished with potatoes, beets, and a salad. Doctor Newton had seemed unconcerned that he was last in the food chain, but at receiving each dish, his chubby little hands had gone to work digging out as much as his plate could politely hold. If anyone else had noticed his eagerness, they did not reveal it.

As she watched the elderly practitioner, she felt an icy stir in her belly. A man she had *once* admired, but no longer. Why? He was a very old friend of the family, and had probably expected a hug and grand welcome from her. But she had managed only a smile — and knew why.

He was the first man to probe her, to discover her every secret — every secret but one. He had not uncovered her sterility. For all those years, he had never informed her she would be unable to have children. So the question came like a dagger. Had he always known and kept it from her, or had he missed it completely? Worse yet, the thought of her condition alienating yet another loved one was something she wasn't quite sure she could endure. But the anger did not dissipate. In the end, in silence and in guilt, she returned her attention to her plate, her question unanswered.

By the end of the meal, the discussions became separated by interest. Janet, Patrick, and Avilon continued reminiscing, while the two doctors hit it off, against Tom's initial reticence, and were in turn listing the advantages and disadvantages of city and country medical practices.

Beside Janet, Cathy sat quietly, listening. She had heard the stories of her father's school days before, so she tried to concentrate on the new guest. She sensed her father's antipathy toward Doctor Newton, but, to her own surprise, she found she liked the older man. He reminded her not so much of Santa Claus, whom she knew to be a fake, but of a kindly old uncle, like the doctor she'd seen on "Bonanza" on TV. Gentle, kind, with a throaty chuckle and a childish whim about him, she thought him nearly irresistible. Still, the thought of feeling close to any man other than her father slightly worried her, and she strained to keep a level head about this new male.

The conversation between the two doctors had sounded interesting at first. There were words she did not understand, processes and techniques she knew nothing about, but the enthusiasm each man showed was contagious. Cathy giggled when she tried to pronounce some of the words Tom was answering with. She got halfway through "cardiopulmonary" before Newton and Tom stopped and stared at her. When Cathy's grin disappeared, they chuckled and shook their heads. Cathy crossed her hands on the table and put on her best innocent expression.

Perhaps feeling a natural break in the evening, Avilon excused herself and returned with dessert, vanilla ice cream with chocolate syrup and nuts. She apologized to Cathy for not having a cherry to put on top, but she promised to get some next time.

The subjects started up again as they ate. Cathy tried once more to listen to the medical talk, but her interest in her ice cream won out.

With a final spoonful midway to her mouth, she suddenly froze and shook violently. Painful needles stabbed the back of her eyes. She pushed on her eyelids until the slivers went away, and silently wished she hadn't eaten in such a hurry. Still, it was not for nothing. It brought back a memory that chilled her further.

61

She looked over to Newton, who was transfixed with his own double scoops. *He's a doctor,* she considered, *and knows a lot about these mountains. Maybe . . .*

"Doctor Newton," she said carefully.

Newton and Tom paused again to look at her. Patrick noticed the annoyance on their faces and leaned toward his daughter. "Cathy, don't interrupt—"

"I wanted to ask him about the clearing," she said in a low voice, but not so low that she wasn't sure the two doctors had heard it.

"Forget about it," hissed Patrick.

"He can help," she answered.

Patrick's reluctance was like a magnet to Newton's curiosity. The plump man leaned forward in his chair, folding his hands before him, and smiled pleasantly at the girl.

"It's all right, Patrick," he said. "Now, what did you want to ask me, Missy?"

Blood rushed from her face as she looked around the table. Once again, she was the center of attention.

After stumbling through the first few words, she took a breath and began again. "Well, you've lived here for a long time, right?"

"Almost my whole life."

"So you've been here a *real* long time and you really know the forest."

Newton ignored the child's unintentional slur and smiled. "Yes, I know Harkborough pretty well. Is there something you want to know about it?"

"Well . . ." She paused to look up at her father again, to make sure she was not making some horrible mistake. He was frowning, but nodded for her to go on. "Well," she said, faster now, "when I was out walking yesterday, I found a weird hole in the woods. There was no grass, no flowers, no trees, and not even any bugs inside it."

"A hole?"

"That's what my dad says."

"It's a clearing," Patrick clarified.

Newton leaned back in his chair, stroking his chin as though a beard were there. "And, uh, where is this clearing, hon?"

"Down the trail." She pointed out the veranda window.

Patrick spoke up, trying to keep his voice casual. "It's about two hundred yards down the back path."

"Yes," Cathy continued, "and today me and my dad and Doctor Howards went down to in-vest-i-gate. We found some round grass and some cut trees. I found an ant and I put him on a stick and put him in the clearing. He hopped off the stick like it was hot and ran back to the grass."

Patrick and Tom both leaned toward the girl at this news. "Cathy," said her father, "you didn't tell us that part."

Cathy looked down at her hands. "I forgot."

Tom asked her to explain exactly what had happened and Cathy tried to remember everything. As she spoke, Patrick and Tom exchanged nervous glances. They had felt the same as that ant.

When she was finished, Tom quickly updated Newton on what else they had found at the clearing. The elder doctor seemed entranced, though his eyes were difficult to read behind the thick spectacles, and when Tom related the high branch that had been cut, Newton raised his hand for a pause.

"Did you inspect the inside or the edges of the branch stub, to see if it was cut, burnt, or broken?"

Tom shook his head. "No, it was too high. We'd've needed a ladder."

Newton was silent then, and everyone's eyes were glued to him. With great care, he shifted his body in his chair until he was comfortable, lit a cigar, and considered the information he had been given. Finally, his eyebrows arched and he searched the faces around the table, only now surprised at the attention he was receiving.

"Well," he said, "I can't reach any conclusion from what

I've heard, but I have a few theories. Could be vandals—maybe some kids from another school about to play our kids in some football game—using chemicals, maybe fire, but it certainly sounds man-made. I'd like to take a look at this place tomorrow, if I could. I'm intrigued. Never have many mysteries up here—medical or otherwise," he added, casting an amused eye at Tom.

So it was planned. Tom and Patrick volunteered their services immediately. Janet wilted, wishing her husband would stay at the house, but decided if she were to be with him, the only way would be to join the party.

It all came down to Avilon, then. She shrugged and said, "What the hell. The walk'll do me good, and I'm anxious to see this place that's been dirtying up my yard."

It was assumed all along that Cathy would go, even insist upon leading the way. But she sat pale as she listened to their plans for a merry picnic down the trail. It was strange, but she wasn't looking forward to tomorrow. She didn't want to get near the clearing anymore. She felt—*knew*—that this time the clearing would *want* her inside it.

She thought of the ant, and wanted desperately to run and hide.

Chapter 4

Tom woke the next morning, gently stirring Janet in the process. That was too bad. He had wanted to make a point of waking before her, so that he could watch her, study her sleeping form as he had not done for months, and think about what had happened the night before — and what it meant.

They had stepped into their room around ten that night, and he had realized immediately that neither wanted to attempt a repeat of the night before. But they couldn't help coming together — through talk, touch, and mere presence — to somehow close the past seven months of distance.

They talked about little things, and laughed, unaware they were undressing for bed, since the act had become a chaste habit by now.

But then came the kiss. And another. And the long, deep look into her eyes that revealed surprising depth and an irresistible pull.

And then they were in each other's arms.

There was no hesitancy now, no embarrassment or fear, as there had been the night before. Without even thinking about it, he knew his body was responding . . . as was hers.

His hands made the smooth journey up the middle of her back, arching her closer, their lips melding, tongues probing and meeting anew. What was left of their clothing was gone in seconds. Every aspect of the past was forgotten. There were only these wonderful, warm, breathless moments. Not even the voice in his head could get through.

As he entered her, he whispered, "We'll find a way. I swear we will." He tasted her tears then, and listened to her whisper his name and her love for him, until the whisper became a stifled scream, a song above his low, ragged, quickening bass.

Afterwards, they held each other close, allowing the sweat to cool their bodies while they recovered. Finally, as he began to drift off, she turned her head to look at him. Moonlight illuminated half her face. It was enough for him to recognize the pain in those lovely eyes.

"You blamed me," she said, her voice so soft. There was no hate behind those words — only the flatness of truth.

He nearly turned away from her — actually felt something grab and twist him — but he latched onto those eyes. They held him, as they had when he'd first fallen into them a year ago.

"I guess I did," he said quietly. "I couldn't help it. I hated myself for it, though. I still do."

She touched his cheek. "Don't."

They lay that way for a long while, their bodies cooling, watching each other. Several times Janet tried to speak, but she couldn't get the words out until her eyes moved to the dark ceiling.

"What about adoption?"

He sighed.

"Are you still completely against it?"

They had talked about it once, after the honeymoon, and he had dismissed it immediately. *The child, a lie, a deception!* the deep, guttural voice had insisted. He felt that voice creeping back, but he managed to suppress it. Looking at Janet helped.

"This whole thing," he began. "It's . . . it's just the *shock* of it. We didn't even suspect. It was like a punch from your best friend."

She turned to him again, her eyes glistening. "And on our honeymoon."

"Yes." He tried to conceal the sadness in his voice, but it was impossible.

They had embraced then, and talked no more that night.

Now, with the morning light breaking through the frost on the window, they lay again, silent, their bodies entwined, eyes meeting and holding. They had reached a beginning. He thought that some of the good words and feelings had probably been expressed in the heat of passion — but, holding her now, it didn't really matter. The beginning still existed.

An hour later, they dressed and made their way to the kitchen. Avilon was up, making coffee. Neither could hide their good mood from her, but she did not comment. She only looked relieved.

Cathy bounded down the stairs a few minutes later, followed wearily by Patrick. Twenty minutes later, Doctor Newton was at the front door, eager to get started.

In fact, everyone was anxious — except Cathy. She felt now the uncomfortable tingle that had, just yesterday, been reserved only for her steps within the mysterious clearing. Even more terrifying was that the sensation was taking on a conscious meaning. It spoke to her, like the whisper inside her head when she would think. And it was whispering something horrible.

Her eyes focused once again on the party as they rallied together, hooting and carrying on as if this were a family picnic — which, for some, it was. The only difference was the paraphernalia accompanying them and the ominous destination.

Patrick, for example, did not cart around a basket full of sandwiches, but held a ladder, collected from the attic, above his head. Tom and Janet each carried flashlights, innocently assured that they would penetrate the forest's secrets, along with some mason jars in order to hold whatever samples they might take. Avilon carried a measuring tape and gave Cathy a pencil and paper for writing down the figures. Doctor Newton carried nothing but his own considerable girth and, in his opinion, his inestimable knowledge of Harkborough.

It took a good fifteen minutes to reach the clearing. Cathy led the way, of course, toting her pencil and pad in one hand while trying with the other to help her father with the ladder. Patrick, smiling, carted most of the burden, even more so as he tried to keep in step with his daughter. Behind them, Avilon was talking speculatively with Newton. Tom and Janet took up the rear, talking quietly, carefully.

At the clearing they did indeed look more like a small group of picnickers than a scientific expedition. However, their eagerness would have been evident to any passer-by as Patrick set the ladder down and the others gathered round, hands on hips, waiting for orders.

Newton was the first to survey the area. Patrick, Cathy, and Tom had already seen it and the two women did not realize they had reached their destination. While the corpulent doctor ran his eyes over the oddity, he rumbled, "Yes, yes, the grass is leaning, Tom. And there doesn't appear to have been any fire." He glanced at Cathy and grinned beneath his mustache. "Doesn't appear to be any ants here, either."

Patrick waded to the opposite side of the clearing and pointed up at a neighboring pine. "Up here, Doctor. Here's one of the branches that was ripped away."

Newton stepped into the clearing and, uncharacteristically, bowed his head and crossed himself. As he trudged on to the location, Patrick retrieved the ladder and leaned it against the tree in question.

"Ah, yes," said Newton. "Always look to the heavens for the answers. Here, Patrick, bring the ladder around here . . ."

It was soon done, and as Patrick and Tom steadied the ladder, Newton climbed. The black earth gave the ladder plenty of traction, so Patrick thought it safe to back up a few steps, to watch the doctor's progress without suffering a stiff neck.

Nearly ten feet above, Newton studied the bark of the severed branch. "I'll take a sample from the tree," he finally called down, "so I can study it better back home in my lab. We'll get other samples from the grass and dirt when I get back down. I want to make sure we get proper specimens."

Tom bit his lip, not mentioning that he was fully qualified to do the same.

On the other side of the clearing, Janet, Avilon, and Cathy watched the doctor's examination with wary curiosity. Actually, they were more concerned with Doctor Newton's safety, for it was quite obvious from their perspective that the ladder was not made for the doctor's girth. As his examination continued, however, and his safety seemed secure, the three began to advance. They crossed into the clearing and all three shivered. Cathy, who had had enough of the chills and wanted desperately to concentrate on something other than her own fears, began to point out some of the other oddities that characterized the area. Soon, Avilon and Janet also forgot their apprehension and followed the girl with interest, checking only occasionally on Newton's progress.

Their exploration soon proved successful.

"Tom," called Janet over her shoulder, "I thought you said that this clearing was a perfect circle."

"Wha—?" said Tom. He didn't finish, for Doctor Newton, atop his tower, had also turned at the question, shifting the ladder's foundation and forcing Tom to compensate.

Patrick called, "What was that? You found something?"

"Here," said Janet, pointing at the edge of the clearing, "there's an arrow going off on its own, almost touching the circle."

Patrick hurried over to them and studied the "arrow" in silence.

It was an arrow of sorts, really just a triangle, and the dirt inside was identical in content to the clearing, but he was certain it had not been there the day before.

"What is it?" called Doctor Newton.

"It's an arrow," called back Avilon, "didn't you hear us?"

Patrick added, "It looks like an acute triangle — an arrow — pointing away from us. There's only about an inch of grass separating it from the circle."

"Don't move. I'll be right down!" called Doctor Newton.

"Maybe sooner than you think," mumbled Tom, still struggling with the ladder.

"Tom," Patrick called again, his voice taut, "I'm positive this wasn't here yesterday."

Janet touched his arm. "Pat, are you sure? It couldn't have just appeared —"

"I think this whole thing just appeared, but I don't know why."

"Well, I'd certainly like to know why," grumbled Avilon. Her arms circled around herself reflexively, her mind still ignoring the unnatural chill. "This is my land, and I want to know who's been vandalizing it. Why, I remember all this used to be dense with trees."

"Dense with . . . ?" Patrick's mouth continued moving but nothing more came out.

By this time, Tom and Doctor Newton were approaching at a quick pace. "Don't touch anything," warned the elder doctor, "just back away so I can see."

They did as he asked, and he leaned down at the base of the triangle, twitching his head back and forth, birdlike, in order to see it from different angles.

"I think," he said finally, "we should take some samples of this dirt and compare it to the ground in the circle. Would someone hand me a couple of mason jars, please?"

Tom bit his lip again, trying to keep the words, "No shit, Sherlock," from being said in company.

As Doctor Newton's chubby fingers worked feverishly to push both top and bottom soil — though there seemed little difference — into a mason jar, Patrick's voice came back to add another disturbing piece to the puzzle.

"Avilon, if you're certain about this clearing once having been filled with trees—"

"I am," Avilon said indignantly, her eyes glued to the doctor's activities. "I should know my own land. This trail went for a mile or more before reaching any wide open land. When you people talked about a clearing, I was thinking of a little circle where the sunlight had snuck through the branches. I didn't realize someone had mowed down my trees!"

"But that's just it. If someone had, wouldn't you have heard them? I can see the cottage from here. And if you were away or something at the time . . . well, where'd they put the damn things? Where do you hide or carry off a half dozen pine trees?"

Everyone was staring at Patrick now but Doctor Newton, who was intent on his samples.

"God," said Janet, "how could they be taken away? How can you uproot so many trees without anyone knowing?"

"Perhaps," stated Doctor Newton as he stood and screwed the lid on a jar, "the answer is in this container. I'll study it tonight. Not many secrets can be kept from scientific study, even the mountain-hick kind."

Tom did not rise to the bait.

But Janet thought, *Not all secrets, Doctor*—then pushed the venomous accusations from her mind.

As Doctor Newton busied himself shoveling dirt from the circle into another jar, the others stopped staring at each other and spread out, searching for more clues.

They found them soon enough.

"Over here," shouted Avilon, waving, "I've found another arrow."

"Here, too," called Tom.

"And here," said Patrick, the enthusiasm noticeably absent from his voice. To his logic, the number of "discoveries" was becoming ridiculous, and he suspected that someone was playing a practical joke on the group. It was a family reunion, after all; what better time to have some fun on some old friends . . . or, perhaps, to wreak a twisted but harmless revenge on some old foes? Still, the longer he thought about it, the theory seemed to fall out from under him, for he could think of no one person or family that would fit the bill, either now or from the past.

But when all the "discoveries" were found, his assurance that it was all a joke was solidified. In all, five identical triangles had been counted, all evenly spaced about the circle, pointing outward.

And he was positive, without a doubt, that they had not been there the day before.

So who had put them there?

The question, he felt, was academic. He was tired of the whole business, now that he was certain it was just a joke, and he wanted to get back to the rest and relaxation he had been looking forward to for so long. He grumbled, trying not to act selfish, when he discovered that the others would not be so placated until more extreme — undoubtedly Doctor Newton's scientific — evidence had been brought forth in his defense. They were, he thought grumpily, living in the shadow of a doubt.

Cathy could not see her father's face, but her own enthusiasm echoed his. She was not bored, just couldn't find the discoveries as exciting as she found them terrifying. To her mind, the triangles were a part of the evil here, which meant the circle had grown during the night, stretching its tentacles further into the world. What would it resemble tomorrow? Or would tomorrow be too late?

Too late for what? she asked herself. But there was no answer.

She considered searching for another ant so that she could demonstrate to Doctor Newton the unnatural power the clearing contained, but when she realized that would lead to her stepping into the clearing herself, she dismissed the idea.

Instead, she waited until Doctor Newton was finished scrounging samples, hoping that he would suggest they leave for home.

"Well," he reported, "I've got quite enough of the dirt, but we need some parts of the grass and flowers bordering the area."

Cathy shuddered, held herself against the internal cold, as Doctor Newton continued.

"I'm not a botanist, really," he said, gazing up at the tree he had been inspecting earlier, "but I'd say that that missing branch was ripped off, probably sideswiped. The bark has small strips hanging past the break, bent the same way as the grass. I'd like to get some samples of the bark now if someone would hold the ladder for me."

Cathy did not catch Tom's groan, but she would not have smiled if she had. She wanted to get everyone away from here, back into the warmth of the cottage. Even better, she wanted to be back in her own bed in San Francisco.

"Doctor," her father was saying, following the old man to the pine, "do you have any idea what may have caused all of this?"

Newton stopped and stared at him blankly, as though he were shocked by the question. Then he said, "For the life of me, Pat, I've no idea — as of yet." He raised the empty jar that would soon hold the twisted bark of a pine tree. "As of yet," he repeated. "However, I can tell you that whatever did cause it, it wasn't a natural event. Not fire, not chemicals. Nothing that nature could produce . . . that I know of."

As the adults continued listening to the old doctor's guesses, Cathy's hope slowly shrunk from ever pulling the others from this place. *God, what if it grows while they're in it? Will the earth shake? Will the ground open up, fold out, spit up? Maybe it'll just burn —*

Then she hit upon a new idea, one that chilled her so deep that she had to sit down to catch her breath.

What if it has already grown? Maybe this isn't the only clearing created? What if there are more nearby?

She looked helplessly at her father, now holding the ladder alongside Tom. Should she speak? There was no real reason to believe there were other clearings, but she couldn't shake the suspicion that she hadn't walked far enough down the dirt trail. There could be several spaced out along the path, perhaps some larger than this. And if there were, she would have to warn everyone.

"Daddy . . ." she called.

Patrick glanced over at her sharply, then back up at the doctor's progress. "What is it?" he snapped.

He'll never go for it, she thought. *Not now, maybe not ever. He's as sick of all this as I am scared. And the others, they're all huddled together, they can't break away from this place . . .*

"It's a prison . . ." she whispered to herself, and a wind tickled her spine.

"What is it, Cathy!" Patrick called, grunting to save the ladder's stability.

"Daddy, I'm going to go farther down the trail, all right? I won't go far, I promise."

"Why?"

She couldn't tell him that she wanted to search for another clearing. He'd get angry, think they'd end up sniffing around all day then. And she couldn't muster up her nerve to tell him that, most of all, she wanted to move away from this clearing. Far, far away.

"Just to look around," she told him.

He stared at her for a moment, that exasperated look that said, Give her a circus and she's bored in an hour. Cathy tried to appear eager so as to foster the thought. She didn't really care how she got away as long as her escape was immediate.

"Okay," he finally called, "but you stay nearby. Within calling distance."

Cathy agreed and took off.

The trees converged, blocking off the adults behind her,

74

but instead of feeling chilled and alone, she was relieved. The effects of the clearing were gone now, merely distant warnings in her mind.

As she traveled down the trail, lower and deeper into the forest, her mood lightened, for it appeared she had been completely wrong about more clearings existing in the area. She would have felt them by now. They would have been an intrusion so forceful that the forest would be unable to hide the change. *Thar be no lions here,* she thought.

She continued on, unafraid, finally falling into the spell the forest had cast just for her. The dew had stopped falling and the sun streamed through the curtain of branches, still glowing sharply. She was curious again, wondering, examining, appreciating the marvels presented to her. Home and bed were the farthest things from her mind.

However, the charm of nature did not release her from her agreement. When she thought she had gone a good distance, she knew enough to go back. And although she was not looking forward to leaving the glitter for desolation, she was anxious to report to the others that there was only the one clearing to worry about. Only a single wart that she hoped Doctor Newton and his lab could soon burn away.

So relieved, she turned to retrace her path.

Her body locked, and the chill of a distant warning once more leaked from her bones.

The forest had changed. The sun was outcast, the woods were dark and still. Only the thin grey eyes clutching at the leaves above provided illumination, and above them their roar was sounded.

It's a storm. Clouds covering the sun, rumbling with thunder.

But the eyes growled again, and she could not help reflecting on a darker explanation. She ripped her own eyes from their gaze and faced the ranges to the east. The trail was sprinkled with yellow rays, but they died quickly as a vague, dark line rolled over and devoured them.

Her body twisted now, unaware of any direction but "here"

and "there," unable to distinguish any colors but "black" and "grey." Night had followed her along this trail, and she could feel it expanding across the mountains.

"Daddy," she whispered.

It had been following her since she'd departed the clearing. The others had been left behind, arguing about the origin of the clearing that was no longer a circle.

It knew the answer.

It had chosen the old and the young first because of their extreme weaknesses. One suffered from melancholy and a contempt for life, actually welcoming death in some form. The other was mere innocence, having had few lessons to learn from.

Of course, It had changed all of this.

It had shown them that love was not something to be sought or cried over, but something which was easily avoided. It had shown them that to follow life was so much simpler than leading life, and a much sounder foundation for the evolution of powerful ideologies and brilliant, *immortal* races — ones who sought nothing but the final, great peace. It had shown them that an eternal death was so much more fulfilling than a short, painful life.

After all, that was Its right now that the War had been won. The foundation was set. Now It had only to build the empire to its ultimate, explosive destruction.

Creation, It knew, was made up of small steps, and that was why It felt no shame in hiding in the shadows. The little girl was frightened, It could see that, and It could experience her shiver the same way the living experience a breath of fresh air. It smiled. It would feed upon her fear, develop it until it had evolved into an understanding and a united goal. Then she would be a part of the darkness.

But first It had to whisper the sweetness through her veins and purge her of the life and love that haunted every man.

It would feed. And the little girl would grow even colder. Until she understood and thanked It.

Terror jolted her, a finger slamming up her spine and rippling her muscles. Every nerve screamed for her to get away. But there was nowhere to go. Darkness surrounded her.

The figure approached, and she caught Its faint outline against the dark crests of mountains miles away, then rising above them, a jutting slab pushed up from the earth's angered core. But It could not be from so deep, she knew. It was cold, like the clearing, and she felt the strength emanate from Its eyes, growing and pushing past her reserve with the unswerving power of a glacier; black disks, swirling orbs that slammed past her lids, but gentle once inside, so *cool*, a pond beneath a tropical waterfall, to protect from the sweltering heat, and, oh God, how she wanted to dip into those pools—

Abruptly, she tore her eyes away. She realized, with an internal understanding that came with the cold, that if she were to gaze into those eyes long enough . . . she would become a part of the darkness forever.

Like this man.

From and of the shadows.

Shadowman.

Like from a child's nightmare, but the title seemed to meld easily with the thing now beckoning her.

And although she wanted desperately to join the legions those eyes promised, one thought broke above all others: If she was a part of darkness, she would never see her father in the same light again.

That feeling of loneliness startled her more than the approaching shadow. Cautiously, she squinted at the stranger and saw that the figure had taken the shape of a man, dressed in black from boots to striking suit to ruffled cape. It was almost upon her now, nearly within touching distance. Cathy concentrated on the cape. Somehow it was a part of this creature, almost another limb, almost like — wings?

It stopped. If It jumped forward It would have her. But It would not try, it seemed. It was merely waiting for her to reach a decision.

Cathy understood all of this, and she suddenly was awakened to all that could be hers if she touched this creature and called It by name.

Still, her father would be taken from her, never to be loved or comforted again. She could not bear this, no matter what the rewards.

Its lips parted, perhaps sensing the rejection, and she was allowed to see the incisors thrust through raw, pale gums. Above this transformation, Its nostrils flared wide with a dead breath, so much like an animal who had sensed an enemy. Or food.

Her eyes inevitably wandered toward the orbs, but she kept herself in check. Instead she watched the silhouette of the monster grow, every muscle tensing to take her into Its world.

The decision had been made for her . . . and she moved.

Avilon, Janet, and Patrick had finished picking choice grass blades and flowers along the border of both the circle and the surrounding triangles and had meticulously labelled each jar the samples went into, when the elder doctor called it a day. At last they were brushing off their hands and knees, preparing to return home, and not one of them did not dream of some cool water and a soft pillow. As Tom got a head start carting the ladder home — pleading that it was now permanently attached to him — Patrick cupped his hands over his mouth to call his daughter home.

A child's scream interrupted him as it broke through the dark forest's grip.

Patrick's heart clenched. He first mouthed the name in

panic, then stumbled toward the path, finally screaming, "Cathy! Cathy!"

Another scream answered him. "Daddy! Daaa-deee, *please . . .*"

"Cathy!" Patrick broke into a sprint, kicking up dirt along the path, as good as bread crumbs for those following him. *"Cathy, where are you?"*

Another scream, only farther away. Patrick blindly followed it, lurching over the hurdles of rocks and roots in his path. He barely heard Tom scream out over the pumping of his own heart, "Everyone stay together! Don't go off the path!"

Patrick squinted through the wind rubbing his eyelids raw. He still couldn't see her, but she couldn't be far. She had only been gone for a little while.

Cathy was running.

The figure had been surprised by her scream and sudden reflex to escape. It had paused, Its deadly smile disappearing. The orbs had blinked, unable to comprehend how such a little girl could have so much control over Its trance. And while It stood there confused, Cathy's legs were moving, trying to pull her as far from the nightmare as possible.

The legs of a ten-year-old are not so long, their stride not so wide, but Cathy's legs now belonged to someone else, for she was flying. When she took a second to glance down through her tears, she saw that she was not on the path. It didn't matter, not now, not with what was behind her. She blinked rapidly and eventually her vision cleared enough for her to search out wisps of sunlight. She had to get out of the darkness. The darkness was Its home. *It* was the darkness. *It* had brought the overcast and the chill. And somehow, she knew, *It* was responsible for the clearing.

"Daddy . . ." she whispered, but it came out as a wheeze. Behind her, she heard the granite footsteps grind into the earth, racing after her. *What was It?* When she had looked into the thing's eyes, she had known the answer, all had been plain to her from conception to goal. Even now the words and ideas struggled to cross her tongue, but she bit her lip and kept running.

Adrenaline still coursed through her, but it was dying. Her breathing was raspy, hard to contain. Her body was covered with cuts and bruises from the slaps of low branches and shrubs. Still, she could not stop. Even when the stench hit her full in the face, forcing hot acid up her throat, she did not stop. She knew that if she did, she would never feel anything again.

Sounds of struggle surrounded her—her arms swatting at obstacles, her coarse inhales, hidden animals fleeing the rampage she brought. Over it all, there was the ticking of her heart, faster and faster, pushing energy through her veins until there was none left to give.

Then there was a new sound—water running over rocks. Would the stream be big enough for her to swim, travel downstream? Did the thing behind her like water or avoid it?

The questions were pointless, however. It was merely a tiny brook, sufficient to carry a frog gently through the woods. She jumped over it without a second thought—and heard a heavy foot smash the water behind her as she landed on the opposite bank.

Inches!

It was on her heels!

A frigid, stinking breath rolled down the back of her neck. It forced a scream to rise in her throat, rolling, waiting to explode when those dark hands reached for her . . .

But her scream was shattered into a huff of lost air, and she suddenly found herself sitting in the dirt. At first she thought she had run into a tree or a wall, but as she struggled to regain herself, she recognized, through puffed eyelids, that the obstacle had been a man.

Not *the* man, but a stocky, robed man with his hands

sandwiched in his pockets.

Must be near another cottage and he heard my screams, she thought.

Quickly, melting before the giant, she crawled to the man and wrapped her arms around his bare legs.

"Please don't let him get me! Stop him! Call my daddy!"

She dared a glance behind her. There was no one following. Could it have been—*no!* She had *not* imagined it. But the breath on her neck, the foot in the brook . . . could it have been her panic producing those effects? Raw with emotion, she realized there was no time to ask questions now. There was only time to cry and hold this stranger and beg for his help.

The man she held spoke softly. "You'll be all right. Some-one chasing you?"

"C-call my d-daddy," she stuttered between sobs.

The man stroked her hair. "I can't do that, Cathy. Not now."

Ice filled her soul. Her eyes wiped clean of tears, she now stared at the man's bare legs. They were white and dimpled. Scratches marred the surface, but there was no blood. Only empty white veins.

Cathy's bottom lip quivered uncontrollably as her gaze rose up the man's body, to his face. It was pale, like pure snow, a grey beard that looked fake etched out on his chin. Dark circles hung from empty eyes—eyes that watched her. The grey lips parted then, and a black tongue flicked out, licking the gleaming canines that reflected the girl's terror.

She was stone cold, ready to die, but somehow she made it to her feet. Her eyes were glued to the teeth. They were the only living things on this body. The man—the *thing* made no move toward her, but continued standing calmly, prepared to watch her and the next few centuries pass him by.

Electrical impulses impossibly made it through her marble body, and her legs began to carry her backwards. Her stom-ach, too, was alive, for it was rising in her throat, forcing her

81

to double over. She wouldn't let her eyes move from those teeth, though. Somehow she had to turn and run, but she couldn't let loose of those teeth.

She swallowed hard. Her fists bunched up. Vomit hung from her lips. Her eyes felt so wide they would soon burst. She had to let go, she decided. It was the only way to get back to the sun, back to her—

Was that a voice calling my name? Daddy? It was so distant that she could barely make it out, but she sensed the general direction, and that was good enough to move on.

With lightning speed, she tore away from the stranger and raced back the way she had come, toward the voice calling her.

She ran right into death.

Her forehead slammed into a large jewel, its center as red as blood, the gold framing dull in comparison. It was hanging about the Shadowman's neck, over Its chest. It covered where a heart should be encased, but where only a dark secret existed.

Upon contact, Cathy screamed and backed away, unsure of who or what she had bumped into until she saw the clear, black orbs staring back at her. They called to her now, whispering a song, twinkling and winking at her. There was no pain there, they told her, no worries or cares. There was no love, of course, but that was the very root of all pain, wasn't it? Here there rested only a simple obedience, without fear of punishment.

Cathy's scream was her only way to fight it. She latched onto the scream and pushed it hard against the jewel, against all that followed the Shadowman. It locked her jaws, squeezed her own eyes tightly shut, and it was only after the release that she could turn again and run.

As she rounded a small clutch of trees, heading for a boulder field, Adam Louis looked to the Shadowman for instructions. None was given, but there was an expression of confidence there, and finally the lips parted to calmly speak.

"She is ours."

Patrick was hoarse, but he ignored the pain and continued calling his daughter. He had been shouting Cathy's name for what seemed like an eternity. He had heard a few more screams in answer but now there was nothing. He slowed his pace, trying to think, trying not to panic. Silently, he prayed that Cathy was doing the same.

Tom and Janet were the only ones to catch up with him. Avilon and Newton had gone back to the clearing, in case the girl should show up there or at the cottage.

Patrick tried to calm himself, but his actions were clearly hysterical. Lumbering back and forth, whispering his daughter's name, then suddenly crying out—these were actions he did not think about, but went through naturally.

He found Janet standing in front of him, pushing the hair from his face, searching his eyes. Her lips moved, but he couldn't hear anything. He tried to speak.

"Where is she, Janet? *Where is she?*" He called Cathy's name again, but it came out crusty and weak. "Where is she?" he asked again, but Janet's mouth was no longer moving. What could he do but try again?

"Cathy, where are you, hon?"

Silence held her from him.

Tom appeared before him, offered, "Look, she couldn't have gone that far. She was only gone a few minutes and she promised to stay close. We might have passed her. She's probably off the trail and scared. She might even have found her way back by now."

Patrick was shaking his head furiously. "No, no . . . the—s-screams, her—s-screams, were coming up—ah-head. S-she's somewhere—ahead. She wouldn't—l-leave the trail, I—"

Janet was stroking his cheeks again, and this time he heard a voice.

83

"Easy . . . breathe deeply . . . you're getting too excited . . ."

Her soothing was interrupted by another scream. A little girl's scream. *Cathy.*

Patrick forgot his companions and was running again, moving deeper into the forest, away from the trail.

"Cathy! Honey!"

He was hyperventilating, he knew, but he forced the screams through the forest. His lungs were filled with concrete and getting heavier. The world was spinning. Still, there was nothing to do but scream and search for a blonde head amidst the shadows.

Janet and Tom followed, also screaming the little girl's name. They were not as sure as Patrick as to which direction they were going. As far as they could tell, the scream could have come from anywhere.

Cathy was forced to slow, her breath coming in short, painful gasps. She tried to think clearly, but the cold from behind always pushed her on into darkness, increasing her panic. She wasn't sure what to do, except to run and scream. Both were becoming impossible, though, as her body was near exhaustion. The figures were so close behind she could feel them, and somehow they controlled the movement of her legs. They would get her if she didn't do something different soon. Dizziness hit her in waves, scrambling her thoughts, and she doubled over, her hands and arms pushing her legs up and down, keeping that lifeline moving.

Almost blind from tears and pain, she stumbled through a maze of thin aspens. Then, when those were gone, her world tilted sporadically. She was crossing a field of rocks and boulders.

Have . . . to keep . . . moving . . .

Or do I?

She glanced back. Nothing was following her, at least that she could see. Still, she felt the cold, and knew they were near. If they couldn't see her yet, she'd have a chance of hiding . . . *if* she had enough time.

As the thoughts slithered through her already jumbled mind, her legs finally gave way and collapsed, making her decision for her. She hit the ground hard, then lay perfectly still with her face in the dirt, her breath creating a minuscule whirlwind of dust. Her eyes darted in their sockets. Sharp boulders surrounded her, high enough to hide her from view of anyone standing a hundred yards off. But it wasn't enough! The Shadowman wasn't tracking her by sight. She had to get closer to the rocks, become equally still and sturdy.

She turned her head tightly and found twin boulders to her right, about five yards away. They were wide, gouged deep in the land, both nearly touching the other so that, unless they were investigated closely, the hole between them would appear to be nothing more than a shallow crack.

Collecting her remaining strength, she crawled on her stomach until she was well behind the rocks. She paused for precious air, then forced her legs into the hole. Her torso and arms quickly followed, and finally her head. Once safely ensconced between the two giants, she attempted to control her gasps and heartbeat which drummed in her ears like so much construction noise.

It will hear.

She thought of those gleaming teeth, and tried to still her heartbeat completely.

Must calm down . . . whispered a voice in her head. The voice talked to her for a long time, now that she was alone. It promised her everything would be fine if she stayed hidden between the rocks, remained silent, and waited for her father to find her. He would come looking for her, and when she heard his voice, she would run faster than she'd ever run in her life, smack into his warm, strong arms. The voice repeated the story several times, differing only a little, and always the same outcome. After the variations had been exhausted, however, the voice also grew bored, and fell silent.

Minutes passed like hours. The sun began to dwindle behind the clouds, creating dark, ghostly shadows in the sky. Observing them through a crack, Cathy concentrated on their shapes, wishing all monsters could be as distant.

When her body was rested—though not relaxed, no, never relaxed—she held her breath and listened. The night wind answered mournfully, but there was no hunger in its voice. Had the monsters finally left? She doubted it. Darkness was their home; why would they leave now?

She took in air for a while, then held her breath once more, this time listening to her own callings. Joints creaked whenever she switched position. Her eyelids were puffed and dry, seeming to snap each time she blinked, like two twigs slapped together. Her heart was no longer the roar it had once been, but she still felt its warm pressure pulsing steadily, building new strength.

She breathed once more, and took inventory of her surroundings. There was nothing but varying sizes of rocks, dirt, and a far-off forest. Whatever had been behind her, she could no longer see. Her muscles gave a little, and she shifted into a more comfortable position. She was deep inside the field, amongst hundreds of identical boulders. They might search for a while, but she was as dark as the hole she hid in, and would hear if they came too close. They might sniff for her odor, but she was so covered with dirt and weeds and twigs that, if she lay on the grass in plain view, they probably would overlook her. They might even surround the area and wait for her to pop up in search of food or water or aid, but she was certain that her father and the others would find her by that time.

Yet there was that doubt. And doubts can be very powerful.

What if Daddy passes by without seeing me? What if he's tired of calling my name, tired of looking, and decides to go home? He may be passing me right now!

86

She realized it was a doubt that had dangerous implications, but she vowed to be careful. Safe or not, though, she had to get a better view of the outside. The small crack in the rocks' side did not provide much landscape to study, but she felt that if she stuck her head out of the entrance in back of her . . .

She recognized how badly the thought of open, *free* space made her want to escape her niche. But she had promised to be careful, and she would. Mindful then, she peered out the small crack at the side, to see if the Shadowman was lurking anywhere in that direction. There was no movement but for the grass dancing with the wind. Then she peeked out the entrance hole, scanning very carefully for any intruders. As she saw none, she thought it safe to move out — slowly.

First, her head slipped through the crack. She twisted her neck this way and that, but there was nothing to see that she hadn't seen already from within the shelter. Her shoulders wiggled forth, followed by her arms. As she sat up, her legs still safely tucked within the hole, her perspective rose about two feet — still not high enough to see over most of the larger boulders, but enough to catch the border between forest and field. No one moved, no one called.

With deliberate calm, her legs were plucked from the trench, then her back pushed against the twin boulders. She wondered which action would be the best to follow next. Stand up quickly so as to get it over with; or do it slowly, blending in with the land. She chose the latter, for it had served her well so far.

It was difficult to keep from moving faster, but eventually she was standing at a crouch, looking out over the field and to the forest beyond. Not even the grass was moving now, as the night sky — she assumed it was night and not just a pall brought by the Shadowman — had stolen the wind. There wasn't much light with the moon tucked behind the blanket above, but her eyes had adjusted and her vision was now nearly perfect. Not that it made much difference. There was no one to see. Just more rocks and trees.

But then the importance of her actions became clear. The malevolent presence had not abated. She wanted more than anything to crawl back into her hole and wait for Daddy.

Without thinking twice about it, her knees buckled, and she was sitting again with her back against the twin boulders.

As her legs began to slither back into the hole, a disturbing thought caught her all at once, and she froze. She had searched in every direction for her father and the Shadow-man—every direction but one. She had not looked on the other side of the twin boulders. And if someone was waiting for her there until she crawled back into the hole . . .

She left the thought incomplete, certain that the ending her mind would create would send her body into convulsions. Instead, she tensed the muscles in her legs, prepared for swift flight, turned her face to the wall of rock, and began the slow ascent.

Her eyes twisted this way and that, making sure nothing was near, that nothing was sneaking up on her. Her hands rested lightly on the rock face, but as she rose from her kneeling position, that pressure grew stronger and imprinted the crust onto her palms. Higher, higher she panned over the boulder's face, her eyes now locked onto the hard design of swirls, pebbles, and glistening grains. Her chin drifted softly over the bumps and pores. The face bent back, revealing the new world on that side of the rock.

Higher . . . higher . . .

Once during the climb she heard a snap, but it was due only to the painful extension of her legs. She did not hesitate, though, for she was nearly to the top of the mountain. Her eyes were ready to clear the pinnacle and all she could think was *there will be nothing there . . . there will be no one there . . .*

Then, disturbing the hypnotic silence, her ears rang with a familiar voice.

"Cathy, where are you?"

It came from behind her! She gasped and turned her back

to the rock again, her eyes searching wildly for her father.

"Daddy! Over here! Over he—"

From behind, two hands, as big as shovels, cold and pale with age, gripped her head, popping both of her eardrums with the pressure. Cathy was pulled upwards, away from her little hole in the ground, and lifted into darkness and the monsters in the sky.

She didn't have time to scream. The pain was fast and the shock dulled it further. She could only close her eyes and experience ironic joy as all feelings were sucked from her, replaced by black ice . . . and an understanding.

Near the end, Cathy Simon wrinkled her freckled nose and smiled.

Chapter 5

Twenty yards away, behind another rock, Patrick stumbled into the field, looking frantically for any sign of his daughter. His nose was full, so he was forced to breathe quick, irregular gulps through his mouth. Through blood-shot eyes, tortured by tears and sweat, he saw only blurred, white outlines. Through ears that throbbed with his heartbeat and struggling lungs, he heard—could have sworn he heard just a few moments ago—his daughter calling out to him.

He paused in his rampage to listen again, but through the sobs that jolted his body he could not make out the sucking sounds.

"Patrick!"

He turned, wiping saliva from his lip. It was Tom, calm Tom with his rational voice. Patrick chose not to hear and turned back to the field that held his daughter.

Tom rested a hand on his shoulder, but Patrick also chose not to feel that. He called out her name again, but the field did not answer. Compassionately, hopelessly, Janet and Tom gathered around their friend, blocking his view of the world.

"Let's go back," they cajoled.

Evening covered the mountains. The sky was black and

restless, stretched across the distant mountains, covering the world.

At Patrick's insistence they searched the field before leaving. When they found nothing, they doubled back to the trail and checked the surrounding forest on the way home. They finally met up with Avilon and Newton, who reported that they hadn't heard from Cathy either, back at the clearing.

It had been Patrick's last hope, and the words were as fatal as a dagger through his heart. He tried to scream, tried to shove her name into the night once more, but it only materialized as a prolonged sob.

While the others circled around to help bear his weight, he tried unsuccessfully to deal with the surge of emotions assailing him. For the last few hours he had been dead, numb with shock. But now it all came rushing back, and he closed his eyes, trying to see the patterns, to organize them.

He was angry. Angry at anyone that would do this, angry at the God who would allow this, angry at the forest and the vacation and the ideas.

He was depleted, a dark vermin gnawing at his strength, at his stamina. *There was no way to rebuild that,* he thought, *and it will only hurt her more.*

Also, there were the varying degrees of guilt for having let her go off alone; the embarrassment over allowing these shadowy emotions to escape from their long sentence; and the irreconcilable struggle between obsessive love for his daughter and intense hatred for whatever power had taken her away.

That was as far as he could go, for the remainder of his thoughts were tangled, looping forever over the same should-have-dones and why-couldn't-it-have-beens.

He tried a last call, not to his daughter, but to some higher power that could help. But even that had to contend with the wall of emotions, and the rush of air was released in a slow, vengeful hiss. He began to cry uncontrollably that this fleeting hope had been denied him. He cried on as they helped him to the house, unable to stop and not sure he wanted to.

None of them could believe the little girl, so full of life, so real, was now gone — perhaps forever. The hike uphill was silent, interrupted only by Patrick's sobs and the wide, terrified gazes exchanged by the others.

Once in the cottage, Doctor Newton gave Patrick a sedative. He was scowling when he administered the injection; all those years of carrying that damn bag around everywhere he went, and now it had tragically paid off.

The sedative worked almost instantly. They helped Patrick upstairs and soon he was hurrying toward a peaceful sleep in his bedroom, next to an empty pillow with golden hair sprinkled across it. That sight stayed in his mind during the night, keeping the current horror from his dreams. There was only Cathy as he remembered her. Smiling. Straw hair. Freckled nose. Chubby arms reaching for him.

"Margie . . ." he whispered, and then he was out.

Downstairs, Tom called the Sheriff while Avilon made coffee — the only contribution she could think of. Later, the four adults settled into their seats and prepared for a long evening.

But not their longest.

Sheriff Mark Kinkade arrived near seven o'clock that evening. He was a tall man, settling comfortably into middle age. He didn't even bother to cover up his receding hairline with a hat. His uniform was a bit too large for him, but it had been that way for the last ten years. At the moment, it was covered with dirt and sweat, and when he entered the cottage, he looked everyone over with dark eyes and a tired scowl. No introductions were offered; he'd met everyone in the house at one time or another and he had always been good at names.

"Good to see you people," he nodded to the Howards. He then turned to Avilon, who brought him a cup of coffee without her usual cheer. "What happened here tonight, Ave?" he asked.

"May be best if you talk with one of those two." She gestured to Janet and Tom. Kinkade knew Avilon well enough that, if she didn't want to talk about something, she must be very upset. He didn't press the matter.

The Howards explained all that had happened, to their knowledge, from the discovery of the clearing to the disappearance of Cathy Simon. The sheriff listened quietly, his scowl deepening, his eyelids twitching with irritation and exhaustion. At the end of their account, he stood, shaking his head.

After a moment of thought, he confronted Newton. "Is he upstairs, Doc?"

"Yes, I gave him a sedative. He'll sleep, God willing, until morning."

"Damn it," grumbled Kinkade. He patted his coat pocket, searching for a cigarette pack. His nerves were frayed, his thoughts disjointed. He'd always left duty to others whenever he'd felt this way in the past, but there was no way he could go home and rest now. Unable to find a pack, he stalked to the front door, feeling the family's eyes on his back, pushing for an encouraging word, a miraculous solution. He had none to give, and felt his heart sink even lower.

He stopped and stiffened, deliberating. Finally, "I gotta tell you folks something, but I don't want it spread around. I don't want a panic on our hands on top of everything else." He sniffed, wiped at his eyes. "You people ain't the only ones in Harkborough that've reported a missing person."

The others moved closer, anxious for more. Kinkade grumbled something under his breath, then continued.

"I've been running all over this damn village, from Frank Reynold's place to Hickory Lane. The station's been swamped with calls about missing husbands, wives . . . children." He had their attention riveted. It made him shrug, a little embarrassed. "Well . . . you know, by swamped, I mean swamped in Harkborough terms. At last check, I think we had nine cases. There were twelve, but the other three showed up, mostly kids lost in the woods again." This created a vibration through the listeners. There was hope, then. Their faces implored it. The little girl could only be lost, soon to find a road or a cottage.

Kinkade couldn't bring himself to mention that those other kids had been found within two hours of their disappearance.

"Anyway," he continued, "we've got calls from friends and relatives—even kids running in the station, saying their parents were gone." He wiped a long hand down the length of his face. "You folks, I hope, are the last ones."

"Mark," Dr. Newton interjected quietly, "when did all of this begin?"

"Got the first call this morning. Adam Louis was supposed to meet someone and never showed. Went out to

94

his house and didn't find a thing. Clothes are still there along with all of his belongings, so he sure as shoot didn't decide to take a trip all of a sudden."

The room grew silent again. Faces looked pale in the glow of the two lamps illuminating the room. Shadows hid their eyes. They could taste the fear falling over them, heightened by the sheriff's own ghostly features: If authority was afraid, everyone was afraid.

Tom was the last to find a seat. This was becoming too much for him. Though he'd dealt with pain and loss before, it had always been from a professional position. Then his eyes rested on Janet's weeping form, and he grimaced at the falsehood of his thought.

Doctor Newton leaned forward on the couch and said, "My God, Mark, hasn't anyone been found yet besides those wayward kids? I mean, *adults* lost in the woods? Adults who have lived here for years, maybe all their lives?"

"Doctor," said the sheriff, staring down at his muddy boots, "we've had nine reports today, no telling how many tomorrow. There doesn't seem to be anything special about any of them. All I can figure is maybe someone is . . . well, taking them."

"Why?"

"I don't know. Maybe some creep from the city came up for some fun. Thing is, there doesn't seem to be any pattern. Hell, we haven't even found any bodies. For all I know right now, these people might all be gathered down at the liquor store playing poker." He glanced up, and it was clear that he was embarrassed to admit this to anyone. His eyes held shame. "I've . . . never handled anything like this before. Things are always so peaceful up here. I . . . I trust you'll give me your full cooperation.

I'll do everything—everything!—I can to find your little girl."

Avilon reached for his hand and squeezed it. "Of course. Anything we can do, Sheriff."

Kinkade seemed to perk up at the sound of the title. His voice was strong now, in control. "I'll be by early tomorrow to talk with Pat. In the meantime, I want you to lock up your house tight tonight. We've been spreading the word that there's a burglar on the loose so the neighbors will lock up without any panic." He paused to stare out the den window, his eyes glossed over. "There's something bad out there and I don't know what it is. But I swear, eventually either I'm going to get it or it's going to get me."

" 'It'?" asked Doctor Newton. "Why 'It'?"

Kinkade stared at the elder man for a moment, his lips working slightly as though struggling to form words. Nothing materialized, however. The sheriff merely turned away and headed for the door. Over his shoulder he reminded them to lock up everything and perhaps keep a single light burning in the living room.

During the drive back to the station, he thought about what he had said in the cottage. He *had* said "It" without hesitation, sure of his choice. Why? Was it the mystery surrounding the culprit—if there was a culprit—or was he merely generalizing everything he felt he knew about this menace in a single abstraction? That answer also eluded him. He was too tired to think further, and his mind turned to the comfortable cot resting in the office.

He pulled into the station and dragged himself in. Some office, he thought. A quarter of the station, separated by a half-inch of cardboard and wallpaper. He smiled and whispered to himself, "Well, what do you

96

expect in Harkborough?" He'd never expected much . . . certainly not the disappearance of nine of its citizens in one day.

How many tomorrow?

Shaking his head, he threw his gun belt over a splintered chair and flopped down into its worn arms. Forget the cot. He wanted to be ready to *move*.

Feet kicked up on his desk scattering missing-persons reports, head thrown back, arms folded behind his neck. Nothing to do now but watch the phone and hope that it would never ring again.

That night he dreamt of holes in space and tentacles.

Pauline Davenport carried the cake into the middle of the festivities and was welcomed with a unanimous roar. It had taken her a week to plan the big birthday bash: sending invitations to the Johnsons, Kirbys, and Simsons; buying and displaying the decorations; and preparing the multi-layered, extravagantly designed cake she now held in her hands. But it was worth every bit of effort to see the smile it now brought to the little girl at the head of the table.

"Happy Birthday, Corine, Happy Birthday, Corine . . ."

The dark-haired girl brimmed with excitement, not the least bit embarrassed at all the attention she was receiving. In fact, her eyes were wide, reflecting the light from the seven candles on the magnificent cake. She had never seen such a masterpiece of eggs and flour in her life, and she felt a momentarily pang of sorrow that she would have to help tear it down and digest it until it was gone forever. Then she remembered that birthdays came *every* year, and that next time would probably be cause for an even larger prize. Confident then, she took in a breath to blow out the inferno, noting humorously that, beside her, two of her best friends were just as mesmerized with the sight, so much so that they could barely mouth the words to the song.

About to blow, she giggled instead, and her friends beside her, unknowingly the cause of Corine's laughter, watched her and joined in. Just then, the song ended and the guests applauded. Someone over fifty said, "It would take me eight tries to get those candles blown out. One for practice." Someone else under ten sang out, "And many more, on channel four," which didn't make much sense, but was accepted in good humor.

Corine was about to begin another assault on the candles when Pauline rushed up and said, "Wait! Let's put the lights out first! Have to do this properly!"

The lights were killed, and the room was illuminated by only seven candles, giving the once lively celebrants a ghostly tinge, even more eerie that they were smiling.

Corine shivered at the sight and closed her eyes. Behind the lids, she dreamed of limitless toys and games and powers, some of which she might receive before the night was over. She was happy at that moment, truly happy. She couldn't see the golden death masks of those standing around the table. She couldn't see the puzzled expressions on their faces as the candles mysteriously fluttered into oblivion. But when the room fell into complete darkness, her happiness was also lost, and she felt the damp cold of fear.

The party stood there a moment longer, confused and afraid of the sudden darkness. The other girls ran to their respective parents, squealing with mock fear. They weren't sure what was happening, but they knew, as everyone did, that the lights would return soon. What agitated them was that "soon" was taking a very long time.

Finally, Pauline spoke over the group's confusion. "Uh, don't worry. I'll get the lights on as soon as I find the switch. Then we'll try the candles again." She passed her husband David and whispered, "And close that damn window. If I have to keep lighting those candles, we'll end up eating wax!" David agreed, but didn't move immediately, as he could have sworn he'd closed the window before the guests had arrived. Slowly, he stumbled in darkness toward the end of the room.

"Okay," called out Pauline and hit the light switch.

The darkness was not put off.

She flicked the switch again and again, the only sound in the house, but nothing happened. She tried a nearby lamp, but again nothing. "I'm sorry," she told them. "I don't know what's wrong." Her guests laughed nervously.

Jim Simson held his daughter tight, trying to control her very real shaking. "It's probably just a temporary blackout," he said. "It's those winds down on the main road. Always blow the poles over." Others in the room grunted their agreement, but his little girl strengthened her hold around his middle.

David returned from the depths. He did not want to compound the mood, so he moved carefully to his wife's side. "Pauline," he whispered, "the window *was* closed. There's no way that a breeze could have gotten in here."

The whisper was not silent enough. It carried through the cavernous darkness and reached innocent ears. Frank Kirby was one of them. "What breeze, David?" he asked.

"Oh . . ." He paused, wishing he could glance at his wife before continuing. If he chose wrong, there would certainly be another damned fight later in the evening and he'd get little sleep again.

Ah, what the hell. Better than dead silence in the dark.

"Well, you saw it," he said. "The one that blew out the candles. It's probably just a draft from a vent or something." His hand sought Pauline's arm, but it grasped cold air.

Isabel Johnson sighed, a most unmistakable sigh for those who knew her. "Well, all we can do is wait for the lights to come back on," she offered. "I hope it hasn't ruined your night, Corine."

They all stared into darkness, at the end of the table, expectantly. There was no sound down there. Pauline, absently flicking the light switch up and down again, snapped, "Corine, did you hear Mrs. Johnson?"

No stir. No whisper. No breath.

Pauline started toward her daughter, angry at the additional pressure put on her. David managed to grab her arm, pulled her back and held her still against him. She stared up at him questioningly, but stopped from saying anything when she made out he was looking elsewhere. She felt his body stiffen.

He knew she was watching him, but he didn't acknowledge it. He was too afraid of what was at the end of the table.

"Corine," he said cautiously, "don't play games now, okay?"

Another cold wind flashed through the room. One of the little girls began crying, followed by a soft *shh* and a muffling of the sobs.

David, his eyes still locked on something, pushed Pauline behind him and crept toward the end of the table. His wife called his name, pleading for him to come back, but she did not make any move past where he had left her.

100

As he advanced, the darkness grew thicker, like a fog, and his breath became more labored. Then he stopped. He could barely make out the outline of his daughter sitting in her chair, illuminated by the thin lines of moonlight allowed to slip through the north windows. He hesitated, his eyes adjusting, until he saw her smile. Her teeth reflected an unearthly glimmer.

"Corine, you're not hiding. We can see you. Now come here." He held his hand out, angry at the fear his daughter had stirred in him. His own daughter!

In seconds, his hand was holding something cold and hard. The shadow gripping him was not his daughter's hand. It was too large, too rough. The ice spread, and his arm went numb.

"Corine . . . ?"

The figure in the chair stood. It went past the four feet of his daughter, even past his own six feet. It nearly touched the ceiling. Behind It, a pair of wings wafted in the still, cool air.

David tried to scream as the smile he thought was his little girl's mutated into the snarl of an animal, dripping with slick, black goo. David knew instinctively it was the blood of his daughter.

The scream finally made it past his lips.

The party, standing far back, nearly hidden, watched and heard in horror. They made out a huge figure whose mass slammed through the darkness's fog. It was lifting David Davenport off the floor and into Its greedy mouth.

Pauline rushed forward, trying to grab hold of her husband before he disappeared forever, but she was pushed back by a sharp fist in her belly. She slammed against the ground. Tiny explosions of yellow light blurred her vision. She must be dazed, but there was something else, something heavy and sticky covering her sight.

She stared at the ceiling and blinked several times before realizing the ooze melting down her face belonged to the creature above. A new creature. It was pale, almost glowing, smelling of death. Its face came closer, so close, *too* close, to her own. The black eyes, the white skin, the wrinkles splitting the face — and the only living part, the *teeth* — inched, slowly, inexorably, toward her erratic jugular.

But none of this was equal to the true horror that Pauline finally recognized.

This creature was her daughter, Corine.

Pauline's scream was cut short as the girl bit into her neck with a savage force. She smiled as the sucking sounds grew louder. Ice filled her heart, but she was with her daughter now, forever more, and that was all that really mattered . . .

A few feet away from the embracing forms of mother and daughter, the Johnsons, Kirbys, and Simsons were forced back by fear and disgust. They tried to protest, tried to think of something logical and reasonable, to act correctly, but terror slashed their minds, cutting everything away. As quickly as darkness had come, panic and pandemonium erupted. Isabel, Jim, and Frank ran to the aid of their neighbors. Bill Johnson, Harriet Simson, and Lisa Kirby, the latter two clutching their screaming daughters, ran to the front door, trying to escape.

Nobody made it.

Isabel and Frank were taken quickly. First they were moving forward with purpose, then they were yanked into the darkness by powerful hands that were just as quickly hidden by the darkness again.

Jim, however, managed to evade the hands and continued on to where he'd last seen the Davenports—though with only a fraction of the confidence he had had when there were two others backing him up.

Near the front of the house, his daughter Melisa watched him from deep in her mother's arms, snatching hurried, panicked glances at his progress. She saw the clawed hammers long before her father did.

The first caught him in the middle of the back, as Melisa had once seen him hit her mother, only this time a lot harder. So hard that she could hear the bones snap back in reaction and shatter. So hard she could see the blood catch the moonlight leaking through the darkness as the liquid sprang across the room. So hard that this time she wanted to explode with the hate and fear she had always checked when it was her father doing the hitting and her mother the suffering.

But there was no time. She and her mother were at the front door now.

Bill Johnson, leading the party, reached for the knob, but it flew open before his hand was even close. The door arced around, crashed into the wall but did not bounce back, the doorknob now imbedded within the concrete. At the same instant, the windows of the cottage imploded, cutting and gouging those still alive, a mild shower to those of the darkness.

Bill, his upper torso covered in blood from his many cuts, thrust his arms across the exit before the two women and their daughters could hurry through. They pushed and pleaded to get past, but he knew enough to be careful now. He did not want to run into anything like what was inside. Hastily, he searched the dark street with his near-blind eyes.

A bearded face suddenly sprang in front of him, and a white, blue-scarred hand clutched his throat. Bill tried to cry out, but his larynx was torn clean away by the stranger. He fell to the ground, dead. Pale, grinning figures soon covered his body like vultures, constantly pushing their grey hair away from their meal.

Lisa, Harriet, and their daughters backed away from the horror; some screaming, some merely mumbling unintelligibly. More dark figures passed the torn body of Bill Johnson and strolled calmly toward them.

Long fingers pulled at the front door until it was released from the wall. It slammed shut and locked.

Outside, the cries from the living merged with the thunder overhead. Lightening ravaged the sky only once, then silence was forced onto Hickory Lane. The pretty little cottage nestled at the end of the road was as dark and quiet as the other houses on the street. Their walls echoed with screams that no one was alive to hear.

The Army grew.

It was 5:00 a.m. the next morning when Johnny Ryan peddled his bike around the corner of Ivory Street and into the gloom of Hickory Lane. He rode from one curb to the other, tossing papers onto the porches of deserted homes. It unsettled him that he had to ride across and back the width of the street, as the mist was so thick he couldn't tell one house from the next until he was a few yards from it, and his wariness grew as the journey progressed.

There was something very wrong here. The Kirbys

were usually up at this hour, as he worked in the city and it was at least an hour's drive there, twice that in this gloom. But the Kirby windows were dark when their newspaper slapped the porch, and Johnny was so shaken by the loneliness of the house—why, the whole street for that matter—that he almost didn't hear the voices that called out to him from beyond his vision.

They were haunting, yet comforting voices, not wails of torment or cries of despair; but a solemn, almost angelic song that welcomed him into the shadows.

When he was sure of what he was hearing, Johnny's feet pushed against the bike's pedals and skidded him to a halt in the middle of the street. An unearthly cold, rising from the asphalt like insects crawling to the surface of dirt and mud, slithered up his pants leg, up his shirt, up beyond his neck to fight behind his eyes. He shook, gripped his handlebars until his knuckles were as pale as the air around him. He knew two things immediately. There was no warmth to be found here, as this was no place on earth. And there were no sleeping, contented bodies within those homes.

Such thoughts spurred him to attempt action, but for the first time in his short life he was scared stiff. His joints, pushed and pulled by weak muscles, ached with the cold. For an eternal moment he thought the only part of him that *could* move were his eyes, for they were turning wildly about within their sockets, straining to see beyond what the mist veiled.

Then they stopped and he stared straight ahead. He knew now that this was not so deserted a street as he had once believed. Someone was watching him.

A gate snapped shut somewhere yards behind him, and it was just the impetus Johnny needed to break free of his trance and take off. He didn't bother to look back but moved straight down the middle of the street—a speeding train with only one possible direction. His legs pumped faster than they had ever tried, and the vague shadows of houses, rising out of the fog like bloated monsters, were merely a blur.

But still it was not fast enough.

He dumped most of the newspapers remaining in his satchel. Not fast enough. He ripped off his bulky rear-view mirror, leaned farther over his handlebars. *Still not fast enough.* Then his lungs sprang to attention, burning as the stench of miasma hit him full in the face, mixing with his own putrid sweat. Yet on he rode, faster . . . *faster* . . .

And as he rode, he listened. He phased out the drums of his racing heart. He ignored his ragged, hurried breaths. And what was left was that cry of welcome, growing louder, adding voices and ranges, all to the click-ety-clack beat of the cards flapping against the spokes of his wheels. *The cards!* he thought wildly, wishing to think of anything other than those voices calling him. There were three cards: two jokers and an ace for good luck. God, how he needed that luck now.

. . . *faster* . . .

He pedaled, breathed, listened for hours, for days, a single voice in his head finally screaming out: *Where is that corner? Where is Ivory Street?* If he expected it to appear suddenly, like a mirage in a desert, he was fearfully disappointed.

Instead, one of the shadows, until now maintaining a hazy periphery, came alive. It swam out of the fog with sudden speed and barrelled into Johnny's side, nearly knocking him off balance. He would have been lying in the street if his feet hadn't jumped out and caught the ground in time. It wasn't instinct, however, that had made his legs splay, but a sight. As he was hit, he had looked into the face of the woman and had seen a ghost, scarred without blood, and teeth that were distinct even in this gloom.

Mrs. Kirby.

"Oh, God! Please, God!"

He must be nearing the corner, he told himself, where the fog had begun. A borderline. Safety. He pushed harder, ignoring the screams of his legs as effortlessly as he ignored the song around him. The mist seemed thicker as he advanced — *God, am I going the wrong way? Am I going deeper?* Darkness closed around him, creating the illusion of stillness, yet the tops of the houses on either side were still visible, passing like waves in a storm.

Should I turn around? Should I go back the way I came? But what if that's the wrong way? Think what will be waiting for me back there. Strike that. Don't think of that. Just — keep — pedalling —

— faster!

Along with the darkness and the mist came the cold, the biting, hungry ice that hung heavy in the air but was as prickly as a pin in its attacks. The stench was worse, but he grew used to that, expected it of this place. He merely breathed through his mouth now.

The face came back to him, and for a moment he thought he would scream because the image appeared in the fog as before. It was only his memory though, and he quickly turned to studying it, wondering what could have changed such a nice woman so quickly. He'd seen similar faces before, of course. In horror movies the dead people from hell that ate everyone always looked at least that bad. But the song he was trying to ignore didn't sound like the malevolent cries those movie-ghouls made, and it certainly didn't sound like it came from any hell.

As a matter of fact, it sounded quite pleasing . . . almost enticing . . .

Pedal!

Through the pinpoint of darkness he now concentrated on ahead, Johnny watched the growing detail of a grisly pale man, covered with scars and dried blood, doing what he could to stumble into the bike's path. No, Johnny decided, he wasn't stumbling. This was no slow-moving, retarded zombie on the loose. This guy was actually dodging back and forth, waving his arms in order to capture the bike and rider.

By the time Johnny saw the whole picture, it was too late to swerve. He ran straight into the thing.

He tried to keep his balance as the man was ruptured by the bike's front wheel. Although the pain should have been enough for him to lie out of the way somewhere and suffer, he managed to get his arms hooked onto Johnny's handlebars and hold on. His feet dragged to the sides, attempting to slow the bike, but Johnny's feet were still firmly planted on the pedals, and he pushed with all he had, his grunts and cries marking each revolution.

Eventually one had to give, and the creature's newly discovered powers were not as mature as Johnny's determination. So, with swift agility, the guy gave up on one method and tried another. His feet came together, slapped the ground, and hurled his rotting body over the handlebars, growling not with pain or exertion, but with unmistakable *hunger*.

The act took Johnny by surprise. He was not quick enough. The thing had aimed for his neck, but Johnny twisted his head at the last second. Its teeth grasped his ear hard, but after the initial pinch there was no pain. He was sickened, though, by the warm blood streaming under his shirt and down his chest. He listened for the inevitable sucking sound, but none came. All he heard was his heartbeat pounding in his head—and the song growing louder and louder.

The creature continued ripping at his flesh, tearing most of the ear away. Then the mystery happened. The creature flinched. It paused in its mad devouring, then shook in spasms, and finally opened its maw to release what it had taken in hunger. Its head moved away from Johnny, and he saw the thing spit, mumbling, as if it had had some undercooked meal. It might have been funny if Johnny weren't missing most of his right ear—and if the horrible encounter had not continued.

Now the creature was spitting out more than flesh and blood. It was shaking its head ferociously, and part of its lip slid off its face, followed by yellow teeth. Johnny's vision was blurring, but he swore he could make out *smoke* erupting from the thing's mouth, pushed out by its horrible cries of pain. For a moment, the thing looked into the boy's eyes and seemed to try to say something. The next, its tongue lolled, slipped out of its mouth, like syrup poured from a container. Its cries became unintelligible.

As most of the creature's lower jaw glowed with green fire and melted into the bike's newspaper satchel, Johnny screamed as loud and as long as he could. And in the middle of his cry, the pain came. For some reason he could never explain, he was grateful. The pain cleared his mind, filtering out the disintegrating thing in front of him and the voices of welcome and the angelic song. His eyes sprang open, and he saw a rolled newspaper vibrating

109

half-in, half-out of his satchel—untouched by the goo of the monster. In one swift move the paper was in his hand and he was ramming it into the creature's face. The newspaper became limp with the creature's melting flesh, but it finally found its purchase and forced the volatile mess farther and farther back. From the short distance, Johnny managed one final glance at the dissolving man's face. It nearly stopped him dead in the street. He swore it looked familiar. It was put together wrong, the color was gray, and the bubbling, steaming surface disfigured it enough to be foreign, but Johnny was certain that under all that glaze there was a *person* that he knew.

But with such thoughts the song of these creatures rose again. Johnny wisely shook them and returned to business. A final push and the dead man fell away, erupting further into a quivering, screaming lump.

Johnny held his ear. His fingers touched a stub covered with something warm and sticky. He tried not to think too hard now, didn't want to pump so much blood into his head. Adrenaline would take care of the legs. *Pedal, pedal.* He passed the sign that read JUNIPER STREET, and the fog was gone. It occurred to him vaguely that the dark mist had floated over all of Ivory Street, maybe covered other directions too. *Faster.* It was not a time to think of the fog and its horrors. He was past it, and he felt confident that nothing could touch him now that he was in view of the early morning light.

But there was another kind of fog to worry about. He fought to retain consciousness, above all to force his weakened muscles to keep pedalling. *Those people are from somewhere near hell, but this ain't no movie,* he thought. *It's real . . . so real.* He could feel the blood throbbing between his fingers and, oh God, he could feel the *pain*. This was all

110

too real.

Tears welled in his eyes at the thought of his family having to face those creatures. An image flickered before his eyes, but the pain washed it away. He would never remember that his own father had just tried to kill him.

Eventually his mind closed completely and his eyes glazed over into shock. Still, his legs kept up their revolutions, inexorable as the hands of time mounting the clock. His direction had been chosen long ago and would lead nowhere else. It was the nearest safe place he could think of, a place that was open with a phone and a man who would help.

Art's General Goods was open for business eighteen hours a day ever since Art Billings took on an apprentice. Billy Upton was a good kid, hired for his knowledge of displays and inventory, his head for figures, his interest in management, and, Billy suspected, his dating the boss's daughter, Amy. However it came about, Billy was grateful for the experience and he proved his worth to Art every day.

He'd been working at the store for about six months, naturally volunteering for the graveyard shifts so he could, on his own, learn as much as possible about the inventory and stocking of the back room. He was becoming skilled at it, almost to the point where it was second nature, as it was with Art Billings—though he also knew that it probably wouldn't impress Art very much. The boss knew what he could do behind the store. His main worry was how Billy handled things up front. Working with people had never been Billy's strong point—the inevitable drawback of having a voice that wavered in monotone and occasionally stuttered—but he'd been working on it with Art's help, taking a few of the day shifts just to get in some practice. He'd improved a little, and the confidence was giving range to his character, if not his voice.

Amy liked that, too.

Still, all the confidence in the world couldn't have prepared him for the visitor he confronted that early morning.

Johnny Ryan stumbled up the wooden planks and groped for the door with a blood-slicked hand. He had just entered the dull light of the shop, the bell above the door announcing his arrival, when relief covered his face and he fell to the floor face first, unconscious.

Billy came around the corner of the counter as quick as light. His mouth gaped and he began to reach for the boy—then stopped, remembering something Art had once warned him about. The kids around there loved to play practical jokes and some burglars from the city played all kinds of games to get the storekeeper out from behind the counter. Billy frowned, wondering what action to take. The kid was so pale, and it didn't look like his chest was moving, though it was hard to tell with him lying on his stomach. He debated whether to back off and just wait a while to see what happened.

Then he saw the pool of blood spreading across the floor.

Chapter 6

Patrick woke early the next morning, but decided to lie in bed until noon. He didn't want to face the others—not yet. He curled up in a ball, on his side, and held himself to keep warm. There were covers on the bed, but somehow this was more natural, more comforting. The cold was tangible. It was so bad that it nearly fogged his breath. More harrowing, it held him prisoner, prickling his skin if he dared move.

His mind wandered elsewhere, though, and he closed his eyes and tried not to dream.

Downstairs, breakfast was finished and the dishes were nearly put away. It had been a late breakfast for everyone, as they had all had difficulty falling asleep after the events of the previous day. They waited now with trepidation for the arrival of Patrick. None of them were sure how to handle the situation. The rash of disappearances, combined with their direct involvement with Cathy's, confused and hurt them more than even Avilon would admit, so they did not look forward to handing out sparse portions of hope to the grieving father when they themselves were starving.

They sat silently, exchanging glances, sighs, and pastries.

Janet's hand did not move once from beneath Tom's, but neither glowed with the warmth of the touch.

The only interruption came when, a little before noon, Avilon remembered (or probably hoped) that she was running low on food and needed to go shopping. Janet volunteered to accompany her.

On the driveway, heading for the old Cadillac Avilon had owned for twenty years, Janet expelled with relief, her muscles magically healing their aches. "God, I thought you'd never get me out of there."

Avilon's mouth drew up tightly. "Once a week we'd do this, whether we needed the food or not, remember?"

"It wasn't *that* long ago," Janet said, nudging her mother in the shoulder.

"Well, it feels like it was. I haven't been out like this in a long time. Sometimes people just have to get up and leave a difficult situation, look at the rest of the world."

God, thought Janet, *I know how true that really is.* Not only did she want to get away from the verdict of death the family had passed úpon Cathy, but there was the added problem of Tom. The tragedy of a missing *child* had put a damper on their reconciliation. It made her angry. She couldn't deal with both tragedies. If she hadn't gotten out of that house when she did . . .

But they were out, and everything was faraway for a while. In the car, the borders of the wilderness racing by, Avilon tried to start a conversation, but Janet could not get interested or even fake her way through. Against their will, the same silence they had fled was still with them.

Janet scowled. Her mother needed this as much as she did, so why was she being so damned selfish? She looked at Avilon; the short, squat body, the unfashionable glasses, the pale lips, tiny nose, and nondescript eyes staring out the dirty windshield at the world they should be appreciating. "I love you," was on Janet's tongue, ready to spring into the silence, but Avilon veered the car to avoid hitting a scurrying deer, and the words were lost.

Instead, Avilon was speaking. ". . . was it doing out here?"

Janet blinked. "What?"

"No deer would run across the road like that with the sound of a car nearby. We haven't had a deer hit for decades. They know the town as well as the people."

"Maybe something was chasing it."

Avilon nodded, and the pall of death returned.

They arrived at the store twenty minutes later, and were surprised to find Art Billings, owner and manager, mopping his steps. When Janet was a girl, the storekeeper would always give her something to eat before leaving. Candy if her mother didn't see, but more often than not an apple, or even a sandwich if he was in a very good mood. But one thing she never remembered him doing was work. There was always hired help for that. From what she'd heard, he'd narrowed the help down to one young kid who had managed to impress even the boss.

Avilon rolled up to the store front and parked. Janet peered out the window. The place hadn't changed much. Maybe a new coat of paint, some new signs—and she was certain that had been done by the new employee. Still, her eyes were drawn irrevocably to the lean figure bending over a pail and squeezing the dark water from a mop. She couldn't get over the surprise. Inside, *that* was his pride and joy. He'd once hired five boys to keep up the displays during the summer when the tourists had flocked here after a Boulder paper had done an article on the town. The inside of the store was his home, his life, a flourishing business. He'd been heard to say that he didn't give a goddamn what the shell looked like as long as there was a pearl inside. Of course, when queried by local politicians who had formed a commission to clean up Harkborough,

115

his answer was a bit more diplomatic. He had to retain the quality *inside,* and the *outside,* he was sure, would enter his schedule sometime in the (distant) future.

But now, wonder of wonders, the old man *was* outside, and he *was* working. Even Avilon slowed her pace at the unfamiliar sight before them.

They approached the storekeeper with polite smiles glued beneath wide eyes. "Good afternoon, Mr. Billings," Avilon managed. "You're . . . mopping." The statement was as meaningful as if she had said, "You're . . . dead."

Still leaning over his pail, Billings squinted through thick lenses. A few seconds elapsed before he realized who he was answering, and a natural smile curled his lips.

"Oh, Mrs. Jersey. How are you today?"

"Fine, fine, but what's with the mop? The closest you ever come to mopping the outside porch is when you spit on the stoop and rub your shoe in it."

Billings' laughter was like gravel shaken in a coffee can. "You haven't heard, eh? You remember the Ryan boy? Johnny Ryan, delivers papers hereabouts?"

"Yes, of course. I see him once a week, when he comes to collect for the paper."

"Right. I'm cleaning up his blood."

He stood straight then, busily pushing the mop around the porch while the two women took in the news. As he had hoped, their expressions were now filled with horror — and something else that he couldn't quite describe.

Janet caught the joy in his voice, and was flooded with other memories of the storekeeper: telling her he occasionally kept worms in the apples; that candy would rot her teeth to the naked nerves; that he kept wild raccoons in his basement and sometimes threw sandwiches down to them when they scratched at the door. . . . He had his kind ways, but everyone had to have a release, and his was a perverse joy in confusing and shocking people. Billings

116

cackling over the tabloid papers, Billings guffawing at the latest gossip whispered to him over the counter—these images passed by Janet's eyes at a dizzying speed. She was not shocked by them, only amused at how she had been deceived again. He was always like that, she told herself. It gave him an edge over the others, something that he probably craved even more now in his final years.

Still, the statement *was* intriguing.

The initial horror had passed, replaced by a repulsive throb in their stomachs. They stared at Billings, waiting for more, but he kept his back to them, mopping, plainly enjoying the situation a little longer than he should have. Then, when their suspense began to turn to anger, the old man explained, in uncensored detail, just what had happened that morning between Billy and Johnny. Billings livened it up a bit, no doubt, but the facts were exactly as Billy had told him earlier.

When it was over, the ladies looked ghostly white. This nearly initiated another cackle from Billings, but then his business side took over and he asked if he could get them anything to calm their nerves.

They didn't answer. Janet was the first to regain her color. Out of the corner of her eyes, she saw the old man waiting. She was glad he had not recognized her because it would have caused only more delays. Quickly, she maneuvered behind Avilon so Billings would not get a good look at her. In her mother's ear, she whispered, "Don't think of it now. It hasn't happened to Cathy. The boy probably just had an accident."

Avilon nodded imperceptibly, but color was returning to her cheeks.

The idea that maybe the boy had met with an accident led Janet to think of Dr. Newton. She put a hand over her eyes to shake the sun—and disguise her face—and asked, "Where'd they take him, Mr. Billings? It sounds serious."

"Oh, it was, it was. Took me half an hour to clean up inside."

I'll bet it did . . . "Where'd they take him Mr. Billings? To Dr. Newton?"

Billings stared at them a moment, his own mouth agape. He'd been shocking people with the news of Johnny Ryan all morning, but these were the first two who hadn't even asked if the boy was dead or alive. Finally he said lamely, "Well, like you said, it was pretty messy. They got an ambulance up here and took him to North Camp General, I think." Then he shrugged, as if the entire discussion were academic, and opened the door to his store. He gestured to his customers. "All clean inside, ladies."

Avilon shook her head, looking sick again. Janet took her by the arm and led her back toward the Cadillac. "I think we'll come back some other time," Janet called over her shoulder. "My moth—Avilon isn't feeling very well right now." They climbed into the car, feeling worse than when they had left the cottage.

"Damn!" snapped Billings to himself, his scrawny head peeking out the store door, "thought this would bring in business, not turn them away!"

Just ten minutes after Avilon and Janet left for the store, Doctor Newton drove up to the cottage in his old Chevy, his large cigar leaving a trail of smoke behind almost equal to the amount pouring from the exhaust pipe. When he knocked at the front door, he was greeted by Tom.

"Is he up yet?" was his first question.

He rumbled in and made himself comfortable in the den as Tom continued to the kitchen to get some coffee. *Strange,* the elder doctor thought, *how people change roles after a tragedy.*

From an overstuffed, over-aged chair, Doctor Newton repeated his question. Tom returned, a cup in each hand, steam rising from them. "No," he nearly snapped, "he's been sleeping all morning. At least, I hope he's been sleeping."

"Not anymore."

The voice came from behind them. Patrick stood on the stairway, in the shadows. The dark likeness of Patrick wiped sleep from his eyes and clawed at his disheveled hair. He had not changed his clothes from the night before and they were wrinkled and hedged up on his limbs. Even his voice sounded unchanged and dirty.

Then, before anyone could react, he stumbled into the daylight, becoming just another distraught human being again, and flopped into Avilon's rocker.

Newton watched his patient with calm interest. Patrick stared back, eyebrows arched, awaiting the verdict.

"How do you feel, Pat?" Newton asked.

Patrick laughed, the sound forced like a sob. He hung his head in exhaustion and said, "Fine, just great." The laugh lines disappeared and he leaned forward, eyes boring into Newton like two fists. *"Anything?"*

"Kinkade's been out looking, but we haven't heard from him." Newton paused, then added in a whisper, "I'm sorry, Pat."

Patrick said nothing. He closed his eyes and sat back in the rocker, dead to the world around him.

Tom tried to lessen the silence by clearing his throat. Newton sat complacently, studying his subject. Then, the younger doctor remembered something.

"Pat, the sheriff, Kinkade, is going to drop by today. He wants to ask you some questions and give us an update on everything that's been happening."

"You mean everything about Cathy?" Only his lips had stirred.

Tom looked to Newton for help. Newton shrugged and sipped his coffee. "Well," said Tom, "it seems that Cathy

119

was not the only one who was reported missing . . . or lost. There's been others. A lot of them."

Patrick's eyes opened. They were as large and white as eggs, and they stared through Tom, through the wall, to the land outside. "I know," he hissed.

The two doctors exchanged glances. He knew? *He knew!* How?

Patrick's gaze swept the room. He recognized the puzzled expressions and shook his head, looking for an explanation through the haze that filled his mind. "I don't . . . when I was sleeping . . . it came to me . . ."

"What came?"

"A feeling . . . a, uh, understanding . . ."

Newton barely heard the words. He was debating whether he should tranquilize Patrick again. A minute of observation passed before he was satisfied Patrick's words were not the beginning of hysteria. Still, there was something horrifying in them, something that gripped his spine and made the cup in his hand feel like a big rock. He wondered if it would benefit or injure if he were to bring up the matter of Johnny Ryan.

He decided that Patrick would hear about it eventually, so it may as well come from him. Neither men knew the boy anyway. "There's been . . . something else," he said slowly. "I don't know if . . . well, I *think* it's relevant, and so does the sheriff." Then, hastily, "But this doesn't mean anything has happened to Cathy, you understand."

Patrick's eyes were thin slits again, peering at him as a bird aims for its prey. "What."

Newton saw the glitter of knowledge in Patrick's eyes. Yes, somehow, someway, he already knew. He was so damn close to his little girl. Could it be some sort of telepathy?

Quickly, he stated, "Johnny Ryan, the newsboy around here, was found injured in Art Billings' store."

He left the revelation open, waiting, dreading to see if

Patrick's cracked lips would form the words: *"I know."*

Tom, however, was quicker. "When? What happened?"

"The smart boy Billings hired, Billy Upton, said Johnny came in the store early this morning, bleeding and crying something about monsters and being . . . captured. Then he fainted dead away. He's lost some blood but he'll be fine."

Newton paused to watch Patrick push himself farther into the cushions of the rocker, into the tiny shadows that rested there. The doctor's voice dropped to a choked whisper as he continued.

"His . . . his ear had been ripped off. He could have bled to death if we hadn't found him in time." Then, as an afterthought, he added, "I think it might be wolves. We've never had any serious problems with them before, but I've heard—"

Tom's voice nearly startled even Patrick's limp body. "You *think* it *might* be wolves? You're not *sure?*" He was scared, that much was clear. Something was tilting the natural balance. It was in the forest, in the village, in the cottage, even in this very room. He wasn't at all sure what it was, couldn't even place his finger on the uncomfortable emotions it triggered, but he was certain he didn't ever want to confront it. The potential for destruction was too great.

His eyes met those of Patrick's, traveled down the shriveled, ghostly body. Yes, he was absolutely certain he did not want to confront it.

Newton sipped his coffee calmly, but the steam had disappeared. "There was no way I could be sure," he said, laying the cup aside. "I'm only telling you what it could have been. They took him away a second after I got there, so I didn't have time to examine him. He's at North Camp General now. They've got fine facilities there, and the injury wasn't too serious."

"Are you going up there soon?" Tom asked. An answer was not really necessary. He saw the spark in Newton's eyes. The old boy was close to something, but he wasn't giving it up until he was sure. *Typical medical paranoia,* Tom thought bitterly. But he had to admit that the spark had ignited something in himself, and he knew then that neither of them would be able to stay away from the boy. The boy had *seen* something—and survived. He was their only link to the menace.

"I should get something on those samples we took yesterday by tomorrow." Doctor Newton's voice was dull, underlying the terror. Neither spoke again until Avilon and Janet returned.

During the interval, Patrick pushed farther back into the rocker, into the tiny shadows that pinched like tiny teeth. *Oh, yes,* he thought, *the boy is close . . . but I am closer.*

When Avilon and Janet walked in, they found Doctor Newton stirring uncomfortably in his chair and immediately began to drain him of every detail they could concerning the Ryan boy. Mostly what they received was speculation on the part of a trained physician. When the discourse and exclamations were at an end, it was Patrick who broke the mood by asking for a cup of coffee. To the hurried questions asked him, he replied only that he was feeling "fine."

Sheriff Kinkade arrived a little past one that afternoon. He appeared to have aged ten years over night. His eyes were continually blinded by aching veins and tears, and when he spoke, he was interrupted now and then by his own yawns. The grey hairs surrounding his dome were uncombed and he needed a shave. Still, when he entered the den, he was all business, moving immediately to stand before Patrick and pitch questions at him concerning the day before. To the sheriff, they were particularly routine questions. He'd recited them to at least twenty people in the last two days.

Patrick's responses were cold and short. He obviously felt uncomfortable with his family standing about, staring at him, but they could think of nothing else to do, because they, as much as the sheriff, wanted to hear Patrick's answers.

After the session, the sheriff was no closer to resolving the mystery than he had been twenty-four hours ago. He accepted the usual cup of coffee from Avilon (oddly, he remembered the day her husband had died, and how she'd spent the entire day fixing gallons of coffee for those who came to comfort her) and told the others about the phone calls he had received that morning.

"It's like someone's trying to kidnap the entire village," he said. "And that's the only explanation I have, because we haven't found a single body."

Janet squeezed her elbows. "What about Johnny Ryan?"

His shoulders drooped, and he looked more depressed than he had been already. "Things just don't stay quiet around here for long," he muttered, almost to himself. "All right," he intoned, louder, making it quite clear he would say this only once, "all I know is that at about quarter past five this morning I was called in by Billy Upton—he's the night watch at Art Billings' store. You see, Billings got some strange notion in his head that a village this size needs a twenty-six-hours-a-day grocery store like they do in North Camp. A greedy bastard if I ever—"

"Yes, Sheriff," said Avilon, mildly surprised to hear Kinkade go on like this. "It's only open eighteen hours and we know all about it. We've been to the store and talked to Art."

Kinkade didn't seemed vexed by the interruption or surprised by the information. He merely continued with his

123

report. "Anyway, I got a statement from Billy, the ambulance came about ten minutes later—Doc Newton here was helping out for a little while—and they took the boy to North Camp General. Then Doc and I went over to the diner down the street for some coffee." He lifted the cup he had now and smiled at Avilon. "Always calms my nerves."

Tom stood, something tugging at him. "Sheriff, you know that boy could be the key to this thing."

Kinkade eyed him warily. He didn't need a young, hot-shot doctor telling him his business. He had an old, fat one that did just fine.

"Yeah . . . ?" he drawled noncommittally.

"You have a guard on him?"

"Why?"

Tom glanced at Newton, saw the nod of approval. "Well, don't you think it would be wise to put a guard on his room . . . just in case?"

"Just in case wolves start taking over the hospital, you mean? Just in case they read the directory and take the elevator to Johnny's room?"

Sheriff Kinkade was standing now, the cup set aside and his fists balled up, ready to strike.

"What do you think you're getting at, huh? You don't think I know that some foul play could be involved?"

Tom backed away. He could take the man, he didn't doubt that, but he would certainly come out of it with some very large bruises and missing teeth. Besides, why would he want to? What was making the sheriff so wild?

Avilon's hand rested on the big man's arm, and he jerked as though electricity had run through him. He looked at Avilon, then at the others, finally lowered his eyes and sat again.

"I'm very sorry about that. I . . . haven't slept much."

No one said anything. Avilon's firm grip on his shoulder was enough.

"Don't worry," he said, looking up at Tom. "I'm going up to North Camp right after I'm done here. He's on the third floor, in the middle of the corridor. He's got a guard on him, plus he's surrounded by other patients and a full city staff, so he'll be okay 'till I get there." He stood abruptly. "You're right on one count, Dr. Howards. I think Ryan is the key, and I'm not going to let him out of my sight."

He gave his thanks for the coffee and passed the threshold of the Jersey cottage for the last time.

Many hours later, while the sheriff drove over the Harkborough boundary, leaving behind the churning clouds that promised a storm to the mountains, the Shadowman's army was gathering on a hillside at the foot of a massive boulder the creature used for a platform. They moved close to each other, for they were one, a unit that, together, was the very breath of their leader. Now their dead eyes stared intently at the pinnacle of the great rock, waiting, feeling the darkness and understanding grow to a climax more powerful than anything they had ever felt in life.

Overhead, purple clouds joined hands and rumbled with the mating. Lightning licked the sky, illuminating the clouds so quickly that, for that brief second, their dragon souls were revealed.

Then the rumble died away, falling like a curtain. The wait was over.

A shadow appeared at the top of the boulder. The shadow raised Its clawed hand far into the sky—not to quiet Its army, but to demonstrate the power and who held it.

It was pleased. It had taken nearly a tenth of the village's inhabitants in less than two days. Tonight, *the* night, the masses would disperse into the battle zone, recruiting family, friend, and stranger. And they would all drink to a better future, a future of absolute peace—a future that had been rightfully won.

The plan, It considered, was logical. Start small, with limited communications, and grow, mature, spread like parasitic pioneers. It was a whole new land ripe for the taking—and this It also knew to be a seductive proposal for those who would be recruited. There weren't many great challenges left in life, but when you had an eternity to change a world . . .

The numbers would grow during the night. It knew that, at some point in the future, it would become difficult to hide, and they would even lose a few members. No harm done. It would all be in the name of a final victory.

Of course, there was a threat to the next step in the plan, but It was confident that would be taken care of tonight. The boy would not be a problem, might even make a good soldier. It was something worth considering seriously.

The plans for tonight covered four centers of concern: the post office, which handled all communications, including telephones, letters, telegraphs, and radios; the small graveyard on the edge of town, where reasonably viable bodies would be needed for additional strength; the sheriff's station, of course, to eliminate any organized effort against the Army; and, surprisingly enough, a small cottage to the east, which housed a strength that somehow threatened the eventual success of the plan. Though It suspected, the Shadowman was not sure what advantage they had. But It did understand they were much too close to the truth to be allowed to wait for the darkness like the rest of Harkborough. They must be taken care of immediately.

Thinking of the cottage, It was reminded of someone. It must thank the little girl who only recently had joined the ranks. Her contact with her father had been invaluable to their strategy. As a form of dedication—and to make sure that such a fearsome opposition was efficiently exterminated—It decided that It would take care of the cottage dwellers personally.

There, too, It knew, the girl would be a great aid.

Ah, but there was one more concern facing them: the church. How could It forget the lonely, half-crazed priest who spent more time contemplating his life's purpose than working out a strategy. It sensed the man's fear and failing faith, but there was still a force to contend with there.

The fact that the priest believed God was behind him and would see him through with confidence did not bother the Shadowman at all. As a matter of fact, It found It had to work to control a chuckle.

"Let him pray," It said to no one. "He will pray, but only to convince himself. That is the strength of prayer. But here, I think, it will have an advantage only to me."

The crowd below stirred. Was their leader talking to them? No. It shook Its head and spit on the boulder's surface. The spittle bubbled and hissed, and dissolved into steam.

It looked out at the crowd. It could see the edges today, but soon not even a telescope would reveal them. Here was the spine, here were the nerve endings of the body of the new world.

And the heart of this new body stood atop the boulder . . . and instructed them.

Three miles to the south, in the boarded church of Harkborough, Father Tilkan readied himself. It was his final night in church. This was *his* night, he kept telling himself. He wouldn't admit it, not even to the Lord, but the last few hours had been the most difficult in his life. Here, tonight, was the only chance he would be granted to destroy the evil.

Oh, there was no doubt in his mind that the evil was ready for him. The clouds jostling the sky, the slicing wind riding on death's breath—all of it foretold the arrival of the enemy. He would surprise no one. There would be trickery, he was certain, and betrayals and destruction and finally death, but it must be a death that is final, regardless of the enemy's growing strength.

And yet, with this rising foe, the priest could only shrink, could not protect his strategies from dissolving in the face of so many questions. *Why did It pick this town?* he had prayed, cried, and screamed for hours, *Why here? Why me?* And he had trembled when there was no answer.

Well, what do you want, the statue to rise up and pat you on the head?

No, not that, of course not that, but something like that. Some sign. Some signal that the Lord God was truly behind this mission and that he was not rushing forward like a fool, endangering the hundreds of souls in Harkborough, the millions in the state, the billions in the world.

Still, there was no answer.

Fear had begun its hold many hours ago, pinning his faith, filling him with the venom of doubt. He had prayed and would continue to do so, but now the warmth he had felt for so many years during so many calm services lasted only a few minutes, if that. He remembered the times, during his youth, when he would take the Lord's name in vain without flinching, would regularly break the Commandments, would often get drunk with high school friends, thought priests were merely men who could not get dates, and wanted to do *something* with their wasted lives.

Those were times long gone, in shadows better left unexposed—yet now that reckless, youthful apathy came back as if it had always been with him—and perhaps it had. Could he be so sure that he hadn't been fooling himself all these years, that he hadn't taken up the priesthood in order to hide this disinterest with life, to cover the fact that *he* had been the one wasting his life?

Is that a wicked voice whispering in your ear?

This has to stop.

But it couldn't, because it was part of him. And it wasn't just the feeling that startled him so badly. It was the fact that it sank beneath him with such casual, almost comforting, ease. He was *accepting* it.

"God, what am I fighting?" he had asked so many times that day, truly expecting an answer. When none had come, he had asked another question, or the same, receiving only his echoes in return.

It isn't fair!

The thought was strangled upon its birth, but the vehemence that remained shocked him. He shouldn't be so upset. He was the pillar others would lean against. But plunging into a mission that would upset a world of God's children. . . What possible form would the beast take? . . . a dragon, a man, a plague . . . ? *A lot of good my holy water and faithful mutterings will do against a plague.*

Perhaps a priest.

He prayed, and the whisper died.

Another shiver started over him, but he could control them now, and gritted his teeth to the effort. When it had passed, he opened his eyes wide and stared at the feet of the figure on the cross. He prayed. His hands were sticky and unsteady, but they remained together, clasped in an embrace that no terror could break.

"Where are the answers?" he asked for the hundredth time.

There was only darkness.

He breathed deeply and busied himself for the next ten minutes laying vials of holy water in his bag. It looked very much like a medical bag—how bloody symbolic, he thought bitterly—and that was because it had once been used as one. It had been a gift from Doctor Newton. He'd said he'd worn it out, but Father Tilkan found its frame and skin to be quite stable, though not soft enough inside to safely hold several glass vials. They were protected by a soft, velvet cloth used for draping the pews.

When this was done, he stood reluctantly. He was about to make his obeisance to the altar, but he hesitated and touched the cross round his neck. It was a blessed cross, a gift from his father who had died a Christian of forty-seven years. It was a symbol that had always beckoned assurance within him, and it did not fail him now.

Ah, but would confidence be enough? Would faith be enough? He was certain that this fight would not be the last, but it would be an important one, one that would be fought to the death. Somehow he knew that he was important to the fight, and he took solace now, for that might be the sign he was looking for.

He stared blankly at the tormented face of Christ atop the steps. "God Almighty, would you look at me?" he whispered, surprised at the smile that pulled at his lips. "All of this from a priest who came to Harkborough for a quiet practice and gave sermons every Sunday on 'How things will look up for you if you will look up to Him.'" He chuckled at the thought, unafraid of the echo that surrounded him.

He bowed deep, nearly facing the statue on the left, pushing all his weight onto one knee. There he stayed for a full minute, praying, wanting, receiving.

It's only a statue . . . rock . . .

The thought struck him hard and he stood shakily. He backed away a few steps, then returned, determined, and rested on his knees again. Only words of strength filled his mind, he made sure of that. His father's cross dug into the soft flesh of his palms, but his thoughts did not waiver. As the pain grew, so did his faith. *After all,* he thought with just a trace of pride, *if He did it, why shouldn't I?*

At least *something* rose in him at that moment. Was it the Holy Spirit, or merely courage? He couldn't be sure, didn't want to be sure. Whatever it was, it gave him comfort. Now all he asked for was an answer.

Off in the distance, almost outside his range of hearing, there *was* a sign. He slumped in relief.

So, after all of this exertion on my knees, the answer finally comes with a telephone call.

Jake Smitz was an important man. His fault was that he knew it. If he had known who else thought him important, though, his faults would have disappeared so fast that wings and a halo would have popped out of his back and head.

However, an angel's life had not been the path he'd taken to attain his current status, and he seriously doubted such a path would have ever led him anywhere. He'd started out as a night watchman. Not the most prestigious job, nor the best hours, but it had impressed the bosses when he'd *volunteered* to work late and learn during the slow periods. Of course, it had also helped to spread a few nasty rumors about some of the day crew, and coming from such an upstanding citizen such as himself, what with his dad being a cop and all, why, who was to doubt him? As planned, the night watchman's job had lasted only five years. He'd watched employees come and go, most wanting just the extra wages above minimum the job paid, a few aiming their sights at what Jake Smitz considered his goal and rightful trophy: head custodian of the village cemetery.

All right, all right, he'd told his father, it's not the best career in the world—but his mother had supported the idea by pointing out his school grades for the last five years and the less-than-slim chance that he'd be accepted to even a junior-junior college. That had broken the old man's opposition.

So five years had passed living like a vampire, until old Man Richter died suddenly right outside his office door. Some had suspected foul play when he was found with his skull caved in and one of the twin marble statues from the top of his office lying in pieces nearby. But then Jake had pointed out that those statues had been crumbling health hazards for years, just ask anyone, and all doubt had been neatly swept six feet under—allowing Jake to slip right into Richter's job.

He considered it a worthy position, so the first thing he did was change his job title. Custodian was a very unkind word, in his opinion, and caretaker was too morbid. He was more of a guard: the watcher from the tower, making sure everything was A-okay for the troops below. The job certainly wasn't any more difficult than when he'd worked the night shift, and he still worked odd hours occasionally, but the pay was quite handsome, especially when he'd hit the council up for a raise right after the mayor's son had died in that car accident. Such a lovely boy, he had to be taken care of right, but with the way the facilities were now . . .

He could even say he took pride in his job, and after a while that pride grew into an assurance that he was a Very Important Person in Harkborough. After all, there were plenty of day-care centers for the babies, and big hospitals and convalescent homes for the sick and elderly, but who'd take care of you when you wanted to rest for eternity in the village of your birth? Only one man, that's who.

But having pride in his job didn't keep Jake from filling his office hours with the inevitable morbid questions of life—and it didn't help with him being so close to death. He wasn't morose, he was sure of that. It was an honor to be trusted with the final wishes and protection of the dearly departed, an honor he took seriously. He realized most people would feel ill at ease working around dead people, but they were just people that didn't happen to move, talk, laugh, fight, or enact other harmful rituals that were so common to the living. To him, they were better than the living, because they were helpless and relied completely on his kindness and experience . . . and that was certainly something they should pay through the teeth for.

Of course, he never admitted to anyone that his first year at the place had been a bit different. It hadn't taken him that long to get used to the bodies, but what had had him sweating were ghosts. His mother and father, in complete cooperation with the neighborhood priest, had filled his head with spirits and avenging angels and a burning hell where the souls cried out. *That* scared him. But after thirty years, he hadn't seen even the tail of a ghost, and his beliefs in such matters had been drastically altered — something that would have killed his dear mother and father and the neighborhood priest if they weren't already dead and buried in the very area he protected.

Still, although he'd had thirty years of scoffing and shrugging off the haunted, this was the kind of night he hated most: a sky filled with angry clouds and thunder that could jolt his eyeteeth. He knew the association with the supernatural had been programmed in him by mom, pop, priest, and television, but the rationalization did not calm his nerves. Come a storm in a graveyard, he got the jitters, and nothing in the world would get rid of them.

He was shivering with them at the moment as he cursed and pulled his oilskin coat on. It was starting to rain now, so the remains of one Donald Guttenburg, killed in a messy car accident last week, would have to be moved, and Jake would have to finish the digging of the grave tomorrow, if the rain let up by then.

Grumbling as a man will with a duty he would like to put off, he opened his office door and pulled it shut against the driving rain. Then he began the long trudge up the ramp.

He still marvelled at the originality of the building. It had been built practically underground with only the roof and high, squat windows bobbing above the mud. Jake had tagged it a long time ago, and the name had stuck forevermore: the Bomb Shelter. Naturally, that's what everyone thought it was, but Jake had taken the time to look through the library down in North Camp and found that it had been built long before there was ever a need for such a bunker. His own theory was that it had been constructed above ground and that over the years, with the rain and snow levels that Harkborough suffered, dirt and mud had been pushed up higher and higher. Eventually, he figured, the building would be completely covered, but that wouldn't happen until years after Jake was gone, he'd make sure of that.

There used to be stairs that led to the office door, but he'd had them covered over and built into a ramp so he could roll his coffin carriages ("body 'barrows," he called them) down through the office and into the extra storage compartment in back. It wasn't that the main storage area was full — as a matter of fact, Mr. Guttenburg was Jake's only customer for the week — but it leaked badly and he didn't want to contend with the cleaning process of an uncooperative body.

As Jake emerged from "the pit" — another tag he'd thought up, since the ramp lowering to his office door formed a sort of chasm — he turned to glance back at his twin luck charms. After Mr. Richter's unfortunate accident with one of the two previous statues, the council had granted money for new monuments to be erected where the first had sat. Jake had demanded that the statues be identical to the ones they were replacing, and the council had complied. Some of the other villagers had commented, impolitely, that twin serpents did not make for an angelic setting, but Jake pointed out that they sat above either side of the deep end of the ramp, hidden from the graveyard, even hidden from the street. No one but him would see them. After awhile the complaints (or the complainers) died and the serpents still overlooked the office door, like two venomous sentinels. Jake loved them. Not only did they give the place a royal appearance, but just knowing they were there seemed to frighten away most of the mischievous young'uns in these parts, particularly the ones who knew what had happened to poor ol' Richter.

He found himself staring at them now, longer than he had intended. Dark raindrops were bleeding across their snouts, sliding off their fangs. *Yes,* thought Jake, shivering, *it's going to be one hell of a night.*

The carriage that held the remains of Donald Guttenburg was only a few feet from the maw of the ramp, at the tail of where the sidewalk began to snake through the graveyard. The coffin, lying on the carriage undisturbed, provided a bass to the rhythm of the raindrops.

Inside, the remains of Donald Guttenburg shivered.

Thunder growled again, closer. Jake grumbled to himself, mocking that which he feared, but knowing it wouldn't do much good. He had the goddamn jitters again.

So he busied himself, hoping the task and the trouble would take his mind off the terror. He picked up a bag of garbage he had collected from the grave sites—a bunch of dying wreaths and assorted aluminum cans and food wrappers. For a second he thought it kind of lucky that it was raining, otherwise he'd be smelling that stuff right now. Thinking of luck, he glanced back at his twin beauties. They smiled back, fangs glistening. He turned away quickly when he thought he saw one move.

The rain dropped harder as he moved around the carriage. He couldn't possibly hear the soft scratching from within the casket.

Jake piled the garbage bag on top of the coffin, but with the jostling of the wind and the pushing of the rain, he could not get it to stay. He cursed again, realizing it would take him two trips just because of a bunch of garbage. "Well," he finally said to himself, chuckling so as to stave off the jitters, "that's what I get paid the big bucks for."

He trudged down the ramp, careful not to slip on the waterfall of rainwater cascading down the walls and streaming down the ramp itself. He remembered once when the rain had come down hard and the drain at the foot of the office door had been clogged with old leaves and garbage. He'd spent a very wet night unplugging that mess, but he'd made damn sure it never happened again. Pride again, and he smiled.

His mind otherwise involved, Jake's foot stepped where it shouldn't have and he slipped. As he tried to regain balance, his attention was diverted again when he heard a sharp scrape behind him. He fell on his butt, then got his back against the wall and pushed himself up. His eyes were locked at the top of the ramp. He couldn't see very well, it was so dark and the rain made things fuzzy, but he was certain there was something up there.

Just then, a hand of lightning swept the sky.

Jake sucked in a breath and held it. The jitters had him bad now.

At the brink of the ramp sat the carriage, the mahogany casket staring down with hollow eyes.

Thunder began to laugh.

Jake dropped the bag of garbage. His face grew pale. He felt the beat of his heart increase, doubling its steady rate. Cold rain fell from his forehead and off the bridge of his nose, mixing with the sweat. His scattered hair lay flat

136

against his head like a spider web. Beyond the casket, where his eyes were still locked, he heard a cold wind call from the trees.

The wheels of the carriage creaked forward.

The guard of those old patrons of Harkborough spun around and pulled at his office door. He didn't understand exactly what was happening, but he had the jitters *bad,* bad enough that his heart was knocking to get out, and he didn't want to be anywhere but inside his tiny, warm office.

He cringed, nearly screamed, when he heard the click of a lock on the other side of that door. Jake sucked in air, but it wasn't enough to satisfy the monster in his chest. Eyes wide and bloodshot, they glanced over his shoulder.

The carriage's back wheels were passing the peak.

He fumbled for his keys but realized, in a stomping fit of fear and anger, that he had left them inside on the table, as he did every night. He tried knocking, but the wind and rain hit him so hard that he couldn't tell if he was making any noise. Even if he was, *who would be there to hear it?*

He turned, his hands fending off the spikes of water that thrashed at his face. He tried to look up the ramp, but everything was so difficult, so slow. Rain and tears filled his lids, and his vision blurred.

Still, he could see the dark outline of the carriage creak over the edge of the ramp and start to roll.

Above the scene, thunder and lightning were berating the sky now, as though they were gods who had always owned the world.

But louder than the thunder, eclipsing the lightning, even above the rain and water echoing off the walls, Jake heard the slow, low crackling near his head. He felt small bits of . . . hale? no, it was gravel, sprinkling his bald pate. Then the crackling grew to a creak, and the creak grew to a rumble, more horrible than the thunder's voice because it was so much nearer. Jake stretched the veins of his neck to

137

look into the sky from where God was throwing rocks.

The slick face of a marble serpent looked down on him, flicking its still tongue. Crumbs from its foundation fell onto Jake. Then, abruptly, the sky or the statue — Jake was not sure which — cracked sharply and the serpent leaned farther over him. The tiny gravel bits were now small blocks of marble, crashing down like hale. Jake raised his hands, trying desperately to ward off the attack, when the creaking of the carriage wheels filled his head again.

The goddamn thing's coming right at me —

They were all the thoughts he had time for before the shadow began to cover him and he took action.

His fingers gripped the slippery skin of the serpent as it fell toward him. He grunted, the weight forcing him down into the inky black waters swirling and sucking at his knees. Words, haunted words, screamed in his mind, grinding, revolving in a circle like the wheels of that damned body 'barrow: *Should have jumped out of the way! Should have jumped* . . . But things were happening too quickly for an old man — for any man.

At last, the statue held. His fingers were white with the strain, his wrists and arms about to pop their veins, but the serpent was stilled. Jake looked around wildly. He knew he wouldn't be able to hold it for very long, and he had to find some escape —

But as he searched the pit, the statue became a secondary terror. The carriage was rolling, unhindered, down the full length of the ramp. It was gaining speed, somehow guided toward the helpless figure of Jake Smitz.

He tried to scream but it was caught short under the weight of the serpent, forever pushing toward him to crush his final breath. His legs splayed out, trying for a wider foundation, and the statue was brought to rest once more. But the scream still wanted out. The sound of the carriage wheels were drawing nearer. Jake opened his mouth to bare its power—

The mouth held open, but the scream was lost in a whimper.

The coffin, rolling irrevocably at him, had its lid open. A flesh-worn corpse, only half of its vital organs still in place, rose from the comfort of its eternal bed. Yellow teeth grew from pale meat on the right side of its face, where it had been burned during the final moments of life, but then it smiled and the rest of the devils were revealed. One eye was gone, along with part of the skull. The other eye opened and crinkled with silent laughter. The bony hand— the one that did not hang from a limp, oddly bent arm— lifted a shovel that had been lying on the carriage. It was a shovel that had dug half its grave and would probably be used to dig the other half, but not by Jake Smitz.

The carriage slammed into the guard of the cemetery, breaking his hip and smashing him against the locked door. The scream in Jake's throat was drowned out by warm blood as the shovel sliced through his stomach and lodged in his spine. The serpent, unattended, struck. It crushed the skulls of both Jake and Donald, but only one of them felt it. The carriage also split with the weight of the statue, and the bodies of all fell to the depths of the concrete pit.

Rain continued falling. Soon the water covered the carnage that lay at the door of Jake Smitz's office. The proud owner himself was blocking the drain.

Above the pit, a shadow crept across the graveyard, feeling joyous and at home.

Sheriff Kinkade was in a less than joyous mood. He hated hospitals. He had seen the inside of every ward in the neighboring counties, mostly as an investigating sheriff, twice as a patient. He didn't like the smell of the rooms, or the blazing white walls and sheets and uniforms, or the ghostly groans of sick and injured people echoing down the endless hallways. He'd rather visit a tomb. At least there he knew there was no suffering.

Still, the mission he was on now managed to steer his thoughts from the repugnant, and forward with determination.

He knew Johnny Ryan and had talked to him a few times over the years while both were making their morning rounds. They were almost clandestine meetings, since no one else was up at that hour. He knew it excited the kid a bit, having a few secret words with the sheriff of the town, and Kinkade now had to admit that he probably enjoyed it just as much.

But now it scared him. This was a rendezvous he was not looking forward to, no matter how necessary it was in catching the person or animal that had hurt the boy.

At least security was adequate, he thought. The nurse escorting him had proved obdurate, even at the flash of a badge, and that was good no matter how much it irritated him. It meant no one was getting in or out without being watched.

The nurse mumbled over her shoulder that they were approaching the boy's room — private, as per orders. It was at the end of a mile of corridor, a single door, cold and distant, but easy to keep an eye on. They stopped in front of it and Kinkade read the number — 354 — for future reference and smiled at the understated sign that hung on the doorknob: DO NOT DISTURB.

Without preamble, the nurse twisted the knob and opened the door a crack. She stopped suddenly, remembering something, and turned to face Kinkade before he could step past her. "I'll have to ask you to keep the questioning short. Doctor's orders."

Kinkade nodded reluctantly — actually he would have agreed to anything to just step into the room — and re-

140

turned the pleasant smile when his escort opened the door wide and shuffled out of his way.

He stepped into darkness. He was startled by the inability of the strong hallway lights to penetrate even an inch of the room's shadows. He backed away, just a little, and was surprised to find himself leaning against the door for support. His eyes blinked several times, but they were adjusting to the dark very slowly.

"Aren't there any lights—?"

His voice died in a whoosh of air as the door he leaned on catapulted him back into the hallway and slammed back into its frame.

"Oh, God," he stammered excitedly. It wasn't the door that had dropped lead into his stomach, but the sight he had seen just before the door had closed: a figure standing over the boy, eyes black, glowing . . . and teeth.

He swung around to the nurse. "What the hell's going on? Who's in there?"

The nurse shrank away, unsure if she were more frightened of what was behind the door or Kinkade. "I . . . I don't know," she stammered. "No one could be. We've kept check . . ."

It suddenly hit Kinkade. "Where's the guard that's supposed to be here?"

"He was here . . . I swear, I swear . . ."

Kinkade grabbed the doorknob, turned and pushed. It didn't budge. Didn't even creak. He pounded on it, finally slamming his body against it. The door held, as though the darkness beyond were a monolith of concrete.

"Open this goddamn door!" he shouted. "Who's in there?"

The nurse was still staring at him, her face white as her uniform, her eyes watering and tinged with red lids. "This is a hospital . . ." she began, but the words continued only as thoughts translated into facial expressions. *This is a*

141

hospital, where soft shoes are required, where everyone speaks in a whisper, where rooms are built to be "sound proof," yet you, this giant, are screaming at the top of your lungs!

Kinkade flushed. He noted that others behind her were gathering in the hallway watching him as though *he* were the monster. The nurse was even backing away, no doubt for fear a doctor might race around the corner at any second and catch her with this madman.

"Goddamn it, someone get some help!" was all Kinkade had to say to them, and he turned back to the door, pounding with as much fervor as before, hospital etiquette be damned. "Open this door *now!* This is Sheriff Kinkade! I'm a police officer."

He stopped pounding when he realized it wasn't having any effect. The door wasn't even dented. He put his ear to it, searching, listening. He held his breath, waved for others whispering in the hallway to be quiet.

At first there was nothing but the hum of a nearby ventilation shaft, but eventually, as his eyes had, his ears accustomed themselves to the thick black beyond the door, and he heard—

—the *bip* of a heart machine . . . a slight, strained breathing . . . the steady rhythm of the respirator . . . a movement, a definite stirring . . . and then a hurricane of violence in a single, powerful voice, a voice that could not possibly belong to the boy—

"NOOOOO!"

The door shook with the volume of the scream. Glass shattered within the room, followed by gales of wind.

And then silence.

A cold finger sprung up Kinkade's spine, forcing him to stand straight. He stared at the door dully. After what he felt to be too long, he pushed at the door once more. From the side of his eyes, he saw the nurse start *running* away, full sprint, either out of fear or a snap decision to look for help.

It didn't concern Kinkade. He pushed the door and it gave a little, then a little more. Inky blackness peeked out at him and he pushed again. A crack opened. It was silent inside. The heart machine was off or broken, the respirator too. There was no movement as far as he could see, which wasn't far.

Seconds elapsed, and an army of doctors and interns were rushing to his side. Kinkade wasn't sure whether they were there to help or hinder, so he made a decision and leaned his full weight against the door.

He crashed into the room. The blinding hallway lights followed him, cutting into the shadows. Kinkade looked around and stifled an involuntary scream. He thought there were tiny animal eyes staring at him, but then realized that they belonged to the various machines about the bed, their little lights blinking soundlessly. Beyond them, the room's window frame held only a few sharp pieces of glass, like glittering teeth in a maw that led to the dark storm outside. Rain sprayed through the opening, spitting at the sheriff.

Kinkade moved in closer, followed by the terrified men and women behind him. He could now make out the single bed in the middle of the room, pushed up against one wall. It was littered with crumpled blankets . . . and a tiny form pushed against the headboards. It was then he realized that the room was no longer silent. He heard the soft sounds of a child sobbing.

"Johnny," he asked the person in the bed. "You okay?"

The people crowding the doorway would not move beyond the threshold. There was a deathly cold that kept them at bay, only to stare frantically at the boy in bed. Kinkade alone moved closer, trying to get a good look at him.

"Johnny?"

And then he saw it: the wide, frightened eyes that

143

seemed to glow in Johnny Ryan's head, looking at him with—not shock or injury, he determined, but absolute determination. Kinkade felt himself wilting under that gaze.

"Johnny?" he whispered.

"Get me out of here," the boy demanded between ragged breaths. *"Now!"*

Paul Zimmerman finished filing the next morning's mail and relaxed in his office chair with a warm cup of brew. It was late in the evening, but the old man didn't mind; he slept late, liked to watch the old black-and-white shows on TV when they came on at eleven. It was late enough that he didn't have to worry about the switchboard, so he leaned back, content, and smiled as he always did at the cluttered office around him. The sole manager of communications in Harkborough. It was a damn important job and one he'd handled more than competently for the past twenty-five years. No complaints—no reasonable ones, anyway—and a clean record for accuracy and honesty. He sipped his brew, smacked his lips. His eyes strayed to the mail slots. Not too busy these days, not like in the days of the Vietnam War when tons of mail came in every day—the Hey! Days he used to call them because he'd stop practically everyone passing the station with a call and hand them a letter. No, unless the Prez had some crazy plan to send some of the local boys to South America, things wouldn't be that busy again. However, Paul took pride in the fact that if it did happen, he would carry on just as skillfully as he had fifteen years ago.

Sipping his brew again, the twinkle of remembrance was blown out by a chill that shook his whole body. *Damn weather,* he thought, and considered moving from his chair to make sure all the windows were closed tight. Rain was crashing down on the tin roof and he could begin to hear the opening strains of water pissing through old cracks and leaks. Still, the chair was damned comfortable, the brew so warm and tasty . . .

Come on, Paul, where would a communications office be if the mail was soggy and the wires burned out? So, cursing absently, he rose, his old bones cracking in unison, and trudged over to a cabinet where he kept six rain buckets. They were soon placed in their usual places about the room, and Paul once again retired in his chair.

Ten years ago he had asked for a new roof—his first real encounter with the town council. Oh, he had heard rumors from people, stories relating the horrors involved in dealing with elected officials, but his good friend Jake Smitz had told him otherwise. Why, they'd sprung for two worthless statues for him, and even if one of the old ones had killed a man, it hadn't meant the council had *had* to grant money for replacements. It'd been damn nice of them, and Paul had figured they wouldn't even blink an eye when he asked for a new roof. Hell, anyone could see it was practical. The post office was Harkborough's lifeline to the outside world.

He'd never been so wrong. Instead of a new roof, or even some tar to cover up the holes, the officials, in their infinite wisdom and alleged reason, had granted enough money for five new rain buckets.

Although angry and disillusioned, Paul had taken the money without argument. He knew that if he complained he'd probably get *three* rain buckets and a black mark on his file. So he'd accepted the results, bought four rain buckets and a transistor radio, and since then had made sure that all the mail addressed to members of the council was just this side of soggy. Obviously the council didn't open their own mail. The ploy had yet to work in ten years.

Thunder laughed with Paul at the memory. He checked the clock behind him, then sprang into action. It was half

145

past ten, thirty minutes before the late movie, and time for some music to make the heart young once more. He pushed his cup of brew away and snapped on the old reliable sitting on his desk, bought with money meant for a bucket. He didn't have to twist the dial to get the station in. There was only one signal that Harkborough received. It was a small station down in North Camp, an antenna high enough and close enough to squeak its waves over the top of the mountains and trees to settle undisturbed in any Harkborough radio. Fortunately, in Paul's opinion, the station was a good one, balancing its program for different tastes. During the day, the sunshine was filled with soft rock. After six, the tunes turned to the forties and early fifties, mixing the night air with Frank Sinatra, Joey Fisher, Paul Anka, and countless other legends.

Paul listened happily, abosrbing the light melodies, remembering the days when songs had more than four lines of lyrics and were pleasant to hum. His eyes closed in contentment. He kicked his feet up on his desk, scattering yellowed papers farther into the shelves, and picked up his brew. The night was always his to enjoy alone. This was the only retirement he foresaw in his future. He hummed along to the familiar strains of Sinatra.

As he sang and dreamed, his own little world was impervious to the creak of the door behind him.

A shadow fell over the old man, and he soon entered the land of deep darkness, where his songs could go on forever.

The radio fell uncaringly to the floor. It provided gentle, unhurried music for the night's work.

The idea crept into Patrick's head like a disease. At first unnoticed, only mildly irritating but causing no concern. Then it scratched, giving warning of its presence and growth. Finally, it hit him hard and would not let go no matter how many times he tried to turn his thoughts to other matters. At last he accepted it, studied it, tried to discard it, but it kept coming back again and again, crashing through his reason like an ocean of waves, always taking away some of the reason while retreating for another assault.

By the end, inevitably, it had won.

Avilon was the first to notice her nephew's queer expression and eventually all eyes were studying him. Avilon, the born instigator, was the first to speak. Her voice cut through the tense atmosphere, causing nearly everyone to give a little jump.

"Patrick? Are you all right?"

"Yes," he replied immediately. He then stared into the warm, compassionate eyes of his aunt. *How can she be so in control of herself all the time?* he thought. *Always so soothing and . . . clean.*

He had always been fond of her, could never remember a time when he'd actually been angered by any of her actions or words. She loved him, he knew, but had never spoiled him. He wondered, if he had not received everything he had wanted as a boy, not even his true parents, how could he look back on that childhood with such happiness? The answer was succinct: Avilon. She was a wonder. And he knew now, beyond a doubt, that she could help him.

"Aunt Avilon . . . I need a favor. A rather large one, actually."

She didn't even flinch. "Well, of course. What is it?"

A tongue flicked across his lips. "I want you . . . I *need* you to conduct a seance tonight."

Worried glances were volleyed across the dining room table. Avilon remained still, as though she hadn't heard the request. Only Doctor Newton voiced his opinion, and it was limited to a grunt of disapproval. He then returned to the last of what was now a very late dinner.

Janet reached for Tom's hand. It was there, warm and strong. It allowed her to lean over and place her other hand atop the grieving father's.

She said gently, "Patrick . . ."

His eyes were watering, but he maintained his composure. He found himself gripping Janet's hand tighter as words poured from his lips.

"No, no . . . I'm serious. I mean it, Avilon. I need you to conduct a—"

"Patrick," broke in Tom, "it's late, you're tired, you're . . . upset."

"I *need* this—"

"You need sleep," commented Doctor Newton. He looked as if he were reaching under the table for his little black bag of wonder drugs.

Patrick hurried on. "No, please, I know it can be done. Tell them, Auntie, tell them you've done it before. It's not all show. We've laughed about it"—this helplessly to Janet—"but we've also wondered. You know you've wondered about it. We've just never discussed it seriously."

Janet's lips parted but she couldn't think of anything to say. Instead, she nodded almost imperceptibly.

A grin tugged at Patrick's lips. *Hope!* But out of the side of his eyes, he saw Doctor Newton sorting through his black bag. He shot his attention back to Avilon.

"Avilon, *please!* Tonight, in this room—"

"No, Patrick." Avilon's words severed his words as effectively as a hatchet.

But seeing the injection the old doctor was preparing pushed Patrick onward.

"Please, *please,* it's the only way. If you love me, please do it. It would mean so much to me. It . . . it would make me sleep so much easier."

He had planned the last and couldn't help shifting his

148

eyes about the room like a crime boss gauging reactions to his plan.

Doctor Newton was lowering the injection back into his black bag. Next to him, Tom stared, jaw jutting forward, his face unreadable. Janet and Avilon were watching him with a mixture of fear and compassion.

He was desperate. He felt the hot tears roll down his cheeks, but controlled the sobbing that welled in his chest. He was tired, as the doctor had said, but he also felt exhilarated. The idea, the chance, did that for him. It certainly wasn't an unreasonable demand, as she had done it before. Only now it would have to be more real than it had ever been. There could be no faking, no joking or pantomiming. It was his final hold on his daughter, and if anything could aid his getting a grip on her again . . .

He watched now, barely breathing, afraid it would cover the answer.

Avilon was rubbing her forehead. Her eyes squinted with pain and indecision.

"No," she said finally. "I'm sorry, Patrick—"

His hand left Janet's, flying across the table to squeeze Avilon's into a twisted prey. "*Please!* If you don't do it now, it will never happen." His eyes darted to Doctor Newton and Tom, then back again. "I have to be sure. I have to cover every base. This may be the last . . . chance . . ." He was breaking up now, and he cringed as the others moved toward him with concern.

"*I'm all right!*" he shouted, and they backed away. Far away.

Then, through the cold, empty room, Avilon's voice cut through again. "I'll do what I can, Patrick."

"Mother!" Janet whirled on the elder woman. Her back to Patrick, she mouthed, "What are you doing?" Avilon looked away.

"I think you're being unreasonable, Avilon," said Tom

evenly. "You know it won't do any good. It's not wise to put these false hopes into his head."

"She's not!" snapped Patrick.

Doctor Newton set his black bag back under the table and leaned closer to Patrick. His voice easily barrelled over the objections of the others. "It's bunk, Patrick. Get that straight. Of course it won't help. Avilon's been doing the act for years, just to entertain you kids."

Patrick turned on him with wild fervor. "You're wrong! She *can* contact Cathy, I know she can!" He whirled around to his cousin. "Janet, you know it's not an act! You *know* it! We've seen her do it, not all the time, but now and then she came in contact with your fath—"

"Stop!" Janet spat the word out, her eyes squeezed shut. She continued more softly. "Please, Patrick . . . we want what's best for you, but to rely so heavily on this . . ."

"You've seen her do it!" Patrick insisted. "You *know!*"

Doctor Newton's laugh startled them all, it seemed so out of place in the tense atmosphere. It died into a cough when he realized he was the only one laughing.

When he'd settled back in his chair again, tiny eyes peeked over the top of his glasses. His face revealed uncertainty. Finally, he said, "Avilon?"

Her hands wiped a furrowed brow of sweat. When she lifted her eyes to meet the old doctor's, she blinked weakly and said, "I have done it before . . . I think. I've at least convinced myself that I've talked to the dead. But . . . but to assume Cathy is . . ." She looked to Patrick. "Please don't insist. It would be very painful for all of us."

He caressed her hand, the withered limb he had nearly broken minutes before, and said reassuringly, "It'll be all right, Auntie. It'll help, I'm sure. Even if it turns out bad, I need to know." He paused, searching her eyes. "Do you understand?"

"Avilon?" repeated Doctor Newton. His gaze was more

intense.

The older woman took a deep breath, let it out. This entire vacation had been a disaster from start to finish. She had planned it, she had invited the guests, and all she could do to ease the pain was make coffee or speak gently or hold a hand. But now, yes, *now* she could make the pain easier for Patrick, maybe offer encouragement to the others. She might even be able to find out, if she tried hard enough, if little Cathy Simon was still alive.

"Yes, Patrick," she said, looking deep into the man's eyes. "I'll do it for you."

Chapter 7

Rain scratched its fingers against the dark veranda windows, creating thousands of writhing snakes on the surface. Droplets caught the glimmer of candlelight from inside and appeared as glowing eyeballs peering in, watching, waiting.

Inside, the room was illuminated only by candles. They had once been bought in case of emergency, and now seemed as good a time as any. Their purpose tonight, however, was more to lend a mystic atmosphere than a practical aid. No longer was the room a place to eat and trade amusing stories. It was an arena of magic, brimming with skeptical contacts and sustained hopes.

All brought together for Patrick's final chance to reach his daughter.

He and Janet sat at one end of the long wooden table, clutching hands. Their arms stretched across to the other side, touching the fingers of Tom and Newton. Their eyes were closed, their faces contorted with concentration.

Patrick's face was the most intense, his face already covered with a thin sheen of sweat. Janet, the only other one to have experienced Avilon's supposed powers, was busy perpetuating her past experience. Perhaps to placate his wife or to join in a final hope with his family, Tom managed to cooperate without rolling his eyes or feeling the least bit stupid. Doctor Newton did not comment during the preamble, but he did hide an insatiable urge to chant, "Ohm . . ."

Their varied degrees of effort were directed toward the one person seated at the end of the table. Though the candles supplied ample light, Avilon still looked darker somehow, sunken and skeletal. Her eyes were the only ones that were open, and they were wide and unblinking, staring at the flicker of the single candle in the center of the human pentagon.

She couldn't throw the morbid image that they were praying over some massive coffin.

To her left, Janet peeked between closed lids, still worried for her cousin's safety, as well as her mother's. When Avilon's eyes rolled back into her head, it sent the same chill down Janet's spine as when she was a little girl. But it hadn't mattered back then. She'd had a father to comfort her and tell her everything was okay; even after he was gone, she was older and wiser. Now she was little again and all she had was a despondent husband who saw her as less-than-perfect and a family that was going loony one-by-one.

Tom felt his wife's hand increase pressure steadily, but he made no gesture of concern. *God*, he thought, *dear God, what the hell am I doing here?* He looked at Patrick and answered: *Helping a friend.* But he still had problems with Janet he wanted to work out. Why did this have to happen now, at all times?

You better work your fears out, you bastard, so I can get to mine, he thought bitterly, staring at Patrick.

The grieving father was shaking. His eyes were open now, staring at the candle with Avilon, but he did not feel the warmth or peace that she did. He wasn't quite sure how he felt, but he knew it was close to the cold death he'd known when his wife had died. No . . . this was worse. He *knew* Margie was dead. Everything had been released when that reality had hit him. But with Cathy only missing, he had to keep it all in, just in case . . . just in case . . .

153

He sighed when he felt Janet's thumb caress his knuckles, trying to calm him. He looked to her, saw her attention was on Avilon. He stared at the candle for a moment longer, then also turned to the older woman. Eventually, the two doctors followed suit.

Even the eyes on the windows watched.

Exertion was plain on Avilon's face. She was trying, oh, God, how she was trying. But there was nothing. Maybe something rough, something *alive* just below the surface, but it wouldn't break through no matter how she coaxed, pleaded, or baited. A blazing moment of pain flashed before her when she thought of how much her failure would hurt Patrick. But not even that threat would bridge the contact.

She blinked and was surprised to find her vision blurred by tears. *I've done it before,* she thought bitterly. Her pain grew further when she turned to look into Patrick's face.

"I'm . . . I'm sorry, Patrick. I . . ."

And then her voice was cut and her world went dark.

Her wrinkled lids closed, inhaling images, truths, lies, sifting, sorting, until they snapped open again. Terrified.

Janet leaned forward, alarmed. "Mom?"

Frail lips whispered a name. It came out so mournfully that Patrick began to cry.

"Cathy." She inhaled deeply, her nostrils expanding in pain. "My God . . . *why?"*

Doctor Newton's expression revealed his alarm at the physical change in Avilon. He wanted to speak calmly, but his voice failed, cracking.

"Avilon?"

She did not hear him, or did not choose to hear, for she was listening elsewhere. She was in another world, watching its development, its pain, its escape and ultimate destruction until there was nothing left but the candle's flame—and the evil.

There was pain. There was war. There were cries of death. There was revival. And she knew now what the darkness held.

Her voice was not strained, but it carried with it an urgency that jolted the others in their chairs.

"It was here! From the womb . . . from the core . . . but not born . . . not reborn . . . It has been here since the beginning."

"The beginning of what?" Tom's voice cut in abruptly.

"Mom, please—"

"It has taken so many . . . so many . . . they're confused. They can only follow because they are part of it. Because It has already won . . . or thinks It has . . ." Her words trailed into sobs, and tears washed down her cheeks like the rain on the windows behind her. Still, she did not blink.

Doctor Newton finally noticed this, and it scared the hell out of him. "Avilon, that's enough! No more of this nonsense. It can be dangerous if you let it get out of hand, so just stop—"

He tried to stand so as to shake the old woman, but Patrick's grip was vice-like, buckling the doctor.

"Don't break contact!" he warned. He was clearly angry, at the brink of a breakdown . . . or violence. Inside, though, Patrick knew differently. He was on the edge of an answer and he wouldn't let anyone pull him away from that.

His glare forced everyone to clutch hands. They gave themselves over to the power the contact held.

Janet stared helplessly at Tom, found her confused terror returned. They remained silent. Somehow, they too felt that an answer was near. Anyone could look into Avilon's eyes and see that this was no game.

"What's here, Avilon?" Patrick demanded.

Avilon shook her head, either out of despair or strain. "It has Cathy . . ."

"What does?" Patrick nearly stood at the outburst, but he

155

did not break contact.

"It wants us all . . . it has already won the war.."

"What war? Where's Cathy?"

"Gone . . . gone . . . gone . . ."

Patrick blinked away the sweat from his eyes, tried to keep control of the explosive sobs that shook his body. Across from him, Doctor Newton wondered if he should make a grab for his black bag.

"Where is she, Avilon?" Patrick was nearly screaming, his every word pushed out by sobs. "What is It?" His voice fell suddenly to a quivering whisper, nearly out of control. "Please, *please,* who has my baby?"

The candle flickered, waved with tension.

"The evil. The . . . Ssshhhadowman."

The answer was simple—that's what scared them all. The room temperature dropped. A fog, previously hidden, began its twisting rise from the floor.

Of them all, Tom was the one who tried hardest to record the events logically. His colleague, Doctor Newton, had his tiny eyes aimed at Avilon and was aware only of his concern for her safety. Tom followed his gaze, glared at the old woman. Something—tension?—was rising steadily, and he couldn't explain it unless he considered the power of suggestion. But all of this seemed too real, too threatening for that. So what was left?

Avilon did not acknowledge their attention. She couldn't, not with her eyes rolled into her head, sifting through her subconscious and its secrets.

Tom needed to speak and decided whispering would not seem so ridiculous right now. "What is the evil, Avilon? What is It doing here?"

Her answer was drawn out, her voice guttural. "To take us. To purge us of the curse of life. The war has been going on for so long, and they have lost so many battles, but now . . . now . . ." She shivered in apparent terror, which unsettled the audience even further.

"You say 'they.' Who's 'they'?"

"Evil."

Tom frowned. "They must have a leader. Is that the Shadowman?"

Doctor Newton roused himself from his study of Avilon. He was caught up in the atmosphere just as the others, but now he leaned over and spoke *sotto* to Tom. "If she says Satan, I'm leaving."

They both turned back to Avilon. Tears poured from her eyes. Her breathing was regular but heavy. When she shook, it actually trembled the table.

Avilon herself could feel her hair moving over her skin, affected by the power she now held. She could see the answer in her mind. She tried to escape so as to watch it all from a distance, but it was too late for that. Much too late for anything.

"Avilon," she heard again from so far away, "who is the Shadowman?"

She sighed, and slumped as though her soul had left her.

"God," she whispered.

Outside, shapes began to move. Shadows joined, multiplied, separated, unaware of the rain and cold. *They* were the storm.

And the air was charged for their arrival.

Pandemonium broke out around the table. Arguments grew loud, skepticism and belief clashing, and in their midst Avilon still sat, quivering. A few wasteful minutes passed before their attention gravitated back to the end of the table. Avilon still hadn't blinked and her breathing was quicker. Concern for her health suddenly became paramount, but when Janet and Doctor Newton tried to stand, they found their progress stymied by a powerful grip.

Patrick was not about to let go now, not with the answers so close.

"The leader is God?" he demanded.

Janet looked to Tom for help—his were the only hands that were free—but he made no move toward Avilon. He was as glued to her words as Patrick. Janet half stood and pushed at her husband's shoulder, but still he would not move, as if he were in . . . *a trance!* His eyes were as glazed as hers—

Her frantic thoughts were interrupted by Avilon's answer. "Yes," she barked through chalky lips. "Yes, yes, I can feel it . . ."

Patrick shook his head, unable to believe. "But how? How can God—"

"It is One who calls Itself God. It has won that title . . . so It believes."

"I don't understand. Does It have Cathy?"

"Yes."

Now Patrick was seething. His jaw clamped so tight it looked about to crack.

Before he could stand, Janet jumped to her feet, still grimacing at Patrick's grip, and said, "Mother, has this god taken the other people of this town? The ones that are missing?"

"Yes."

"Can we . . . can we stop It?"

"No."

Patrick's jaws unclenched. "But you know where It is, you know what It's doing! You know how It feels and how It thinks! Don't you?"

Avilon hesitated, then gave a slight shrug. "Yes . . ."

"Then you can stop It! You can stay one step ahead of—"

"No," the old woman said strongly.

"But you know all these things, so you know what It will try in the future. You can find Cathy for me and—"

"*No!*" She was adamant now. She sucked at the air with great effort.

"Why?" shouted Patrick. He slammed Janet and Doctor Newton's hands against the table, finally releasing his hold. "Why not, *why not?*" He sank back into his chair.

Avilon seemed about to answer, but stopped, her mouth half open. Behind her, the veranda windows began to shake, warning. A huge wind, growling its hunger, scratched at the cottage walls.

"Why, Avilon, why?" Patrick was nearly weeping now. Awkward fingers wiped tears from his eyes. "Why can't you beat It? Why can't I get my little girl back? It has my little girl. Why can't we stop It before It's done with . . . with . . ." He could not go on. He didn't know what else to add.

Avilon was still shaking; the pupils of her eyes finally peered from beneath her lids, black holes without life. "Because," she said, "because, because . . . *It is already here.*"

The room froze for a long second, then everyone was on their feet, reaching for the older woman or Patrick. But what they began was never finished; they were forced back into their seats by a cold shove and a blinding wind of darkness.

The veranda windows had blown open, shattering the glass from its frame. The room sucked in wind and rain, howling, scattering paper, clothing, hair, and limbs in its twisting dance. Shadows rolled in, filling the room. And evil. They could all feel that, more than the wind or cold or darkness, and they searched the room for its source.

The Shadowman stood at the window with Its cape blowing wildly in the wind, looking like a black aurora above the creature's head.

After a moment at the threshold, It moved forward. Its height was maintained where it should have stepped down

159

the few steps leading to the veranda windows.

Around the room, the candles flickered, and the five people were sure that they had gone out. But the wind eventually died to a whisper, followed by silence, and the candles bloomed to life once more.

Still, the darkness crowded around them.

The creature moved around the table now, behind Avilon, who still had not fully recovered from the trance and had her head bowed in weariness and terror. Janet prayed she wasn't dead.

The figure glided into candlelight and out again, creating long, veiled shadows across Its face. Its height was now fully appreciated by those at the table: well over six feet tall, if indeed Its feet were touching the ground. Its hair was the color of Its clothes: dead black, without depth, without shape, joining as one with the shadows that crawled over Its body. They caught what seemed to be a hole in its chest, but was actually the dead reflection of a crystal that hung there. Janet choked back a scream when she saw it. It resembled exactly the jewel protruding from the forehead of the beast in her dream. *This is it,* she thought wildly. *The connection! The beast!* Instinctively, she rose from her chair — and was immediately pushed back into it by a pale figure behind her. She pushed her lips together to keep the scream inside, and reached across the table for Tom's hand, gripping it hard.

The creature seemed to watch her with amusement for a moment. Its face looked unfinished, but this was because it so closely melded with the darkness. In truth, the face was deathly pale and almost glowed in its purity. White death and darkness, milk and ink.

When the examinations reached the creature's eyes, the audience was forced to look away. They were huge animal irises, quivering in their lids, searching for the helpless and the weak as all predators search for prey. But they did not

160

search out the strength or beauty or intelligence of the victim. They could *feel* beyond this and look deeper than any of the five could bear.

It waited a few moments longer to insure that Its guests' cursory investigations were at an end. Then It smiled. It knew Its pale lips parting would complete the prehistoric image they all held.

The audience, as predicted, was stunned. They simply could not believe they were prisoners of this powerful, pale nightmare anymore than they could believe Its name was God.

Patrick was the first to speak. He was too scared and confused to acknowledge the danger he confronted. He could concentrate on only one thing now, and he knew that this creature had the answer.

"Where the hell is my daughter?"

The creature stirred but did not answer. When It was still again, It didn't even appear to be breathing.

The smile was scraping at Tom's nerves. Patrick's outburst had had no reaction, and he thought if he said something . . . if he were a bit more solicitous . . . But the silence and the staring just couldn't go on. He couldn't handle it.

"Who are you? What do you want?" He silently cursed himself. He had wanted to sound calm, but his voice had quivered like a taught wire.

But there was a reaction. A tongue flicked from between Its canines, as though clearing a passage for Its words.

"I am God."

It then moved, swiftly, gracefully, so that It might have been floating, though no one could see the floor to make sure. It came around to Avilon's right, started to lay a hand on her shoulder until she trembled with disgust, found its place on the chair's back.

"I am here for you, sir," It said. It looked around the

table. "For all of you."

Tom winced with pain as Janet's fingers locked around his. He glanced at her, and nearly lost his own composure when he saw the absolute panic in her face. Just the sight of the creature seemed to suck the blood from her body. Her eyes were wide, unblinking, tearful. She shook, her lips trying to control the low moan that escaped her. Panic. Hysteria. He thought he heard her hiss, *"Beast . . ."*

There was nothing he could do but hold onto her hand and cover the union with his other. He couldn't watch her anymore, for fear his own panic would explode into a confusion of fear and anger. *What's happening here?*

The Shadowman moved to the opposite side of the table, across from Avilon. Tom suspected It was sizing them up just as they were studying It. As It passed Doctor Newton, Tom glanced at the man. The old codger was as pale and terrified as Janet. He wondered if the man would have a heart attack soon.

Then what? What could I do but watch him die?

Something pulled him forward. Janet was shaking violently now, her limbs occasionally jerking toward her spasmodically to lock her in a ball. She groaned, began hyperventilating. Her eyes seemed to vibrate in their sockets, all the while glued to the creature.

Tom leaned across the table and pulled her toward him. "Janet! Janet!" She couldn't see him. The white underbelly of her eyes rolled up to greet him. Tom stood and slammed the table with his free hand. "*Stop* it!" he blazed at the creature. "What are you doing to her?"

The Shadowman wasn't even looking at her. It waved a hand. "Perhaps she recognizes me. Try slapping her."

"*You're* doing it. I can feel it. Now *stop!*"

The creature's eyes narrowed. "Or what?"

Tom moved, nearly made it over the table before two pale figures grabbed him from behind and held him to his chair. He struggled and went on struggling even after he realized he wouldn't rise again unless they let him.

But the Shadowman had made Its point. It blinked, and Janet's body went lax. She doubled over, eyes squeezed shut, sucking air with one long gasp after another. She would not be fully conscious again for several moments. Still, she knew enough to stay in her seat.

Tom wanted to hold her, to let the relief wash over him, but he knew it would be a hopeless act. Instead, he grabbed his chair's armrests to stable himself, and let loose with a demand not even the creature could ignore.

"What the hell do you want here?"

"I do not fear telling you the truth," the creature said calmly. Its velvety voice startled the others back to their senses, to the very real threat that now confronted them. "There is nothing you can to do stop us now. We have fought a million battles, raged a single, cataclysmic war within the bowels of the earth. And now, in our victory, we have joined to create a peaceful planet." Its tone was clear and deep, but it seemed to echo, as if stereo speakers had been set in the hidden corners of the room.

No one moved. No one said anything. But they could all sense some truth in the creature's words—and the cold fear growing in themselves.

"The enemy lies dead, defeated, in the bowels of this planet," the Shadowman told them. Its voice rushed on before Its audience was lost to panic. "Now all I must do is take the land and the people and begin the process of true peace."

"Why haven't we been aware of this war?" Dr. Newton managed to get the words past a throat constricted by terror. "You said yourself that it was massive."

"But you *have* been aware!" shrieked the Shadowman, making everyone jump in their seats. "It isn't as simple as the ideological fight between Good and Evil, but that will do as a comparison. There are two forces who have fought since the birth of this planet. I expect that the sudden image of Satan and so forth will spring to your minds, but believe me when I say that is merely your own imagination at work. There is no entity called Satan or Devil or Scratch from where I come, neither on my side or the other. Perhaps you have been unconsciously aware of the war, though, and have placed these images in your mind to somehow alleviate, even deal, with the truth."

The creature was moving again, and It grew close to Janet, almost upon her. Tom stiffened. Should he try to jump, try to attack? But Janet was already taking action. She looked away from the creature and inched her chair away from It. She tensed, waiting for Its touch before loosening a scream. Tremors possessed her body.

Don't go over the edge, Tom thought desperately, watching her, wanting to reach for her hand. *Please, dear God, sweet Jesus, please don't let her go over the edge . . .*

The Shadowman stopped and looked down at her. "I startle you, I know," said the creature. "To you, we are, perhaps, the graven image of these demons you think of." It paused again. "Perhaps I can make it clearer to you."

Why? Tom wondered, but he was grateful for the time — and for the distance now growing between It and Janet as the creature moved to the head of the table again.

"When the planets came together, they were all made of the same material, like brothers and sisters. Each planet has two . . . well, 'souls' if you wish, who are in constant turmoil throughout the planet's life."

Tom could no longer keep silent. "You talk as though an entire planet were . . . were . . ."

"Alive?" the creature answered smugly. "And why not? Tell me that the planets don't live. Tell me that they don't have their own movements, their own temperaments, their own personalities. Look at Mars! The war there has been waged for millenniums, and you can see how it has affected the planet. Now there's nothing but cold sand, dead landscapes, raging winds!

"Why? Because that planet's souls are more savage than this planet's. We—my side and the other—agreed that life should remain on this planet, that you should grow and develop into the spoils of a war whose outcome has only recently been decided."

Doctor Newton asked harshly, "So we are nothing but spoils of war? Millions of years of evolution, and we are only trophies that the winners pick up at the end of the game?"

"*Game?*" snapped the creature. "This is not a *game,* sir! You should be grateful for the time you've had! There would be no life here if we had not created the proper conditions!

"You are fortunate," It continued, Its eyes growing darker. "You must know that there was once life on Mars, billions of years ago. The souls there did not allow it to continue. Their continued volcanic activity made it impossible. They are obviously *savages,* and prefer a primitive war." The creature trembled and seemed to grow straighter, taller . . . darker. "And I give you, as proof of their barbarity, the fact that they are *still* at war."

"What of the other planets?" demanded Doctor Newton. "Jupiter! Venus! Saturn! Neptune, Pluto, Uranus, Mercury! They've never even had a chance to bring forth life."

The figure shrugged. "They deal with different personalities. The wars of Mercury and Venus are fought under much harsher conditions, and I'm certain that they are even more barbaric than the souls of Mars. Jupiter and Saturn are . . . mysterious. They cloud their fighting from the rest of us."

Tom held Janet's hand tighter—he could see she was on the edge of panic again, her eyes commanding him to stand

and run away with her, *so tempting*. But he turned his head from her and managed to utter, "Perhaps those souls are not fighting at all, but have come to some peaceful resolution."

Sharp, glistening teeth smiled back. "I'm afraid they *must* fight until one wins out."

"And the others?" Doctor Newton demanded. He seemed to be trying to stand up. He leaned forward, white knuckles bunched against the table top, his face red with rage.

Here we go, Tom thought, and prepared himself.

"The others," the Shadowman replied, "are cold and harsh and desolate. They are tired of war. But still they fight. Those planets are very close to achieving a winner, but still they must fight."

Slowly, some realization broke through the elder doctor's puckered face, and his voice wavered over the final questions.

"What about . . . what about the moons of the planets? Do they also suffer this schizophrenic turbulence?"

The Shadowman chuckled, a dark, echoing clip-clap. "Yes. Oh, how nicely you put that. The fact is that a planet could not survive without two souls in battle. It would crumble and die. There would be no action, no movement or life of any kind. The majority of moons in the system are lucky enough to have dueling souls. Others were born to this system with just one soul. They are dusty, grey bones floating in space."

Doctor Newton spoke even slower now, framing his question carefully. "Did . . . did our moon . . . Earth's moon have two souls?"

The black orbs set behind crinkled lids of moonlight. "Yes," It whispered, "it did once."

"And . . ." Doctor Newton paused to swallow, "and one side won."

"Yes."

"Which side?"

The dark figure shrugged.

"And now it is . . . nothing," stammered Doctor Newton. "Just a dead, dark world without movement."

The others seated around the table slowly came to realize the implications of what Newton and the creature were discussing. Janet's hand grew cold inside Tom's.

"So," said Doctor Newton, now very weak and barely able to take one breath after the next, "since you have won . . ."

The statement did not need to be completed, but the Shadowman did so anyway, for the sake of those who stared at him forlornly.

"We have won the war, so now it is time to clean up, take our spoils and be done with it. And it *will* be done, with the help of my army, until there is nothing left. Believe me, the end will not take very long. We started here because this place has the advantages of being isolated, yet filled with people. It won't take long to expand now, and it will all be for the good of the planet. We will achieve the final peace I speak of."

The creature's eyes widened, as if to gauge the reaction to his next words.

"My friends, after more than four billion *hard* years, it is finally Earth's turn to rest in peace. To *die*."

The answer came crashing down around them. They did not call out. They knew it would be hopeless, that there was something very powerful in this old planet that they had never taken precautions against, and now it was jumping up to rip their throats away.

So embroiled were they in the fate of mankind that when Patrick's outburst broke the silence, they were at first confused, then almost angered.

But Patrick couldn't contain himself any longer. The steam had been building since the creature had spoken of planets and their "souls," and he really didn't give a damn about any of it. What he did care about had been taken from him and he wanted her back now.

"Where is my daughter, Cathy?" he demanded, and further shocked everyone by standing. He was forced, by the pressing darkness, to slump over, so he bunched his fists and slammed them against the table, staring with cold, hard eyes at the thing that had just pronounced the end of the world.

"Where is she?"

For a moment, reason came rushing back to those who were afloat in terror and anger. They momentarily forgot what the Shadowman had told them and joined Patrick in glaring at the towering monster of darkness.

Evil, they thought, and for the first time they sensed a lie in the Shadowman's words. They indeed felt the ancient derivation of Evil in that room and in that figure who dominated it.

"Goddamn it, where is my little girl?"

It was the last time the question would be asked before violent action was taken. They all knew it, and prepared for it, some clenching their fists, others whispering silent prayers. Perhaps the creature also sensed the threat, for It cleared Its throat and answered sharply and succinctly, as a businessman explaining why he took certain avenues that didn't pay off.

"My army is made up of paupers and kings, rich and poor, beautiful and ugly . . . perverted and innocent. I must take everyone, so it doesn't really matter who goes first. The Army must be built—"

"Where is she?"

The Shadowman clamped Its jaw tight, twice, three times, controlling some inner fury that the living knew they would not survive if released. At least, their *living* beings would not survive . . .

The check of temper ended with a smile and a shrug. Then the arms opened wide, the claws extended to the shadows, and the deep, deadly voice spoke.

"You fear what I have to offer. But believe me, it is more beautiful than this life. It is easier and will be easier yet when the end comes. Then, we will all sleep. Finally."

There was an honest exhaustion in the creature's voice as it continued.

"However, since you are still living and concerned for the living, I feel I owe you a little something before it is your time to go. For that, I will show you the common people I have chosen to prove what leaders you will become next to them. Oh, yes, I have special positions for each one of you. Please, look around. See for yourselves what I have built for us."

They did look around. There was no illumination of the shadows, no spotlight that grew in intensity, but slowly their eyes adjusted to the darkness and they saw movement. At first, there was only the blurred outline of bodies— people standing near the doors and windows, posted as guards no doubt—and their vague, almost puppet-like, movements. But they were only torsos, nothing that the name "human being" could be applied to. They waited for the faces to materialize, but they remained in the shadows.

There were bodies standing behind everyone at the table—except Avilon. Apparently, she was of no harm to anyone. An old lady in a trance-like state was hardly a convincing threat, even to the most paranoid.

In the end, as the realization came that they were surrounded and that escape would be impossible, as the uncontrollable fear and panic began to rise again, their eyes rested on Patrick, and they waited for the inevitable. He greeted those stares with determination, a mad certainty that the approaching period of violence would save them all, one way or another.

Not even Tom believed he could stop the man. He prepared for his own descent into hell.

The outburst was cut to the quick, however, by the creature Itself. It saw that Patrick, for all his pounding and heavy breathing, was weak. His eyes were bloated, like a crying child's and his limbs were quivering with the approaching breakdown.

A sharp tongue darted out again and the two black orbs widened. Just as Patrick was opening his mouth to shout again, It said, calmly, hypnotically, "Look behind you, Patrick. Just turn your head and look behind you."

The ominous command fell like a block of ice, glistening with a myriad of cold images. Patrick visibly shook. He wrapped his arms around himself.

The others watched him, transfixed. They did not want to peek at what waited for him in the shadows.

Carefully, Patrick turned, his grip around his chest constricting as if a giant snake were squeezing the life out of him. And it was a snake of sorts, for no matter how hard he tried, his arms would not move back to his side. The cold was too great and he needed that warmth, even if it crushed him.

Tears streamed down his cheeks as he tried to focus on the figure behind him. All he could make out were small, skinny legs hanging from the darkness and what looked like a thousand twitching waves upon them.

The Shadowman gestured for the figure to come forward into the candlelight.

Unable to stop himself, Patrick watched the tiny feet move forward without a sound on the hard floor. A dress appeared between two skinny, white arms. The arms were scratched but the wounds were empty. Then he saw the locks of golden hair. And, for some reason, over it all, there was a constant movement, as if the image were on a television screen and he was sitting too close—

The tears were wiped away now and he could see it clearly. The girl, his little girl, Cathy Simon, was covered with a thousand twitching, crawling bugs, a myriad of insects that bit and tore at her flesh, though she acted as if they were kisses. Some of the bugs attacked each other, devouring their prey in the hidden recesses of the girl's dress or in her hair where they could get a good hold and begin ripping.

And during it all, Cathy did not utter a sound or jump or flinch. She was a true part of nature now.

A scream rose in Patrick's throat.

A familiar, sweet face peeked out from the shadows; two unfamiliar, animal eyes blinking in innocence between the passings of the various parasites. Absently, her hand went up to her hair and ran her fingers through it like a comb. They stuck and pulled. The golden curls were matted, twisted with twigs and dirt and blood.

Patrick couldn't breathe. *This is my little girl? What have they done to my little girl?*

He suppressed the scream. He stood his ground, trying desperately to resist the urge to run away from his child, his only little girl. All that was left of Margie.

"C-Cathy . . . ?" It was a whimper, a question he prayed would never be answered. He realized now the Shadowman's trick. If this was really his baby and this was what now awaited him, he would have been better off not knowing.

The girl's eyes had squinted in recognition of his voice. The eyes were so dark and wide, he couldn't tell whether they moved. But she crinkled her nose and Patrick's fear was, for an instant, lifted, his memories returning to earlier, happier days: laughing in the pastures, giggling, dancing with butterflies, singing, "Daddy, Daddy . . ."

The girl seemed to sense this and her lips parted in a smile.

"Daddy."

A beetle hindered her tongue, but it crawled onto her lips and up past her eyes by the time the word was completed. Then the blue lips pulled back and revealed two small, razor-sharp teeth poking out from her gums, still tinged with blood.

She raised her arms to show off her live collection. "Look, Daddy, they all love me. I'm really their friend now. I couldn't be before, but now I can. This is everything, Daddy. Come with me, *please*."

She kept talking so sweetly, even while Patrick was screaming and crying and scratching at the air, trying to blow away this image that could never be his daughter. None of his friends could rise to hold him, chained to their chairs by horror and an even stronger power.

When his hysteria was finally spent, he fell to his knees in front of her. But the fall did not end at his knees. He plunged quickly and irretrievably into a darkness of his own, sobbing.

Throughout, the Shadowman's smile never faltered.

Doctor Newton was the only one not watching the pitiful sight across the table.

Since the creature's arrival, he had been searching for something in his pocket. He had been gripped by a primitive terror from the beginning, but he had also kept a skeptical view of the proceedings. Now, however, the fear washed everything else away, its intense cold jerking him straight in his chair, and he knew with wild certainty that this terror was closer to the truth than he could ever admit. He had scoffed at the Shadowman's explanation of Its existence and the fate of the world, but he had also seen the way the creature had glided through the room, had seen Its eyes and fangs, and these had ominous and familiar callings.

But now his attention was drawn, *pulled,* to the sweet little girl he'd met earlier and those bugs eating her alive and her giggles—and suddenly his emotions pressed against his heart, trying to suffocate him.

They could be the "souls" of Earth, or they could be demons or even the vampires that they resembled so closely. Whatever their true identities, he was certain of their species: that of Evil. Newton believed strongly in a Good and Evil in the world, and if this were to be taken literally, as the creature had professed, then so be it. The creature wanted war. Well, he would do what he could to be a worthy opponent.

Finally, his hands found the object in his jacket pocket. His fingers wrapped around the instrument and his lips formed a final prayer. God, how many times had he used the power of this emblem when his own scientific powers had failed him? How many times had he been the last warm body a dying person had touched? How many times had he himself had to recite the last rites to patients, if not for their sake, then for his own?

And now it would be used one last time for his own final blessing.

With determination and a bravery he never knew his faith could produce, he stood and shoved the cross forward, the blessings of the rosary beads chattering right behind it.

Tom and Janet were crying—for Patrick and themselves. Tom's tears were masked by anger as he tried to stand, tried to help, but found himself impotent. Janet was near hysteria, her fingers clawing at her ears, her eyes, trying to make the world around her fade away.

Tom stopped struggling in his seat when he grew aware

of the motion beside him. Doctor Newton stood and was now moving inexorably toward the Shadowman, one arm thrust forward like a shield. Then he saw the golden cross, supported by a thumb and fist, and the tiny brown beads dangling below it.

His first impression was one of insanity on the part of Newton. How could a man who believed so absolutely in science, who had devoted his entire life to the study and cure of invisible parasites that the religious had once considered God's Hand—how could a man with that sort of background be moved to a faith-inspired superstition for his salvation? But then he remembered the man crossing himself before entering the clearing, and those words spoken half in jest: *Look to the heavens for the answer* . . . So he was a religious man—for all the good it would do him.

His opinion changed, however, as he watched the retreating figure of the creature calling Itself God.

There was fear on that ghostly face.

Doctor Newton was screaming, a mixture of pain, fear, and faith. His heart was pounding faster, flushing his face a deep scarlet, yet on he screamed with more fervor and conviction than with each previous attempt.

"I know what you want! I know what you are, you bastard!"

"Oh, yes," the Shadowman answered calmly, though Its face told another tale. Behind the forced smile there was a tremor on the lips and the teeth were hidden. "Oh, yes," It repeated, "oh, yes, I *am* a bastard. A child of the Earth's loins, just as you are, just as the Other Souls were." The creature planted Its feet and stood unmoving.

Doctor Newton did not hesitate in his advance. He too saw the hidden terror in the Shadowman's face and he was driven by it. It did not once cross his mind that perhaps that is what the creature had wanted all along.

The trembling mouth, the concealed teeth, the knitted

174

brow — they all disappeared in an instant and were replaced with a hard, probing glare with two black bullet holes in the center . . . and a hungry smile.

Doctor Newton froze in place and suddenly felt very foolish standing before this towering creature, holding a trinket up to Its face. *What happened?* he thought. *How can I be so calm?*

"You see, sir," said the Shadowman, "these events were chosen to happen long ago. I rule this world now because I am its leading soul. I am God. The God of your bible, I'm afraid, was written by men, but if there was a creator of planets, then He is *my* creator, not yours, and you cannot call upon Him to save you."

As the creature spoke, no one noticed that Avilon had snapped out of her trance and was witnessing all of this as one horrible, sweeping image: Janet clutching her hand so tight, both her and Tom's face contorted with horror, Patrick sobbing uncontrollably on his knees at the feet of a tiny ghostly figure, and Doctor Newton screaming at that — at that — The word eluded her. But she knew what the darkness was and she was the only one who was not afraid of it because she also knew how to hurt it. She was about to speak out when her attention was irrevocably drawn to the tiny ghost approaching her.

She very nearly screamed, ruining it all.

My dear god, the bugs! And Patrick, following her on his knees, crawling like the insects, as if he too ate from her flesh — Cathy! My God, is that Cathy?

From there, all thoughts of salvation were lost.

The creature was circling the doctor now, remaining a safe distance from the cross, but never breaking eye contact. Its orbs seduced the old man, writing his name in the darkness, making it bold, then small and cramped, then nearly invisible, his emotions bending to the images. Newton winced at the manipulation and clutched his chest tighter.

Still, the other hand held out the cross.

"There is, however, an Armageddon," resumed the creature, Its voice rising to a climax, "for all good things must come to an end, and the Earth's has already been decided. Let the other worlds continue their wars. Ours is done with, in a very civilized manner considering the havoc the others have wrought, and for this you should be thankful. After all, think of the pain the world would have suffered had we waited for you to bring about your own holocaust."

Newton convulsed, shook the sweat from his eyes. His mouth was gaping.

"Yes . . ." said the creature, nearly hissing. "You understand now, don't you, Doctor Newton?"

The elder physician froze solid at the mention of his name. There was not a joint that would bend or straighten, not a lung he could fill, not a heartbeat he could hear. His own thoughts and the vision brought on by this creature had constricted enough to hold him tight. He stared into darknesss — until he felt the waxy white hand reach out and grab the cross.

God smiled. Teeth glistened, tongue flicked. "*This is Armageddon. It's time to rise up now. You should obey. You should follow without question. And you should say . . . my . . . name . . .*"

Doctor Newton's scream nearly covered the grinding of his hand in the Shadowman's grip. The cross fell to the ground, impotent, and the doctor dropped to his knees beside it.

Tom and Janet were on their feet immediately. A force tried to keep them seated, perhaps the soldiers standing behind each, but they were much too quick and determined. Still, once on their feet, neither of them rushed to Newton's aid. The formidable sight of the Shadowman's approach was just too great an obstacle to overcome. They backed away and were easily led to their chairs. Janet looked behind her and saw the ghostly outline of a body, its face in shadows. Beyond this soldier, there were several other bodies waiting in the corners.

She turned away, feeling the hysteria rising in her chest and throat, and looked to where Patrick was staggering back into his chair. He did not lift his eyes. His face was completely blank of expression. If it were not for the dirty tears that streaked his face, Janet would have mistaken him for one of the soldiers. But he was very much alive and doing his best not to hear the words his daughter called to him with sweet innocence:

"Daddy . . . please come with me, Daddy . . ."

Avilon met her daughter's expression of mute horror, but did not panic. The sight of Cathy and what they had done to her had nearly been the end of what reserved strength she could draw, but, like Patrick, she pretended that it was a false image, that the sweet little girl, so pink and lively, *had* to be somewhere safe waiting for the rest of them to find her.

She shook her head violently, erasing any doubts, purging all fears. She had to keep her mind clear. That was most important for the attack. She couldn't be intimidated or she would be caught off balance. She knew how to kill It, that's what she had to remember and put her faith in.

She found her weapon readily enough: a butcher's knife lying on the sideboard. She took it in her hand, feeling its power, revelling in the strength that came with knowing where to plant the blade. Ready, she squinted into the moving shadows around the table, searching for the soul of darkness.

The creature was standing above Newton and tightening a hand around the doctor's neck. The man's screams were choked off, allowed to escape only intermittently as squeaks and gasps.

"The end is not here yet, my friend," shouted the Shadowman. "You shall not die in the complete sense of the word. You will go on for weeks . . . months . . . as long as it takes. Until we start to feed on each other, and then the glorious end will bring this world to a close."

Newton struggled for breath, but his face turned red, then white, with failure. The creature's grip was so tight that the claws were ripping into the man's throat. They did not tear, but resembled injections, forcing cold, blue-ice into his veins. With his small eyes turned to the face of his god, Doctor Newton could not see his own blood running down the creature's arm in a torrent.

Neither did he see that the creature was staring at Its arm and the doctor's blood—and was frowning in puzzlement. Its rage rose unhindered now, and would have built to such a peak that everything would have been over in seconds had things not occurred as quickly as they did.

At the table there was finally action, but it was not for Newton's cause. Tom jumped over the table, scattering candles onto the floor, and grabbed hold of Janet. She screamed and pulled away at first, but then held him just as close, wanting to bury her head in his shoulder and rub away the images. Tears came in storms now and she knew she'd never be able to stop.

Having her firmly in his embrace, Tom released one arm, sending Janet into hysterics until she saw that he was placing the other firmly about the hollow shell of Patrick

Simon.

Behind them, Cathy Simon moved toward the Shadow-man and the doctor. Newton's blood was covering the ground, its warmth causing steam to rise as it touched the icy floorboards. Cathy watched, transfixed, and she darted a small black tongue out to lick her lips. A spider nearly flipped off her chin by the action.

In the middle of the room, the center of attention, the Shadowman easily turned Doctor Newton's struggling body around so that all could see him. The living in the room held back screams and clutched each other closer.

The doctor's face was a light purple now, as though his entire head were one big bruise. Blood dripped from his silently moving lips and his eyes were bugged, probably the first time anyone had ever managed a good look at them. In a succession of spasmodic jerks, his arms rose up imploringly to those seated at the table. The crushed hand dropped oddly to the side, bone and flesh mixed into a red pulp flecked with slivers of white.

"Now, Doctor Newton," cried out the Shadowman, all joy in Its voice gone, "*Who* am I? *What* am I?"

Tom held Janet and Patrick closer. Avilon readied herself, pushing her chair away from the table.

Doctor Newton's arm fell back to his side as if he were a puppet whose strings have been cut. He looked up and recognized the hunger in the creature's eyes, knew that that hunger could not exist if the end were truly here. But how could he communicate that to the others? Besides, he was so tired, so very tired, and those big, black eyes were so comforting . . .

Blood bubbled around his vocal chords and he sputtered, "God."

The creature's expression did not change. It brought the doctor's head closer, as if to lay it gently against Its breast to comfort him.

Doctor Newton felt his pain ebbing. Soon there was only the cold, and he joyously fell into the darkness.

Janet screamed and felt Tom tremble. She turned away and concentrated on her husband's face, only on his expression. She watched his nostrils flare, then pinch nearly shut as he sucked air. Tears erupted from his eyes, but he would not blink them away. She tried not to listen to the sucking sounds behind her and the occasional *crunch* as the fangs searched deeper into the veins, but it was all too loud, too impossible to ignore. She would have to listen and try to erase it later.

Then, suddenly, a figure catapulted into view. It was a ghost, dressed in flowing white, racing toward the center of the room. It was seconds, long unforgettable seconds, before anyone realized that the figure was Avilon. They barely noticed the knife in her hand.

None of the soldiers standing about the room tried to stop her. The creature had prepared them for such an attack, but they also had been instructed to let the Shadowman handle it alone. Besides, they were all too busy licking their lips, agonizing over the meal set out before them, waiting in forced patience for the Shadowman to finish with Doctor Newton first. To her credit, Avilon was silent and quick as she crossed the room, and it was doubtful they could have done anything to prevent her from reaching her goal anyway. Not in time.

Then, in that final second, they saw her. And something *shifted* in the soldiers when they witnessed the force she wielded behind the knife—and where it was aimed.

The blade connected. They had all seen the black crystal stone inlaid across the Shadowman's chest, just below the ribs, though they didn't know about the identical one in the middle of Its back, hidden by Its cape. But now everyone in the room also *heard* it.

The knife sparked the surface of the front crystal, then

jumped upward and down again into the flesh. By the angle, the edge had managed to squeeze in behind the area the crystal protected.

The creature slammed Its claw into Doctor Newton's face, destroying the features in a pink cloud, and the body fell away, to be quickly swallowed by the floor's shadows. The creature writhed in pain, both meaty hands now on the hilt of the knife, Its shuddering voice shouting and crying out words unknown and never before spoken on the surface of the planet.

And It was not alone. The other soldiers in the room also were crying out in pain, their fingers digging at some unseen agitator within their own bodies.

Patrick closed his ears to the scream of a little girl.

Though a man of hard science for most of life, Tom understood that somehow the magic of Avilon had hurt this demon. There was something behind that crystal that was important and Avilon had struck at its heart. But would It now die? The suspense was numbing to him.

He realized, however, even in his delirium, that they could not wait here to find out. Whatever Avilon's hope of killing the creature, she had acted first to offer a chance of escape.

He looked to her now, as he gathered up Janet and Patrick and pushed them toward the veranda windows, and she answered him silently, with tearful eyes and a slight nod. She stood between the raging beast and her family, unafraid.

At last, he could read on her face, *at last I can really help.*

And he was not about to let the gift pass. Without another look back, he pushed what was left of his family through the broken windows. Janet was screaming unintelligibly, although Tom was certain it was about her mother. Patrick was still dazed, his emotions raw and numb, but he darted through the window just as quickly as his cousin.

181

Behind them, Avilon stood her ground. Behind her, the Shadowman exerted some inward strength, grinned, and, as if by the pressure of the growing smile, the knife was driven from its chest. As Its fangs protracted from the widening mouth, the knife fell. There was no sound of it even touching the floor.

A huge hand, as powerful as a lion's paw, reached out and grabbed Avilon. She closed her eyes calmly, knowing she would never fall under the spell of darkness. She knew too many of its secrets. The Shadowman knew this too, so It mollified Itself by digging its claws into her eyelids, through her eyeballs, into her skull. A split second later a clawed thumb slipped into her mouth and punctured the roof. A thick, green smoke erupted from the destruction.

Tom was the only one to hear the sickening symphony of cracks and pops, the only one to hear what it sounds like when a person's face is ripped from the rest of the head. As he stumbled outside into the raging storm, he thought of the safety of his wife and his friend and of what life would be in a world that was ending—*anything*, so that he would not have to stop and cry out in despair.

Chapter 8

Lightning raped the sky. Her cries were heard for miles, a throaty explosion that shook the land. Her tears struck the earth like meteors, stinging the skin of those pitiable creatures that roamed the forest.

It hadn't taken Tom long to catch up to the other two. Janet was sobbing, nearly screaming, and her words were unintelligible. *She must know her mother is dead,* he thought, *but did she see what happened . . . or hear?*

It was too much to think about now. They had to get away, far away, just keep moving until they reached somewhere safe, wherever that may be. But they couldn't wander the woods the whole night, not in this storm. And the Shadowman's army could be waiting somewhere near. No, they had to find shelter and hide — fast.

He grabbed Janet's shoulder to slow her progress and scream a question in her ear, but she shrieked when he touched her and wrestled away, continuing on after Patrick. Their leader, Tom noticed, was stumbling. His face was hard to see in the rain and darkness, but it didn't seem to move. It was numb with horror, trying to contain emotions that would surely destroy the man inside if not soon released.

Tom didn't touch Janet again, but ran up next to her and called out, "Patrick! Patrick, wait!"

The big man did not even pause. His headlong journey to nowhere was unswerving. His eyes were not looking outside but in. There was too much to think about, too much to try and forget and pretend never happened.

Tom grimaced at his own memories of the little girl and tried not to be sick.

"Patrick!" he screamed. His voice was hoarse, but it still managed to break above the cries of the sky. "Patrick, come back, we have to find somewhere to go! We have to find shelter!"

"Patrick!" This from Janet. When Tom looked at her, she began to cry again. Still, there was a facsimile of composure there. She was trying hard to regain control.

They continued calling Patrick's name, but he would not stop. His feet stumbled on, trudging some path that the land had carved for him that would lead him safely to . . . where? It didn't matter. He wasn't there anyway.

Tom cut in front of Janet and faced her. They didn't stop—at least he didn't think they did—because the land moved around them. Maybe it was just the storm.

"Look," he called into her face, "we have to find some shelter somewhere. They have their people out here. We have to find a place where we can hide and shut ourselves away. At least until the storm ends."

Janet didn't answer. Her arms were wrapped around her quivering body. The rain had soaked through her cotton apparel, making it stick against the skin. She was as wet and as cold as if she had jumped into a stream.

She was no longer crying, though. And her eyes eventually met her husband's.

"Where can we go?" he yelled. "You and Patrick know the area. Where can we go?"

She stared at him a long time. He couldn't be sure

whether she was thinking, or had gone into shock. Her expression was the twin of Patrick's. The thought of the other made him twist briefly. The squat, broadly muscled figure was pulling ahead, but could still be seen clearly through the thick brush.

"There's a cabin nearby."

Tom turned back to Janet. "A cabin?" he prompted.

"Yes. It's not very big, though."

"It doesn't have to be. We just need to get out of this rain, out of this forest."

She stopped suddenly. Tom was taken by surprise and tripped backward, then recovered quickly. Janet pointed off to the right.

"Over that way. Greg Wesson used to live there. I think he still does."

"Good! Let's go." He approached her hesitantly, but she folded into his arms without flinching. They started making their way to the south, up a steep hill. As they started up, Janet stiffened.

"Patrick! Where is he?"

Tom looked over his shoulder. The man was gone. "Damn it! I'm sorry. I thought . . . I assumed he'd stop when—"

"Where is he?"

Tom couldn't help backing away at the hysterical cry. *She can't stand to lose him too,* he thought, then lowered his eyes. *Hell, neither can I.*

"I'll look for him," he said and started off.

"No!"

She ran at him, and for a moment he thought she was attacking, but her hands wrapped themselves around his thick forearm and he understood that they'd be locked tight until the end.

"We stay together," she said. "It's too dark out here. The storm and those creatures . . ." She shook her head of the thoughts. "We have to go together. As one."

Tom nodded, put his arm around her shoulders, and they stepped into the darkness together.

Their calls were not answered. Their fears would not abate the thunder or lightning. Every leaf became an eye, every branch a grasping arm. They both screamed again and again, sometimes alone, sometimes in unison. Soon their throats hurt with the screams and the cry of a name, and finally they allowed despair to pull them under.

They tried hard not to cry, but amidst the pounding of the rain neither thought the other would notice, so they weeped freely. Their sobs mingled with the shivers the icy wind brought on. Their sniffs and muttered curses and prayers were muffled by the sky's own blasphemies.

That's why they were so surprised when they finally did find Patrick. They were on their way back, after they had accepted defeat for their friend, still determined to reach Wesson's cabin, when they nearly ran into the man. Or he nearly ran into them.

He halted at Janet's startled squeal, but did not back away. He stared at them, holding each other like terrified children, and nearly smiled.

"Hey, it's only me," he said.

Janet was first to show her anger. "Goddamn it, Pat, where have you been? How could you leave us?"

"I'm sorry. God, why do you think I kept going? I didn't know where I was headed." He blinked rapidly, breathed deeply for a few moments, then concentrated on his cousin again. "I was scared when I thought I'd lost you two. The panic sort of woke me up. I'll be okay for a while. I think so. Just don't say . . . anything."

"Patrick, why—" She was cut short as she moved toward her cousin. Tom held her back firmly. She stared back at

186

him, her face contorted with confusion, but willing to wait for an answer.

Tom had his eyes glued to Patrick. He was waiting for lightning to strike. He didn't have to wait long.

It was hard to tell. In this weather and under these conditions, even his own dark skin looked pale. He thought the eyes would give it away, but he couldn't be sure of that either. Besides, Patrick's eyes had been dark and sickly since he'd seen his child . . .

"What's wrong?" Patrick asked. He stared back at Tom unwaveringly.

Tom pulled Janet a little closer. She laid a hand on his chest and looked closely into his face.

"Tom, what is it?"

"Where've you been, Pat?" he asked.

"I told you. I'm not sure. I've just been wandering. Goddamn it, Tom, goddamn it, you saw what they—you saw what happened—Jesus . . ." He was breaking again. His face had been molded into concrete, but the cracks were widening now and Tom realized he had been wrong. And perhaps his doubt had been the cruelest attack upon Patrick. He was with them, *alive,* and they had to stick together.

"All right, come on!" he shouted, covering his anger. "We've got to get to Wesson's cabin, fast."

Janet was still staring at him with that crazy look in her eyes, eyes that read, *I can't believe what you just tried to do!* He ignored them.

Patrick, on the other hand, seemed to pull himself together again. It was the action, the pace, that kept him going. As long as he had something else to think about, something important like his own survival or the death of those spooks back at the—but he couldn't think that far back.

"Wesson's cabin?" he shouted, trying to click his mind

back into a safe niche. "Wesson's cabin. That's about a half mile southeast of here."

"Yeah," said Tom, "but which way's south? I'm all turned around. How do we tell?"

"The ridge rises evenly all along this spot," Janet said. "We just head uphill then down again. Then it'll start being a problem. There's a path in the woods leading to the cabin. If we find that—"

"We played on that path as kids," said Patrick. "Wesson was always shooing us away."

Tom and Janet watched him with concern now. He did not look up from the ground. He was staring into his past, before he had been a man, before he had brought a little girl into the world, before he had believed in honest-to-God monsters. He was slipping away from today.

"We always went back, though," he continued, " 'cause he figured we wouldn't dare after the hollering he'd given us. We used to hide in the forest and spring up on each other."

His voice died in the rain. Janet's grip tightened on her husband's arm. Tom didn't move.

Then, very gently, Janet's voice filled a lull in the wind. "Pat. Let's go back there, okay?"

Patrick's hands were bunched into fists, striking the head of some invisible object. "If . . . if I just don't think about . . . all those times we played in the forest . . . hiding . . . getting caught . . . just don't think . . ."

Soon his lips stopped moving and his face was cement again. He stared levelly at them and Tom made a gesture to move on. The storm was winding up to hit them again. They had to get out of it while they could.

They climbed the slope and down the other side and moved on into the thick woods beyond. The nightmare of a thousand eyes and arms reaching out returned, but they clung to each other. If one went, the others would, and they'd be holding on to someone alive. Somehow that was a comforting thought, and their screams of panic became much less frequent.

They discovered the path ten minutes later. The rain was slashing hard again, falling onto their exposed skin like pins and needles dropped from a great height. Still, the sight of the muddy path's channel and its ultimate destination was enough to keep them going. They followed it east for nearly a quarter of a mile, dragging each other along, looking like a six-footed alien who was slightly drunk.

The cabin was not very big at all, but more than enough for their needs. From the outside it looked fairly sturdy. The frame was still erect and neither the walls nor the roof seemed to sag very much. Black spots covered the roof, most likely tar to keep the rain out. So someone was living there. It looked big enough for one person, no more. Perhaps a main room, a tiny kitchen, and a bedroom, but that was all.

That was plenty. They heaved their bodies onto the porch and Tom was the only one with strength enough to slam his fist against the door.

The three breathed deeply, Patrick nearly heaving, while they waited for an answer. There was none. Tom knocked again. Janet called out, "Hello?"

Faintly, a ghost whispered back, *"Go away!"*

"Please," called Tom, "we need your help. Please let us in."

"I've got a gun!" came the muted voice behind the door. It was old, obviously panicked.

"We've got nothing. Please, we just want to come inside. You can lock the door after us."

There was a longer pause this time. The three waited

tensely.

The whisper finally returned. "I can't."

"Why?"

"I . . . can't be sure."

"Of wh—" *Stupid question,* thought Tom. Hurriedly, he said, "We're not part of them. We're like you. We're scared and need shelter and warmth."

"No. I can't be sure."

Patrick suddenly broke away from the threesome and slammed his entire body against the door. The frame rattled, the door sagged, but held.

"Goddamn it, what do you want me to do, cut my damn wrists so you can see the blood?"

Even if Tom had had the strength, he wouldn't have been able to stop the man's attack. He understood the angry frustration only too well. Still, the ferocity of Patrick's words surprised him.

The initial outrage had been spent, though, and Patrick was trying to grab enough air to keep from passing out when the whisper came back, louder now as the old man within came closer to the door.

"Yes," the voice said, "yes, let me see your blood. I just need a little. Not on your lips! Prick a finger or something. I can open the door a crack—I've got chains on it— but if any of you slam against it like you did just now, I'll blow your damn heads off!"

Tom's mind was reeling. "Okay . . . I . . . wait . . ." He looked at Janet. "Hon, have you got something we can use, something to cut . . ?"

She searched herself, but with her shirt and slacks plastered to her body, it was obvious that she was all but naked. They looked to Patrick, still leaning against the door.

"Hey, Pat, get away from there. He's going to open up a little and you can't be pushing against it."

190

Patrick backed up a step. His body spun in tiny circles, trying to find a balance. "Jesus, he wants us . . . to stab ourselves . . ."

"No, no," said Janet, "just a cut. Look here, we can use part of the wall. There're splinters on it."

Tom spat out, "That's not enough to make us bleed—"

"Well, think of something else, goddamn it!" Her eyes flashed at him and the lightning backed her up.

"I'm opening the door now," said the man within. "You folks get away from it. Just put up your hand and I'll shine a light on it."

"Okay, wait a minute," called Tom. He searched his pockets. Nothing but coins. Nothing worthwhile in his wallet. Couldn't even get a paper cut, the rain had soaked everything in it. "Just wait, we haven't got—"

"I'm opening up now," said the man behind the door, "and you better show me your blood quick, or I'll blow your damn heads off."

"Wait a minute!" yelled Tom, but he knew it wouldn't do any good. He could hear the locks clicking open on the other side of the door. "Shit," he said to the other two, "we've gotta find something. There's gotta be something—"

"I'm going to rush the door," said Patrick.

"No!"

"Pat," Janet pleaded, "you heard what the guy said!"

His face was concrete again. "I nearly had it the first time. I can get it if he opens the locks."

"Damn it, Pat, he has a gun."

"He can't fire when he's undoing the locks," Patrick answered stonily. "He can't aim it."

Tom grabbed the big man's arm. "Pat, listen to me. All we have to do is show him we bleed and he'll believe us. I don't want to prove that to him with a gun wound."

Patrick's eyes never left the old wooden door. "I can do it."

191

The locks unsnapped one by one behind the door. There was a pause, then two more came undone.

Patrick started to crouch, like an animal about to pounce. Tom pulled on his arm, trying to get him to stand straight again.

"Pat, listen, Pat, damn it, *he's got a gun*." Over his shoulder he said, "Janet, get something, anything, to cut us. Hurry!"

"There're no rocks," she snapped back. "Everything's mud!"

"Goddamn it, Pat, stand up," Tom whispered violently.

The voice behind the door called, "I'm opening up now. Don't get too close—"

Patrick was ready to attack.

Tom tugged and pushed, trying to throw him off balance. *"Pat, you fucking idiot!"*

"—or I'll blow your damn heads off."

"My nails!" Janet whispered urgently. "They're long, long enough to cut."

Tom let go of Patrick and put one arm out. "Hurry! *Hurry!*"

"Nice and slow now, folks," commanded the voice beyond the door. "I've got the gun aimed right where you'll be, so don't try nothing."

Janet scraped her nails across Tom's arm. He gritted his teeth, then brought his arm up close to his face. He scowled. "It wasn't hard enough! There's only a red line. No blood!"

"I can do it, Tom," Patrick whispered behind him, crouching still lower so that the man behind the door wouldn't see him until it was too late.

"Pat, put your arm out *now!* We can show the old guy—" Tom grimaced again. He brought his arm up. This time there was a thin line of blood.

Janet was already at Pat's side. She held his arm gently

192

with one hand. "Pat, please," she said softly, "I'm going to scrape you. Then all we have to do is show our arms and the old man will let us in."

"Hurry," Tom demanded, "or he'll shoot anyway!"

They heard a creak amidst the roar of the storm. Light stabbed onto the porch. The door was opening. And behind it was a loaded gun.

"Do it!" Tom's voice cracked.

She dug her nails deep. It took only one swipe for the blood to come to her cousin's flesh.

"Now do your own. Fast."

As she cut her own arm, Tom stepped in front of the widening shaft of light. He prayed that his being in Patrick's way would keep the man from charging.

The door opened as far as it was going to go. A series of chains crisscrossed the opening at various levels. Beyond that, two creased eyes framed by scraggly white hair stared out at him. And below that, Tom thought he saw the muzzle of a shotgun.

"Let's see your arm. Quick, boy," the old man growled.

Tom brought his arm up, squeezed the skin around the wound to show that the blood actually came from within. The man inside nodded, seemed satisfied.

"Next."

The gun did not lower an inch. Tom kept an eye on it as he carefully stepped out of the way and allowed Janet to take his place in front of the door, still in Patrick's way. She showed her arm, also squeezing it.

The old man nodded. "Anyone else?"

Tom licked his lips. "One more." His eyes roamed to the other side of Janet.

Patrick was still crouched down, but his face was no longer a slab of numbness. There were tears or rain streaking his cheeks, his nose red from constant sniffing, his eyes weak, the lids quivering. He looked very much alive.

A pause passed on the porch, and Tom thought sure the old man in the cabin was going to give in and start blowing their damn heads off.

But Patrick stood and lumbered to the crack in the door. He let the light shine evenly on his pale arm, where the blood spilled from a long, thin line.

The old man nodded, but remained silent. He seemed to be deciding something, wondering perhaps if this were proof enough to open his house to strangers. Tom felt himself shiver violently. It wouldn't have been enough for him. He couldn't even guarantee that he wouldn't have shot them by now.

"Any more?" the old man asked.

"No, that's all," answered Tom.

"I saw three arms. Any more than three people come walking into this cabin and I'll kill you all. Understand?"

Tom nodded. He felt numb all over.

"We understand," said Janet. She took hold of Tom's arm, careful of the scratch.

The door closed. Patrick looked back at the other two. His expression did not hold confidence even while the shifting of chains went on behind the door.

Tom and Janet didn't say anything. They just breathed, kept sucking air. They were alive, that's what mattered.

But something on Patrick's face disturbed them. They kept coming back to it, he wouldn't let it drop or fade away. He was staring at them, deciding something. Then the words behind the glare came out:

"How do we know *he* isn't one of them? Maybe there's a bunch of them in there and they want to make sure we'll go rushing in without thinking."

Tom and Janet stopped breathing. The life just flew out of them. It was ridiculous, wasn't it? Why would the old man wait so long to let them in? Why would he have them cut their arms first? Why act so suspicious?

Maybe he wanted to make sure we were bleeders. Maybe he wanted to make sure we would rush into the middle of the room before realizing we were surrounded by them. Hell, they'd take a little place like this before they'd take a big cottage like Avilon's . . . wouldn't they?

The answers swarmed around them just as the final chain fell. There was a long silence as the three turned their scrutiny to the door. They waited and waited. And as the time passed, their thoughts hurried toward terrifying conclusions.

"All right," said the voice from inside the house. It was farther away now, barely heard above the rumble of the sky. "You push the door open real easy and come in one by one. I want to see your faces. I remember them. You just come in one by one, and when there's three of you, you close that door and use all the locks on it. I'll put on the chains."

Glances were exchanged around the tight circle. Patrick made the first move toward the door. He gripped the knob and turned carefully. There was a crunching noise as the bolt withdrew from its hole. The door was resting on its hinges now, ready to be swung open.

Patrick aimed a pained look over his shoulder and pushed the door forward. It stuck for a moment. Then, with the wind's help, it was flung wide. The wind continued its push, making the door tap out a heart-pounding rhythm against the side wall. Beyond, there was only an abyss of darkness.

Tom and Janet came up behind Patrick and each laid a hand on his shoulder. He shrugged them off and stepped into the cabin. His figure disappeared into the shadows of the room. If he had gasped then, or choked or began to scream, they wouldn't have heard it over the storm.

Tom started to go next, but Janet stepped in front of

him, kissed him lightly on the lips, and turned to step swiftly inside. She, too, was consumed by the darkness.

The wind laughed. The sky cried and cursed. The door beat against the wall. Tom stood, shaking, looking at the weathered porch, the dirt road behind him, the rattling forest to the sides, the tiny room of void awaiting him.

My wife's in there, damn it, he thought bitterly, and stepped forward. The wind's howl was immediately bitten off. The dark of the unconscious consumed him.

He felt so alone.

"Janet?"

No answer.

"Janet?"

"Close the door behind you," insisted the voice. Its sudden volume made Tom stumble in the darkness. "Do it *now!*"

He could think of no other plan, so he followed the voice's command. Once closed, he remembered to click the door's locks in place. He hoped he had gotten them all.

When he turned to confront the darkness once more, the room was suddenly illuminated. The light was soft, emanating from a single lamp which the old man had clicked on, but it was enough to show the terror on Janet's face. She sat next to Patrick against the wall with the old man's shotgun trained on their heads. Patrick's concrete expression was back, but Tom still recognized the burning anger in those eyes.

The man holding the gun on them, and now turning it toward Tom, was thin and wrinkled, his clothes faded and years past fitting his frame. When he spoke, it was through gums that held only a smattering of yellow teeth, like isolated gravestones upon a hill.

But those teeth were not pointed. Tom breathed a little

196

easier—as easy as anyone could with a gun aimed at his chest.

"Sit!"

Tom followed the end of the shotgun to sit next to his wife against the wall. He was relieved to find her hand in his before he hit the floor. It comforted him more than he would have thought.

But all feelings except terror quickly dissolved when he realized that the old man was not letting his gun drop from its study of their faces.

"We . . . need your help," he tried.

The old man licked his lips. He squinted at them, looking comically like Popeye. "What's your names?"

Tom and Janet told him theirs. Patrick said nothing, just stared at the old man as though he were waiting for a chance to bulldoze forward without being shot. Janet gave his name for him.

The old man nodded, but kept a watchful eye on Patrick. "My name's Wesson. Greg Wesson. You folks aren't from around here."

"No, we—" began Tom.

"We used to be," said Janet, her voice eager to please. "You must remember Patrick and me, you chased us off your land so many times."

"I've chased a lot of kids off my land." The gun barrel paused in front of Patrick. "Shot a few, too."

"I'm Avilon's daughter," Janet said hurriedly. "You know Avilon Jersey, don't you?"

Wesson's eyes blinked wide open. "Mrs. Jersey? You're . . . the little one?" He balked at the big man. "And Patrick? That you?"

Patrick did not respond except with his eyes. They could have killed on their own, given enough time.

"Who's this, then?" Wesson nodded his head at Tom, but kept the gun on Patrick.

"My husband," said Janet. "We were married a little while ago."

"Nearly a year," amended Tom.

The old man seemed to be searching his memory, but by the expression on his face, he grudgingly believed their story. Finally he nodded a few times, as if to reassure himself, then set his mouth sternly.

The gun still did not drop.

"Well, that's all well and good. Didn't know you folks too well, but guess you were good enough. Still, I've . . . well, I've known . . . I *know* . . ." He faltered like this for a long while, until his voice was nearly a whisper. It must have been a powerful memory: his eyes were torn from Patrick and wandered to a door across the room.

Tom braced himself against the wall, uncertain as to what Patrick might do with the old man preoccupied.

The eyes came back, perhaps just in time. None of them noticed Patrick edging his body forward or how taut it had become, but they did see him relax and fall against the wall again when Wesson's attention had returned.

Wesson's voice was sharp now. "I knew some fine folks, but they're gone now. Not really gone, but the good in them's gone." He seemed to lean a little closer, his voice becoming conspiratorial. "Do you know what I mean?"

They stared at him for a moment, stunned by their own memories. Tom finally answered calmly, "Yes. We know. We've seen."

"Good! Then you won't mind me asking you all to give me a great big smile, hmm?"

The request did not sound so ridiculous since they had all been studying his own dentures for quite some time. They smiled, even Patrick, although his could better be called a sneer.

Wesson strained to study each pair. As he did so, his gun prompted each one to stand and step off to the side.

Tom was first. Janet followed. But Patrick's face was strained for a much longer time as the old man blinked and drew closer, blinked and studied again.

His gun did not drop from Patrick's head.

"I don't know . . ." he whispered.

Tom and Janet's attention was inevitably drawn to Patrick's sneer. They immediately understood why the old man questioned him. His pair of upper canine teeth looked a bit too sharp for comfort.

"I don't like it . . ." whispered Wesson. The others recognized the tension in his voice. He was really scared.

"It's okay," said Janet. She reached out to touch Wesson's shoulder, but thought better of it. Her fingers remained curved in the air. "Some dentists file them like that. You must have seen it before."

"Can't say that I have . . ." said Wesson. He cocked the shotgun.

Patrick's face glowed with sweat. The anger in his eyes had completely disappeared, replaced now with rising terror and a picture in his mind of what his head would look like when the explosive force of two shells pelted it.

"Hey, come on," Tom said hurriedly, trying to keep his voice from cracking, "come on, Mr. Wesson, his teeth are a little sharp, but they're not long enough." He tried to think of the Shadowman's fangs—no, he didn't want to remember what had happened back in the house. Still, even a cursory glance back was enough to picture those teeth. "Not *nearly* long enough," he said again.

The old man began to nod, the bobbing-like motion increasing.

But the gun barrel was now planted firmly against Patrick's forehead. His lips quivered around that ghastly smile.

"How can we be sure?" asked Wesson.

"He showed you the blood on his arm," said Janet.

"He didn't squeeze it like you two. It could have been wiped on."

Patrick tried to raise his arm, to squeeze as much as the old man wanted to see, but the gun barrel pressed above his eyebrows.

I could jump him, Tom thought wildly. *I'm behind him. He's an old man and I could take that gun away before he even thinks about pulling the trigger.*

But he knew the reason he wouldn't try. He wasn't as sure about Patrick as Janet was.

The man accused was quivering now under the strain of supporting a loaded gun against his forehead. His face was deathly pale and his eyes were turning up into his head, trying to see the end of the gun's barrel—none of which helped his case in trying to prove he was a living human.

"Please," Janet whispered in Wesson's ear. She was so close now, she could put her arms around him if she wanted to. Tom wondered if she would try to take the gun away. He doubted she'd be so foolish, but if there was any doubt about Patrick, he could always give her a light push into the old man, make him pull the trigger, later explain how he was trying to prevent it . . .

"Please, please," Janet continued to whisper, "please, don't do it. You'll be destroying one of us, I swear it. And we need as many of us as we can get. You don't want to become one of them. You know that. That's why you're hiding up here. That's why we're all here . . . Patrick, too. He could have taken Tom and I a long time ago, if he were one of them."

There was a long pause.

Wesson didn't look like he had heard her, but slowly he lowered the gun. After what seemed like an endless arc, it was safely pointed at the wooden floor.

Patrick released the air he'd been holding. If anything had helped convince Wesson, that did. Patrick's face was

200

now beet-red. He was helped up off the ground by Tom and placed in a chair in the corner near the front door.

Wesson moved slowly to a stool in front of a crude table. "I'm really sorry about that, folks," he said, his voice surprisingly soft, even gentle. "You're right though. I gotta protect myself and anyone else like me. Them things out there . . ." He shook his head, his disbelief not finding words.

Tom approached him. "Mr. Wesson, we just came from Avilon's house. She and Doctor Newton were . . . taken." In an even lower voice, he said, "So was Patrick's daughter. She was only about eight or nine."

"God A'mighty," said Wesson. "I . . . I'm sorry. They've been taking so many, but when it's someone so close . . ." His eyes brimmed with tears and he turned away to hide his face in the shadows.

Janet leaned against her husband and took his hand again. "Mr. Wesson, you've lost someone, too?"

There was no immediate reply. When he turned around, the tears were gone, but his nose and eyelids were red. "Yeah," he said, his words clipped so as not to reveal too much. "A good friend." He stood awkwardly. "Can I get you folks something warm to drink. You look like you just swam the Pacific."

They chorused their thanks, even managing grins.

Wesson reached for a kettle on a plank nailed over a stove and began to fill it with water from the sink's pump. "You say they have the Jersey place, hmm? You're sure they didn't follow you?"

Tom and Janet exchanged uncertain glances. Janet said, "Uh, we're pretty sure. We didn't see anyone. If they had followed, they could have taken us any time."

"Don't be so sure," said Wesson. "Maybe with their leader backing them up, but on their own they're not so dangerous. Just a bunch of uncoordinated muscle spasms

201

trying to appear human."

This time Tom was struck hard by the implication. "How can you be so sure? Their leader talked as if they were a crack unit. Calls them the Army."

Wesson dug in the cupboards for some tea bags. "Yeah, well, I've seen a few."

"You've actually fought with them?" Janet couldn't have stopped the question if she'd tried. And she didn't want to try. She wanted to hear that they could be beaten, that they were not indestructible.

Wesson seemed to pause in his search. When he resumed, his voice was calm. "I've run into one or two. Didn't get much more than a bruise. 'Course, I hear their leader can be quite a sweet talker."

Tom and Janet exchanged a glance. *You can say that again.*

"Mr. Wesson," said Tom, "what if . . . well, what if they *did* follow us here for whatever reason. Are we reasonably safe in this house?"

"Don't worry. These walls are strong, even if they sag a bit. Kinda like me." He turned away from the stove and stalked across the room to the front door. He then busied himself draping more chains across the door. The front window beside it was boarded up.

Tom looked around. There was a door on the opposite wall. "What's in there?"

"My bedroom," said Wesson. "Nothing in there."

"No window?"

"Last storm blew a branch through it. Had it boarded up. Figured it was for the best anyway."

Tom kept staring at the door. It was in shadows but he could still make out what looked like fingers crisscrossing the front, attached to the frame. He moved a little closer.

They were chains.

He wasn't sure he wanted to know why, not right now anyway. There was already too much going on. So he averted his eyes, turned them on something bright and cheery and familiar, in opposition to those dark chains barring the bedroom door.

His gaze fell upon a familiar board lying on the single table in the room. It took some concentration before he recognized it. Tom asked the question before ever suspecting how important it actually was.

"You play checkers?"

Wesson stood straight, as though someone had just poked him in the ribs. His eyes rose into shadows, but the fire could still be seen burning through the black veil.

"Why?" he snapped.

"Just asking." Tom made a show of inspecting the game pieces. "Just wondered if you played, that's all. We may have a lot of time to spend up here."

"We can't stay here, Tom," Janet broke in immediately. "You know we can't. Not with those—"

"I was just wondering." He exaggerated the words. Janet sat back, crossed her arms, and looked away. Tom cursed under his breath and faced Wesson again. "We can stay, can't we? Did you have any other plans?"

"Hell, no," the old man said. "I ain't moving from this spot. Least this way I know where everything is, where it might come from. Out there . . ." He jerked a thumb over his shoulder and shook his head. The other three knew what he meant. They'd just been through that particular hell.

"Well, then" said Tom, "I figure as long as we stay here together, we have a chance at keeping alive . . . at least until day breaks and we can better see what the hell is going on around—"

"Who do you play checkers with?"

The question came from Patrick. His eyes were hard, still holding back a fury that would eventually break him. Janet noticed how fiercely his fingers dug into the crumbling chair's armrests. She looked to Tom, but he was staring at the large man calmly. The old man, Wesson, however, was anything but calm.

"What do you mean?" he stammered, almost like a child trying the words for the first time.

Patrick looked like some behemoth god carved in stone. His face was deathly pale—though no one wanted to admit how dead it looked—and his eyes were sunken, almost hidden behind the overlapping brow. When he spoke, only his grey lips parted, like a Saturday morning cartoon character.

"It looks like you have that board out to play with someone," he continued. "I can see the box you keep it in lying on the other stool there. You don't play by yourself, do you?"

"Maybe I do," said the old man.

He sounds so weak, Janet thought, but it wasn't Patrick she was concerned about, it was Wesson. His words were weak and did not sound convincing.

"What do you mean, maybe?" asked Patrick. "Either you do or you don't. I don't think you do."

Wesson gulped, his face flaccid. "Well, I do, and who the hell are you to—"

"You don't smoke, do you Mr. Wesson? I've never known you to." This came from Janet. She was staring at the table. Everyone's attention followed hers until they reached the ashtray set on one corner.

"I just use that to hold down stuff," said Wesson, his voice growing stronger the faster he talked. "When the window broke in my bedroom, there was a wind—"

"There're ashes in it," Tom added simply.

"Show us your cigarettes or pipe, Mr. Wesson," said

Patrick. His voice was perfectly flat now. It drove shivers through Janet and no doubt did the same to Wesson by the expression on his face.

"I sometimes have a guest over to play checkers," he finally admitted.

"You were expecting someone tonight?" Patrick asked.

Tom looked at the man in the overstuffed chair in the corner. He knew. He had to have seen the chains over the bedroom door. Wondered what they were for.

"Were you?" repeated Patrick. His voice did not rise in impatience, but his fingers dug deeper into the armrests of the old chair.

"Yes," the old man said faintly.

"And he came, didn't he." It was a statement. Patrick was staring at the bedroom door now. Janet and Tom did the same.

Wesson noted their gazes and his shoulders drooped, a burden lifted from him. Still, with that burden went the control he had had over his nerves, and he suddenly began to shiver and shake, becoming the quintessential old man. "God, I'm so sorry, I'm so sorry," he whispered fervently.

"What are you sorry about?" demanded Tom.

"I'm so sorry . . . sorry . . ."

Tom decided to go with all he had. "What are the chains doing over that door, Wesson?"

Wesson looked up at him as though he had just asked what two plus two equalled. "To keep the monsters out," he answered simply.

"I mean the ones over the *bedroom* door."

Wesson nearly breathed the words, his vocal chords cut with some sharp memory. "To keep the monsters out. . . ."

"You said you boarded up the bedroom window," Tom pointed out. "How could the monsters get in through there?"

Wesson bowed his head. His next words were barely

heard.

"My friend is in there."

There was a long pause. The room would have been silent had it not been for the occasional crash of thunder and the constant rat-a-tat-tat of rain on the roof.

Janet's harsh contralto was the first to inject itself. "Mr. Wesson, is your friend one of those creatures?"

Wesson looked up and the others were momentarily stunned by the anger that blazed in those old eyes. "Why the hell do you think I've got chains over the door? You think it's some sort of giant chastity belt I put over my bedroom . . . at . . . night. . . ." He couldn't finish, the anger was too much for him. He didn't sob, but merely allowed his voice to die.

"Are we safe?" asked Patrick.

"Yes." Whispered.

"Who is he?" said Tom.

"Adam Louis. The guy I play checkers with. He came tonight. He was . . . missing. I . . . we were supposed to play yesterday, but he never showed, and I figured there was something wrong. Then he just shows up at my door tonight. Of all nights." He pushed himself to the table, dragging the shotgun by the barrel behind him. He fell onto a stool and every muscle seemed to relax. The other three waited for him to topple onto the floor, but he remained steady. Only his expression fell, as did his color. Next to him, even Patrick looked tanned.

"Good Christ, I've never seen anything like it," he continued. "It was like he was an animal." He rubbed his shoulder, and for the first time the others noticed the torn cloth there.

Tom leaned in close to the old man, trying to keep his voice calm. "How did you get him into the other room? How did you trap him? Are they weak?"

Wesson's eyes lit up. "Weak? God, no! He was like an

animal, I told you. A goddamn *animal.* And he came at me—I kept saying, 'Adam, Adam, get ahold of yourself! Where you been? What's wrong?' But he wouldn't answer. Just kept coming at me. And then . . . God, I . . ."

They all knew what was coming next, what Wesson had seen next.

"Those teeth," he hissed. His eyes bore through them, not realizing that they could understand the horror of that sight. "Those teeth," he said again. "God, they came at me and I didn't have my gun with me, but . . . I . . . there was . . . he was clawing at my shoulder, trying to get at my neck like some wildcat, and I took . . . *that* . . ."

He nearly spat the word. A gnarled hand extended a claw and pointed toward the sink. Beneath it, under a stained rag, rested some sort of tool. The wooden handle peaked out from under the cloth.

When Patrick and the Howards turned back to the old man, he was shivering, tears brimming, then cascading down his cheeks. His jaw quivered with the words, threatening to just shake on, silently, forever. "An . . . an axe . . . I had to confuse the son of a bitch . . . *he wasn't human anymore!*"

He grabbed Tom's shoulder. Tom nearly fell over, but managed to remain calm and balanced, merely covering Wesson's grip with his own stronger hand.

"He wasn't human anymore," Tom stated.

"He wasn't! I swear! There was nothing else to do so I . . . I confused him!"

"Confused him," repeated Tom.

"Yeah," drawled Wesson, his eyes wide, his pupils gaping wider. "Yeah, then I dragged his body into the bedroom and—"

There was an immediate eruption in the room. Voices over voices, questions over questions, all trying to get to the same point. Finally, Janet's higher tone carried through.

"You *killed* him? How did you do it? We've seen them and how they . . . well, they're already dead, aren't they? How could you kill one of them?"

Wesson looked up at her. His face was stretched wide, his mouth agape, and he looked upon her as if she were an angel descended. He wasn't going to provide answers. He wanted answers *from* her.

"How?" he whimpered.

"How!" screamed Patrick. "How did you get the body into the bedroom?"

"How did you confuse it?" Tom clarified.

They waited for the answer. They were anxious and terrified and tired, but they could have waited forever for the answer in that warm room, with the rain and cold and monsters outside, behind the chains.

Inevitably the answer did come. "I . . . chopped off his head with that axe."

Tom released his grip on the old man's hand. Wesson had stopped holding Tom's shoulder for some time, but only now could he take his hand back. He cradled it in the opposite arm like a dying baby, sniffing and keeping his head bowed so that the tears fell into the palm.

Tom looked at his wife. Beyond the horror, he saw the need and dependence returned in her eyes.

They turned to Patrick at the same instant, but he was staring at the bedroom door. His jaw was extended and they could actually see the blood pumping in his temples.

He had that look he'd conveyed when he'd been about to break through Wesson's front door.

Tom stood up and moved in front of him. He knew he'd make a formidable wall and hoped Patrick, in his rage, would realize it.

His back protected only by his wife's warnings, Tom addressed Wesson. "Is that how you confused him, Wes-

208

son? Is that how you managed to drag his . . . body back into the bedroom?"

The old man nodded.

"What about the head?"

"I rolled it in there, too." He looked up. "Before you came," he said, "sometimes he'd call out to me. He'd call my name! He'd plead with me to open the door so we could play the game." He looked at the checker board. "He kept saying he was sorry, kept apologizing for attacking me, but he was hungry and cold and had been lost for a while. He wanted to play now. Just set some pretzels and a cold beer in front of him and he'd be fine."

"What'd you do?" asked Janet.

"I opened the door."

"Christ!" This from Patrick, who was looking more sick now than determined.

"Only a crack," the old man insisted. "But the second it was open enough, he stuck his fingers through and grabbed the door. I pushed and pushed on it, all the while staring at those sick, white fingers pushing the other way. God, they were strong. I don't think Adam's *ever* been that strong."

Tom felt Janet's hand on his shoulder and was grateful for its warmth. "So you finally pushed it back?"

"Sure. But it almost got the door open enough to step out. I was sweating it. Nearly died right there. I saw . . . God, I couldn't believe I'd cut Adam's head off. I just couldn't believe it! That's why I opened the door again. I just couldn't believe I'd done it! But when he pulled the door open enough . . . there . . . there was the head, looking up at me from the floor near the bed, calling my name over and over again." Wesson sighed and for a while it seemed he would never breathe in again.

"I finally got that damn door closed, locked it from the outside, nailed chains up as fast as I could. Then I did the

209

front door. Couple hours later you folks arrived. He's been
. . . he's been calling me every now and then, but I figure
he's tired of it now. Figures I'll eventually be his, I guess."

Tom moved to Janet's side on a ratty couch. He sank
into the cushions. His mouth was open just a bit and his
eyes were blank, thinking.

Janet recognized the expression. He was struggling with
some idea, so she waited patiently, gesturing for Patrick to
do the same. Wesson just continued to sob.

All at once, Tom stood and began moving in circles
around the room. His words were just as scattered, but
forceful. "We have . . . several choices. I don't like any of
them, but we've got to choose one.

"The first is that we make a break for it. We run like
hell until we meet up with some normal people, and that
might not be until we reach North Camp. Anyone care to
run that far in this rain with those things out there looking
for us?"

No one answered. They didn't have to.

"Okay. The other is that we stay holed up in this room
and wait for those things to find us."

"The sheriff, maybe some officers from North Camp,
might get here first," said Patrick.

"You really think so?" said Tom. "I'd figure those things
have already got the sheriff. Of course, he was in North
Camp last, so maybe he's still all right, but I don't figure
on him staying that way. He'll drive up alone and those
things will be waiting for him."

"Tom!" He stopped and stared at Janet. She cleared her
throat and said, "I'm sorry. Just get on with it."

"Right. Well, we have one more choice. It's the one I'm
voting for. But this has got to be unanimous because I'm
going to need everyone's help.

"I say there's got to be a way to beat these things.
Problem is, we have no way of knowing what it is without

doing some experimenting of our own." He looked hard at the heavy chains on the bedroom door. "It seems to me we might have the perfect candidate for such an experiment."

"Good Christ!" Wesson whispered harshly.

Patrick's face was dimpled with worry. "Hey, Tom, hey, I don't know . . ." Tom could only marvel at the sudden change in the man's attitude.

Janet didn't even flinch at the suggestion. She nodded her encouragement and it helped Tom to continue. He wasn't particularly looking forward to the experience — wasn't even sure they'd all survive it, especially the old man — but it was the only alternative they had. He wished he could convey the importance of that to them.

"Look, it's confused. It has its head chopped off. Now, how much trouble can a headless corpse be?" *Don't be patronizing*, he thought. *This is serious stuff. We have to be together on this, one-hundred percent.* "The head's no problem," he continued. "If we rush the body, we can tie it to the bed" — he looked at Wesson questioningly — "right? You have bed posts, don't you? Good. We can tie it to the bed and then I can proceed with a primitive examination. Maybe we'll come up with something."

"I'm not going back in there," said Wesson. His eyes pleaded with Tom. "I can't go back in there. That's my friend."

"We need your help. Everyone has to help. We don't know how strong this thing is."

"But it's Adam —"

"He's not your friend anymore. Your friend is dead. He died yesterday, probably before that. Now he's a monster. You don't want more of them here, do you?"

Wesson shook his head. Still, there was anger growing in his eyes. "What the hell do you know? How are you going to tell what can kill these things or not?"

"I'm a doctor, Mr. Wesson. I know these creatures aren't

your regular everyday corpses, and I'm going to have to apply a lot of liberal imagination to my knowledge of facts, but we might come up with something. *Something!* Dear God, isn't that better than waiting for these creatures to come knocking at our door?"

The old man was about to refute the argument when, as if on cue, a strong arm started pounding on the other side of the door — the *front* door.

Chapter 9

The unseen hand hammered away a dozen times before anyone in the room moved. Patrick was first to the door, his jaw set, eyes wary with that look of desperate destructive power. He would survive no matter how scared he was. Tom and Janet clasped hands and stood together, their eyes glued to the web of chains that kept the monsters outside.

Only Wesson appeared calm, and as he pushed his way to the door, the shotgun once more in his hands, he cried out, "That you, Father?"

"Father Tilkan, yes," came the muffled reply.

The answer seemed to satisfy Wesson. He lowered the shotgun, nodded, and made motions for the other three to move out of the way.

No one moved.

"Come now," said Wesson, anxious not to keep the Father waiting. "You heard him, it's Father Tilkan." When the three still did not move, he said, a bit more harshly, "Well don't you recognize his voice? Come on, little Janet, you know the Father's voice."

The others looked at her uncertainly. She gulped and nodded. "Yes . . . yes, it does sound like him."

"Greg?" called out the voice of Father Tilkan. There was

obviously fear behind it. "Greg, are you in there? Are you all right?"

"Be right with you, Father." Wesson turned to look at Tom. "Well, are you going to get your damn grunt out of my way and open up for the Father?"

Patrick let the slur pass. He stood straighter, though, perhaps aware that his stature influenced the old man, and said, "What's a priest doing out on a night like this? To play checkers, maybe?"

Wesson matched his glare. "I called him before you folks arrived—uninvited I might add. Seeing how it was an emergency, the Father said he'd be right over. And it was lucky I called him when I did—right after, the phone went dead." He gulped uncomfortably, looked off to the side. "Either the storm or those things, I guess."

"This was after you locked your friend in the bedroom?" asked Tom.

Wesson nodded.

"How do we know Father Tilkan isn't one of them?" Janet offered.

"We don't." Tom looked hard at the door and the chains. Were they finally here? Were the monsters waiting outside for them? He couldn't believe those chains would hold against the creatures, let alone the rotting wood of the wall—and he felt the injection of paranoia stab at him.

Wesson stared at the three uninvited guests as though they were the monsters. Finally, he let loose his anger.

"What are you folks talking about? He's a priest, for Christ's sake! He's a man of the cloth. That's why I called him, to exorcise the demon from my friend Adam."

"We still don't know for sure," said Tom.

"*I* know for sure. No demon can take over a man of the cloth. They're holy, mister, *holy.*"

The priest's vocation seemed to satisfy Wesson on all

214

counts. Tom wished his words were as tranquilizing for the rest of them. Still, he knew that, although the belief was enough to calm the old man, it could also move him to violence. Swiftly, with an agile grace he didn't think possible after all he'd been through, he reached forward and plucked the shotgun from the old man's hands. He aimed it at the door . . . and a tad toward Wesson.

"I'm *not* sure, Mr. Wesson," he said. "You're going to have to open that door just a little and have this Father Tilkan show us he can bleed, just like we did for you."

Wesson staggered. "You're . . . you're kidding." Janet and Patrick moved around behind Tom, their expressions grim. "No," murmured Wesson, "you're not. You're very serious. You actually want me to tell the Father to cut himself so we can watch him *bleed?*"

"You made *us* do it," snapped Patrick.

"I couldn't be sure about *you!*" returned Wesson. "*You* people aren't bound by the cloth, *you* people aren't messengers of God!"

"No," Tom said slowly, "but I *am* holding the shotgun."

Wesson looked at the weapon as if he were seeing it for the first time. "So you are," he said.

"Greg? Are you coming?" shouted Father Tilkan. "I'm getting soaked out here."

Wesson stared up into Tom's eyes. His jaw was set in grim determination. "Well?"

"Open all the locks, but keep the chains attached. Then crack it open and tell him we want to see his arm bleed." On Wesson's scowl, Tom added, "If he knows what's been going on here, he won't question the request."

Wesson still didn't like it, but he turned and did as Tom ordered. When he had the door open, the four saw a pale but expressly human face peering back at them. Father Tilkan leaned against the door and seemed more perturbed than puzzled that it wouldn't open any wider.

"Sorry, Father," said Wesson. "I've got guests."

Tilkan's expression grew worried and he stepped back. "Oh, God, Greg . . . it's not them . . . not—"

"No, no," Wesson told him, "they're right people, but they want to make sure you are. *I* know you are, Father," he emphasized, "but these others want to make sure." He then whispered, "One of them's a doctor," as though that explained everything.

Apparently, for the priest, it did. He smiled briefly and nodded his consent. "What do they want me to do?"

"Well . . . I'm sorry about this, Father, but they want you to cut yourself and show that you can bleed."

Father Tilkan took it in stride, though his mouth grew thinner with distaste as he performed the operation. When he'd finally drawn some blood on his forearm with the end of his cross and displayed it through the crack of the door, the nod was given, and the chains were removed to usher in the very tired, very wet holy man.

Hasty introductions were made, then not another word spoken until Wesson had them securely locked away again. Tom was embarrassed to find that he was still holding the shotgun on the priest and, with what he hoped was a surreptitious move, managed to lean it against the table.

"Father," Janet was saying, "do you know what's happening here?"

He was small, even more so dripping wet, and hardly seemed a man with whom one could trust one's entire salvation, yet his smooth face and wide eyes conveyed an innocence so powerful that the others in the room felt a subtle comfort, as though they actually had a better chance of survival with this man's help.

Or perhaps it's that two-cent collar, thought Tom.

"I'm sorry, I don't quite understand what's happening,"

216

said Father Tilkan, then continued hastily when he recognized the agony in the other faces. "But I did have a premonition that this would occur. I knew it several days ago. I've been preparing for it ever since."

"Preparing for *this?*" stammered Tom. "How the hell do you prepare for something like *this?*"

Father Tilkan started to explain about the holy water and his prayers, but then he remembered that, before leaving the church for Wesson's cabin, he'd thrown away the water and left his prayers unfinished. He had known, without doubt, that they would be useless for the task ahead.

Standing before these strangers now, he tried to appear confident, and patted the bible held securely under his arm. It was the only thing he owned that he still considered a weapon. "This has most of the answers," he said. "I believe that God is using me in his fight against these creatures." His eyelids trembled and he wondered, *Why did I hesitate?*

Tom was staring at him with almost open disgust. "You mean you think all this is just the Devil and his demons? You think you can wave your book and chant a few Latin phrases and everything will go away?"

"No. I have faith in the book and what it teaches, but I also have an open mind, sir." He leaned forward, speaking almost conspiratorially. "Do *you* know what these creatures are?"

Tom shook his head. "*They*—or rather the leader—says It's a soul of Earth—a representative of one half, anyway."

The priest stood a little straighter. "You've talked with this leader?"

"Very briefly." Tom licked his lips and looked to Janet for some help. She touched his fingers. "It's inhuman, I know that. And it somehow has power over cadavers." He remembered the agony of Doctor Newton. "I think there's some vampirism involved, but that could merely be—"

"—the irrational ~~acts of a psychotic~~ projecting his own nightmares," finished the priest. He grinned at Tom's surprise. "Yes, I know the term. I've studied more than one book, sir. Tell me, do they seem inherently evil. What I mean is, do they seem to embody evil, or do they convey some strain of compassion?"

Tom thought this over. He didn't want to make any snap judgments at this stage of the game. But the only one he could think of who had shown any signs of compassion had been that tiny little voice calling for her daddy. And even she had been calling for him to join her in that horrible afterlife. They had used her sweetness.

He looked up. "Yes, I think they're completely evil."

Father Tiikan nodded. "Then there must be an opposite. A good soul or souls."

"No," said Janet, "Father, you're wrong. They said they had defeated the other side. They said it wouldn't matter to us who'd won since the results would be the same. Both sides are evil. At least, to us they are. They both want the same thing. That's why these creatures are up here. They've won and they're here to bring this world to a close."

"No, I can't believe that," said the priest with finality. "There cannot be evil without good. The good must be somewhere."

Tom asked, "Where?"

Father Tilkan shrugged and made no move to answer.

Patrick moved forward in the silence and said, "Father, have you seen these creatures? Have you actually seen what they do to . . . what they look like?"

Father Tilkan lowered his head, his eyes crinkling shut. "I . . . was on my way here. I left right after Greg's call, but my car wouldn't start. Someone had pulled the battery out. They've been watching me for many days, but they haven't touched me." He looked up and into Tom's eyes, grinning slightly. "I have no delusions about my collar, sir. I am a man like any man, only following a personal faith that I feel guides all men. For some reason, they would not touch me. So I began walking. The people I saw . . . the children that ran by me screaming and laughing . . . one little girl with insects crawling all over her—"

"Stop!" Patrick's eyes stared into space, the rest of his body rigid. The only signs of suppressed rage were his white knuckles as he clenched his fists and the sweat rolling down his temples.

"Please," said Janet, gently, "go on. Did any of them try to touch you?"

"None. After a while I grew very bold, even managed to bump into a few of them. It didn't seem to harm them in any way. I'd say they just ignored me . . . or pretended to. After a while, I thought they might know where I was going or try to follow me there, so I thought it best to avoid them, perhaps double back a few times." He looked over at the old man. "I'm sorry, Greg, that's why it took me so long."

Wesson merely nodded, his head bowed in exhaustion and despair.

"I'm pretty sure no one followed me here, so we should be safe for a while yet."

"What do you think they are, Father?" asked Janet.

"Demons." This from Wesson, who did not balk when everyone turned to frown at him.

Father Tilkan answered gently. "I don't know. I wonder if what this leader told you was true. Maybe he came up here—"

"We call the leader the 'Shadowman,' " interrupted

Patrick, "and 'he's' an 'It.' "

The priest actually smiled at this. "Shadowman. Yes, very good. But I wonder if It came up here, killed these people, and prepared the bodies for possession by more of Its ilk. But then, what makes the Shadowman so special? Why not just invade dead bodies that happen naturally throughout the world? Why did It have to come first?"

"It's just happening here," said Tom. "I haven't heard about other disappearances in, say, North Camp, or Boulder, or anywhere else in the world. So maybe it's something special about this place."

"Harkborough is isolated," said Janet. "It could be setting up shop here until things get rolling. Who would know, until it was too late?"

"And as for something special about the Shadowman," Tom said, feeling an edge of excitement, "perhaps we can exploit it. It might be a weakness."

"Might," the priest said darkly. "But it might also be something that could destroy us all."

"Well," Tom asked, trying not to sound petulant, "what exactly do you suggest we do?"

Father Tilkan wet his lips. "I was going to suggest that we make a run for North Camp, but that's out of the question. I'm not sure I can protect any of you, let alone myself, now. They might be stronger. So, I think our only recourse is to wait here and perhaps try and find a cure for this madness." He held his bible again. "I have confidence we shall know the answers soon."

"Exactly my idea," said Tom, grateful for the unsolicited encouragement. "You know about Mr. Wesson's friend?"

"Adam, yes. I assume he's behind that other door there."

"Right. I think we should experiment. I'm a doctor and you're a priest, so I think we'd have all bases covered if we both made our own examinations."

The priest hesitated. "Um . . . you're sure he's one of them?"

"Father," said Wesson weakly, "I cut his head off and he was still laughing at me."

Father Tilkan nodded. "Okay. It sounds like a good idea to me."

I wish it did to me, thought Tom. *But what the hell, what else can we do? Maybe the priest will come up with some magical liturgical solution. I could believe in miracles if it would get us out of this.*

"All right, then," he said, standing with the others to face the bedroom door. "Let's give it a whirl."

No one wanted to make the first move toward the bedroom door. Wesson even moved out of the way and got behind the others. It was finally left up to Tom to go first, which he did quickly. He pulled at the chains crisscrossing the door, noted the locks off to the side, and turned to Wesson, asking for the keys. The old man handed them over without a word. Five minutes later all but one of the chains were unlocked.

"Mr. Wesson," said Tom, his voice forced down to a whisper in case the two ears in the bedroom were against the door, "does this door have a lock of its own?"

Wesson nodded. "Yes . . . but it's on the inside."

"Damn." Tom turned back to the single chain still on the door. "All right, then. This is our only defense against this thing. We'll need two people to stand guard here. One to hold the chain ready, the other ready to clamp the lock on and snap it home."

Janet and Wesson volunteered for the jobs before they were asked, and took their places.

"Fine," said Tom. "Now, Mr. Wesson, is there a light

221

switch in the bedroom?"

"Yes. It's on the right after entering. About chest high. It connects to a single bulb ~~in the middle of the room.~~"

~~Patrick peered~~ at the floor under the door. "It's not on now," he reported. "Are you sure it's still working?"

Wesson stared back at him blankly. "Them creatures don't like the light, mister. He probably just turned it off."

Tom nodded. "I'll be first to go in," he told them. "I'll hit the lights and bend low. Patrick, you come in behind me, make sure you hit anything that might be attacking. Hit him high. If I can, I'll hit it from below."

Patrick nodded, looked to the priest. "What about him?"

"He's last. You and I will be hitting, he's gotta be around to help us maneuver the creature around to the bed. Mr. Wesson, you got some rope?"

Wesson left his position and hurried back with a single long coil of rope. "It's enough to go around the bed a couple of times. It should hold him . . . I hope."

Tom balanced the rope in his hand, then tossed it to the priest. "Yeah, it should do. I don't think these things have superhuman strength. You say this Adam was a big guy?"

"Real big. Had a hard time sitting in the chair to play checkers. And I figure a good part of it is muscle, except for the stomach." Wesson smiled wanly, his eyes drifting off into space. "He sure did like his beer. . . ."

Tom glanced at Patrick. "Hit him in the stomach." Then he turned back to the door and rested his hands on the single, thin iron chain. "Everybody ready?"

No one said anything, so Tom inserted the key and turned it till the lock popped open. The small click made everyone in the room jump. As he carefully removed the curled metal from the links of the chain, the others were glued to their positions, holding their breaths, waiting for the slightest sign of trouble.

222

The lock was free. He handed it to Wesson whose hands were trembling. The end of the chain was given over to Janet.

Tom touched the knob of the door. It was cold and he nearly drew his hand back. But then, with some emphasis, he secured his fingers around it and knew he would not let go until the door was opened. And to do that, all he had to do now was turn it.

The sound of the bolt sliding back was like a rifle crack in the small room. They remained alert for any violent motion. Tom pulled the door back and a light fog drifted about an inch into the room before it evaporated, a ghost finally released.

The door was open three inches now. Enough for the creature inside to know someone was coming. If it was going to attack, it would do so now. Tom knew he had to act fast—should have acted faster than this—but his nerves wouldn't let him leave this haven for the dark of the unknown without taking another glance around to make sure everyone was prepared.

Janet stood holding the loose end of the chain between two white fists, ready to drape it across the door at a moment's notice. Across from her, Wesson stood with the lock to complete the trap. Behind him, Patrick and Father Tilkan were drowning in their own perspiration, but they were bent at the knees and their eyes were already checking for movement beyond the door.

All of this passed in less than a few seconds. They'd have to make sure it didn't take much more than that to subdue the creature if they hoped for success.

Feeling his fingers beginning to slip off the knob, Tom took a deep breath, held it dear—it might be his last—and thought: *Now!* He jerked the door open and rushed in, Patrick and the priest on his heels.

His fingers slapped for the light switch and he almost
lost his nerve when he stood there for nearly three seconds, his hand still searching frantically for anything on
that goddamned wall — *Ah!*

The single bulb in the room erupted like a blinding sun,
changing the cavernous abyss into a small ten-foot-square
room. There was no wind or movement to send the bulb
swinging, but the shadows in the room seemed to jump
and hide anyway, perhaps startled by the hurried entrance
of the three strangers.

From his bent stance, Tom could still see the entire
room, what little there was. Occupying the center was a
stained, sagging bed with an iron head-board and foot-
board (perfect for tying limbs to), and, filling the corners a
dresser cabinet, a night stand, a mirror, and a stool. But
no sign of the headless cadaver they had expected.

"What — ?" started Father Tilkan, but Tom waved him
quiet. He stood straight and the other two followed him
farther into the room. Behind them, Janet peered around
the corner and watched for any movement they might
miss.

They covered every visible inch of the room. Nothing.
Now for the invisible. Tom's stomach jumped at the thought.

"It's not here," whispered the priest. "Perhaps it left
through the window."

Tom checked the wood boarding it. It was still secure.
Nothing larger than a small rat could have escaped that
way.

He looked at the others and quietly shook his head. He
then gestured to the bed and the dresser cabinet. Patrick
nodded as Tom stood before the bed. Father Tilkan also
readied himself, although he was more concerned with a
quick escape. By the look on Patrick's face, he didn't think
the big man's plans were very much different.

Tom was on his knees, at the side of the bed, but in a position where he could get up quickly if it became necessary. He leaned toward a fast escape also, especially now that they no longer had surprise on their side. Still, they had to determine whether the creature was here. If it wasn't, it would warn the other creatures, and then there would be no hope of escape anywhere.

His fingers almost touched the ends of the bedspread on the floor. Quick was the way to do it. Lift fast, take a peek, then run like hell before the thing got up. Outside they'd be able to think of a new plan. So just a quick peek . . .

He had just touched the bedspread when he heard a slow creak behind him.

He was on his feet in an instant, turning, a scream half torn from his throat. The cabinet's door opened wider, kept on coming, but Tom's feet were glued to the floor. His eyes stared hard into the darkness, waiting for the huge form to come charging, a pair of numb but powerful hands ready to squeeze the life from him.

Patrick was the first to notice the small shape emerge from the foot of the cabinet door. The shadows were still playing tricks, but he knew immediately what the object was, and he made a grab at Tom.

Tom saw it now, too. He'd never met the man, but it was obvious this was the head of Wesson's friend, Adam. And it was staring up at him now, smiling and blinking.

"Gotcha!" it cried.

As the word sprang from its pale lips, a hand shot out from under the bed and grabbed hold of Tom's leg. Tom screamed and tried to back away, with Patrick's assistance, but the grip was just too strong. With horror, he watched the creature's other hand emerge from under the bed and struggle to grab his other leg.

225

Both Patrick and Father Tilkan were groping for Tom's arms and shirt and hands, trying to pull him from the grasp of the creature growing from under the bed. They could now fully see the dead organs hanging from the severed neck and the other meaty hand searching furiously for Tom's free leg.

And all the while, the head that had spilled out of the cabinet was laughing and screaming, creating the panic and hysteria that the three men had wanted desperately to avoid.

Tom could feel his calf going numb where the creature held it. The vice-like grip would never come loose, he was sure, and if that other hand got ahold of him, he knew this creature would have the strength in death, as it had in life, to tear him in two. His own panic rose rapidly. He could now see Janet over the shoulders of the two men helping him. Her pleading eyes, her numbing screams, all of it forcing him closer to doing something foolish. *And that body under the bed!* Dear God, seeing, actually *witnessing* the organs that had once held blood and muscle hanging lifeless from the thing's neck — and that other hand *grabbing* — how the hell could it see to — *Wait!*

A small shot of reason was enough to save his life. He concentrated on it, pushing away the panic, and he realized then that something had to be guiding this creature, directing its path.

With his free leg pushed on by the last reserves of free will, he kicked out at Adam's head. The head saw it coming, but was in no position to run. Tom's foot connected, and the head screamed and rolled under the night stand, its eyes pointed away from the action. Desperately then, Tom kicked at the free hand grasping for him. It went wild, searching blindly for something to hold onto. And in that moment of confusion, Tom landed his heel down hard on the hand that held him. He grimaced at the sound of bones shattering. But the hand let go.

Tom was up and out of the room before the other two men. He dove across the bed and ran straight for his wife. Behind him, he heard the bed crash as the creature's body stood and bolted after them. Patrick was last out the door and the body was nearly upon him when Janet slammed the door tight, draped the chain across, and Wesson snapped the lock home. The door banged once, twice, bulging at the hinges even with Patrick's and Father Tilkan's backs against it, then stopped. A second passed. Then the light piercing the floor under the door went out again.

"*Shit!*" screamed Patrick. "I'll be *damned* if I'm doing that again!"

Janet slumped against her husband on the couch. Both were sucking air, exhausted, but it did not hinder them from putting their arms around one another. "What do we do now?" she asked.

Tom swallowed. "We go back in."

Patrick's eyes bugged and he spoke slowly so that any idiot in the room could understand him. "Maybe you didn't quite hear me the first time. Read my lips, *No way!*"

"We have to," Tom said. "What other choice have we got?"

"Why don't we take Mr. Wesson's shotgun," Patrick offered, "and shoot the damn thing into a million pieces?"

"And how am I supposed to conduct an experiment that way? We have to have the whole body."

"In case you didn't notice, buddy, that ghoul is already in *two* pieces. What harm's a few more separations."

Tom leaned forward. "Exactly! It's running around without a head, but that doesn't mean that some laws of biology still don't apply, although this is the damnedest

227

extreme I've ever seen."

Patrick swallowed a few times, still catching his breath. Finally, he muttered, "What are you talking about?"

"It's what saved me. Look, you saw how clumsy the body became after the head lost sight of us, right? It was grasping like a blind man—*because the head couldn't see us!*"

"So?"

"So, we already know that that God or whatever It is—"

"The Shadowman," supplied Janet, softly.

"Yes. It's got some sort of hold over these creatures. Sort of like one brain governing the decisions, the actions and reactions, of all these bodies. And It does this from a distance."

"So? snarled Patrick.

"So, the individual bodies must still retain some individuality, like our bodies have involuntary actions that govern our breathing and regulate our heartbeat or make us pull away when something hurts. The principles of a regular body are still in effect with these creatures, except the nervous system and optics and muscles and brain functions are instigated, not by an electrical impulse system, but by . . . some other system, one that can operate over a distance. That's why the body was blind when the eyes were turned toward the wall. It's still somehow connected to the head."

"Which means?" Patrick growled, annoyed that he wasn't getting it.

"Which means," said Tom as calmly as he could, "this time we steal the head."

"Shit!" Patrick cursed disgustedly. "*Now* I get it!"

The second time went much smoother. Before Janet even had the chain in hand, the three men were through the door and the light was snapped on.

This time, the creature was surprised.

Its body was holding its head, twisting it in different directions trying to choose a new hiding place. It was facing away from the door when the three men burst in. Apparently its ears still functioned since it twisted soon after they entered, and began to yell.

The body swiftly laid the head on the night stand and charged the three men. Fortunately the sight was not new to them. Tom had the forethought to bend again and pummel its belly and groin while Patrick and Father Tilkan took turns punching its upper torso. The blows seemed to have no affect except that the power behind them pushed the body farther back.

Tom waited until he was sure the priest and Patrick had the body under control, then made a mad dash at the head. His fingers splayed open to pluck it from the night stand, but he drew back when the thing gnashed its teeth, trying to bite him. Carefully, Tom grabbed it by the back hairs and rolled it, much like a bowling ball, right out the door.

Janet kicked it for good measure, and it was gone from sight.

The body stiffened and began to grasp violently for any hold. It was no longer punching, but gripping shoulders, arms, whatever it could find for some support.

Patrick knocked its legs out from under it and Father Tilkan, calling on strength he never thought he had, pulled the torso up until the body was lying on the bed. The priest silently gave thanks that the bed had not been upended after the creature's previous burst from beneath it.

The Father tied the rope around one of the thing's wrists, circled it around the metal bedposts at the head,

229

and tied off the other wrist. Then he went back and tied both arms more securely.

By the time he was tying the legs, the body knew what was going on. It began to thrash. The men thought they heard a hollow scream as air vibrated over small remnants of vocal chords still in the throat, but they ignored it. At least until the job was done.

It took fifteen minutes of tying before they felt safe. The body still thrashed—apparently its muscles could no longer become tired—but eventually it realized it was captured, and the fight went out of it.

Tom rolled up his sleeves, looking toward the door. Janet reappeared and nodded grimly.

"What did you do with it?" he asked her.

"Put it in a bucket of water."

Tom returned his attention to the body and briefed the two other men on what he was going to do. The body, he believed, could be killed if there was some way of disconnecting the physical impulses the Shadowman was sending to it. He theorized that there must be some sort of "relay receiver," something that caught the Shadowman's messages—though he secretly wouldn't have been surprised if he was completely wrong about this. This was, after all, new, bizarre territory.

Hiding his uncertainty, he went on to explain that he was going to try to find this connection by performing a few minor operations. Hopefully.

What he didn't tell them was that he was not a surgeon, knew only a little about cutting people open. He just prayed he didn't get sick in front of them.

With the body before them, Patrick nodded and the priest grimaced. Father Tilkan was not comfortable with the thought that, in torturing the body, they might also be torturing the imprisoned soul. But he did not object. It had to be done. And when the doctor was finished, the priest would do his part. Perhaps together they would find the answer.

Wesson handed Tom a penknife from his back pocket and for a brief moment Tom considered sterilizing it. He shook away a small laugh that was growing in his throat — he was afraid that once started it would not stop — and bent over the prone body.

"I first want to make sure that it's not breathing. If it is, then either it has to breathe to survive or there's some reason the Shadowman wants it to."

The penknife dipped into the jumble of flat arteries, vessels, and bone sticking from the body's jagged neck. No reaction from the body. Did it feel pain? He tried to clear a way for the trachea with the knife. He thought he had it, but no matter how carefully he listened or watched, there was nothing. No wheezing, no movement of the chest at all. He waited a long while to make sure, then leaned back again.

"No breathing. And there doesn't seem to be any blood in the arteries at all. It looks to have been sucked dry." He indicated for Patrick to move to the opposite side of the bed. "Take hold of the creature's hand. Father Tilkan, would you take this one? Good. Now, I'm going to cut the wrist to be sure that the body is completely dry."

"Why not just check its pulse," offered the priest.

"If the heart were pumping blood, then it would be shooting out of the neck. But I still want to be sure the body is absolutely dry."

"Why?"

Because I remember seeing computers on television that used water to transmit information, but you'd laugh if I said that because even I think the idea of information being received and carried by liquid in a human body over a distance is ludicrous . . .

231

Tom shook his head. He looked at Father Tilkan and frowned with regret. "Sorry, Father. I'm afraid this is the quickest way." And he left it at that.

Father Tilkan nodded, and then he and Patrick strongly gripped the body's hands. The pale fingers struggled and groped impotently, never achieving a hold on anything.

Tom forced the penknife into the skin and made an incision across the wrist's width. The wrist opened, parting like two ghostly lips, but nothing spilled out.

This time, however, there was a reaction in the body. It stiffened, shook in two, three spasms, then collapsed. It didn't move again, even when Tom prodded it.

"Good God," whispered the priest, "is it dead?"

"I . . . I don't know."

Patrick drove his fist into the body's ribs. There was a crack, but the body did not stir.

"It's gotta be dead," he muttered.

Tom scratched the back of his neck, looking down on the body skeptically. "I don't know. Why would it die when I cut the wrist and not when it lost its head? Both are major arteries and both appear to be empty. So what's so special about the wrist?"

Patrick just shook his head. "You're the doctor."

"Maybe it has nothing to do with the artery," offered Father Tilkan. "Maybe the Shadowman knew the body of Adam was in trouble and decided to let go."

Tom nodded. "Yes. But we can't be sure. We can't just go around cutting these creatures' wrists, hoping it will have the same reaction on all of them. I've got to make a complete examination, or as complete as I can under these circumstances. There're still some questions I need to answer."

"Why bother," said Patrick, letting the dead hand go. "It's dead. We know how to kill them now."

But Tom ignored him. He had to be sure about the nature of the body before he could be absolutely certain what might kill it. And he still wasn't satisfied that the body was completely without life.

He was lowering the knife over the pants legs to slice them back to cut into the femoral when the body erupted. The energy it had apparently suppressed the past few minutes was suddenly released in a steady stream of spasms that threatened to knock the bed apart.

One hand, although tied, managed to get a good hold on Father Tilkan's hand. The priest screamed as his bones were crushed.

Patrick yelled, "Tom!" but the other man was too busy cutting away the body's pants legs. Moving with an agility that owed much to his shortness, Patrick was soon on the other side of the bed, forcing each finger of the body's hand back until they snapped and he could no longer close it around the priest.

Not that it mattered to Father Tilkan any longer. He was nearly unconscious. The pain was a constant throb that filled his sight, his hearing, his breathing. He could concentrate on nothing else. When he saw that his hand no longer resembled a hand, but rather a meshed glob of red bone with undefinable digits growing from its center, his vision went from white to grey to black. He hit the ground about the same time his hand was finally freed.

Patrick flipped the priest over his shoulder and hurried to the bedroom door. Janet was waiting to help, her face streaked with tears. Behind her, a bucket of water gurgled with bubbles of laughter—the creature's head.

As Janet helped the priest to the couch, she called over her shoulder, "Tom, come on! *Hurry!*"

But Tom was in no hurry. He couldn't believe what he was seeing. The body was still thrashing, but that made

233

the blood ooze from its femoral artery that much faster.

Blood.

Human blood? Animal blood? Was it Adam's own or was it ingested? Could his theory about liquid capturing information be true? He hurried over to the night stand, took an ashtray, and placed it beneath the wound he had made. Blood curled slowly into the dish, looking much like syrup except for its crimson darkness.

When it was half-filled, one of the body's arms managed to snap one edge of the bed's headboard. The hand slipped the rope under the iron post and began grasping at the remaining imprisoned hand.

"Tom! Come out there, damn it!" Janet.

Tom watched the dish, steadied it by placing his arms between the body's legs. He glanced sideways, saw that the other arm was nearly free.

The ashtray was three-fourths filled. Tom prayed it would be enough.

He grabbed the sample and scurried for the door. Behind him, the other arm broke free and the body flipped onto the floor. Its legs were still tied to the floorboard, but it had enough strength to crawl toward Tom, dragging the bed behind it.

Tom stepped out of the room and the door was instantly shut and locked behind him. He held the ashtray up for everyone to see. Then he noticed the unconscious form of Father Tilkan on the couch. The priest's crushed hand was buried under one arm, attempting in his final seconds of consciousness to keep the limb in one piece.

"Is he all right?"

"Yes," Janet snapped. She grabbed his shoulder and turned him around violently. He nearly lost the ashtray. "What the hell were you doing in there? You were nearly killed!"

234

He held the ashtray out. "I got this."

She grimaced. Her arms circled around and held herself close. "What is that?"

"Blood! Janet, that goddamn thing actually *bled!*"

She looked into his eyes, studying him for a moment. "I thought they didn't have any blood, that they were sucked dry."

"That's what I thought. But I knew there had to be some part of the Shadowman that was governing the body."

"You mean that blood is from the Shadowman?"

He met her incredulous gaze with a smile. "I don't know. It might be from the Shadowman or it might be Adam's and the Shadowman somehow perverted it. But I'll bet it's very receptive to capturing some sort of electrical signals, somehow routing it directly to muscles." He broke off, realizing he was confusing everyone with this crazy babble. He added, "It's important. I'm sure of that. I have to analyze it."

"Analyze it?" Patrick was wrapping an old rag around the priest's crushed limb. He stopped now and stared at Tom. "How the hell are you going to analyze that stuff. Where can we go? Any of us?"

Swallowing hard, Tom said, "Doctor Newton has a lab at his office, I'm sure. We could use that."

Patrick's stare was long and hard. When he was done, he turned back to the priest's hand and muttered over his shoulder, "Lots of luck."

Janet added, "Tom, Doctor Newton's office is at least a half-mile from here."

"Doesn't matter. We can't stay here. We have to do whatever we can to find a solution to this." He raised the dark liquid above his head. "This is the best we've got right now. I *have* to get to that office lab."

Janet's eyes left his. As she watched Patrick bandage the

235

priest, Tom realized just how much this experience had aged her. Her hair was matted with dried mud, her eyes were bloodshot and underscored with dark lines, wrinkles he'd never traced before shot through her lovely face.

At that moment, he wanted to drop the damn ashtray and wrap his arms around her and take her to some warm place to hold her.

She looked back at him. By the concern in her eyes, he imagined he didn't look much better.

"I'm going with you," she said.

He nodded once. There was no possible argument, he could see that. "I know."

She looked back to the couch. "What do we do with the Father?"

"I haven't got any first aid stuff here," called Wesson from near the bedroom door. "I haven't even got any rubbing alcohol."

"He'll be fine here," said Tom, his voice subdued. He tried to sound comforting to Janet, but in truth he was afraid that Patrick or Wesson might hear the tremor in his voice. "Really," he lied, "this is the best place for him now."

She sighed. And agreed. She knew it was a lie too, but there was nothing else they could do. Not until help came. If it came.

"Patrick," snapped Tom. "You coming with us?"

"Well, I'm not staying here."

"Good. Do the best you can with the Father's hand and let's get moving. We can't afford to waste any more time." He turned to Wesson. "Do you have some sort of container I can pour this blood into?"

"Sorry. Didn't do my shopping 'cause I was worried about Adam. Don't have a thing in the house."

Tom looked around, saw a plate in the kitchen. He fit it over the ashtray. It would do until he got to the office lab.

He then walked over to where Wesson's shotgun lay, hefting it into the crook of his arm. "Mr. Wesson, I'm afraid we're going to have to take this with us."

"Why?" Wesson looked shaken, no matter how he strived to control his voice. "It won't do any good. It ain't going to stop them."

"It might slow them down, though," Tom replied.

Wesson scrambled forward, grabbing for the gun like a child grasping for his toy. "No! You can't take it from me! It's mine!"

Tom backed away. "We need it. We have to leave—"

But Wesson was still coming. Tom couldn't fight him or he'd spill the blood. Providing a useless defense, he continued to back away. Wesson easily caught up and took the shotgun from his arm.

"It's mine. I'm keeping it."

To illustrate his point, he pointed it at the three of them.

Patrick stood, rubbing some blood off on his pants. "I think this is where we came in," he mumbled.

"You're free to go if you want," said Wesson, gesturing to the door with the barrel. "I ain't stopping you. And I'll take good care of the Father."

Tom sighed. Patrick glared at him. The muscles in his arms bunched, demonstrating what he could do to Wesson. Tom shook his head and frowned. Either the old man or Patrick would get hurt or killed, and that's the last thing they needed now. The old man was probably right anyway. The gun wouldn't stop any of those creatures, wouldn't slow them down enough to make any difference.

"All right," he said. "The gun's yours. You be sure to lock the door up tight when we leave. Don't let us back in unless we prove to you we're alive."

"Then don't come back!" Wesson snapped.

Tom glared at him, but Wesson held his gaze. Shrugging, Tom made his way to the door, followed by the two cousins. Patrick started to undo the locks around the door while Janet shuffled off to the side. Tom kept his eye on Wesson and the shotgun.

The door was nearly open when Janet's quivering voice broke the silence.

"Tom. You'd better come here and look at this."

He sidestepped over to where she was, still keeping one eye on the gun. When he looked into the bucket she indicated, he forgot about the old man and passed the tray of blood to his wife.

Very carefully he lifted Adam's head from the bucket. It stared back with blank eyes. A purple tongue filled the mouth like a wad of cotton. Laid against it were the teeth—those nightmarish fangs, alone in the gums, that would stay in their dreams forever, should they ever survive this. Tom looked close and saw the raw nerves sprouting from the gums around the fangs, where the rest of the teeth had been pulled out. He nodded. This, too, seemed to be devised by the Shadowman to increase the legend, and the panicky fear, of the vampire. Making demons again. But now he could see they were merely teeth. The two canines were normal size, but they seemed larger because the rest of the front teeth had been removed by the creature's powerful fingers. Their sharpness was natural, as they were in most people, but their isolation against the red, raw gums made them appear unnatural.

The revelation did not shock him. He somehow had expected a reasonable answer. What did disturb him, however, was that the thing was lifeless in his hands. Dead. Just to make sure, he swung it into a wall. No reaction at all.

He threw it back into the bucket and looked across the

238

room, to the bedroom door. Slowly, he made his way there, holding his hand out for the key to the lock as he passed Wesson. Wesson kept the shotgun trained on him but gave him the key. He backed away hurriedly as Tom undid the lock and released the chain.

Janet whispered angrily, "For God's sake, Tom, haven't we had enough of that?"

He mouthed the words, *I have to be sure,* and threw open the door. The body of Adam Louis lay prone across the floor, its legs still tied to the posts of the bed. A small trickle of blood ran down its leg, around its thigh, and into the cracks of the floorboards.

"He's dead," he announced. He turned to Janet with a hint of a smile on his face. "Let's keep that blood safe. Once we figure out whose it is and what it does, we'll be closer to beating them."

He started toward her, holding his hand out for the tray. He made it halfway before freezing.

Around them, the cabin's walls began to vibrate, and a thousand tormented souls screamed out in agony and hunger.

The Shadowman's army had finally arrived.

Chapter 10

Nobody moved for quite some time. Then, like a stick disturbing a pond's tranquility, they all broke into action at once, scattering in their various directions. There were screams, then muffled whispers. There were people drawn to another, and others who drew away. Finally, only a single voice and a single command was followed to the letter, and that was because it was Greg Wesson commanding and he held a loaded shotgun.

"Lock that goddamn door, mister!"

This was directed at Patrick, who had just backed away from the front door at an incredible speed. He now moved warily back again, waiting, just *knowing*, that some*thing* was going to push through the single chain now securing the door and start playing squash with his head. The voices and cries that grew from the other side were fodder for his nightmare.

"Hurry it up! *Hurry! Now!*" Wesson brought the shotgun up to his eyes and aimed. He meant business, and there wasn't anyone in that room, including Wesson himself, that doubted he would shoot Patrick's head off if he didn't reach that door in two seconds.

Patrick made it in one. He draped the chains across the door and locked them in under a minute. Then, sweating and cursing, he once more backed away.

But the urgency was not at an end.

"The bedroom door!" Janet shouted, pointing, and Tom was closing it and draping the chains almost as soon as she'd finished.

Then they were quiet. They gathered closer, gravitating to the center of the room, all eyes searching the walls protecting them.

"All right," Tom said, breaking the quiet that suffocated them, "let's just keep calm. They're not in here yet."

"Yet!" snapped Patrick. He took a second to wipe his face with the front of his shirt. It didn't help much. A minute later, he was slick with sweat again. "Damn it, Tom, what the hell do we do now?"

It took everything Tom had left to keep himself from throwing down the tray of blood in disgust. "*Damn it!* We were so *close!* If we could have just made it to the lab, I'm positive that—"

"Well, Doctor Fuckup," Patrick screamed, coming at him, "we can't make it now, so why don't you think of something we *can* do!" His face was inches from Tom's. The two men stared at each other like hungry tigers. They would have been at each other's throat by now but for the nightmare outside.

A hand rested on Tom's shoulder. "Please," said a voice, a voice he recognized and loved, so powerful that it broke through the rage that had welled up. He looked into his wife's face. "Please," she said again, "let's do something. We can't fight each other. We have to find a way out of here and we need both of you." Her gaze turned to Patrick, but he would not meet it. He finally turned away, lost in thought.

"Well, I think the plan you folks had was a pretty good one." The words were harsh and gravelly. The three turned to stare into the corner's darkness. The face could not be

241

distinguished, but the sleek weapon puncturing the shadows, pointing at them, was unmistakable.

"What're you talking about?" demanded Tom.

"I said, I think you folks better leave," Wesson answered. "Just like you planned."

Tom's anger took hold again. Its suddenness made his arms and legs quiver so much that he put the tray of blood on the table for fear it would spill.

"What're you saying?" he said again, barely containing his screams. "You hear them out there, don't you? We can't leave."

The gun barrel rose. It was at eye-level again, although they couldn't possibly see Wesson's eyes in the shadows.

"Get out," the old man said. "For all I know, they just want you. Maybe you'll get somewhere and they'll follow you. Anything to get them away from here."

Tom was about to scream back when Patrick suddenly rumbled forward. "Look, you lousy son of a—"

The shotgun fired. Splinters erupted from the floor, inches in front of Patrick.

"Out!" shouted Wesson. There was still one shell left in his gun.

Tom wasn't to be put off so easily. He couldn't control the overpowering anger, an emotion he'd not dealt with for a long time—at least not since that phone call so many months ago. It left him feeling reckless.

"You idiot!" he shouted. The gun rose toward him. He didn't even flinch. "You selfish piece of shit!" he screamed. He could feel Janet's fingers tearing at his shirt, his own hands constantly pushing them away. "You freaking madman, how are we supposed to *survive* out there?"

Fortunately it wasn't the gun that answered. But Wesson's words were just as deadly. "I don't give a damn. Just get out of my house. *Now!*"

"Come on, Tom," pleaded Janet, "come on." She pulled, cajoled in whispers, even maneuvered her body into the line of fire.

Tom couldn't hear her. All he saw was that asshole's double-barrelled snout pointing at him, accusing him, sending him and the woman he loved to their deaths. There wasn't enough air in the cabin to keep his anger alive, but it struggled, as all live things do, pushing his heart *faster*, his lungs *faster* . . .

"Please, Tom, please, come on. He'll shoot us. All of us. We have to go . . ."

The words were drowned in the cries outside, bantering with the storm over who would crush the world. They infested Tom's thoughts, took hold of his attention—their cries and that goddamn metal finger pointing at him. He stood rock solid. He knew there were tentacles trying to pull him away and down into the dark waters, but he wouldn't budge. *Just keep staring at the hand behind the finger. Just keep listening to the cries of those who have let the tentacles pull them away. Just keep sucking oxygen—*

"You got five seconds, mister, and then I'll kill you! I swear it!"

The voice was familiar but the words didn't mean anything to him. He wasn't moving.

"FIVE . . . FOUR . . ."

"Tom! Tom, he's going to kill you! For God's sake—"

Stronger hands clutching him. Patrick? *"Hey, man, you want to take him?"*

Those were words he could understand! "Yeah," he answered.

Janet again, nearly hysterical, screaming, "What are you saying? Are you both crazy?"

" . . . THREE . . . TWO . . ."

"We don't stand a chance out there with those things!" shouted Patrick.

"He's going to shoot you!" she cried. "You want to fight some dead people, or a bullet?"

Patrick was looking at the figure behind the gun. His stare was as maddening as Tom's. "He's not going to shoot anyone."

" . . . ONE . . ." came the reply.

"Please!"

If the plea had come from Janet, it was doubtful it would have changed anything. But the voice was new and took everyone off guard. It was Father Tilkan, sitting up on the couch.

"I think this is what the doctor would call panic," he said calmly.

"I don't care what it's called," growled Wesson, "I want them out of here." He paused. "You can stay, Father." His voice hoped that this offer would make a difference.

The priest rocked his head back and forth. It glittered with the sweat of pain. "No, Greg. If they go, I go. And then you'll have it on your conscience that you sentenced a priest to death — or worse." He held back a satisfied smile. It was wrong to play on a man's guilt, but this would certainly come under the heading of an ecclesiastical emergency.

Wesson was silent for a long while. The wails of anguish outside made battle with the harsh breaths of the living inside. Then Wesson's cracked voice came back again. "Then you'll have to go, Father. I'm sorry, but they have to go and so do you."

Father Tilkan took this in without any change in expression. "The dead haven't broken in yet," he said finally. "And they've been here quite a while now."

"Doesn't matter. They can come in anytime."

"Yes," said the priest, "and you think that all of them will go chasing off after the four of us? You don't think they won't search the cabin just to make sure that—"

"I don't care!" The outburst was followed by gasps for air. The metal finger drooped a bit. "I don't care," Wesson said again, only softer, less convinced. "It's a chance. I need that chance, Father."

The priest said nothing more. After a while he stood and looked at each of the people in the room. As his eyes met theirs, his good hand surreptitiously removed a key from the table. Then he walked stiffly to the front door, his mangled hand stuffed securely in one pocket of his jacket.

Wesson's voice was on the edge of hysteria again. "Where you going, Father?"

"Out. Like you ordered." He started to unlock the chains with the key. The cries outside seemed to grow louder every time a lock snapped open.

"What about the rest of these folks?" The gun pointed at the other three. They watched the priest in silence.

Father Tilkan waited until he'd undone all but one lock, then turned. "Greg, if we have to go outside, then I'm the best choice to go first." He looked at Tom. "Maybe this time I can do something useful."

When the three started moving toward him, he added, "Trust me," and whipped off the final chain. The key fell to the floor with a clatter. A second later, the priest was gone, the door shut solidly behind him.

Outside, the cries of despair ended on a single note. Once more there was the silence of a storm in the land.

"We've gotta stop him!"

Tom pushed Patrick aside, preventing him from opening the door and rushing out. Quickly, he strung a chain across the door and locked it—only one chain, in case the priest made it back. But there were no great odds on that.

The key was plucked from the floor and pushed into Tom's pocket. He turned back to the others and said, "We're not going anywhere until we see what the Father has planned." He narrowed his eyes and stared hard at Wesson, daring the old man to order otherwise.

"Maybe it's a diversion," said Patrick. "Maybe he's going to get those monsters' attention so that we can escape!"

Tom shook his head. "He would have told us. I think he just wants us to watch him. To see what, if anything, happens." Silently, he wished he was as convinced of his words as he sounded.

Moving cautiously in the rattling void left by the voices outside, he moved to the window and began prying at the boards. Eventually he found one that was loose, and with Patrick's help they managed to unnail one end and pivot it around so they could see through the crack.

"What's happening?" Wesson whispered urgently. The gun was at his waist, limp, but still pointed toward the other two men.

"None of your damn business," snapped Patrick.

"Hey! I sent him out there! I've got a right to know—"

"Whether you've killed him or not?" finished Tom. "Whether you've sentenced him to a future more horrible than death?" Tom licked his dry lips and returned his attention to the crack in the board. "You just stay hidden in your shadow, Wesson, like the ghouls outside. We'll tell you whatever we want you to know."

At that moment, Wesson could have ordered the two men away from the boarded window and taken the position himself. Or he could have shot them and taken their place. Or he could have threatened Janet. But he could do none of these now because the gun was ten times as heavy as it once was and the old man's eyes were too blurred with tears. All he could do was watch the two men watch the

Father, and pray that he would not be responsible for the destruction of a good man.

When Janet saw that Wesson wasn't going to try anything, she moved up behind Tom and Patrick and crouched so that she could see between them.

Father Tilkan looked like a very small man through that slat. And the monsters still looked like monsters.

They had lined up, not in single file, but in a group that remained well behind their leader. The Shadowman's teeth glistened unnaturally, almost iridescent, and Its eyes were wide with—Surprise? Joy? Hunger?

Those alive would soon find out.

The priest stopped five feet from the leader of this degenerate army. He could have moved no closer even if he'd wanted to. Something in his blood, in his very soul, forbade him from getting too near these things. They were an ungodly enemy, an unnatural and incredible evil, to be sure, but they were something more to the Father. Something that he had just recently come to terms with and understood. Something that finally gave him the faith for which he had searched his entire life.

"Father Tilkan," said the pale creature, wrinkling Its nose, "come closer, please."

"No. I will not." Good. The voice sounded strong, confident. It didn't matter that his body was drenched and shivering in the cold rain.

"Very well." The Shadowman's clawed hands opened wide in front of It. Father Tilkan noted that one was horribly deformed, as if it had melted. The creature's voice pulled him from the sight. "You certainly did not come out here expecting to reach some sort of compromise or to negotiate a treaty with the undead. So what is your purpose? Nothing violent, I trust."

Father Tilkan paused for a long moment. He was stunned by how the creature's entire manner was that of a beast of the wilds: the searching, piercing eyes constraining black orbs the size of quarters; the quivering nose scenting the human flavor; the teeth, so obviously canine; the muscles taut and ready to break into action at any second; the claws so willing to rip through flesh and muscle and bone with a single swipe.

It was all so clear. It had been foretold so many times. Born of a jackal . . .

No! No! That was wrong. It was the wrong way.

"Something troubles you, dear Father?"

The priest looked up at the resonant voice. He winced as the sudden motion sent pain throbbing through his hand.

Quickly, he said, "I had a small accident inside the house."

"I know," said the Shadowman, his nose twitching. "I can smell the blood."

Father Tilkan smiled at this. He said, "You would like a closer look, I presume?"

"Of course."

"This you shall have soon enough. For now, though, let's talk."

The creature laughed abruptly, a bark in the moonlight. "A sermon, Father? For me and my gang? I'm sorry, but the undead are untrustworthy and considered to be generally delinquent. And you know how delinquents feel about church."

Holding up his good hand, the priest said, "Not a sermon. You may have noticed, however, that we have never met, yet I am not surprised by your existence."

"You perhaps see me as a devil? Maybe *the* devil that you priests hunger so intensely for. Why do you search so

248

thoroughly for an enemy that can assuredly destroy you? Is it, perhaps, because of your celibate background, that you find this sort of self-inflicted pain parallel to masturbat—"

"There's no need for blasphemy!" shouted Father Tilkan. His voice did not reach out of its range or sound uncontrolled. In fact, it was authoritative enough to cut off the Shadowman without even a smile.

"No," continued the priest, "blasphemy does not become you. You seem intent on playing a part so as to undermine my attack."

"You're attacking, are you, Father?" asked the creature in Its best Irish accent.

In spite of himself, Father Tilkan couldn't help smiling. "Yes, I am."

The creature slapped Its chest. "Give me your best shot." The priest noted that, in slapping Its chest, the creature did not touch the jewel inlaid there. He nodded his head imperceptibly and tugged his soaked jacket closer around him. For a second he wondered if he would catch pneumonia in this weather, then laughed the thought away.

"Something's funny, now?" asked the Shadowman.

"I have known of your arrival for quite a while. I was warned of it and have been preparing. My position in the church allowed me to have full run of the hallowed surrounding to nurture my strength and faith in God."

The Shadowman glanced back at his brethren. "Please, Father. You're scaring my kids." The Army's faces were blank, however, and had not even shuddered at the mention of the Holy One.

Father Tilkan swallowed hard and continued. "While I was there, in the church, suffering and learning, a Voice came to me in the night."

"Now Father, you said this wasn't going to get religious." The rain was coming harder now. Father Tilkan's voice rose above the torrent. "The Voice told me how I could defeat you. The Voice told me how I could control this unholy battle."

"If I had a soul for every time a priest has said God talked to him . . ." the creature shouted back.

Father Tilkan's mouth clamped shut. His eyes met the Shadowman's. They stared at each other for several minutes, until a smile creased the features of the priest.

He said, "I never said the Voice was that of God, did I?"

All traces of amusement that might have occupied the face of the creature a moment ago were now completely banished. Instead, a black mouth opened, and a bloated purple tongue lashed out around the edges.

"What do you mean?" asked the creature darkly.

"You know what I mean. My faith in God made it easier for me to understand and accept. And now my role in all of this is clear. There's nothing you can do to stop it."

The creature was breathing hard now. Or, rather, it looked like It was gasping, but for all the observers knew, that was *real* steam erupting from the demon's nostrils.

"Liar!" It called.

"No."

The creature took a step forward. *"Fucking lying priest!"*

"You know it's true." Father Tilkan tried hard not to back away. He couldn't just turn away now.

"You are lying! Look!" It glanced back at Its followers, pointing furiously at Father Tilkan. "Look! You can see it in his eyes! He is a living human being!"

Father Tilkan struggled to control his voice. "Then make me one of you." The chilly spasms were coming faster now, but they were soothed by the sweat that covered him, its sticky warmth trickling down and around his body.

God forgive me. God protect me.

He revealed the dark pulp of cartilage and muscle that

250

had once been his hand and forced it into the demon's face. "Lick it, then! Suck *this* blood! Turn *this* flesh into one of your numbers!"

"You lying filth!" screamed the creature. It sprang at him, Its massive claws rising with the power of a horror worse than death.

If Father Tilkan had wanted to get away, he knew it would have been impossible. But still, he would have tried if his conviction had not been so powerful. And with that conviction came a great sense of satisfaction and relief. Yes, he was relieved now. Relieved of his position and his life.

Back in the cabin, they couldn't hear the words because of the storm. They caught small snatches near the end, because they were yelled, but they weren't sure exactly what was happening until they saw Father Tilkan draw his hand from his coat pocket and push it into the Shadowman's face. The creature was on him in seconds. The priest's head was swiped from his body in one swift motion, then left to lay upon the muddy pavement.

Janet and Tom fell deeper into the cabin. Janet was in tears but under control. Tom was screaming at the old man with the gun. Wesson, for all the power he wielded, was taking the verbal battering like a child. He cried and swore to God he was sorry, and never once thought of raising the metal finger again and telling Tom to shut the hell up.

Meanwhile, Patrick remained at the niche in the window boards and watched with growing puzzlement the scene being played outside. He had been waiting, with dread and a morbid sense of curiosity, for the priest to rise, pick up his head, and make his way toward the cabin with the rest of the Army.

But now he saw that the Army was walking *around* Father Tilkan's remains. None even stopped to lick the blood spilled at their feet.

"Tom!"

Patrick motioned toward the window. Tom left the sobbing old man and peered through the hole. A second later he was looking at Patrick, questioningly.

"They're not drinking," he said.

Janet moved up behind them. "What's wrong now?"

The two men continued to stare at each other for an indecisive instant, momentarily caught up in a male bias. But then it all came back at them. She'd seen everything else, had lived through it all just as they had. She had a right to know.

Tom pulled close to her and said, "They're passing the Father by. He's dead, but they're not drinking his blood. They're not turning him into one of them."

"Why?"

"I don't know."

"Is it because he's a priest? He wasn't waving a cross at them out there. Is he somehow holy?"

"I don't know," Tom insisted. "Please, just listen. They're coming closer to the cabin. We haven't got a chance unless we figure out how to fight them."

"They've got blood in them," Patrick injected. He was at the front door now, busying himself with locking more chains across it. "If we cut their legs like you did to—"

Tom whirled around. "With what? And how do we know they all keep the blood in the same place? It could be moving around in their bodies."

"They don't have heartbeats! How can it move around?"

"I don't know! We can't even be sure that what they have is blood."

"But you would have felt a pulse. You checked for it in

252

that monster in there!" Patrick pointed with a fist at the bedroom door. "Those veins were flat! There wasn't even air going through them!"

Maybe they can regulate their heartbeats, Tom thought, but he put his hands up and said, "All right, all right . . ."

"So, *Doctor,*" Patrick ordered, "let's grab some knives or something sharp and start cutting their legs or necks or whatever we can get ahold of."

"All right!" shouted Tom. "That's enough!"

Patrick backed away, breathing hard. In the harsh silence that followed, they all looked to the walls of the cabin. The haunted wails were beginning again. The creatures were hungry for company.

"Shit," muttered Patrick, "let's do *some*thing."

Janet watched her husband walk back and forth, his face pinched with concentration. She saw how troubled he was, knew how the pressure would destroy him, but she couldn't help asking, "Tom? What'll we do—"

"I don't know!" he snapped.

She laid a hand on his arm. His face seemed to lighten a bit. At least he stopped pacing.

"I just don't know," he said again, this time more calmly. "If we could have gotten to the lab with the blood . . . I don't know. Maybe nothing. But it would have been worth trying."

"We can't leave here," said Patrick. As he said it, the creatures outside began knocking on the walls, on the roof, even on a few of the floorboards. "They want in, I guess," he growled.

Tom sat at the table, next to the ashtray. He looked into the inky darkness that rested there. Blood. Human blood or otherwise? Did it matter now? The creatures would get in soon—these old wooden walls couldn't possibly hold them back for long—and they would merely sip this blood along with everyone else's. Such a waste. But what was that saying? What's good to one man is another man's poison. And soon they would all learn to love that same poison.

They waited there, the four of them, lost in the jaws of defeat, each absently wondering how long it would take before they, too, would be hammering on a neighbor's wall, asking for a handout, or a footout, or a headout. . . .

Then, just as suddenly as they had begun, the cries and hammering ceased.

The four humans inside looked at each other, then around the room.

Nothing.

A minute passed.

Still nothing.

As they started to move from their places, however, a single voice broke the static of the rain.

"Daddy . . ."

Patrick's knees nearly gave out. He grabbed the back of the couch to steady himself.

"Daddy, let me in. It's cold out here."

"Oh God, oh God, no . . ." He stumbled to the door. His hands were on the chains, but he made no move to unlock them.

Tom started toward him, feeling panic anew, but Janet stood in his way. She looked into his eyes a moment, enough to silently communicate something, then they both stood back and watched their friend.

He still hadn't made any move to release the chains. He was crying, though. They could see his head bowed and his shoulders heaving. Finally, he looked up at the door and drew in a ragged breath.

"Go away!" It was meant to be a shout, but it was more throaty air than voice.

The tiny utterance that came from the other side of the

door seemed to get weaker.

"But it's cold out here, Daddy. I'm wet. I think I'm catching a cold."

"Go — *away!*"

"*Daaadddeeeee* . . ."

It was such a pitiful voice, so filled with fear and vulnerability, that Janet wanted to rush out and grab the child. She managed to control herself, and just stood with her husband, hugging his arm, and letting the tears spill from her eyes.

Tom felt his own tears. The words of the little girl were ones he'd wanted to hear all his life. But even now he couldn't answer them. He would never be able to hold his own child. He thought he knew very well what Patrick felt.

"*Daddy, please* . . ."

The tension broke. Patrick picked up an axe — the bloody axe that had removed Adam Louis' head from his shoulders. He hefted the deadly implement in his hands and stood in front of the door for the longest time, sucking air and trying to blink the tears from his eyes. It was too long, however, because the rage was spent. He dropped the axe before the girl spoke again, and never picked it up again.

"Daddy?"

Patrick stumbled to the couch. Janet broke away from Tom and helped him into it. Without a word, he rested his head on her shoulders and began to weep.

"Daddy? There's a big man out here. He said he wants to hurt me."

Tom approached the door. He felt the anger rising, but he couldn't allow it to blind his thoughts. Not now. He turned suddenly and sat beside Janet.

"Daddy? The big man says he's going to break my arm so you can hear it. Don't let him do that. Please don't let him do that. Come out with me, Daddy."

255

Janet held her cousin closer. He was still crying, growing more vulnerable, but she felt the tension rising in his body. Softly, she stroked his hair, hoping it would calm him.

"He's got my arm, Daddy. He's holding it in his hands. His hands are so big and cold, Daddy. I'm scared. He said if you don't come out, he's going to break my arm."

Janet's hand covered Patrick's one ear and held his other securely to her breast. When the *snap* came, and the cry of the little girl, Patrick was still sobbing, his nightmares undisturbed by the greater horror.

"Doctor Howards?"

Tom stirred abruptly on the couch. The voice on the other side of the door was new. But familiar.

"Doctor Howards, are you there?"

Yes, familiar. But somehow different. There was a peculiar accent to it, perhaps an impediment.

"I need to talk to you. To you and your wife. It's about the two of you having children."

Tom looked at Janet. Her face had gone ashen.

"Shit," Tom spat and stood to confront the door. "What do you want, Doctor Newton?"

"Ah. You recognize my voice. I was afraid you wouldn't. Not after the nasty . . . accident I had. I'm afraid my nasal cavity has had some extensive reworking. Good thing I don't sing, eh?"

"Go away, Newton." Tom's voice was as tired as his body, which slumped back into the couch. "Just go away, please. We're not coming out."

"Oh, but I don't have any need for you to come out, Doctor. I just came by to relate some bad news to you and your wife. Some very tragic news, I'm afraid. It seems that she can't produce children—ever."

I should have known, thought Tom. But he'd been through it so many times that it wasn't as painful as the creatures had hoped. It just made him more tired. He started to lean on Janet, wanting to put his arms around her and hold her.

She was there for the first few seconds, but then her support was gone. He looked up and saw her jumping off the couch, leaving Patrick in a quivering heap, and rushing at the door.

"You son of a bitch!" She nearly made it to the door before Tom caught her arm and spun her around. She continued the momentum and whirled back toward the door again. Tom held on to her waist with something like desperation. Her fists were flailing the air and her legs stamping and jerking as she cried, "You son of a bitch! You knew! *You knew!* All this time!"

Her words degenerated into tears, and soon after that she fell limp, exhausted. Tom held her close, whispering comfort in her ear. He felt her tears touch his neck and shoulders, and wished he could hold her closer.

"Yes, I'm sorry, Janet," came the voice of Doctor Newton, "but I've known for years. Even since you hit puberty and came to me for your first gynecological exam. Of course, I couldn't tell you. I just couldn't upset you or your mother. Too bad your husband had to find out the hard way, eh?

"Oh, and by the way, Doctor Howards," the creature continued, "if you had any plans of visiting my office or my lab, I'm afraid the housekeeper hasn't done a very good job. There's glass and chemicals all over the floor."

The voice eventually ran itself out. Perhaps it was too difficult to force air out of a mouth with so many punctures in it. Whatever the case, the couple stood in the room holding each other for a very long time.

Their moment was broken only when a sharp snap of wood sprang behind them.

Wesson, once lost deep within the shadows, suddenly

leaped into the light and aimed his gun at the bedroom door. "Good God," he cried, "they're in the bedroom! *They're in the bedroom!*"

Tom broke away from his wife and started toward the door. He stopped when he heard more wood snapping and then some scraping. Then silence again.

"I think they've gone now," he whispered.

Wesson didn't take his eyes from behind the end of his shotgun. "What do you mean they've gone? They're coming in!"

"No. I think they just came in to get Adam. They dragged him out. They're gone now."

"Why?" asked Janet, but she knew she wouldn't get an answer.

Tom shrugged. "For some reason, they want us to open the door to them, to make it easy for them. I don't know why. You've seen what the Shadowman can do. We wouldn't have lasted this long if the Shadowman—"

"I tell you, they're coming in!" shouted Wesson. His finger twitched on the trigger.

"You blow a hole in that door and they *will* come in," snapped Tom. "Get ahold of yourself. They just entered to retrieve that guy's body."

"Tom."

The voice was so small and filled with fear that Tom wanted to grasp out and hold it.

"Tom," Janet said again, "that's all they got, was his body. We still have his head." She gestured to the bucket of water.

"Get rid of it!" shouted Wesson. "Toss it out the door!"

Tom shouted back, "You want to open the front door? You go right ahead! We'll close it again as soon as those creatures pull you out!"

"We'll get that head out somehow. Make another hole in the window boards."

"No." Tom approached Wesson again, this time wondering why he hadn't taken the gun away from the old man sooner. He was on the edge of hysteria, ready to kill anyone that stood in his way. And he was the only one with a weapon.

"No," he said again, "Mr. Wesson, they can get the head when they come in here. And if they come in here, we're going to slash their eyes out because without them they're blind. Do you understand me?" He was nearly there. His fingers stretched out, preparing to grab the cold metal.

"Yes, yes," mumbled Wesson, his eyelids and chin in a race to see which could vibrate faster. "Yes, we'll . . . we'll put out their eyes. We blinded the other one, we can blind them . . . yes . . ."

"That's right, Mr. Wesson." Tom kept his eyes glued on the barrel of the gun. It wasn't pointing at him, but a quick swerve could change that. And he certainly didn't want that valuable last shot to be wasted on him. Not yet, anyway.

"Shoot their eyes out . . ."

"No, no," said Tom, "don't want you to waste that last shot, Mr. Wesson. Just keep it aimed at that door. If they come in, it'll be through there." He stopped, slowly, so as not to startle the old man. His muscles tensed.

Now!

"Yes, through that door . . ."

"Kill them if they come. Protect us." Before he was finished speaking, Tom jumped forward, grabbed for the gun's barrel. He didn't have far to grab. In less than a blink, it was pointed right between his eyes.

"Back up now!" commanded Wesson, his tone darkly savage. Tom did as he was told and backed into Janet's arms. "Should have shot you when I had the chance," the old man growled.

259

Tom felt stiff. "Can't waste your last shot."

"Maybe I got more shells." His grizzled face twisted into a smile. "What I can do, though, is what I'd planned from the beginning. I think it's past time for you folks to be leaving."

Tom couldn't speak. He was exhausted, mentally and physically. No arguments came to mind, so he finally decided maybe it was best they did leave. Out there, the pain would only last a few seconds. Then they could just follow blindly. No more pain. No more aching joints or exhausted minds. No more minds.

But the fight was not over. Janet recognized the despair in his face and immediately took up the argument. She pleaded, "Mr. Wesson . . ."

"Don't 'Mr. Wesson' me, girly. Get your husband and cousin and get the hell out of here!"

"Mr. Wesson, you can't. You've known us since we were kids. You've known my mother for ages! How can you do this to—"

"Wait a minute!" Tom whispered. The hiss of amazement was enough to quiet both the debaters. With a swiftness that belied his haggard frame, Tom went to the boarded window. The single board was still pried loose and the glass on the other side remained unbroken. He peered through it.

Father Tilkan still lay there. A gentle stream of rain was swirling his blood into a ditch near the cabin.

"Father Tilkan," he whispered to himself. "And Avilon."

From behind him Janet asked, "Tom? What is it?"

He whirled around and managed a genuine smile. "I think I have an answer."

Janet screamed. Wesson jumped back and aimed the gun at Tom. Tom was about to duck when he heard the crash of glass behind him and felt a hand rip at his neck. The pale, rotting fingers had a firm hold and his world was about to go black when a new sound intruded upon the chaos.

The sound of a horn, growing louder.

Sheriff Kinkade had spent the first half hour of the drive home going through every expletive and unkind phrase he could think of—twice—and his steering wheel had taken much of the abuse. Before that, he'd spent three hours trying to clear everything up with the North Camp Hospital administrators. They didn't like the idea of a law enforcement officer, and not a relative, taking Johnny Ryan from their care. It took a long time for him to convince them that the boy was not seriously injured, that he was not in shock, and that it was unlikely any relative would question his taking Johnny since Kinkade had missing persons reports on the boy's entire family. He also stressed that the boy was very important to his investigation of those missing persons. In fact, he was sure the boy was the key.

For reasons left unsaid, no one mentioned what had happened in Johnny's hospital room. There was no real explanation. Kinkade thought the administrators might have suspected the boy, but they couldn't have been serious about the idea since they didn't keep him for psychiatric observation. Even if they had threatened it, Kinkade doubted he could have brought himself to tell them that he'd seen a—Shadow? Man? Beast? Maybe that's why he hadn't told anyone. He wasn't sure himself.

Whatever it had been, though, he was certain it was after Johnny. And for some reason, it hadn't succeeded. There had been that horrible cry of *"NOOOO!"*—and then just Johnny alone in the room, insisting he wanted out of there. Kinkade couldn't blame him, but he had hoped for something more than what the boy had produced so far.

After his tirade, he'd settled down enough to question the boy about what he'd seen in his hospital room, what had happened on his paper route, and if he knew where his parents were. But the boy's answers were not helpful. He stared ahead, eyes blank, and occasionally shouted "Mom!" or "Dad!" When Kinkade tried to calm him, Johnny would whisper, "Can't touch me" and "Pain."

And then, the most ominous, *"Sssshadowman."*

Now, driving the curving mountain road that led to Harkborough, Kinkade wondered if he should return Johnny to the hospital. The boy should have snapped out of it by now. Maybe there *was* some shock involved. Certainly the doctors back at North Camp could do more for the boy than he could.

But then he remembered the condition of Johnny's hospital room. He couldn't let that happen again, no matter the consequences.

They continued on to Harkborough.

Night had taken the mountains. Hell, night had been in control for quite a while. Kinkade only just noticed it was nearing daybreak, and the need for sleep was close to overwhelming him.

He made sure the road was straight for a while, then took some time to rub his eyes. It was damned cold outside, worse with the rain racking the car, but he broke open a window anyway to let the night air wake his body. He looked at the boy. He was still staring out the front window, eyes glazed, fingers pulling at his bottom lip. Kinkade shook his head worriedly. He tried the radio to clear his mind, but there was nothing but static. Strange. He'd always been able to pick up something in town and he wasn't that far from it now. Maybe the station tower was down.

A few miles later, winding continually upward, he reached Harkborough. It was like plowing into an ocean wave. The fog rolled in thick, moving with infinite patience down the road.

Fog? thought Kinkade. *In the rain? What the hell* . . .

He was startled when he felt something twist next to him. When he realized it was Johnny, that disturbed him more. The boy was excited. He was sitting forward in his seat now, his legs bent beneath his bottom, bouncing him up and down, his pale fingers digging into the dashboard to steady himself.

His eyes still stared out the front window, but now he was blinking rapidly, like some sort of spasm.

"It's here," said Johnny.

Ice danced down Kinkade's body. He grasped for the window lever, but couldn't find it. His eyes were glued to the boy now. The road was forgotten.

"What? Johnny, what did you say?"

"It's here. It's coming." Bouncing. Staring. Pale.

"What is?" Kinkade fought to keep his voice steady. "What's coming, Joh—"

"Look out!"

Kinkade still wasn't looking at the road when the scream came, but he knew enough to swerve the wheel. When he looked outside, he saw the body, waiting for them in the middle of the road, hunched as though to catch them. He slammed on the brakes. The police car twisted, the wheels sliding and screaming. The person in the street disappeared to the car's right. There was nothing but fog to see now, a ghostly white cloud that surrounded the car.

Before the car was completely out of control, Kinkade twisted the wheel in the direction of the skid and accelerated. In seconds, the vehicle's course was steady again, but he had no idea what that course was. He couldn't even see the road now.

"What the hell was that?" he snapped. He tapped the brakes again, taking time to look around the car. The person in the street was gone, hidden by the fog. "What did you see, Johnny?"

Johnny's head slowly shook, the lips pale but silent. He leaned back in his seat again.

Kinkade took some deep breaths. The aftershock of nearly hitting one of his own townspeople took over. The ice he'd felt at Johnny's words were now gone. Sweat broke out on his body, and his arms were rubbery, shaking.

Nearly killed some idiot walking in the middle of the street in the fog. Just what the village needs to hear right now. The man who's supposed to protect them is riding wild.

Don't think about it.

He busied himself asking the boy questions that he knew would never be answered, about the person they'd nearly hit. The hardest part was attempting to keep his voice and manner calm. *No need to get the boy more scared than he is.* But then, *What is he scared of? He said something was here. What?*

He looked out the window again and the thought struck him: *The fog? Did that scare the boy?* It *was* thick. It made Kinkade jittery himself. For a little while Johnny was forgotten. He concentrated on his driving, hoping to find the yellow line that would signify he was back on the road.

He slowed to ten miles an hour, but soon even that was too fast. He was going along at five when he heard the voices. They were crying or singing or something, but all Kinkade could wonder was what the hell they would be doing outside on a night like this.

The car rolled to a stop. Kinkade opened his window a little wider, trying to discern the various sounds.

"Close the window," said Johnny, suddenly alive again.

Kinkade held up his hand. *Now he talks.* "Quiet for a

second."

He licked his lips. His ears strained to listen. It sounded like . . . like people *dying.* They were moans of agony. What the—

"Go! Go! Go!" screamed Johnny.

Kinkade turned to him and suddenly he was done listening, because a single voice rose up amidst the multitude and replaced the sound with pain. The left side of his face became wet and warm with an abruptness that shocked him. Instinctively, his foot left the brake, hit the gas, as his hand felt the blood now rolling down his cheek. His fingers touched the wound—only a scratch? But who the hell was responsible?

He glanced at the boy, wanting to say something but unable to think of any words. Didn't matter. Johnny was in another world. His long, thin body was now rolled into a ball on the floor of the passenger seat. He was trembling, sobbing, occasionally yelling something into the cool flesh of his arm.

Kinkade felt panic rising in his own body. *Keep your head straight, goddammit it! Do something!* He searched through the gloom in his side and rear view mirrors for whatever had attacked him. He saw the vague outline of someone running after him. His hand, still wet and sticky, slid down his waist. The gun was ready, in its holster. He slid it out and laid it next to him. His foot rested on the brake again.

"Time to find out what's going on out here." As he'd hoped, his own voice calmed him. Had to be an accident— just had to be, he told himself. Maybe someone delirious, or just desperate to get his attention and had accidentally scratched him. Just had to be . . .

But he felt the warm ooze dripping down his neck, sliding under his shirt. It was a deep wound. Going to need some first aid soon.

Who the hell . . . ?

His question was soon answered. In the bright red of the car's taillights, the woman who had scratched him appeared. She was dead. He knew it immediately. Her skin was white and mottled, her face sunken, and although she was running, there was no trace of warm air erupting from her nose or mouth.

But it wasn't until he saw his own blood on her upraised hand and her war cry hit him full in the gut that he finally hit the accelerator and got the hell out of there. The ghoul was left far behind, but still chasing.

Whatthefuckwhatthefuck . . . his mind raced, as quick and as blind as his car hurling through the streets of Harkborough. But his wild ride was safe. There was no one in the streets to kill anyway. There were, however, figures to hit. And before he even thought of slowing, Sheriff Kinkade hit some of those figures hard.

"Oh my God!" he cried as a woman and her child bounced off his windshield, sending a spider web of a crack across its length. *"Shit Almighty!"* he yelled at the black man who looked a lot like Martin Summers and fell under the two left wheels with a jarring *WUMP! WUMP!*

"Go!" screamed Johnny from his corner. "Get out of here!"

"I'm going, goddammit, I'm going!"

As he struggled to keep the car under control, he managed to see other groups of people rushing to meet his car. And those faces, all of those sunken, rotting, *familiar* faces calling out his name with a mixture of laughter and agony—

"What the hell is going on here?!" he demanded of one woman, Mrs. Kettle, he thought, who proceeded to bury her teeth into his shoulder. He screamed as pain exploded in his arm. With a single punch from his meaty fist he

broke Mrs. Kettle's jaw and drove on.

The pain was numbing his entire left side now, but he still managed to roll the window up. Mindlessly, he cursed the day he had decided it wasn't in the budget to equip the vehicle with electric windows.

More bodies hit the car, bounced away. But there wasn't a drop of blood hanging on the web of cracked glass that obscured his vision. Not one drop.

Squinting through the latticework, his knuckles twisted back and forth at a maddening pace, trying to keep the car on the road. He was moving uphill, he could tell that, but he didn't know which road or which side a steep cliff might appear on. There were fewer than a dozen close calls, where he nearly drove the car into the grey oblivion, but his body was already pumped full of adrenaline and couldn't take anymore.

I'm losing it . . .

"Johnny!" he called through his mist.

The boy didn't answer.

"Johnny, listen to me!"

"I don't know what's going on!" Johnny insisted.

"Johnny, I need your help." Kinkade heard his voice getting weaker.

He could barely see Johnny's head poke up from his balled form.

"Johnny, you have to help me drive the car." Almost a whisper now.

"I can't—"

"Get the fuck up here, Johnny, or I'll run your ass in!" He nearly laughed after he'd said it. The threat had always worked with kids before.

But Johnny didn't move. He may as well have been another dead body.

Kinkade was wiping his eyes repeatedly now. They stung

267

with sweat and tears. There were fewer claws and demon faces jumping from the fog now. Still, every *WUMP! WUMP!* brought home the horrible fact that he had driven over another citizen of his community.

They are the citizens, aren't they? he asked himself in amazement. *That was Miss Johnson with the sagging breasts and the bite taken out of her neck as though it were an apple, wasn't it? That had been Mr. Kiley, the barber, who had stared at him through the windshield, baring blood-stained teeth and one dangling eye before falling off to the side to add to the symphony of WUMP! WUMP!s, hadn't it? And the Daisy twins, laughing as the car plowed into them, shaving them nearly in half?*

My God, I'm murdering half the population of Harkborough!

But, God, after the pain they'd given him, it felt good.

He continued driving and smashing bodies, bodies he knew to be dead, and did his best to keep the car on the road evenly. But he couldn't keep it up. Not for long.

"Johnny," he tried again. "Just put your hand on . . . the wheel . . ." He was going. Images passing him in the dark were doubling, tripling, their outlines indistinct.

Then, when he saw the lights up ahead, he thanked God for the beacon and hit the accelerator.

"I c-can't," he heard from below the passenger seat.

"Joh . . . John-ny . . . please . . . a light . . . ahead . . ."

The light became two, then three. Then too many to count. What was it? And the road, splitting off into as many directions, and high roads and low roads, spinning . . .

The pain came back to his shoulder and he cried out. Tears flooded his vision. The single light ahead now danced in his head, making him nauseous.

He knew he was passing out. He knew he may never wake again. Nevertheless, he was the sheriff and he had to warn the public. Nevermind he was driving his car over the majority of the public, the civilized ones had to be warned. And right now, in his final breathe, he decided that the only civilized people left were the ones that were housed with that light.

As he struggled to peer through the cracked windshield and gloom, he watched his world change forever. Johnny was forgotten, a nonentity. The single light was all — the single light that became a million. The crowd of ghouls that had been surrounding the light made way for him. Then all was black.

He could still move a little, and he managed to press his foot securely on the accelerator and aim the car on an even course. All that was left now was to signal that this was a police emergency.

Racing at the cottage at near sixty miles an hour, he doubled up, unconscious, and his head hit the horn.

Chapter 11

They watched in stunned disbelief as the black-and-white car plowed through the walls of the cabin, scattering planks, glass, and mud in every direction. The wind and the savage twisting of metal and the anguished but somehow triumphant cries of the undead followed. As a flickering fireball, they filled Greg Wesson's cabin, and soon the very human screams of horror joined them.

Then, as abruptly as they had started, the sounds were cut by some invisible switch, all except for one high pitched wail.

Tom was first to regain his senses. He'd managed to tear away from the ghoul's skeletal grip and had run straight into Janet's arms when the car's horn blared behind him. The sound had been so shocking that it had pushed him onward, deep into the shadows, his wife forced back with him.

He looked around now, not at the accident and the disaster it had created, but for his wife. He found her still in his arms. She was screaming and crying intermittently, her eyes straining to stay in her head as they frantically surveyed the damage. She was usually one to bury her head in his chest and turn away from ugly things, he thought. But she was okay, screaming or not, and that's what counted.

He thought of Patrick, and searched his memory as best he could during the next few seconds of commotion. The last place he'd seen the man was . . . *on the couch.*

The couch was gone. The police car had slammed into it, sending it spinning into oblivion. All that remained were some splintered boards with rusty nails protruding, stuffing which still spilled from the air, and a torn covering now hanging from the bumper of the black-and-white car.

But no Patrick.

By this time Janet was also aware her cousin was not poking his head up anywhere. She called his name several times, but her cracked voice didn't reach very far. Tom joined her, and eventually they were answered.

"Over here! By the big wall."

It wasn't difficult to find. There was only one big wall left standing, the others either shells or completely destroyed. Together they went toward the voice. They moved jerkily, panicked. They knew that the silence and shock would not last. The creatures were out there and now there was nothing to keep them at bay. If they didn't move fast . . .

"Patrick!"

"Here!"

A hand caked with blood rose from the ruins. Tom left his wife's side and hurried over to the man. They struggled for a while before Patrick was completely free of debris.

"Are you all right?" called Janet, making her way carefully now.

"Yes," Patrick answered, spitting some blood out of his mouth. "I think so." His face was nearly black, but there didn't seem to be any serious lacerations. His arms were in similar shape—the blood was from a slice across his palm that could be treated later. But his right leg was another story.

A board had splintered and the sharp edge had driven into his calf. It came to neither man's attention until Patrick tried to stand. He winced, held the leg, and Tom bent to examine it. After some hasty and painful observations, Tom decided the tendons were probably severed. Patrick wouldn't be walking on that leg for a long time. He'd be lucky to walk on it normally ever again.

"I guess it could have been worse," said Patrick, surprising the other two with this modicum of good nature. "I heard the horn and it scared the shit out of me, so I jumped off the couch. Could have been a *lot* worse."

Tom nodded and said, "We've got to get out of here. If we support you, do you think you can make it?"

He didn't answer immediately. He looked into the faces standing over him, searching their eyes for some hint of doubt.

"I think so."

"Great. Janet, get around under this arm." Tom continued to instruct her and Patrick until they got him on his feet.

"Wait," cried Janet suddenly, "what about the man in the car?"

Tom paused. She was right. There was a possibility he was still alive. If it was the sheriff, they could certainly use his strength and knowledge just now. But Tom would have to work fast.

He helped Janet lay Patrick on the ground again, then hurried to the car. It was lying upside down, so the driver's side was nearest. He fell to his knees, careful of the sharp wooden edges and nails from the destroyed walls, and looked through the closed window.

Sheriff Kinkade looked blankly back at him. He was dead, definitely. If the crash hadn't killed him, the deep wound in his neck had. Tom was momentarily puzzled because it looked like the dead man was floating between the floor and roof of the car. Then he realized that the sheriff was suspended by his seat belt. Tom suppressed a shudder.

"He's dead," he reported, turning back to Janet. "He's got a deep slash in his n—"

"Help me! Someone, help!"

Tom stiffened in the midst of the destruction. The voice had come from the car, but it couldn't have been the sheriff's. A woman's? A child's?

He peered back through the window, searching the darkness beyond the dead man. He thought he saw something moving on the passenger side, sliding across the roof.

"Hey!" Tom tapped the driver's window. "Hey, are you okay?"

"My arm," called the boy. It was obvious he was trying to control his crying, his words now wrapped in hiccups. "It . . . it hurts."

"All right, hold on," Tom told him. "We're going to get you out." But how? The window looked like it had been rolled all the way up. It wasn't cracked in any way. Would a small-town police car have smash-proof glass?

He stood and peered over the car's bottom, now facing upward like a dead animal's belly. The passenger side had destroyed most of the kitchen wall. One sturdy looking beam that emerged from the wall was rammed against the door. It looked solid and impossible to move. But maybe . . .

"Kid," he called through the closed window, "is your window open on that side? Can you crawl out that way?"

There was a long pause. Tom was about to repeat his question when he heard a faint, "No. That leads to the outside."

No more had to be said. He understood the fear. Besides, the beam looked like it covered most of the passenger window.

Again to his knees. "Okay. Look. I need you to crawl over to the driver's side, over here, where I am. You see me?"

He saw a small head rise from the darkness inside the car. Something white and round covered one side of his head. *A bandage,* thought Tom. Wide eyes reflected what little light

273

existed.

"That's it," said Tom. "Just slide over this way. You can lower the window here and crawl out."

"He's dead," said the soft voice.

"Yes, he is. But he's not one of them. He won't hurt you. You have to hurry, though."

The boy seemed to pause for a moment to think this through, then scurried across the inner roof of the car, until he was sitting just below the sheriff's suspended body. He looked up at Tom with wide, terrified eyes.

Not more than fifteen, Tom thought, and he grimaced at the sight of a blood stain in the center of the bandage. "Good," he said. "Now, reach up past the window. Don't worry about the sheriff! Don't even think about him. Just reach up to the handle."

"My arm," replied the boy. "I can't move it."

The boy was in a better light now. Tom looked down at his left arm. It wasn't bent in any odd shape, but perhaps there was a fracture.

"Okay. Use your other arm. Just keep the one that hurts next to your side."

The boy followed instructions. Slowly, slowly, his good arm rose past the window, inches away from the sheriff. Tom couldn't see the window handle from where he was, so he watched the boy's face. He had told him to ignore the sheriff, but that, quite naturally, was impossible. The boy's eyes were glued to the corpse.

"What's your name, kid?" Tom asked, hoping it would draw his attention away.

"Johnny. Johnny Ryan." His voice sounded stronger, but his eyes were still on the dead man.

"Johnny Ryan?" someone said behind Tom. He turned. It was Janet. Patrick lay behind her, watching, pain evident on his face.

"You know him?" asked Tom.

274

"He was the boy found in the market this morning. The one the sheriff went to North Camp to question. Remember?"

The key, thought Tom. *Jesus.* He turned back to the window.

"All right, Johnny. Just look up at the window handle. Concentrate on the window handle. You have to turn it *now.*"

Johnny nodded and allowed his gaze to move away from the corpse for just a second. His arm kept coming up, up . . .

The sheriff's body shifted. One of his beefy arms swung down. Some blood spiraled down the dead arm, the fingers, to drip against the boy's face. Johnny screamed, drawing his arm back.

"No, no, no!" called Tom. "Don't be scared, Johnny. Hurry. Try it again. Just do it fast. Fast, Johnny, *fast!*"

And the boy did it. He took a breath, shifted away from the drops of blood, stared straight ahead, into the car's darkness, and shot his arm past the window to the handle. He bumped the sheriff a few times as his hand swung the handle around, but it didn't stop the action. After several seconds of this, however, he couldn't take anymore. He drew his arm back again, as fast as the first time, and wrapped it around his shoulders, his body rolling into a ball. He buried his eyes.

The window was halfway open. Enough. Dear God, prayed Tom, let it be enough, because he didn't think the boy would be able to do it again.

"Johnny! You did it! Come on, let's go!"

But Johnny was still rolled into a ball, sitting below the sheriff. He wouldn't look up, wouldn't answer.

"Johnny!"

Still nothing. Just the small form shivering in the dull light.

"*Goddammit, Johnny, come on! We gotta*—"

And then he heard it. Janet's hand was on his shoulder, saying his name, but he knew what she wanted. They looked around the cabin.

The cries of the dead were beginning again. Louder now, because there was no wall to separate them. They were coming.

We gotta hurry, thought Tom.

"Johnny, look we—"

But he was interrupted again. Johnny also had heard the creatures approaching, and he was now poking his head out the window, his legs scrabbling against the roof to push the rest of his body through.

"Help me. Help me, *please.*" All control was gone. His voice was that of a child in the grasp of complete panic.

Tom grabbed his shoulders, to help pull him through, and Johnny screamed painfully. His arm.

"Sorry," Tom mumbled. He reached through the window and grasped the boy's right arm, pulling as Johnny pushed.

Janet also bent to help pull, then stopped. Something caught her eye to the left, coming around the back of the car. Something from outside. Something moving fast.

"*Tom!*"

He twisted to look at her, saw the horror. But he couldn't let the boy go now. Johnny would never get out then. He'd be lost forever.

The key . . .

"I can't—" Tom began.

Janet didn't wait. She moved past him, toward a jagged plank of wood that lay across the upturned car. It had punctured the oil tank, its end slick with glistening darkness. *Dark like the beast.* She didn't pause. She pulled it from the tank—the sound like fingernails on a blackboard—and rushed to confront the creature.

The monster actually looked respectable, as normal as

276

the monsters *could* look. In fact, its elder, male face looked very familiar to Janet, like an old friend, a neighbor she might have grown up with. But she didn't allow herself to think of that. Instead, she used her fear and confusion to ram the plank into the creature's face. The board broke across the bridge of its nose and drove straight through its eyes. Oil, like blood, dripped from the hole.

She doubted she had killed the thing, but the force of the blow was enough to make it fall back. It twisted on the floor, blind but still moving, grasping for the end of the plank still ground into its skull.

Janet sucked air. She had bought them some time and taken years off her own life.

Tom still struggled with Johnny. The boy hadn't pushed more than his head and shoulders through the window. It wasn't open enough, but there was no time for him to go back in and open it more. They had to pull him out now, even if it injured him further.

Janet grabbed another piece of wood—smaller, easier to handle—and screamed for Tom to move over. Tom never let go of the boy's arm, but he moved to his left, allowing enough room for Janet to draw back with the board and slam it repeatedly against the window.

It seemed to take an eternity before it even cracked. It was followed by another, louder crack, one that sent needles of horror through Tom's body. *The car's breaking apart. It's going to fall in on itself and crush the boy, the key—*

But that was impossible, he realized. No, the sound had to come from somewhere else. No time to think about it. He pulled.

Johnny grit his teeth with the effort. His eyes squeezed out tears. A groan was pressed from his body, compacting his chest. Yet *still* he could not slip through the window. Worse, his pushing was becoming less forceful. His feet were slipping against the roof. The sheriff's blood soaked his pants, and the growing puddle below him made it increasingly difficult for his shoes to find purchase.

Then, suddenly, the boy froze. The pushing stopped altogether, as did his breath, and the strange, almost comical, look of surprise on his face made Tom and Janet pause in their exertions.

"Johnny," said Tom, "what is —"

The boy screamed. His body fell back, the shoulders once more in the car. Tom didn't let go of his arm, though Johnny's sudden retreat pulled him forward. Shaken, Tom thought wildly that Johnny must be trying to duck back inside to open the window farther.

"*No*, Johnny, we don't have *time* for —"

Then he saw it. Johnny wasn't going back in the car. He was being *pulled* back by another hand. A hand that had broken through the beam blocking the passenger door — the *crack* they had heard seconds ago. A hand had pushed through the window, and now securely held the boy's bloody right pant leg.

Tom grabbed hold of Johnny's good arm with a renewed strength and *pulled*. The boy was screaming, and kicking at the huge pale hand that was reeling him in. The creature was powerful. Tom, exhausted, his hands slippery with sweat, knew he was losing this tug of war. Johnny's chin began slipping back into the car.

"*Janet! Help me! Grab something!*"

She tossed the wooden beam away and rushed forward. One hand took Johnny's shoulder and the other grabbed his hair. There wasn't time to worry about *hurting* the boy. They had to save his *life*. Together, husband and wife, they pulled Johnny toward them with all their strength.

Johnny's head and neck were sticking out the window again, but the other side was not giving up. The monster dug its fingers deeper into the bloody fabric of Johnny's jeans. It would have taken a chisel to break the grip.

278

Tom winced at the boy's screams. He knew they were slowly pulling him apart. He wouldn't be able to take much more of it. Soon, very soon, they'd be hearing the horrible pops of bones and muscles tearing away from each other.

Yet they still would not let go.

Unfortunately, the struggle did not end there. The police car was unbalanced, ready to move. And with the pulling and struggling and straining going on inside it, it was only a matter of time before the car began rocking back and forth from driver's side to passenger's side.

Janet noticed it first. She wished she had the strength to call out a warning. It wasn't necessary, though. Soon Tom and Johnny knew exactly what was going on.

The rocking increased. Dust started rising from the sides of the car. The vehicle was deep in the wreckage, so it would not turn on its top, nor was the swaying great enough to cause it to upend again.

But with a boy's head and neck sticking out the driver's window, if the rocking increased the car would crush his skull like a melon and snap it away from his body.

Apparently the creature holding Johnny's leg also realized this because it began pushing against the passenger's side to increase the car's pitch. Tom and Janet fought back. He pushed his weight against their side of the car while she continued to pull Johnny's arm and shoulder. Yet the swaying grew slowly deeper. Johnny's chin was now hitting the ground every time the car rocked his way.

Then came another crash—the shattering of glass. During Johnny's attempted escape from the creature holding him, Patrick had made his way, crawling, to the front of the vehicle. He alone had seen the other way out, and was now creating the opening. He lay on his side, grasping with both hands another wooden plank from Wesson's walls, and, backed by the strength wound up in that compact body, battered the front windshield of the police car. It spiraled, concaved, and finally the frame snapped. Patrick used the thick board to push the window in, so that there was a clear passage between Johnny and the outside.

Patrick could just make out the muscular arm pushing through the passenger window to hold the boy's jeans. The rest of the creature was obscured in darkness. No doubt most of it was pressed against the car's door, pushing at it to increase the rocking.

But it was the single monstrous arm Patrick had to concentrate on. He maneuvered the thin beam he held into the car, aimed one sharp end at the creature's wrist, and placed the other end securely in both his hands. Then he pushed the board forward with great force, pulled back, pushed out again, smashing, repeatedly, the thing's wrist. In seconds, his strength was waning and his aim was falling off, but the attack was creating a desired result.

The skin around the thing's wrist broke immediately, though there was no blood. Next the muscles and tendons began to tear. The bones began to snap. In the end, the fingers were helpless. They had to let go.

Still, the rocking did not let up.

And the creature's release of Johnny's jeans didn't mean the boy was free. Now Janet was pulling the boy frantically, and already had his head and chest out when Patrick called frantically, *"Let him go, Janet!"*

Apparently she'd seen his attack on the monster and the hole he had made in the car. Her pause might have been longer otherwise, and thus fatal. However, she let go of Johnny, even helped push him back into the car, before the monster on the other side put its entire weight against the car and rolled it onto the driver's side. Johnny's neck and back would have been snapped had he still been struggling to get through the window.

But Patrick had him now and was pulling him frantically out the front of the car. Janet came around and helped, hugging the boy close, his head buried against her, when he was finally free.

Tom was close behind her. He patted Johnny once on the back, then hurried to Patrick. "Janet! Help me! They're coming!"

She moved to Patrick's side immediately, making sure Johnny stayed near. In seconds they had Patrick up and were moving, fast. Johnny's rescue from the car, though it had seemed an eternity, had taken less then three minutes. Not long, but long enough for most of the creatures to recover outside and begin their attack anew. The nearing wails from outside confirmed their fears.

In the distance, thunder stepped on the world, drowning out the cries of the dead. On that cue, their pace increased. They made their way around the debris, across the bare floor where they could get outside. The rain was blowing into the cabin, washing the blood and their good vision away. Still, they knew the creatures were close. They didn't have to see or hear them to feel the cold hands pushing at their backs.

They headed for the wound the car had made. They moved faster and faster as the outdoors grew nearer. The claustrophobia of the cabin was more intense now that they had a taste of freedom. They thought nothing could have stopped them after that, at least from stepping outside, but they *did* stop when they heard the command over the storm.

"Hold it right there, folks!"

It was Wesson.

He appeared fine, but he had a hidden purple bruise covering most of his right hip. The bone was cracked there, and he found he couldn't stand or walk very well. Still, he managed to lean against the bedroom door and point the shotgun at anything coming near him . . . or anyone trying to ditch him. That would do for now.

Johnny cowered behind Janet, one hand holding tightly

to her clothing, the injured arm laying limply at his side. Patrick cursed lightly, but it mixed well with his grunts of pain. Tom was too tired to argue and, after hesitating, tried to continue forward. But Janet wouldn't budge. She had her head turned, looking over her shoulder at the tiny man slouched in front of the bedroom door.

"We're leaving, Mr. Wesson," she said. Her tone was harsh, almost breaching violence. "There's nothing you can do to stop us."

"I've still got a shell left, girly," said Wesson. "I can take you out so fast—"

"And then what?" she screamed. *"*You waste your last shell on one of us, then what are you going to do? Listen, Wesson. Open your ears. Look around." Then, softly: "They're coming."

Patrick and Tom also listened. The cries were louder than before, as if the dead were singing some strange, grating song. Bare outlines of figures outside could be seen through the rain. Soon the shack would be surrounded, and there would be no escape.

"We're leaving," continued Janet, still in that harsh whisper, barely in control. "If you're not, you'd better save that last shell for yourself."

They stood there for a long moment, staring at each other across the rubble that was once their shield. Something passed between the girl who was now a woman and the old man who had once, long ago, chased her away.

The shotgun lowered.

In the end, though, it didn't really matter. As soon as the barrel touched the floor, a deformed, rotting face rose above a pile of debris to Wesson's right, and Wesson let go with the final shell.

Skull fragments and grey, blotchy tissue splattered everything behind it. The body fell back, out of sight. But it wasn't very long before it righted itself again and headed for

Wesson.

The old man screamed. It was a sound no one, even himself, would have imagined could be produced from such a fragile body.

"Come on," Tom said shortly and Janet clutched Johnny closer to her, turning his eyes from the sight, and fell in step. Patrick made no argument, merely allowed himself to be led into the open.

Outside.

They were outside. Rain. Bitter, cold wind. Thunder reminded them that the Earth was still alive, though not well. And, all around them, rising with a speed and strength that belied their deaths, the Shadowman's army began its second assault on the cabin.

"Where do we go?" Janet screamed.

"The lab," mumbled Patrick.

"No! The doctor said it was ruined."

"We can't trust him."

"It doesn't matter," said Tom, "I left the tray of blood in the shack. It was lost in the crash."

"Let's just move!" The panic in Patrick's voice was shared by the others. Around them, the Army was converging. Soon they'd be visible — and vulnerable.

They hurried forward, moving as one. Their eyes wandered in circles, searching through the storm for anything that might attack. Tom saw something in the distance, something lying flat on the road. To the left of it was a small, round object, easily mistaken for a large rock if not for its familiarity . . .

His eyes focused on a more immediate concern, however, when a creature — a large, elderly, pot-bellied man — stepped out of the mist in front of them and hurried forward, teeth bared and an ugly scream spilling from its pale lips.

Janet screamed and instinctively pushed Johnny behind her. The action unbalanced Patrick, which made him and

Tom stumble backward. There was no way either man could put up an adequate defense in time.

Johnny, however, was suddenly gripped with an urgency he couldn't control, and he broke from Janet's grasp, ignoring the pain to his fractured arm, and stepped forward, into the attacker's path. He tore at the stained bandage covering his ear, and wiped his fingers in the warm stickiness underneath. He had no fear or pain at that moment. Somehow, it was suppressed.

When the creature was a few feet away, charging fast, Johnny made a fist — the blood squeezing through his fingers — and swung at the monster's jaw for all he was worth. The punch alone would have stopped the creature, perhaps long enough to run into the forest, though they certainly couldn't have outrun it once it had recovered.

But this punch was different. Johnny's fist connected, painting the creature's lower face with blood. The strike brought not only a stunning crack to the creature's skull, but a ghostly green steam that seemed to melt away the flesh and tissue and bone of its jaw. The monster made to grab Johnny, but it halted when it realized its entire head was being eaten away by an orange fire. It reared back, screaming, the four living humans forgotten. Bent double, it stumbled off into the woods. Just before disappearing, Johnny and the others could just make out a faint, dark outline, a raging fire of green and orange above it.

The terror and exhaustion Johnny had suppressed for so long now hit him. His knees buckled and he hit the ground hard, screaming as pain bolted through his bad arm. Janet rushed forward to help him up.

"Can you walk?"

He took a deep breath. His vision was fuzzy. Everything looked like a dream, this horror *had* to be a dream, he *never* would have confronted a monster in real life. But he felt strength return to his legs and nodded curtly. "Let's go," he said. The woman managed a smile, then hurried back to Patrick's side.

Johnny moved next to her, Patrick on her other side, and together they started forward. Upon the first step, however, they were brought to a halt. Something held them back.

It was Tom.

He stood, unmoving, still looking into the fog covering the road. At the flat shape lying there. Familiar.

"Tom," called Janet through the storm, "come on! They've seen us!"

Tom caught his breath, looked back at the figures fast approaching from the shack, and made some quick calculations. *That monster that attacked Johnny was put here to guard something. You saw what Johnny did. It must be . . .*

He pushed Patrick onto his wife. "Take him." Suddenly, his face contorted with worry. "Can you?" he asked Janet.

Johnny came around the other side and wrapped Patrick's arm around his scrawny shoulders. They struggled, but Patrick grunted and bore more of his own weight. "It's okay," Patrick said, though his teeth were gritted by the pain, "I'll make it."

Janet began, "But—"

"Down the slope, back to the clearing, the pentagram," Tom ordered.

"Tom, why—how can we make it?"

"Just go!"

In that split second of hesitation Janet saw the desperate hope in Tom's face. She didn't understand it, but she trusted him. Speed was important now. She relented. They were moving. Before their heads disappeared beneath the hill's crest, Patrick turned back, calling, "Tom, what the hell are you doing?"

And they were gone, the forest, the storm, maybe even the world, swallowing them up.

Under his breath, Tom whispered in answer, "Hell if I

know for sure."

He worked fast.

Inside the cabin, Wesson searched a drawer for more shells. He knew he didn't have anymore, it had been on his shopping list for the past few weeks, but he had to search nonetheless. The headless thing was bumping around the room, still searching for him blindly, but now there were other creatures entering and sniffing around. They'd soon have him unless . . .

A *shell!* He found one lodged deep inside one drawer he thought was only filled with old newspaper clippings from his track days. But there it was, grey and showing streaks of rust, but powerful nonetheless. He had no hope of killing all of them, but this one might just be enough to save his life.

He backed away to the bedroom door again, sitting low and pushing his back against the wood. His bony hands slipped and cramped as he struggled to fit the shell into the slot. While he fought with the weapon, his mind went through curses and fears as though an invisible finger were flipping an index card in his head. *Goddamn arthritis! If I were twenty years younger . . . God, those women could scream when I'd hit that finish line!*

A shadow crossed his face. He looked up. His eyes filled with tears, his mouth tried hard to contain a scream.

Stumbling right at him, just a few feet away now, was the headless creature, arms extended, the end of its spinal cord sprouting from its neck and throbbing with excitement.

No teeth there, thought Wesson, but his fingers continued to scramble at the shell. It finally snapped home. He brought the gun up and aimed at the creature.

Don't panic! he told himself. Only this one left. Don't waste it on something that don't have teeth. But God, oh God, look at that thing, just look at that goddamn thing!

The thing closed in. It could sense the fear and the human sweat, and the small jelly bulb hanging at the neck throbbed faster.

Wesson felt the panic pulling every chord in his body, forcing his finger to squeeze the trigger, but he couldn't control it. It was just too much for him. He pushed back harder against the bedroom door, willing his body to go through it and disappear. But there was no time.

Tears touched his lips and sobs began to rack his body. He shook his head, hoping to clear it of this mad nightmare, but the creature continued forward, unabated, hungry.

He couldn't do anything else. He fired.

The shell exploded, sending its hundreds of fragments tearing into the abomination. The creature fell back and brushed wildly at its chest as though a swarm of bees had just invaded it.

Wesson would have screamed if he'd had the chance, but just as his throat was about to release its burden, hands, thousands of rotting, stinking hands, ripped through the bedroom door behind him and raked at his face and body.

By the time they dragged him through, he was dead. But even that state didn't last for very long.

The storm seemed to rage a more violent fight against the woods than the area around Wesson's cabin. The going was tough for the three lone figures. Patrick was occasionally crying out now whenever a branch or even the wind would hit at his injury. Janet did her best, but she was feeling the strain. Johnny couldn't take much of the weight, what with his size and his own injuries. She dreamed of collapsing, of just falling asleep and not waking up for days. Even the mud looked comfortable. But she knew if she gave up now, they would all wake up to a worse nightmare than this.

So on they stumbled, toward the general direction of Avilon's cabin, back to the strange clearing that had started the nightmare. The deeper they went into the forest, the more Janet began to panic. Every tree was beginning to look the same, every trail they took exactly like the one they'd just left. At this point, she wasn't at all sure if they were going in the right direction.

And what of Tom? He didn't even know the way, except vaguely.

Patrick cried out again as she shifted the burden of his arm around her neck. Johnny stumbled with the redistribution, but remained silent as always.

Then, perhaps attempting to ignore the pain, Patrick began to talk.

"Why are we going back to the clearing?"

"I don't know," Janet answered truthfully.

"What's there? You saw Tom. He has something up, some sort of answer. What is it? What's it got to do with—"

"*I don't know!*" But she couldn't help glancing at Johnny. How had he beaten that monster back there?

They struggled on in silence. They took turns looking back, with what each thought was an imperceptive move, unsure whether they were looking for Tom or the Shadowman. They saw neither, but the calls of the dead were still around them and did not diminish no matter how long they ran. They were surrounded, they knew, and for some reason the clearing became a sort of sanctuary ideal for them, too.

They emerged onto a definite path, muddy but discernible. Janet took charge of their direction. "This is right below the cottage," she shouted over the storm. "It leads through the clearing."

"If we're following it in the right direction," added Patrick, but not loud enough so she could hear.

Janet knew the area better than that, though, even when it was distorted by rain, and they soon found the clearing. Exhaustion suddenly caught up with them and they nearly collapsed right there. Hurriedly, Janet worked them over to a boulder where they sat, arms around one another.

"We should be inside the pentagram," cried Patrick.

"Pentagram?" called Johnny, startling them with the strength of his voice.

But there wasn't time for explanations. Janet turned to Patrick. "He didn't say—"

"You know that's what he meant."

Yes, she knew what he had meant, but she couldn't bring herself to step inside that cold place without Tom. Something told her that if she did, she'd never see him again.

But Patrick was adamant. "Come on. Hurry." He pulled his two human crutches now, nearly falling to the ground several times without their weight to support him.

"No," Janet shouted. "We've got to wait for Tom!"

"He may not come!" Patrick's face went as white as hers at the brutality in his voice. He added halfheartedly, "When he comes, though, we should be inside the clearing. He told us to—"

Patrick went on, pleading and insisting, on the edge of hysteria, but Janet stopped listening. Johnny had released himself from Patrick and come to her side, putting a red-stained hand on her arm.

"Please," he said, surprising her with those wide, knowing eyes. "We have to be inside the circle. It's important . . . somehow."

How does he know about the circle? she thought. Yet she was affected by the confidence in his voice. She decided that it might be best, even without Tom. But she had to take one last look back, just to make sure—

"Wait!"

Thunder struck the land, but it wasn't thunder. It was the

ground, something large slugging the earth. It came from up the trail and it was getting louder. Someone — or something — was coming.

"Get in!" Patrick tore at her arm and she stifled a scream of pain. She grabbed hold of the boy and followed without question. Supporting Patrick again, they stumbled their way into the clearing. Janet held her breath before stepping inside, but when her foot landed, then her other foot, and she was well inside the pentagram, she felt no different. They had not been torn from the earth into the bowels of hell. Everything was the same as it had been. Hell was still on the surface, around them.

Except that they were now out in the open, without even the defense of camouflage against the thunder rolling down the hill.

They held each other tight. They watched where the trail disappeared behind a clump of trees. Lightning flickered, creating distorted shadows from their deepest nightmares. Thunder followed, mixing with the rumble of whatever closed in on the clearing.

Then a figure appeared. It was tall, large, with a giant hump on its back. It had at least four arms and was bouncing with what was obviously a great weight.

Janet checked her scream, but her fingers were clawing at Patrick with as much earnestness as his fingers held her. She tried to bury Johnny's eyes against her breast again, but he would have none of it. He held her hand forcefully away. He *had* to see what was coming for them.

Then lightning illuminated the land again, and their fears turned to excitement. The creature was Tom, and he had a body hoisted over his shoulder. As he grew closer, it became apparent that the body he carried was headless, and that the missing part was tucked under his other arm.

They did not rush to meet him. There was something wrong with him, something beyond the cadaver he carried.

290

His face was pale and wide with terror. His clumsy footing should have tipped them off. He'd been keeping the pace for quite some time, and if he slipped once, he'd be finished.

As he reached the bottom of the hill, they saw the reason for his panic. The Army, led by the Shadowman, was racing after him, their dead and, in some cases, broken limbs carrying them as quickly as death and the power of their leader would allow.

Janet couldn't move. Before, she had been afraid to enter the clearing without her husband. Now, she couldn't leave it to help him. It enslaved her, as did the terror. So she watched, helpless, as the man she loved struggled alone to reach her.

Tom was gulping air, nearly drunk from it. He saw his wife and Patrick and Johnny waiting up ahead, in the clearing, but they were just standing there! They must see him! Didn't they realize he was struggling? Couldn't they see what was behind him, praying at every step for him to fall?

What's she waiting for?

But as he grew closer, he saw the terror in her eyes and knew what kept her away. He'd have to call her, try to break her attention from the beasts. If he couldn't . . .

His mouth worked, but there seemed to be a delayed reaction before the sound was permitted to reach her.

"Come on! Help me!" He threw the head into the clearing and Patrick fell to the ground trying to get out of its path. Johnny backed away, his mouth working, unable to believe what he saw.

"Janet, hold the legs!"

She faltered, her eyes still glued to the rolling head. It came to rest in a thick mound of mud.

"Come on, goddamn it!"

She moved. Without thinking of what she was holding, she took the priest's legs and lifted them as high as she could, according to Tom's instructions. She wasn't even surprised that they weren't carrying the body into the clearing.

Tom kept his end low and they began moving around the circle inscribed in the pentagram. Occasionally Tom would scream for her to shake the body and she would struggle to get a better hold on the two handles (she just couldn't think of them as legs any longer). Eventually, as she weakened, he demanded that Johnny help her. The boy stood there, unable to speak or blink or breathe. The scene before him was horrifying. What were they doing with that headless body? But something kicked in inside of him, and he found himself moving forward, to hold one of the priest's legs under his good arm.

They worked fast. Halfway around, Janet realized, though she tried not to think about it, that they were tracing the circle with the priest's blood. The sudden image made her sick, but her fingers clamped harder around the leg and she and the boy shook when Tom told them to.

The circle was nearly complete when the Shadowman and the Army arrived. Not one of them crossed over the circle where the blood had already been laid. *"Scatter!"* screamed the Shadowman, and the ghouls began humping around the circle, looking for an opening.

And there *was* an opening. The circle was not complete. Tom stopped with only a half a yard to go.

"What's wrong?" Janet called.

He looked up at her. "It's dry."

Her head was shaking before the words came out. "No . . . no . . . there's got to be enough."

Tom dropped his end. His eyes whipped first to the fast approaching creatures, then to the incomplete circle of blood. He began to shake and back away.

"We've got to finish it . . . got to . . . my God . . ."

"Tom! Tom, what do we do?"

"Got to . . . got to . . . find a way . . ."

It's all been too much for him, she thought. *The mad run, the severed body riding on top, a terror worse than death at his heels—*

"The boy!" It was Patrick. They looked to where he lay in the mud. "The boy's blood! You saw what it did! *Use him!*"

Tom looked at Johnny. True, that's where he'd gotten the idea, seen it proved before his very eyes. And they had to close that gap now . . .

Johnny saw the glint in Tom's eyes. He dropped the priest's leg and backed away. His hand unconsciously rose to touch the bandage that flapped open over his ear. Tom took a step toward him, then stopped, confused.

Janet stepped between them, staring incredulously at Tom. "What are you doing?" she screamed viciously.

He lowered his face, squeezing his eyes tight. "I don't . . . I'm sorry, I . . ."

The undead screamed. They had spied the opening and were rushing over themselves to get to it, their claws raised high.

"Can we spread it thin?" cried Janet.

"Already . . . thin . . . got to . . ."

Damn it, Thomas Howards, she screamed to herself, her nerves tingling, *now is not the time to lose your—*

"Head!" she shrieked.

"What?"

She looked wildly about. It was lying near Patrick, who looked back at her perplexed.

"Pat! Throw me the head!"

He looked at it with disgust. "No!"

"Throw me that fucking head *now!*"

He saw the creatures rushing around the circle, teeth bared, bumbling over each other in their desperate hunger. For some reason, they wouldn't pass through the priest's blood. In fact, they were making a direct effort to go *around* it. To the opening.

He didn't understand it all immediately, but panic made him act. He grabbed the head carefully, turning the face away from him, and heaved it at Janet.

She caught it, and nearly got sick at the squishy *plop!* it made as her palms slapped its cheeks. She couldn't help staring at its face. It was Father Tilkan of course, just as he'd looked in life. She wanted to scream, but the fear of the creatures was more powerful. Clumsily, she fastened her fingers in the mud-matted hair and squeezed as she rubbed the neck across the ground.

The circle was completed just as the creatures reached it. One tried to grab over the circle, scraping Janet's shoulder before Johnny pulled her back, but the creature withdrew as quickly as it had attacked. Its arms were on fire, raging even against the storm's rain. In the orange glow, its skin appeared green and blotched, like a reptile's, and its black, sightless eyes only added to its ghastly appearance.

What really struck the three captives, however, was the unearthly scream that the creature released. For the first time they realized that it was, without a doubt, a scream of *pain*.

"Are you all right?" Janet heard whispered in her ear. It was Tom. She nodded and he wrapped his arms tighter around her. Johnny was still beside her, holding her hand as if they had always been connected. Patrick came crawling through the mud and lay behind them.

They huddled together like that most of the night, a tight circle within a larger one, watching the various corpses surround them and seal off all channels of escape.

"What now?"

Silence. Patrick did not intend the question to be rhetorical, but the lack of any answer made it such.

The Shadowman's retinue crowded around the circle now. Occasionally a ghoul would get too close to the blood and would burst into flames. Its neighbors would move back and allow the creature to die slowly.

And they did die, there was no denying that. The legs would char so badly that they could no longer support the body's weight, eventually leading to a complete collapse. Then the limbs would stop twitching and the screams would cease. The screams were always the last to go.

"Must be the small amount of blood in the body bubbling and evaporating," Tom would comment. The others would remain silent.

The body of Father Tilkan was left in its two pieces where Tom, Janet, and Johnny had dropped them. Tom kicked some dirt on it from where they sat, then the four of them turned their backs on it.

They now stared into the visage of the Shadowman, who stood on the very edge of the circle, claws on hips, foot tapping in the mud. The rain had stopped after an hour. The Shadowman did not even attempt to speak with the prisoners during that time. It wasn't until a clearing wind began blowing the night clouds toward dawn that the creature finally addressed them.

"We shall wait," It said.

Tom looked up from his wife's face. She had nearly fallen asleep, Johnny cradled in her arm, but the cold voice had awakened her and made her sit up. Johnny, disturbed, rubbed his eyes of sleep. Tom pulled both back, and told the creature, "The storm has passed. It'll soon be day."

"We shall wait. In the shadows. You cannot escape."

Tom nodded his head. There were so many trees around,

it would be too complicated to find a labyrinth of sunlight back to . . . a cabin? Too dark. A phone booth? Too far. So the attempt would be useless without even a destination.

The creatures began dispersing when the sun tipped over the mountains. The land was purple, tinged with the gold of sunlight that the creatures hated. Tom doubted it would kill them to step into the light. He suspected they merely avoided it as humans avoided bitter cold. They certainly weren't what they pretended to be, but he decided to continue letting them believe he believed. Perhaps, somehow, someway, it could be used to their, the humans', advantage.

At seven, the sun was well into the sky. Birds should have been singing. Leaves should have been rustling in the wind. People should have been pushing through the streets, the very blood of this village. But there was none of that. Only the sun to proclaim that there was still an Earth and it still had some life to it.

Tom watched this alien world awake around him with an uncomfortable shudder. Janet shifted next to him, careful not to wake the boy, and looked up. He tried to smile but couldn't make it stick.

"Good morning," he said.

She took a deep breath before answering. "Yes," she said. Then, a hand gripped his, and her voice was more urgent. "What happened last night, Tom? You knew something. You still know something. What is it?" Her expression flickered. "What . . . what was it about Father Tilkan?"

Tom met her eyes; eyes he'd fallen in love with the first time he'd seen them, so long ago. She was everything: innocence, strength, wisdom, love. And he debated whether he should distort that combination with the knowledge he had.

She continued to wait patiently, and he found he wanted to stare into her eyes forever, hold her anticipation. He sensed a softening in her body, in her face. Maybe, if they didn't look around anymore, just at each other—

But another voice interrupted their dream.

"Tom, what was it? Why the priest?" Patrick. He spoke softly so as not to wake Johnny.

Tom glanced at the other man. "How's your leg?" he asked.

"Fine," Patrick answered without pause. "Now start talking." He sat up a bit straighter, as though awaiting an argument, but Janet laid a hand on his good knee, and he relaxed.

Tom nodded. There was no longer any choice. He took a deep breath and began.

"First, you have to understand that these creatures have been here since Earth's beginning. They must have seen the dinosaurs come and go, and have seen every second of human history.

"Well, then they must know what fears we hold dear; what myths we believe in, what superstitions we act on. And they're smart enough to use these things to their advantage."

He stopped, looked around. Most of the circle was clear, as sunlight danced on the blades of grass, but there was a section behind them that was infested with trees—and shade. Figures were visible in those shadows, lurking behind trees or beneath the wild blades of grass and flowers. Tom lowered his voice and leaned closer to the other two.

"They wanted us to believe—as most everyone has—that they are demons."

"Well, the Shadowman is the closest thing to the Devil I've ever seen," commented Patrick.

"Exactly! That's what It wants you to think. But It's not. It's just the leader, or some agent, of whatever army fought in the bowels of this planet, if we can believe even that. But they're *not* demons and they're *not* vampires."

"But the blood," began Janet.

"The only bodies they can take over are dead ones. The bodies can probably be those of animals or bugs or whatever they want, as long as they're dead. To do that, they have to kill, and what better way of killing than perpetuating the idea that they are somehow part of our nightmares come to life?"

"You mean they don't have to suck the blood?"

"They don't have to suck it, but I think they have to drain it from the body, since that's the fuel of any living being. I suspect they have to leave just enough so as to keep the limbs and body animated. I'm not too clear on this part, but I think that little bit might be some of the Shadowman's blood. That's how It controls them. It gives them motion. It gives them voice."

Patrick sat up straight again, then winced and rubbed his leg. "So, as long as they kill the body and drain it, it's still good to them."

"Right. The Shadowman instructs Its army to suck the blood because it's the best way to kill. It continues the myth of vampires and demons *and* it keeps the bodies in good condition. You can't walk around very well or kill other people if you have a broken head or shattered arm or whatever."

Janet looked into his face again, the eyes once more pleading. "But, Tom . . . what they did to Doctor Newton . . ."

"Yes. Let's concentrate on that for a second. First of all, that whole scene in Avilon's cottage, what was all that about?" Janet winced at the name of her mother. Tom continued hastily, feeling like a klutz. "Um . . . I mean the Shadowman. Why did It tell us Its actual identity? If It wanted everyone to believe It was the Devil and Its army was Its demons whose souls had been relegated to hell, why did It tell us Its true background?"

"Maybe you're wrong about them," said Patrick. "Maybe

they *are* what—"

"No. Just listen. I think It had to tell us Its true background because It sensed something evil about one of *us*. I think It was baiting that person, trying to get that one to reveal himself so that It could deal with him separately. The rest of us were going to become a part of the Army anyway. They had us surrounded, we were trapped. Why not tell the truth in order to fish out that important one—?"

"Which one?" stammered Patrick. "Who're you talking about?"

Tom took a deep breath and released the name with a sigh. "Avilon."

Janet did not react as he had expected. She merely stared at him curiously, trying to figure it out. It was Patrick that finally burst with, "Why her?"

Tom's eyes never left his love. "The Shadowman and Its army are not the Devil and demons. The Shadowman is the only agent from below, otherwise the other bodies, if inhabited, would be just as clever and imposing. But the Shadowman is the only one from Its side, and It can only build Its numbers here on the surface through the dead. It stands to reason, then, that there are more of Its numbers waiting below, perhaps for an all clear signal from the Shadowman, and that . . . that the only creature It *does* fear is one from the Other army, the other side. And if the Shadowman can only draw Its human slaves from among the dead, perhaps the Other army draws Its from . . . from the living."

Her eyes spilling with tears, Janet broke the contact and whispered, "My God . . . she was one of them."

"Not one of the Shadowman's people, Janet," Tom emphasized. "She was one of the Others that the Shadowman and Its army are fighting. Or, rather, her body was being used by one of the Other Souls."

"But the Shadowman said It'd already won the war," said Patrick.

"Of course," explained Tom. "The better to bait an actual member of the Other army. But it was a lie, just as their being demons or vampires is a lie."

"Jesus, this is nuts," said Patrick. He winced again and rubbed his leg. He never once looked down at it. His hand was nearly dyed red.

"Not so crazy," continued Tom, "if you accept the premise of two armies—the 'souls' of earth, as the Shadowman put it—battling it out so that this planet can finally die. For some reason, they've brought the battle to the surface directly, rather than affecting it through earthquakes and volcanoes and the like. Maybe the Shadowman is the first of Its members to reach the surface, maybe It's some sort of surprise attack. Maybe the Other army got wind of it and is trying to counter it. Whatever the reason, they're here, and we must accept that.

"Now everything should follow logically. The Shadowman was baiting Avilon—though It didn't know she was the one It was looking for—and she *did* act, but not until the creature was caught unaware. In fact, she almost managed to kill It."

Janet was nodding. "Yes, with a kitchen knife. She tried to stick it around that jewel on the Shadowman's chest."

"Yes . . ." Tom murmured, thinking.

"But wait," Patrick said. "It was Doctor Newton who attacked the Shadowman first."

"Right. And it was Doctor Newton the creature took to be a member of the Other army. He had the creature backing away with a cross and some threats about the Bible. After a while, though, the Shadowman stopped retreating and laughed. It must have realized Newton was not the one it sought. And Newton's actions were perfect. He wasn't the one the Shadowman was looking for, but the sight of It backing away from a *cross* and a *Catholic* . . . well, once again, it perpetuated the myth of demons and vampires."

"But It crushed the cross and . . ." Patrick's voice trailed off.

"Yes," said Tom, sadly, "and Doctor Newton. Out of anger. Doctor Newton was shouting with joy because he and his faith had the Shadowman by the short hairs. But it wasn't true. When the creature realized Doctor Newton was just a regular man, It laughed . . . then, when It saw the conviction in the doctor's acts, the doctor's smugness at the power of his *human* religion over this 'demon,' the Shadowman felt forced to demonstrate, against the myth It had been trying to feed, that It was more powerful than any superstition. I guess for loss of a better word, Its *pride* got in the way. After all, I think It's nothing more than a soldier, and It wanted to show the might of Its side by demonstrating that not even our faith in religion could protect us."

"Kinda makes you wish It really was the Devil," Patrick said.

"But why now?" asked Janet. "If these armies have been below the surface for so long, why have they chosen now to try a sneak attack? And why only one agent, why not the entire army?"

Tom aimed a hard glare at her. "Exactly. Why? I'm not sure, but I think it's because none of these creatures could reach the surface before now. The pressure below the surface of the earth, especially near the center, is tremendous, but they're used to it. Coming up here would be like going to an alien planet for them."

"Then how come there's one here now?" demanded Patrick.

"I don't know," Tom said, but he was thinking of something glittering, something he remembered on the Shadowman. *Jewels* . . .

They were quiet for a long while after this, assimilating all of the information Tom had provided them. He was having his own trouble with gathering it all and fitting it together correctly. There was just so much that they still didn't know . . . or understand.

Finally Janet spoke up. "Tom, what happened to Mom? If she was one of the . . . Other army, did she escape?"

The memory of a skull collapsing pushed at the back of Tom's mind. It created an expression he couldn't hide, and he saw the understanding in her eyes even before he spoke.

"I'm sorry," he said. "I'm sure she's dead. She had the capacity to kill the Shadowman, so the creature certainly had the capacity to kill her."

Her head lowered for a moment, then came back up with renewed hope. "But they can't turn her into one of them, can they? I mean, she can't be a member of the Shadowman's army."

"No, I don't think so. She's the enemy. The true enemy. The Shadowman somehow controlled Adam's body in Wesson's cabin with that little bit of blood, so somehow the Other army controlled or inhabited Avilon's body the same way. And I would guess that each side's blood is somehow anemic to the other." Still, Janet did not look convinced. He added, "And remember, they could have sent her to Wesson's cabin while we were stuck there. They sent Cathy. But instead of Avilon, they sent the next closest person, Doctor Newton. And he was a . . . defective product."

"All right," Janet said, seemingly to herself. "All right." Her body seemed to relax with the confirmation. She pulled Johnny closer to her. "All right . . ."

Patrick's urgency rose above their brief comfort. "Then that's why they didn't take Father Tilkan either," he said. "He was one of them, too. He had the blood of the Other Souls."

Tom nodded. "Or whatever they do to the blood. And I think he knew it. That's why he went out to talk with them. He knew he couldn't become one of them, so he bought us some time."

302

Patrick's eyes focused past Tom's shoulders. "With his life."

Tom bowed his head slightly. "Apparently he felt it was his life's meaning. A higher calling. Maybe it was."

Patrick let his eyes wander. They rested on Johnny. "Tom," he whispered. He waited for the other man to look up. "You saw what the boy did to one of those things."

Janet tried to rise, but settled again when she realized it might wake Johnny. She wasn't sure he should hear what might be said.

Tom, however, merely nodded calmly at the words. "He sort of turned me on to the answer, to the Other Souls. He confirmed what I had suspected about the priest. Without him, I might have hesitated, and if those things . . ." But his voice became choked. He turned away and gently brushed some hair out of the boy's face. Johnny still slept soundly, like any other boy, with his bad left arm held stiffly away from his body.

They grew quiet again, this silence lasting longer. They stayed grouped together, holding one another, agonizing over the waste, wishing for a way out.

"Where do we go from here?" asked Janet, so quiet and scared that Tom wanted to enfold her in his arms and hide her from the world.

"I took a gamble," he whispered. "I picked this place because I figure it's where the Shadowman broke to the surface. He probably added the triangles to the circle—to create a pentagram—to continue the lie that It was the Devil. I figured our occupying this space would by psychologically equivalent to the troops occupying the enemy's homebase. Maybe it will also keep any 'cavalry' from charging to the Shadowman's rescue." He sighed and held Janet tighter. "So now we have a sanctuary. But I haven't thought past this."

Patrick asked, "Do you think the boy knows anything that

303

will help."

"We can ask him." Tom shrugged. "I doubt it. At least nothing he understands."

"But . . ." Patrick paused, looking at Janet. "I'm sorry, but his blood might come in handy."

Janet shivered and held the boy closer. He stirred, eyelids fluttering. Janet hissed, "Pat!"

He looked away, more out of discouragement than shame. Silence returned.

Later, after thinking, Janet looked up into each man's face. "One of us has to leave here and find some help," she said abruptly.

Tom shook his head. "No."

"Well, we can't just sit here," she insisted.

"Yeah, Tom," Patrick added, "they can wait us out here. In a couple days we'll be dead of hunger or exposure."

"We only have about eight hours of sunlight left, *if* we don't get anymore storm clouds," said Tom. "That might be enough to get down to North Camp if we walk there directly, but we'd have to zigzag through the woods wherever there's sunlight."

"It's only for a little while, though," insisted Janet. The determination in her voice was almost enough for renewed hope in the two men. "Once we hit the road, we can stay on that."

"You saw the fog in the village," Tom said. "That may be enough for those creatures to rush out, grab us, and pull us back into the shadows."

"Then we avoid the fog. I'd think it would evaporate in the sunlight anyway."

Tom looked around. The sky was clear. Not even a wispy cloud. "Maybe," he said. He looked at his wife. "Maybe one person could make it. But for all of us to try, it would be the end if we were wrong."

"What about the boy?" said Patrick. Before Janet could

304

give him a look, he added, "The monsters wouldn't be able to touch him. He could make it."

"He's a child!" whispered Janet. "Pat, his arm is injured. He'd probably faint from pain before he found a road."

"He's special," insisted Patrick. "Tom said so."

Tom stammered, "I only meant that an Other Soul may be—"

"The Shadowman can't touch him and he knows the way to the next town." Patrick clamped his jaw in determination.

"Damn it, Pat—" Janet began.

"I'll go." The voice, strong for a child, startled all of them. Johnny rose from Janet's arms and stared at them with wide eyes and ears, awake long enough to understand what was going on. "I'll go," he repeated. "I know the way."

Janet was about to disagree when Tom asked, "How's your arm?"

Johnny looked down at it. Concentration and flickers of pain crossed his face. When he looked up again, he admitted, "I can't move it."

"It's probably fractured," said Tom. "The pain could get worse unless you rest and let me look at it. It won't get better if you're out on the road dodging monsters."

Johnny stared at him for a long moment. He was young, but he could understand reason. Something inside him told him he would not make it to the nearest working phone, let alone North Camp. It would be best for all if he stayed.

"You're right," he said finally.

"Fine," Janet shot, sitting up. "I'll go."

"Absolutely not!" Tom blurted. "I'll go."

"Tom," she said, almost grinning, "you don't know your way around. I've lived my entire life up here. I can't get lost."

"No, there's no argument. I'm going—"

"Tom," Patrick interrupted gently, "Tom, listen. You're right about the boy, but she's got you. She and I used to

305

play in these mountains. We know every inch, every land-mark. You can't go. You'd be lost inside of half an hour. I can't go. I can't even stand with this leg."

"And that leaves me," Janet said, standing and brushing off her pants. Johnny rose to stand next to her. His fingers touched her arm lightly, as if he were afraid to lose contact.

Tom searched their faces. There *was* no choice. The boy looked dazed and in pain. Patrick mirrored defeat and not a little shame at being the cripple when he was needed. Janet was determined and confident, the first time he'd seen her reflect hope since the nightmare had begun.

"All right," he said cautiously, standing to meet his wife eye to eye. "Maybe there is a chance. But, dear God, Janet, *please* be careful. If you're ever unsure of a route, don't take any chances. If you start to feel like you're getting nowhere, head back. Don't be stupid."

"I've never been stupid," she answered. She leaned close to him and kissed his lips lightly. "I married you, didn't I?"

He held her for a long time, savoring the muscles in her back, the softness of her skin, the breath on his neck. Then they parted and he walked with her to the edge of the circle. Johnny remained close, like a helpless animal following its keeper. Patrick stayed where he was and called out, "Good luck."

She gave him a long look, smiling. Then she turned to Johnny and hugged him close. The boy's right arm circled her, his grip strong with the power of fear. She felt tears in her eyes. They hadn't known each other long, but Johnny had shared a lifetime of terror with them. He had even saved their lives.

Tom brushed the boy's hair again. Johnny had proven himself. There was something special about him, more than what the Other Souls had put in his blood. It was his determination and his hold on sanity.

Janet eased away from the boy. She held Tom's hands as

she put one foot, then the other, over the thick, uneven line of caked blood. Behind them, some ghouls began to stir, but they did not call out or make a break into the daylight.

Janet squeezed her husband's hands and smiled. "I'll be back with the cavalry in no time."

"You'd better be," he said, then added softly, "Damn it, love, you'd better be." He moved next to Johnny, anxious for someone to hold.

She had turned and disappeared behind a clump of trees before his tears began.

She was gone nearly fifteen minutes before Tom turned away, alone, and walked back to where Patrick rested. Johnny followed silently, his eyes tilted to the ground, rubbing his left arm.

"You going to be all right?" asked Patrick, trying to sound casual.

Tom nodded. "Jesus, of course *I* am. It's her I'm sick about." He collapsed onto folded legs and patted the ground next to him. "Come on, Johnny, let's take a look at that arm."

Johnny sat beside him, and Tom examined the injury gently. He tried to bend it different ways, watching the boy's face for pain. In the end, he decided there was very little he could do. He applied a primitive splint to the arm, made from two semi-straight sticks he found outside the circle and one of his shoelaces. Not that he thought it would do much good. He explained this to Johnny, advising him to move it very little and keep it relaxed against his waist.

Johnny listened to this without expression. When Tom went to work on Patrick's leg, Johnny whispered, "What happens if she doesn't come back?"

Tom busied himself making another half-assed splint. "I don't know, Johnny. But she will. She will." He continued working, the quiet broken occasionally by Patrick's mumbled curses. Johnny watched them until Tom said, "Go on, lay back. Rest. Keep that arm relaxed." When Johnny was settled, Tom finished with Patrick, sat down behind the other man, and they leaned their backs against each other, like two boys resting their muscles when no trees were near.

When Tom thought Johnny was near sleep again, he wondered aloud, "What happens if she doesn't come back, Pat?"

Patrick shrugged. "I really haven't the foggiest. You and I are in the same position. The women we loved most of all are gone." He paused before adding: "Yours has a chance of coming back safe. Take some comfort in that. Hold that chance as long as you've got it."

Their eyes couldn't meet from their positions, but Tom was fairly sure Patrick's would be clear of tears. He had exhausted his despair long ago. He was merely stating a cold fact now.

Tom went back to tracing figures in the dark earth. "I think she'll be all right," he said.

"I think so, too."

"Have you thought about what we're going to do if—*when* help arrives?"

"Run like hell, I suppose." He glanced at the twisted flesh splayed in front of him. "Of course, I'll have to borrow someone's leg."

There was a long silence between them then, filled by an uprising of wind through the trees. After so long, it couldn't help but remind them that there was still life on the planet, that somewhere in the world there were birds chirping in the same kinds of trees that surrounded them.

"You can borrow my leg," said Tom into the quiet.

Chapter 12

The quiet of the country was not broken again until the sun began its hasty descent behind the mountains. It was not the humans who spoke first, however, but the ghouls as they emerged from their shadows and crossed the land that had been forbidden to them only minutes ago.

Tom and Johnny stood while Patrick shuffled about on his butt, trying to keep all sides of the sanctuary in sight. After a few harrowing moments, it was apparent that the priest's blood was still potent. Only a handful of creatures tried to cross this time, and all of them expired in a green and orange bloom of failure.

Perhaps to revenge their inability to reach the three captives, the Shadowman's army began wailing again. None of them mourned over quite the same song as another, but it was clear that their haunting rhythm was unified and controlled by the single smiling giant who stood behind the crowds, seen only as a striking silhouette except for Its gleaming white teeth.

Tom kept his eyes on that figure. It was the beast responsible should anything happen to Janet. He hadn't even the beginning of a notion as to how he would exact justice from It, but just staring at the visage gave him the rage that he knew he would need for the task.

"How do you think she's doing?" asked Patrick. Tom

looked down at the man, watched as his head jerked one way, then another, like a bird's. His voice was based with fear and doubt. The remark had struck Tom, but he knew it was not meant to upset him. Patrick merely needed confirmation, as he did himself.

"Probably talking to the National Guard right now. How's the leg?"

"Can't feel it. I'm not sure if that's good or bad."

A creature that would have looked familiar if its skull had not been misshapened by some strong and evil hand, went down on one knee in front of Patrick. "B*aaaa*d," it mimicked, its tongue lolling nearly to its chin. "B*aaaa*d . . . not so b*aaaa*d, Patty. Leg be all b*eeee*tter. Promise. Not so b*aaaa*d . . ." It stuck a hand out to him, a hand wrinkled with great age, just beginning to turn black with rot. The gesture was a gentle action, meant to cajole Patrick into joining it in the relaxing other world of the undead, but it resulted in a small burst of flame and a few painful minutes as it attempted to put its fingers out. Some of the ghouls standing nearby began to laugh.

"Jesus," said Patrick, "we gotta get out of here."

"Don't panic," Tom said slowly, "she'll be here." He looked around and moved behind Johnny. The boy was staring at where Janet had disappeared earlier. "She'll be here," Tom said again, putting an arm across Johnny's chest.

By midnight, Tom and Patrick had expected the uproar to become worse. Mysteriously, the opposite happened. As the hour grew later, the crowds diminished. When they realized what was happening, the two men watched the creatures carefully—leaving Johnny alone to look out for Janet—to determine where each member was going. The ghouls marched in the same direction, to where grey smoke rose above the trees and blotted out the stars.

"What the hell's going on over there?" Patrick whispered.

"Don't know. Maybe it's some sort of trap."

Patrick began jerking his head around like a bird again, hoping to pierce the darkness and find the cache where his nightmares lay hidden. "You think they're trying to draw us out?"

"Their yelling and threatening hasn't worked, so why not? You saw the Shadowman watching us earlier?"

"Yeah," Patrick replied, wiping some new sweat from his upper lip. "I thought I'd go crazy. I figured he was using some sort of mind power on us."

Tom whipped around. "Don't *ever* think something like that! I know the Shadowman is something we don't quite understand, maybe something we can't quite believe, but It's *still* governed by certain rules. If It had mind powers, this whole game would have been over a long time ago. Centuries ago!"

"Okay, okay . . . then what the hell was It doing out there?"

Tom took several breaths before answering. His own fear of losing Patrick surprised him. Johnny would be with him, but he still needed that adult strength next to him, a friend who was his age and had been through what he'd been through. Losing Janet was bad enough—even though she'd be back soon, he just knew it. She had to be—

"Tom?" Patrick was staring at him with an inquiring, almost desperate, expression.

"Yes, uh . . ." He struggled for words. His thoughts kept revolving around two questions that couldn't be answered: *Am I going insane? Is this what insanity is like?*

"The Shadowman," supplied Patrick, his concern momentarily resolving his fear.

"Yes, the Shadowman." He twisted and called for Johnny to join them. It took a few moments for the boy to come out of his daze and stumble to where they waited. Tom was alarmed at the dead look in Johnny's face. *He's on the edge. The monsters, the injury to his arm, the pain and fear . . . and the*

311

Other Soul doing something to his blood . . .

He must have gone off into his own daze. When he snapped back at the sound of a voice, he was surprised to find it belonged to Johnny. The boy looked up at him inquiringly.

"Um, all right. Look. Earlier, you saw the Shadowman, right? I . . . I think It was studying us. Trying to figure out how to capture us. It couldn't get us by force because we're safe in here, so now It has to turn to outwitting us. We have to stay alert, guys. We have to keep outsmarting it until . . . until . . ."

"Until help comes?" supplied Johnny.

"Yes. Until then. All right?"

Patrick nodded, but his eyes went back to the fire hidden deep within the forest. Johnny's attention followed his, as did Tom's. Almost imperceptible at first, a music grew from the darkness. It wasn't the abject wailing of ghouls, but a lyrical song, almost like a church choir.

"What is it?" said Johnny.

"I don't know," Tom answered dully.

Patrick, shaking his head, muttered, "It sounds like . . . like the Mormon Tabernacle Choir! Are they chanting?"

"I don't—maybe they're trying to keep us off guard."

"It sounds so *heavenly*, though. How can demons like that sound so nice?"

Tom's anger flashed again. "They're not demons!" He stopped right there, though, knowing that to continue would be useless. All he could hope to do was keep Patrick with him, sane or otherwise.

Calmly, he said, "The song sounds familiar, doesn't it?"

They listened for a little while. "Yeah," said Patrick, "I've heard it before."

"Christmasy," said Johnny.

Tom nodded, the name suddenly in his head. "Of course it is. It's the beginning of Handel's *Messiah*. We, and every-

312

body else in the world, hear it every year at Christmas."

Patrick nearly stood, as if his body had been shocked by an electric current. He addressed Tom, but his eyes and ears were twisted toward the music. "But . . . but *why?*"

Tom was about to answer when Johnny suddenly spoke up, his face still turned to the fire in the darkness.

"You're right," he said. "The Shadowman's trying to throw us off balance. It's the only way It can get to us right now. It's afraid we might find a way out."

Tom and Patrick exchanged glances. Was the boy being supplied answers by the Other Souls or was he just stating an obvious fact? Whichever, Tom felt better hearing his theory spoken with conviction by another.

Patrick apparently believed it was some sort of trance because he moved closer to Johnny and spoke slowly, softly. "Why that song, though?"

"Because it's probably the only one all of those people know," Johnny replied. "They had some conscious, certainly subconscious, knowledge of it when they were alive. Even I've heard the song. The Shadowman probably called upon their memories to find the most calming, most *religious,* sound it could find. That was probably the only one they all knew, except for some lousy Christmas songs. This is much more holy." Johnny turned to look at Patrick, and the short man realized that this was no trance. The boy had a look of deep concentration on his face. "It reminded you of church, didn't it?" he asked.

"Yeah, but—" Patrick stopped then. His head was turned toward a different voice now. Tom held his breath and listened carefully, hoping to find the sound. When he did, his body stiffened and grew inexplicably cold.

It was the sound of running feet. And the voice he loved.

"Tom! Tom, I got them!"

"Janet!"

His voice was an urgent whisper, to not wake the creatures from their campfire song, but it felt to Tom like he was screaming with all his might. His throat even felt raw afterward.

She appeared at the edge of the circle, and he moved quickly.

"Jesus, thank you—"

She was smiling. Dazzling. "Tom, they're on their way. The police in North Camp called the National Guard, the Army, the whole works."

His stride widened now, hurrying him into her arms, wanting only to hold her again, to touch her smoothness again, to feel her breath again—that's all he'd ever really wanted from her.

"They thought I was crazy," she whispered across the narrowing distance, "but some weird things have been happening there and they say Harkborough's been cut off completely. Oh, darling, it's wonderful, isn't it? We're going to be okay."

"Yes!" Tom answered, his words dissolving into laughter. "Oh, yes, we're going to be *great!*" He was almost running now, for her arms were open, ready to wrap her body around him and never let go.

But now something was holding him back. Some claw had ahold of his feet, was trying to pull him back, trying to keep him from the woman he loved. A claw—the *creatures!*

He was about to scream when he looked down and saw it was only Patrick. He was still on the ground, both hands clasped around Tom's leg and his body dragging behind him.

"Tom—"

"Patrick, what the hell are you doing? Let *go!*" He could see the pain in the other man's eyes—his bad leg had been dragged quite a few feet over the black earth, the splints now slightly crooked—but there was something else in those eyes, too. Fear. Revulsion.

314

"Tom, *please!*"

Tom stopped. He couldn't help it, meeting those eyes.

"Tom," Patrick said, also whispering, "ask her to come to you."

Tom froze then, not quite understanding, but sensing the urgency and the absolute terror in the words. His gaze shot up to Janet again. Her arms were still open. She was smiling, her eyes wide with happiness.

But she was still outside the circle of blood.

After several minutes, Tom let out a breath he was certain would die within him. Patrick's grip on his leg loosened, but he did not move forward. Uncertain of what to say or how to act, he merely waited.

"Tom?" said the beautiful woman outside the circle. "Tom, what's wrong? Come here, sweetheart. God, I was so scared. Come and hold me."

He took a tentative step, then revoked it. She was so beautiful, but even that beauty was dissolving in his own tears.

"Come to me," he said. He'd wanted his voice to sound hopeful and full of love, but it came out raw and scratchy. "Come here and tell me everything."

Her smile faltered, only for a moment. Then she moved around the circle's curve, seeming to come closer to Tom, but always remaining on the other side of the boundary.

"Please, Tom. It's so cold out now. I've been through so much, with the police questioning me and the cuts from the trees and my feet aching after so many miles." Her voice softened into sweetness, with just a touch of need, like a child's. "Please, hold me close."

Tom shook his head, started to say something, then looked away and shook his head again.

"Please . . ." he managed to say before breaking into tears.

"I love you, Tom . . ."

315

"God, *please* . . ."

"I need you. Come hold me. I love you."

"No . . ."

He sank to his knees and covered his face with his hands.

Janet shifted her attention, seeing the boy standing behind the two men, his face nearly as pale as hers. "Johnny! Come here, let me see you up close."

Johnny stepped toward her. He moved past Tom, and Patrick was about to reach out and grab his jeans when Johnny stopped. He was at the very edge of the circle, staring across at Janet.

She smiled. "I missed you so much, Johnny. It was like . . . like you were a part of me. We've been through so much together, and your parents are probably gone now. Tom and I have always talked about adopting . . ."

Tears fell down Johnny's cheeks, but he didn't sob or sniffle. His composure remained.

Janet's mouth twitched, and she abruptly changed the subject. "How's your arm?"

"Hurts," Johnny said.

Janet moved as close as she could. "It doesn't have to hurt," she whispered. "I can make the pain go away. Then we could be together always."

Johnny's composure waned. Tom's fingers parted from his face to watch Johnny turn away, Janet calling his name worriedly as he walked to the other side of the circle. He never turned back. It was obvious, as he sat hunched over and his shoulders heaved, that he was crying. Tom wanted to reach him, but he knew he didn't have the strength.

"*Daddy?*"

Tom slowly faced Janet again. Somehow, he knew what he would see.

It was Cathy, but the bugs were no longer on her. In the moonlight, her skin was pale and glowing, like Janet's. Her hair had been combed, twigs and dirt disposed of, and her

316

dress looked like new. She stood in front of Janet, both women smiling sweetly, eyes twinkling with love. A ghostly portrait.

Tom heard the groan from Patrick behind him, but he couldn't turn to meet another despairing face.

"Daddy?" said the little girl again. She looked at Tom.

"She can be ours," said Janet, her face excited. She rested her hands on the girl's shoulders. "It could be the family we've always wanted. A little girl, Tom! And you and I would be together. It's what you've always wanted."

He couldn't cry. He couldn't scream or shout. He couldn't move. All he could do was watch the little girl that he had always wanted and the woman he had always needed. They would be a family if he crossed that line. The family that he'd always prayed for.

God, he thought, taking a step, *they look so damned beautiful.*

And they did. Their smiles were innocent and honest, as if they didn't recognize his hesitation and pain. The little girl's hand clasped that of her new mother. They actually did look related, something Tom had never noticed before. Their pose was like a picture; one of those pictures a family treasures always.

He took another step toward them.

"I've felt so empty for so long," continued Janet, clutching Cathy Simon closer to her. "Even longer than we've known each other, love. But now we can have any child we want. It's *more* than adoption, Tom. Each one is a part of me.

"Please, Tom. Be with me. Love with me." She opened her arms again, waiting for his warmth. "Hold me." Cathy's arms also opened. The child's eyes pleaded. "Hold us, Tom," whispered Janet. "If you love us, hold us . . ."

Tom was truly amazed now at how much the girl resembled his wife. They really did look like mother and daughter. Perhaps . . .

His shaky knees took him another step closer. Then

another. It was getting easier. He stretched one hand out. Out, out, toward the answered prayer, the absolute *miracle*, he would have given his life for. And now payment was due.

"Tom!" called a new voice, a million miles away. "Tom, goddamn it, you leave me here all alone with this possessed kid and I swear I'll become one of those creatures and tear your goddamn head off! *Don't you leave me here alone!*"

And then, from behind, another voice saying his name. Johnny, choking words out between sobs. "Tom, please. We need you here." A pause, for breath and courage. "I need you," he said. The statement was so simple, so honest, that it managed to pierce deep.

Tom stopped. There was no hand gripping him, but something inside made his legs suddenly heavy. And his arm. It came down to his waist. He couldn't go on.

In front, Cathy's sweet, plump hand went out. "Please, Daddy."

Behind her, another hand rose imploringly. His wife's. His lover's. The woman he had sworn to spend his entire life with.

"Please, Tom. Darling."

A small chill exploded in his chest, and he knew then that it was over. He couldn't join them in their new lives. He was already dead.

"No," he muttered, and turned away.

As he stumbled to where Johnny waited for him, he felt his wife and almost-child reach out to follow him. Then he heard the tiny *pppffffssss!*, the muffled screams, and the crackling of fire as it burnt their smooth skin away.

Patrick cried out. He had shut his eyes to the horror, but he heard the moment of his child's death. Johnny and Tom rushed to his side. "Now . . . now I know, Tom," he whispered hoarsely over the crackling of the orange flames. "Now I know for sure." And then the words were choked by sobs once more.

Before them, the night was illuminated. The woman and child remained there, their arms stretched out, their faces contorted with hope, until their bones splintered and their ashes floated into the sky amidst Handel.

Darkness returned.

The three sat huddled together for a long while. Their heads were hidden, bowed deep, and their bodies were still so that, from a distance, they resembled a solitary boulder amidst the clearing's desolation. There was no crying. That had passed hours ago. There were no words, for they were too wrapped up in their own sorrow to care about the other man's. But they held each other, arms around shoulders, with a tightness that never lessened. If they lost each other, they would fall into themselves, forever lost in their own personal insane darkness. Eventually to die, of that they were certain.

Distantly, they heard footsteps approaching. When they stopped, very near the circle of blood, it was several minutes before curiosity forced the three to raise their heads as one.

It was the Shadowman. He was not smiling.

"I'm very sorry about your losses, gentlemen."

"God . . ." muttered Tom. The Shadowman's composure seemed to lighten at the word.

"I understand that you loved them very much. And soon you will join them unless you join me."

"Fuck you!" shouted Patrick, then lowered his head again.

"Succinctly put," purred the creature. "But listen to what I'm offering you. Life! Not a life you know now, but a new one, opening doors that have always remained closed. Gentlemen, your wives are gone. Your children are gone. They will never return. There is nothing but death waiting for you, even if by some miracle you escape this circle. You have nothing to live for." It stepped closer, so very close now. It ignored the small sparks that threatened Its own existence. "Cross this line and you will have a new life. You won't have to remember your losses. You won't feel the pain that's tightening your chests now. You can laugh and love and play again."

"Until the end of the world," snapped Tom, "which will come that much sooner if we cross that line." *Why even speak to It?* he wondered. *Does It have the power to keep us talking?*

"What do you care about the world, Mr. Howards?" It asked. "Your wife has been torn from your grasp forever. What the hell do you care if the world survives or not? Am I right?"

Tom did not answer. But he was frightened at how close the creature had come to the truth.

"The end of the world will be a great celebration. There will be laughter and dancing and love all around. It will not be a sad occasion. We've fought for nearly five billion years. It will be the end of a war that we've won. Of course we will celebrate, and our extinction will be wholly painless."

Tom stood suddenly, breaking away from the group. He didn't know what he was going to do, didn't know what he was going to say. All he was sure of was that this creature was responsible for his wife's death. And that, somehow, someway, It was going to pay.

He approached the beast. The Shadowman opened Its arms and smiled brightly. Tom was startled to see that the creature's teeth did not appear as sharp as they once were. He stared at those teeth, and found he wanted to continue past the border, actually wanted to feel the creature's arms comforting him—but he forced himself to stop inches from the blood in the dirt.

He thought furiously, trying to organize his feelings, concentrate on what he could possibly say to this beast to harm It, to discourage It. But, again, the Shadowman was first to the plate.

Tom felt the wind pulled from his lungs upon seeing the plain, middle-aged woman standing beside the creature. The disparity between them was nearly ridiculous: tall and average, dark and pale, evil and sweet.

But both were smiling . . . and the woman had all her teeth.

"Johnny?" she called lightly. Her hands wrung a dish rag, as if she had just come from the kitchen and was hesitant to disturb anyone.

"Johnny?" she said again.

Tom closed his slack mouth and whipped around. Johnny was looking up now, staring at the woman with something like wonder.

It's his mom! Tom screamed to himself. *It's his mom, oh, Jesus, it's his mom!*

"Johnny," said the woman, a relieved smile washing some color into her face. "Oh, Johnny, we've been so worried about you. We didn't know where you'd gone. No one called us about the accident! I'll speak to the sheriff about that. But—are you okay, honey?"

Johnny's face was blank, more dead than his mother's.

"Honey? Are you okay? Are these people treating you right?" She stepped closer, to the border, and leaned forward with her hands on her knees. "I'll bet you're hungry, huh? Can I make you a sandwich? Peanut butter? You're dad will be home in a while, but I don't think one sandwich will spoil dinner." She held out a hand. "Come on, then."

Johnny didn't budge, but Tom wasn't taking any chances. He stepped in front of Mrs. Ryan, his back to her, and bent his legs to a crouch, ready to tackle the boy should he make a break for his mother.

Mrs. Ryan moved around the border, so that Johnny could see her better. Johnny watched her progress, but made no other movement or sound.

321

"Johnny!" Her voice was sharper now. "Johnny, you're making me mad. You know what happens when you make me and your father mad!"

Johnny's mouth worked, but it was a moment before sound fell out of it. "Switch," he whispered.

Mrs. Ryan folded her arms. "You don't want him to use it on you, do you?" The arms unfolded. She was a loving mother again. "Come on, Johnny. We love you. We miss you. Come home with me. Daddy and I—"

"Dad's dead!" Johnny snapped. He ripped the falling bandage from his head. The glue pulled from his hair sounded like tearing ligaments to Tom. There, exposed, was what was left of Johnny Ryan's right ear. It was more a hole in the head, curved, like what a screw would go into, with a white nub around it. The nub was ridged with scabs that could easily be made to bleed again.

Mrs. Ryan backed away from the sight. Tom, too, fell back, feeling sick.

"Here, Mom!" Johnny screamed. "*This* is what Dad's done to me! He didn't even have to hold the switch! He's the one that tore my ear off, and I . . . I . . . knew . ." His head fell forward, his dirty hands covering his face, and the sobs came hard. Patrick shifted his arm tighter around the boy.

Tom looked at the Shadowman, hidden in the night while the scene played out. Now It stepped forward, hands gripped behind Its back, a distinct red glow of fury in Its eyes.

Mrs. Ryan saw It coming. She moved toward Johnny again, her voice desperate now.

"We . . . I didn't know, Johnny. He was just trying to save you, though. He wanted you to be with us. So that we could be a family again. He wouldn't be spending so much time at work and coming home so tired and grouchy anymore. He wouldn't use the switch anymore. We'd be a family,

322

Johnny . . . for once . . ."

The Shadowman reached her. Tom readied for a sudden swipe of its claws that would destroy the woman. The woman expected the same by her expression, but when the hand did come up, it came slowly, and rested on her shoulder with concern.

"You may go," It said. "I'll bring him to you."

Tom thought he saw tears in her eyes, but when she turned back to Johnny he saw it had only been the moonlight reflected against the dry, dead eyes.

"I love you, Johnny," Mrs. Ryan said. Her voice choked with emotion. It couldn't have been an act. However, it might have been, thought Tom, the first time she'd ever said the words.

As she disappeared into the shadows, Tom watched Johnny. He had never raised his head again, but the sobs were slowing. Patrick's arm still circled the boy's shoulders. The man also had his head bowed. He looked as shattered and hopeless as Johnny.

Tom was about to say something when he felt the cold presence behind him. He didn't turn, but took several breaths before speaking.

"Go away. We're not joining you, and if we have to we'll die in this circle. So there's nothing for you here but a waste of time. Why don't you just go back to hell where you came from?"

"I thought you were of the opinion that I was not from hell."

Tom shrugged. "A figure of speech, you son of a bitch. That, by the way, was another figure of speech, although I can't be sure how much truth there might be in it."

The Shadowman laughed abruptly. A sharp crack, like thunder. "Delightful!" It bellowed. "If you're not filled with sorrow, you're erupting with anger. Oh, you'll make a fine member of the Army, Doctor."

"Never happen!" growled Tom, turning around to look the creature in the eyes. He was startled by how black they were. They seemed to grow as he watched, as if they were dark maws opening to swallow him, but he stood his ground and continued to stare the thing down.

"Oh, come now," the Shadowman said gently, "it's not all that impossible, Doctor. After all, you're the only one I have left to convince. The boy will follow once you're gone and everyone else has come around."

Something in the eyes glittered, and Tom felt a chill zip up his spine and drop a bomb in his chest. Something was seriously wrong. He backed up a step, thinking it was the priest's blood, that its potency had worn off. But the creature did not make a move. In fact, Tom could still make out a few sparks near Its cape, trying desperately to become living, breathing flames.

So it wasn't the blood. What was wrong, then? What was it the creature had gloated over? *Not all that impossible, Doctor . . . the only one I have left to convince . . .*

The Only One!

He whirled around. Patrick was pulling his injured leg over the border. He had separated from the boy when Tom wasn't looking, leaving Johnny stranded in his own emotions. Johnny still had no idea what Patrick was doing. Before Tom could move, the other man was on the outside of the circle. Some creatures appeared from the shadows and approached him slowly, perhaps afraid they might spook him back into the sanctuary.

"*No!* Patrick!" Tom nearly leapt at him, but it was too late. He thought of reaching over and grabbing the other man's leg, but he was afraid his own arm would burst into flames—ridiculous, but panic swayed him.

He glanced back at the Shadowman. Its arms were folded and It answered his glare with a crooked smile.

"I'm sorry, man," Patrick said. His voice was weak, nearly

324

gone.

Tom sank to his knees, only a few feet away from his friend, the blood line between them. It could have been a million miles.

"What're you doing?" Tom pleaded. "You can't leave. We're okay here—"

Patrick was shaking his head. "No, man, no, listen . . ." He took a long breath, exhaled it. The creatures were coming closer, but he didn't turn to watch their approach. "I just can't do it, Tom. The pain and hurt, all those years . . ."

"Goddamn it, Pat!" Tom spat viciously. "You were listening to that thing's drivel! That fucking liar—"

"No, *no!* You don't understand." His voice sank into a whisper, as if he were sharing a great secret. "Tom, when my wife died, a big part of me died. I really, really thought *I* was going to die. There was nothing in my life . . . *nothing!* It was just pain and memories, and it felt like a giant anchor hanging on my heart. Sometimes I couldn't even get up in the morning, I just wanted to lie still forever, let the tears and pain come until it was all used up. But it's never all used up, Tom. There's always more."

"Patrick, listen to me—"

Patrick's fist smashed the ground, creating a small dust cloud. The creatures behind him seemed to be waiting for a message from the Shadowman. "No, damn it, listen to me! The only thing that kept me going during that time, the *only* thing that kept me alive, was Cathy. I . . . I l-loved her more than anything. She became . . . sort of a substitute for Marjorie. But now she's gone. And there is no one else, Tom."

"Pat, there's me. I'll stay with you. I need—"

"No, Tom."

"—you, I need someone close to help me get through this thing. You've been through—"

325

"No, Tom."

"What about the boy!" Tom pointed at the solitary figure near the center of the circle. Johnny looked up, sick and pale, then frightened when he realized what was going on. "The boy, Pat!" said Tom. "Even he's lost a lot, but he's not giving up. He needs you, too, Pat! We *both* need you!"

Patrick swallowed several times while staring at the boy. Tears brimmed in his eyes, and his head kept lowering.

Beyond Johnny, beyond the circle's border, the Shadowman leaned forward, worried. The creatures behind Patrick stirred uneasily.

Finally Patrick's glazed attention rested on Tom. "I'm sorry, man. I can't take the pain again." The tears spilled over. As he spoke, he had to catch his breath every few words. "You and Johnny will survive it together, but I won't. I can't. I don't want to. I'm sorry."

When he didn't say anymore, the monsters were on him. Tom didn't dare reach out over the line of blood. Instead, his fingers dug into the dead earth, clawing, grasping for something to hold. The dirt merely slipped through his fingers.

"Goddamn it, Pat, you *can't* do this to me! You can't leave us here *alone!* You *can't!*"

"I'm sorry, Tom. I'm sorry."

"*No!*"

"I'm sorry . . . I'm sorry . . ."

There appeared to be a brief struggle. Then the apology was silenced forever.

Kneeling in the dirt, the cold wind swiping away the hush, Tom felt the end nearing.

"Tom?"

He didn't turn. His fingers were bleeding from scratching at the earth, yet, despite the pain, they continued mechani-

:ally.

"Tom, are you all right?"

He heard the voice distantly, knew it was the boy's. He wanted to answer, but his breath was stolen by sobs, like hiccups. *I can't breathe right.* The thought revolved in his head. It would lead to panic, he knew, maybe hyperventilation and unconsciousness. He tried to force himself away from the border, but his fingers were too busy eating the dirt.

A black leg, black as death, stepped in front of him.

"Tom, it's a terrible thing to be alone," said the dark voice. "A very terrible thing."

A huge hand, palm up, appeared in front of him. Tom knew the other one to be nearly destroyed after touching the blood of Avilon and the priest. This one was pale and monstrous, but it offered so much. Tom wanted to touch it, to follow wherever it led . . .

"Tom?" called the tiny voice behind him. "Come here, please."

He shook his head. The shock of wanting to be with the creature was enough to force him back in revulsion. As he retreated, his legs hit something. At first he thought it might be Johnny, but he knew the boy was farther back than that. Then he knew.

He smiled at the Shadowman, a drunken smile that held back a horrible laugh he was afraid, if begun, would never end. He reached back and patted the drained, decapitated corpse. "I'm not alone, bastard. I've got the kid . . . and I've got the Father here to keep me company." He opened his other arm, gesturing for Johnny to get beneath it, so that they could pose, the three of them, for this family picture.

The laugh nearly broke through that time.

Johnny stayed where he was, watching Tom uncertainly.

The Shadowman nodded once and turned away from them. It strode several feet from the circle, heading down the path toward a hill in the distance. Then It stopped and whirled abruptly, outstretched arms scattering the night air.

"I've offered you friendship and love! I've offered you the woman and child you've always wanted!"

"They were ghosts," called back Tom, his voice cracking.

"Yes." The Shadowman stared at him for a moment, studying. "Yes," It said again. "We've offered only ghosts. That's what I was afraid of."

Tom was about to call something back, something inane, but the sight that rose before him forced all words and ideas from his head.

For a moment it appeared that the Shadowman was growing into a giant. Not really a large man, but a compilation of two men, one growing from the other. But then Tom realized that the deformation was due to the angle from which he was watching. Another man was actually being raised high on the hill behind the Shadowman, higher and higher, taller than any man could be. The man was stiff, his arms outstretched like a zombie's, every limb extended, in silhouette, by posts . . .

The act was finished and once the Shadowman jumped out of the way, he could see exactly who the figure was.

Patrick. Nails had been driven into his wrists to hold him to the outstretched posts. A single long spike speared both legs just below the shins.

The picture was so strange, so alien, that it took Tom a moment to realize what was actually happening.

Patrick was being crucified.

"Dear God." Tom stumbled toward the tortured figure. His head was on fire with disbelief and hatred. Suddenly, something tugged at his waist, pulled him back. It was Johnny. He looked down, bewildered, and saw that the boy had stopped him inches from the border of blood.

Tom gripped Johnny's arm where it circled his waist, held it for its warmth.

"Tom," said the chilling voice, so near again that Tom's heart nearly stopped. "Tom, we have not taken your friend into the Army. He is still very much *alive*. He fainted when my friends drove the nails into his legs and wrists, but when he awakens, he will be in more pain than he could ever imagine."

"You monstrous son of a—"

"Names will not break my bones," quipped the Shadowman, grinning wolfishly. "This will be interesting, I think. Very interesting . . ."

The creature backed away into the darkness, almost floated. Tom tore his eyes from the horrible figure on the hill and surveyed the area. The creatures were gone. They couldn't even be seen in the shadows.

He and Johnny were alone again, but a friend was in sight.

Johnny's head dug into his back. It reminded Tom of the times Janet tried to hide his eyes by hugging him.

"What do we do?" asked the muffled voice.

"I'm not sure."

"They want you to go out there."

"I know."

Johnny's grip tightened. "Don't."

Tom wanted to say that he wouldn't, but he thought it best not to lie to the boy. Instead, he took hold of Johnny's wrist, loosening the grip around his middle, and dragged the kid along beside him. He stamped around the clearing, trying to keep his eyes from Patrick. There *had* to be something he could do. Why would the Shadowman let Patrick live? Why put him through this torture? The answer was obvious; even Johnny had seen it: to capture Tom. The Shadowman could certainly put off Patrick's transformation in order to bait the last survivors from their niche. But did It assume he would rush outside the circle and rescue his friend without considering the consequences? Apparently

329

so.

And Tom wasn't so sure he wouldn't concede. His plan would be to wait until daylight and help his friend — even though he suspected the cross was planted near the large tree on that hill so that it would always be in shade — but if Patrick woke during the night and began screaming and begging . . . well, Tom wasn't sure how long he'd be able to hold out.

He stopped, turned. He realized that perhaps he wasn't completely helpless. After all, he *wasn't* alone. There was Johnny. He remembered what Patrick had inferred about the boy: *Maybe he knows something, something that will help us.*

Tom sat heavily in the dark earth and dragged Johnny down next to him. Johnny winced at the pain that jolted his arm when he hit the ground, but soon grew attentive.

"Johnny," said Tom, "we're in trouble. You understand that, right?"

"I'm not stupid." He sounded disappointed in Tom's attitude.

"All right, sorry. Look . . ." — his voice fell to a whisper — "you know that you can hurt these things. It's something in your blood, like it was in the priest's, right?"

Johnny didn't answer. He looked alarmed and pulled back. Tom held his wrist tighter, but there was a gentleness in his eyes.

"*Please,* Johnny, I'm not trying to frighten you. I'm not going to make you do anything you don't want to do. We need each other."

Johnny visibly relaxed. "Yes."

"But I need whatever information you can give me about these things, especially about the Shadowman. Do you know anything?"

The boy shook his head violently.

"No."

"Johnny, are you sure? Isn't there some insight, something that could help us. Can you . . . look, would you just close your eyes and try to . . . I don't know, peer inside yourself, I guess. Try to listen to whatever is in you. Maybe there's something."

"I don't know anything," he insisted. He was pleading now, trying to work his wrist from Tom's grasp. "I just feel a little different, that's all. But I've tried to listen for a voice inside me. There's nothing."

Tom felt cold. "You tried? When?"

Johnny looked away and began chewing his bottom lip. *"When?"* He shook the boy. "Johnny, *when?"*

The answer was shouted out, startling Tom.

"In the hospital room! When the Shadowman came!"

Tom thought about this for a moment. The Shadowman had come to Johnny's hospital room. Obviously, It wanted to kill him . . . unless It didn't know Johnny was special until It got there, and then Its original objective would be to make Johnny a part of the Army. It was natural. Johnny was the only one to survive an attack. There was a chance he knew something important, and he was outside of Harkborough.

But was there some connection with Johnny looking inside himself and the appearance of the creature?

"Johnny," he said, "I won't ask you to look inside again. The last thing we need is the Shadowman around. But I want you to try to remember . . . what did you see when you closed your eyes in the hospital room? Was there something that came to mind, maybe an image or a voice . . ."

He let his voice die out, watching the concentration pass over the boy's face. Johnny raised his head.

"What?" Tom whispered.

"A . . . a jewel. I saw it. But it reminded me of a . . . a . . ." He tried to form a shape with his good hand, the word eluding him.

"What? What did it remind you of?"

The boy's hand stopped. He looked into Tom's face. "A shell. That's not the word, but . . . I think . . . something like a shell."

Tom nearly grinned. It was what he had suspected. Again Johnny had helped confirm something that might prove helpful. If, indeed, the uncertain memory of a scared boy could be called confirmation.

He shook the thoughts and decided he'd better prepare for whatever decision he would make. Day or night, he'd need a weapon, even if it only managed to hold off the creatures for a few minutes.

The clearing was, of course, bare, but for the corpse of Father Tilkan, and Tom doubted the priest had anything helpful on his person. His usefulness had been drained from him long ago.

The monsters were gone, though, so it provided him with an opportunity to duck outside the circle for a few seconds. He knew they were watching, preparing their own on-slaught should he make a break for Patrick, so he was back inside the sanctuary before they could send out the warn-ing.

When he came back, though, it was with a thick branch in his hand. He sat next to Johnny, explaining his plan as he pulled out the penknife and began whittling. The point grew steadily sharper.

Sometime after midnight, Patrick began calling Tom. The sound was throaty, more tortured breath than voice, but that only made its effect that more chilling.

When Patrick realized what had happened to him, the pain must have struck, fully awake and raging after its forced docility while he was unconscious. Naturally he screamed, but the words that accompanied the pleading made Tom stand up and wander about the clearing like a caged animal. His name was called several times, in the same vein as a merciful God.

"Have to ignore it," Tom told himself, his own voice barely audible above the screams of pain. "It's not daylight yet." But he had known all along that it wouldn't be daylight when Patrick awoke. That would go against Its plans. It must retain Its advantage.

It had been quite a few hours, though, since the Shadowman had played Its card, and it had given Tom time to think. He had prayed that this situation would not come during the night, but somehow it had seemed inevitable, and he had planned for it. Now it was here and he was ready.

He approached the line, then turned to look at Johnny. The boy smiled back, a smile that held no strain or fear in it. It helped Tom a lot. He ruffled Johnny's hair again— careful of the fresh scabs on his ear—managed a wink, then turned back to Patrick's tortured figure on the hill.

Painted like an Indian, a stained stake in his hand, he stepped over the line of blood into the world of nightmares.

Nothing happened. Nothing tackled him, nothing jumped out and attacked him, nothing sunk teeth into his neck and serenaded him with lyrical sucking.

He took another step, closer now to his friend.

The wind rattled, perhaps trying to ease the tension rising in the world. Trees bent. The moon flickered behind clouds.

Another step. Another. Five.

He looked behind him, ready for whatever creature had snuck up silently. But no, that was Johnny's job. The boy would warn him in time. He could see Johnny now, standing, then stooping, but always with his eyes scanning the area around Tom.

When he looked forward again, for just a second Tom wondered, *Was Johnny outside the circle?* It made him feel so scared that he shook the thought. He had given precise orders to Johnny to stay within the sanctuary. The boy wouldn't — couldn't — break that rule and endanger them all. Right?

Don't think about it. Just keep going.

Patrick had seen him by now and had broken off his screaming. *He must sense the danger,* Tom thought. He moved forward several more steps, ever leary of the enemy.

"Hurry," Patrick called in an urgent whisper, breaking the night air and nearly sending Tom running. "Hurry, please, Tom, hurry . . ."

Tom showed his palm to his friend and signalled for the man to keep quiet. He was afraid to say anything himself.

He was a fair distance from the clearing, starting up the knoll that would peak at the foot of Patrick's crucifixion. The trees were ganging up on him, stretching and reaching with aged fingers. The wind was pushing, trying to make him hurry into a mistake. His own nerves agreed with the elements and pumped adrenaline that demanded to be run off in haste. But he wouldn't have it. His feet moved as if they were walking through a field full of mines.

"God, the pain . . ." whispered Patrick. Tom tried to signal for quiet again, but saw the man was not looking at him. His head was bobbing this way and that, trying to shut out the agony. Tom was close enough now to see the tortured body clearly in the moonlight. He nearly turned away and returned to Johnny, never to look back again.

It looked hopeless. Patrick's arms were covered with blood that had run from his wrists and dried. Fresh blood still ran in tributaries from the wound. The legs, he decided, would never survive. The splint had been ripped away from the broken leg. The damage done by the sheriff's car, the deep claw marks left by the creatures, the giant spike driven into the bones below the shins, combined with the man's struggles to free himself. Well, there wasn't a whole lot left connecting the feet to the body, and the legs looked bled dry. If he had suspected Patrick might be one of the creatures and was only playing the part of a hurt man, he knew now that that was impossible.

He shuddered, suddenly aware that he had stopped to study this sight, wasting valuable time. Patrick was staring at him, perhaps wondering why his savior was hesitating. It took a great effort for Tom to move his legs again.

Finally he reached his friend. Patrick recited his thanks to God over and over as Tom worked at the nails that pinned his limbs. *Stupid,* thought Tom, *really stupid.* He had prepared for a fight, had prepared for his own safety at the hands of the ghouls, but not once had he considered how he was going to pry the nails from the cross.

But as he worked at it, the decision was made for him. He heard, distantly, a sharp cry, but the wind seemed to rise at that moment, carrying the sound away. When he turned to investigate, two powerful claws gripped his shoulders and swung him around and into the air. There they held him, pinned in a crushing vice, forcing him to stare into the blackest eyes he had ever seen.

"You knew it was a trap," asked the Shadowman. "Why did you come?"

Tom didn't answer. He managed to tear his eyes away from the growing orbs, but that wasn't enough. The voice was just as hypnotic, a far cry from its booming malevolence a few hours ago. Now it actually *talked* to him, deep within his mind. Exactly like that guttural voice he'd been fighting for months, the one telling him bad things about . . .

"Why? You had the boy. You weren't alone."

Tom struggled.

"He was your friend," the creature said. "You needed a friend, someone close to your age, someone who'd been through the loss you had, eh?"

He couldn't help answering, "Yes."

"I can be your friend, too."

"I'm not that kind of guy—" Tom started, but the grip tightened and one of his ribs snapped. He screamed, struggled, believed that to free himself from the creature would free him from the sharp pain. But the struggling only made it worse, so he stopped, his legs dangling stiffly eighteen inches from the ground.

"You are holding a stake, I see," said the creature.

Tom didn't have to look down. He still felt the rough wood in his hand.

"You were planning to use that on me?"

"Yes."

"Tom . . . look at your friend."

He didn't want to but his eyes were drawn to Patrick. He had fainted again. The blood looked like ink blotches on his pale skin. Decades had been rubbed into the face. It was a pitiful shell of a man, no more human than the things that were now surrounding the hill.

"That could be you, Tom," said the voice. "If this were a human army, we would nail your body to a cross, or a rack, or an endless number of devices that prolong death. All of them have a common denominator: to make fear and pain the last emotions the victim feels on earth.

"But we're not human or alive, Tom. And you hold that against us. Yet I've been with this planet longer and I'm more a part of the natural course of the universe than you are. More importantly, I can make your last living feeling be that of joy. What more could anyone ask of their final moment?"

"For that final moment never to come," Tom grunted between clenched jaws.

"True. But that's not possible, is it? We all die eventually. Even the planets." Its face came closer. "Even me, Tom."

The hands forced Tom's body around until he was staring

336

into those eyes again. So flat and black . . . and *growing*. Darkness, yes, complete darkness, but a comfortable darkness. Like sleep.

"Yes," hissed the voice. "So close now, Tom. Then your own war and pain will be over. You'll forget about your wife and your friends. No more pain. No more despair."

"Yes," Tom breathed. His own eyes were wide, wanting to dive into the pool of blackness. But something held him back.

"Just lift your head . . . that's it. Now, just answer one little question for me, Tom . . . Who am I?"

"Uh . . . uh . . ."

The grip tightened, bringing pain and humiliation and life back. It would be so much more comfortable to let it all go—yet there was still that thing on the other end of the rope, pulling him back, something just out of reach right now, just out of the corner of his eyes . . .

Johnny, where the hell are you?

"Who am I?" the voice asked again, demanding.

A shithead, he wanted to say, but couldn't form the words. No, only one word was on his lips. A word, an idea, he had never believed in until this moment.

"Who—am—I?"

Then, from the pale human form next to them, the words came:

"Janet loved you."

It was enough. The creature ripped its eyes from Tom, nearly plummeting him into an abyss of unconsciousness, and stared hard at Patrick. "You will die horribly for that—"

Its threat was never finished. As Tom fought to retain his senses, he felt the fire in his side and the pain in his heart instigated by Patrick's offering, and he acted upon them.

The wood was solid in his hand. It rose sharply, at his insistence, and slammed into the Shadowman's chest.

337

Fear clearly crossed the creature's face, but when It looked up from the attack, Its fangs gleamed amidst a smile.

Tom stared at the intended wound. The jewel that protected the creature's chest now held the point of the stake. It would not go any farther unless Tom applied continued pressure and he didn't have enough time or strength for that.

The creature laughed, and several ghouls standing nearby chuckled with him.

Tom, beyond hope now, continued pressing the stake. A small wisp of smoke rose from the jewel and the weapon gave a little, but it wasn't enough. He would have to hit it hard if—

But the creature was squeezing again, and another rib went off like a gunshot. He screamed and let go of the weapon. He struggled, his legs kicking air, his fingers grasping the wind—but he didn't move an inch from the Shadowman's hold.

"Now, you shit, I'm going to show you how terrifying the final moment can be!" The eyes snapped wide, the sharp animal irises puncturing Tom's soul. Slowly the creature's mouth opened, a maw of sharp teeth, blood-red gums, and a tongue that wriggled and rejoiced in the meal soon to come.

With an intended lack of speed, the creature bent Its head toward Tom's neck: a slow, agonizing foreplay of terror before death's orgasm.

Tom screamed and fought for all he was worth. He had taken precautions—Johnny had insisted—but there was no way he could be sure. The creature must see it, must know, yet those tearing teeth were drawing inexorably closer.

The creature did see the stains on Tom's neck and parts of his face, but It thought nothing of them. Perhaps they were used to hide Tom in the dark, or a result of trying to tear the nails from Patrick's limbs. It didn't matter. Soon it

338

would be tasting only warm blood and Tom would be just another member of the Army.

The screams grew higher, almost like a woman's, as Tom felt the warm, sticky drool slip from the creature's mouth and tickle his neck. The night was growing blacker, the moon was turning into spots. He was passing out, perhaps forever. In the distance, he heard someone screaming his name again.

The creature held him a few seconds longer, suspending Its teeth less than an inch from the pulsing artery. The creature smiled. It knew that the containment made the fight that much more terrifying. But that was enough. The terror would not get any higher. It was time to feed.

The teeth plunged into the soft skin. The tongue began to lap and suck.

Tom thought his eyes were going to pop out and his throat explode with his final scream. Only his dependence on a small hope kept him from blacking out. Within seconds, long agonizing seconds, he would know whether it had worked.

The blood was warm, refreshing. The scream from Tom and the terrified contraction of his body was even better. But then the creature stiffened Its own body. Something was wrong. Its lips were on fire. Its tongue was scalding. Its teeth were *smoking!*

Its head jerked back. It released Tom. Almost immediately It knew It had made a fatal mistake. The stuff covering Tom's neck had been blood! *Blood from the boy—*

—and it had worked! Tom felt the earth rise up to meet him and he sat there long enough to catch a single breath. Then he turned and saw the creature holding Its mouth and screaming in *pain!* Johnny's blood was still potent, although it had not been strong enough to keep the creature from puncturing his skin. But if it still worked, why hadn't the stake gone through? Its point had been dripped in the stuff.

339

Allowing only a second's hesitation for these thoughts and to check the wounds on his neck, Tom stumbled to his feet and ran at the creature.

It was swinging in circles, doing what It could to control the pain. When It faced Tom again, he grabbed the stake still protruding from the crystal and jammed it forward with all he was worth.

Some of the blood had clotted and dried, and it had flaked off the stake, so his first attempt had managed to bring the jewel in contact with only a little of the blood. But this time it touched on an area coated more heavily, and the crystal began to melt away.

It was like drilling acid through metal. The sharp *hisssss* from the jewel and the rising smoke alerted the creature. It screamed, this time in terror, but instead of backing away, It grabbed either side of Tom's head and began to squeeze.

Tom closed his eyes, gritted his teeth, and prepared for his world to explode.

Patrick watched through bleary eyes. It was a dream, a nightmare. It had to be. Here was his friend fighting the Devil himself, and he wasn't doing anything to help. He couldn't move. He couldn't even feel his limbs. Then, when he had spoken the words that the knew would startle Tom back into consciousness, the Shadowman had stared at him, glared right through him like a knife, and he had suddenly remembered where he was.

And began to scream.

Neither of the two contenders heard his screams, for they were locked in combat by then. Now it looked dead even. Tom was pushing and shoving the stake farther into the creature's chest (and, even through his haze, it looked like the damned crystal was *smoking*), and the Shadowman was determined to bring Its claws together somewhere in the middle of Tom's head.

Patrick screamed again, but it wasn't acknowledged. He looked around, hoping to find someone that could help, but was met with empty stares from monsters he had once known as people. They were all staring at the fight with glassy-eyed concentration, or perhaps it was with the wide-eyed disinterest of the dead. After all, the Shadowman couldn't possibly have control over them now.

There was another scream, beyond the creatures, but Patrick's blurry vision couldn't see that far. Still, the shape was small and jumping around, holding something . . . Johnny? Why didn't the boy help them? How could he stay in the sanctuary now?

Another scream in the air, this one closer, and Patrick recognized it as Tom's. He tried to reach out and help, but nothing registered in his limbs. No pain, no tightness. He was only a pair of eyes forced to watch the murder of a friend.

Unless.

He closed his eyes and concentrated. A connection still had to survive. Like Tom had said, there was an electrical stream between the brain and every part of the body, even if there was space between the two. Well, he hadn't said quite that, but Patrick knew what he had meant and he did everything he could to put it to use.

He thought of his legs. He remembered glancing at them, seeing the blood and the giant nail, and feeling the pain, but now he remembered that his broken one had been nailed on top of the other. He took a breath and closed his eyes. He thought of that leg, a perfectly regular leg, lifting up. His stomach muscles tightened. He was excited to feel that. Adrenaline pumped into his body, barely replenished since he had realized he was going to die. His eyes cracked open. He still couldn't see his legs, so he closed them again and continued concentrating. It seemed so easy physically, but the mental process was becoming more and more difficult. He now knew what mental exhaustion was, but still he continued the process, thinking over and over, *lift that leg, lift that leg* . . .

Tom had been right. The damage to his legs and feet had been massive, and now the strength of his leg and stomach muscles coupled with the broken bones near the shin supplied the final destruction. His broken leg rose horribly, without the foot still spiked to the cross. If he had opened his eyes at that point, he would have seen a hairy white limb and a bloody stub, raw with the life that was escaping him.

But he still wouldn't have felt a thing.

Tom still screamed, but it wasn't all in pain. He felt like the Incredible Hulk, every muscle about to pop out of his clothes. He had been exerting all the pressure he could on the stake, and it had been giving continuously, though not nearly as fast as he would have liked. Still, it was making progress, and he could still catch a flicker of fear and pain on the creature's face. If his skull—his whining, cracking, whistling skull—could just hold out a few more seconds—

Then something shifted. For a second he was afraid it was his brain giving way to bone shards, but no, it had come from *outside* his head. He didn't give much much thought to it. He redistributed his weight and pushed everything he had behind the stake. It gave a bit more. The jewel hissed.

The creature was momentarily confused. Something white and hairy had just knocked Its grasp from Tom's head. It didn't bother searching for the cause of the interruption. Its more immediate concern was preventing Tom from pushing his weapon further. It could feel the wooden slivers slipping into the coldest region of Its body, so near that terror was actually consuming It for the first time.

It thought about calling Its army to the fore, but It knew

342

It didn't have time. Tom had to be taken care of *now*. It could easily tear the stake from Its chest afterwards, and if the blood ignited Its hands, so be it. At least the real danger would be foiled.

So, as Tom took hold of the weapon and *pushed* again, one powerful claw rose and raked across his head. Tom went flying, finally landing against the tree that dominated the hill. He wasn't unconscious. He was visibly stunned by the onslaught, but the creature still recognized a particular evil in his eyes. There was determination there, and the Shadowman felt a ripple of heat pass through Its cold soul.

It turned, then, realizing It had very little time to do away with the stake before Tom returned. It could see, at a glance, that the boy's blood had not only melted a hole through the crystal—along with the part of Its flesh—but had also managed to weld the wood to the crystal. The Shadowman grabbed hold of it and suddenly felt it pushed deeper, warm blood splattering Its front. It looked up.

Patrick had given as accurate a kick as possible. His bloody stub had hit smack in the middle of the stake, driving it farther. His last thought before the end was: *One for our side!*

The Shadowman, enraged at the attack by this man who should be dead, lost control. It released a tremendous roar, reared back, and struck, slamming a mouthful of teeth into Patrick's exposed throat. When It ripped back, Patrick's head fell forward, connected by only the spinal cord in back. The Shadowman chewed the mouthful of flesh and cartilage with vicious satisfaction.

When It turned back to Tom, It found him struggling to his feet. His vision was blurry, his head still ringing and dizzy from the Shadowman's squeeze. He fell backward, losing all balance, and managed to run up against the tree that was meant to shadow Patrick's cross. It was a thick, sturdy aspen, more than strong enough to prop him up for a while. Not that he had a while.

In front of him, the Shadowman had swallowed Patrick's meat and was now ready for more. It couldn't help laughing at the pathetic figure against the tree, a dark, rumbling laugh that shook every bone in Tom's body. The stake was forgotten. No way Tom would get near it again.

Instead, the Shadowman rushed at him, Its claws raised high, even the twisted one deadly. Its scarred maw opened wide, wider than any human's could, and a row of sharp animal teeth was revealed, strands of flesh and innards still hanging from them and rippling in the wind like a woman's hair.

Tom's knees gave out and he hit the ground hard. He cowered at the massive monster about to swallow him whole. At the last possible moment, he kicked out at the stake with his foot and missed. It was his last attack.

Images rushed at him, filling his world: red, burning eyes, sticky teeth, a deafening roar of wind with the unmistakable smell of blood and the dead black darkness enveloping it all. He screamed—

—and his scream was joined by another, from behind the monster. The Shadowman froze. Tom's world returned to him. The monster above him twisted Its head back, to face the fresh attacks, but It wasn't quick enough. Johnny, running at full speed, blazing with rage and terror, rushed at the creature's back. He carried a long, thick branch, a spear with an unsharpened point painted with his blood. He rested it across his splintered arm and cupped its back end with his good hand. When its bloody point slammed into the Shadowman's back, he pushed with all his strength, crying out with the strain. It was awkward. Johnny's bad arm hindered his aim, and the point of the branch barely broke the surface of the creature's flesh below the back crystal, but it was enough.

The monster's torso raged with orange flames, pulling

green tendrils from the wound. The spear did not go deep, nor did it get near the thing's heart. Still, the power behind Johnny's attack was enough to force the Shadowman forward. Tom, nearly standing again, saw the end of the stake sticking from the creature's front jewel come at his head. He ducked, just in time. Above him, the stake slammed into the tree, that sturdy, ancient, beautiful tree, barely splintering the grey bark of its trunk, and the weapon's point was driven home. The crystal gave way. Johnny's dried blood was forced forward to pinch the cold, black center of the Shadowman, puncture it, set it aflame. At the same moment, the jewel that once protected it faded to a dull grey.

Tom saw it all in less than a second, then he rolled way the hell out of the way.

The Shadowman's every muscle became taut. It was filled with a consuming agony It had never experienced before. It was a pain beyond any human experience. It set the torso and limbs on fire, every nerve a tiny spark, and rolled into the many facets of the body — a body that had long ago forgotten what a demanding mistress pain can be.

The night was filled with screams as nearly a hundred bodies went stiff, tingling with that same anguish. A part of them, hidden very deep, was suddenly torn from their bodies, and their voices turned to a single cry of mourning. Even the trees around them shuddered, blackened, wilted. Then they were silent, leaving only the Shadowman to carry on the tune.

It fell to Its knees. Long, sharp fingers pulled repeatedly at the stake, sprinkling slivers of wood into the air. The fingers slipped and cut, but kept coming back for one more try, whittling away a little more of the branch each time.

But it was too late. The transformation of death began. There was an explosion between the jewels, red and black pulsing meat spiraling out from the center, leaving rings of green smoke. For a moment, Tom thought the rest of the body would go that way and he thought of running. But he couldn't rise, couldn't move. He was frozen by the slow disintegration of the Shadowman. Its head, then Its body, slithered away, like warm water over a block of ice. There was no blood. There were no bones underneath. The eyeballs did not pop and the hair did not burn. But the scream did go on and on, incredible in its intensity.

It was not exactly a grotesque sight, more like a giant plum shriveling with waves of green and black. The fluids seeped onto the long blades of grass, then down into the earth and beyond. Soon only the dark, bubbling heart, expunged from the body in the explosion, lay in the grass, flickering with red rage like volcanic lava cooling, and then that too oozed into the ground to follow the rest. The clothing flaked away, like so many centuries-old rags. Within half a minute there was nothing left of the creature but Its legacy of destruction — and two almost identical grey jewels.

Bodies littered the land like a battleground. They were all quite dead, had been dead for at least a day. Animated, yes, only minutes before, but devoid of any human pulse for a long while.

Tom looked and shook his head, letting the sobs play themselves out. It was over. Janet was gone. So was Cathy. He thanked the heavens that they didn't have to go through what the other bodies had at the end. Patrick was dead. Dead, but a hero and a good friend. Tom steeled himself to bury the man in the same spot where he had been crucified.

But then an image came back to him, through the fog of misery: a boy risking everything to battle the creature, to kill It.

Johnny!

He stood, stumbling, and called the name over and over,

346

until his throat was hoarse. He scoured the hill, especially around the large tree that had killed the Shadowman. Where was he? He couldn't have gone far? He was right here when he struck the monster . . .

Then he saw the boy; deathly pale, lying at the bottom of the hill against a blackened tree, barely discernible from the dead around him. Tom rushed to him, tripping halfway there and bloodying his chin. He didn't stop to feel the pain or wipe the blood. He had to reach Johnny and hold him, see if he was all right.

The Other Souls have taken him away.

The thought drove into him like the stake through the Shadowman's heart. Even holding the boy, feeling his warmth, his body now stirring, the strong pulse in his neck—even then the thoughts circled inside Tom's head, torturing him with panic. He wrapped his arms around Johnny's waist and held him close, whispering, "Stay . . . stay . . ." in his damaged ear.

The night nearly passed before Johnny awoke. He coughed, spitting up a little blood, but that soon passed. Tom just held him, waited for the boy to speak first.

Johnny didn't make a sound for a long while, though. His head jerked around, studying the land and victims around them, unable to comprehend it all. Finally he whispered in a tiny, fearful voice, "What happened?"

Tom licked his lips. *Stay calm.* "You don't remember?"

Johnny shook his head. His breathing was increasing, becoming panicked. He tried to break Tom's hold on him, but Tom held tight. He whispered "Shhh" in the boy's ears until he settled down again.

"What do you last remember?" Tom asked.

Johnny gave this a lot of thought. "Riding my bike."

"Where?"

"I was delivering papers. Then there was fog. I got scared and rode home."

347

Tom waited, gently rocking Johnny back and forth.

"Mom and Dad are dead, aren't they?"

Tom didn't answer. He didn't have to. The boy knew.

"Where can I go?"

"With me," whispered Tom. "I'll be with you now. And you'll be with me. We'll stick together."

Johnny seemed to breathe easier. He leaned back into the older man. "All right."

Tom looked around them, somehow relieved. They were alone again. Completely alone. No secret eyes peering out at them this time. They were, perhaps, the only people left on the entire mountain. He wondered, oddly, how the hell they would explain this to anyone.

But there was proof. He saw the two jewels lying nearby, twins but for the destruction a stake and a brave boy's blood had waged on the one. Tom thought he understood, vaguely, their value to the creature. He speculated that they were somewhat like oxygen masks for deep sea divers. *Why hadn't the creatures come up here centuries ago?* he had been asked once. Perhaps they had, for short periods of time, but this was the first real test. The pressure was different in the center of the planet. Their exposure to the smaller pressure topside without protection was similar to a human flung into space without a spacesuit. The jewels, the life support systems, were once too weak to last very long. But they had improved.

He suspected that he was now looking at the Shadowman's "spacesuit." And when it was destroyed by Johnny, the Shadowman's core, Its heart, had exploded in the sudden pressure drop.

It was over, he prayed. They had the key now, and if they learned how to puncture the jewels quickly, the creatures would have to go back until they found something new. Another thousand years, maybe. And the Other army would help keep them at bay.

348

But he couldn't help shivering with the hope. The Other army had helped them through this. Yet the survival of earth was based solely on the balance of the two factions. What if *they*, the Other army, should one day beat the Shadowman's army? In fact, could he be absolutely certain that Johnny wasn't still . . .

He shook his head. Sometimes there just weren't any good guys. Nevertheless, Johnny was a boy first, his boy, and he knew that he would not allow any specter to crowd between them.

The wind rose, brittle cold. He stood, helping Johnny up, and put an arm around his shoulders for support. Johnny placed his good arm around Tom's waist, careful of the searing pain in the man's side, and together they limped off toward North Camp, across the earth they hoped to see bright and green until their dying day.

And in this they would never be alone.

ZEBRA'S GOT THE FINEST
IN BONE-CHILLING TERROR!

NIGHT WHISPER (2092, $3.95)
by Patricia Wallace
Twenty-six years have passed since Paige Brown lost her parents in the bizarre Tranquility Murders. Now Paige is back in her home town. And the bloody nightmare is far from over . . . it has only just begun!

TOY CEMETERY (2228, $3.95)
by William W. Johnstone
A young man inherits a magnificent collection of dolls. But an ancient, unspeakable evil lurks behind the vacant eyes and painted-on smiles of his deadly toys!

GUARDIAN ANGELS (2278, $3.95)
by Joseph Citro
The blood-soaked walls of the old Whitcombe house have been painted over, the broken-down doors repaired, and a new family has moved in. But fifteen-year-old Will Crockett knows something is wrong—something so evil only a kid's imagination could conceive of its horror!

SMOKE (2255, $3.95)
by Ruby Jean Jensen
Little Ellen was sure it was Alladdin's lamp she had found at the local garage sale. And no power on Earth could stop the terror unleashed when she rubbed the magic lamp to make the genie appear!

WATER BABY (2188, $3.95)
by Patricia Wallace
Her strangeness after her sister's drowning made Kelly the victim of her schoolmates' cruelty. But then all the gruesome, water-related "accidents" began. It seemed someone was looking after Kelly—all too well!

Available wherever paperbacks are sold, or order direct from the Publisher. Send cover price plus 50¢ per copy for mailing and handling to Zebra Books, Dept. 2651, 475 Park Avenue South, New York, N.Y. 10016. Residents of New York, New Jersey and Pennsylvania must include sales tax. DO NOT SEND CASH.

THE ULTIMATE IN SPINE-TINGLING TERROR
FROM ZEBRA BOOKS!

TOY CEMETERY (2228, $3.95)
by William W. Johnstone

A young man is the inheritor of a magnificent doll collection. But an ancient, unspeakable evil lurks behind the vacant eyes and painted-on smiles of his deadly toys!

SMOKE (2255, $3.95)
by Ruby Jean Jensen

Seven-year-old Ellen was sure it was Aladdin's lamp that she had found at the local garage sale. And no power on earth would be able to stop the hideous terror unleashed when she rubbed the magic lamp to make the genie appear!

WITCH CHILD (2230, $3.95)
by Elizabeth Lloyd

The gruesome spectacle of Goody Glover's witch trial and hanging haunted the dreams of young Rachel Gray. But the dawn brought Rachel no relief when the terrified girl discovered that her innocent soul had been taken over by the malevolent sorceress' vengeful spirit!

HORROR MANSION (2210, $3.95)
by J.N. Williamson

It was a deadly roller coaster ride through a carnival of terror when a group of unsuspecting souls crossed the threshold into the old Minnifield place. For all those who entered its grisly chamber of horrors would never again be allowed to leave—not even in death!

NIGHT WHISPER (2092, $3.95)
by Patricia Wallace

Twenty-six years have passed since Paige Brown lost her parents in the bizarre Tranquility Murders. Now Paige has returned to her home town to discover that the bloody nightmare is far from over . . . it has only just begun!

SLEEP TIGHT (2121, $3.95)
by Matthew J. Costello

A rash of mysterious disappearances terrorized the citizens of Harley, New York. But the worst was yet to come. For the Tall Man had entered young Noah's dreams—to steal the little boy's soul and feed on his innocence!

Available wherever paperbacks are sold, or order direct from the Publisher. Send cover price plus 50¢ per copy for mailing and handling to Zebra Books, Dept. 2651, 475 Park Avenue South, New York, N.Y. 10016. Residents of New York, New Jersey and Pennsylvania must include sales tax. DO NOT SEND CASH.

A CAVALCADE OF TERROR
FROM RUBY JEAN JENSEN!

SMOKE (2255, $3.95)
Seven-year-old Ellen was sure it was Aladdin's lamp that she had found at the local garage sale. And no power on earth would be able to stop the hideous terror unleashed when she rubbed the magic lamp to make the genie appear!

CHAIN LETTER (2162, $3.95)
Abby and Brian knew that the chain letter they had found was evil. They would send the letter to all their special friends. And they would know who had broken the chain— by who had died!

ANNABELLE (2011, $3.95)
The dolls had lived so long by themselves up in the attic. But now Annabelle had returned to them, and everything would be just like it was before. Only this time they'd never let anyone hurt Annabelle. And anyone who tried would be very, very sorry!

HOME SWEET HOME (1571, $3.50)
Two weeks in the mountains should have been the perfect vacation for a little boy. But Timmy didn't think so. Not when he saw the terror in the other children's eyes. Not when he heard them screaming in the night. Not when Timmy realized there was no escaping the deadly welcome of HOME SWEET HOME!

MAMA (1247, $3.50)
Once upon a time there lived a sweet little dolly—but her one beaded glass eye gleamed with mischief and evil. If Dorrie could have read her dolly's thoughts, she would have run for her life. For Dorrie's dear little dolly only had murder on her mind!

Available wherever paperbacks are sold, or order direct from the Publisher. Send cover price plus 50¢ per copy for mailing and handling to Zebra Books, Dept. 2651, 475 Park Avenue South, New York, N.Y. 10016. Residents of New York, New Jersey and Pennsylvania must include sales tax. DO NOT SEND CASH.